M. A. Hunter has been a huge fan of [text obscured] young age and always fancied the i[text obscured] That dream became a reality when One More Chapter signed The Missing Children Case Files.

Born in Darlington in the north-east of England, Hunter grew up in West London, and moved to Southampton to study law at university. It's here that Hunter fell in love and has been married for fifteen years. They are now raising their two children on the border of The New Forest where they enjoy going for walks amongst the wildlife. They regularly holiday across England, but have a particular affinity for the south coast, which formed the setting for the series, spanning from Devon to Brighton, and with a particular focus on Weymouth, one of their favourite towns.

When not writing, Hunter can be found binge-watching favourite shows or buried in the latest story from Angela Marsons, Simon Kernick, or Ann Cleeves.

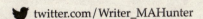 twitter.com/Writer_MAHunter

Also by M. A. Hunter

ISOLATED

The Missing Children Case Files

M. A. HUNTER

One More Chapter
a division of HarperCollins*Publishers* Ltd
1 London Bridge Street
London SE1 9GF
www.harpercollins.co.uk

HarperCollins*Publishers*
1st Floor, Watermarque Building, Ringsend Road
Dublin 4, Ireland

This paperback edition 2021

1

First published in Great Britain in ebook format
by HarperCollins*Publishers* 2020

A catalogue record of this book
is available from the British Library

ISBN: 978-0-00-844330-6

Printed and bound in Great Britain by
CPI Group (UK) Ltd, Croydon CR0 4YY

Content notices: suicide, domestic violence, paedophilia, sexual assault.

Dedicated to all who work in the
UK Criminal Justice System.
Thank you for keeping us safe.

A white well
In a black cave;
A bright shell
In a dark wave.

A white rose
Black brambles hood;
Smooth bright snows
In a dark wood.

— *Incantation*, Elinor Wylie

Chapter One

THEN

Bovington Garrison, Dorset

The spiky twigs scratched at Natalie's face as she raced further into the pitch-black forest, trying to claw her back to where she daren't return. Her chest burned with fatigue, but the burst of adrenalin brought on by the sheer terror of what she'd just witnessed prevented her aching legs from stopping. Pumping her arms, she willed the never-ending darkness to evaporate, but as she tried to focus on any sign of the path she'd come in on, the darkness swallowed up the ground ahead.

She'd known it had been a bad idea to venture out here at the bewitching hour; she'd wanted to tell the others that she wouldn't be a part of it, but they'd insisted and had muttered amongst themselves when they'd sensed her reticence. Whilst Natalie didn't necessarily know what those mutterings were, she knew the other three well enough to understand the grumbling to be about her perceived weakness. And Natalie accepted that as the youngest in the group, she would forever be the weakest link, and in order to gain their acceptance, she would occasionally have to ignore her own feelings.

As another branch scratched at her cheek, catching her just below the eye, she wished she'd never agreed to sneak out in the middle of the night and join them. If her parents ever learned of her deceit, she would be grounded for the rest of her life – and her dad's belt would seek out its own punishment.

'Your parents will never know,' Sally Curtis had said at lunchtime on Friday as they'd stood behind the sports hall, pretending to smoke.

Natalie hated the taste of the cigarettes that Sally pinched from her mum when her back was turned. Every morning, Natalie would promise herself that today would be the day when she told them that she didn't want to smoke, but her willpower would wane when she'd see them exchanging glances, certain that if she didn't go with them she'd inevitably end up as the chosen subject of conversation. At least they weren't brave enough to gossip about her when she was in their presence.

Natalie's foot caught on a thick root, and then she was flailing… falling through the air, with nothing to stop her. Her palms bore the brunt of the tumble, but her chin and chest took up the slack. Every part of her stung, but she was too tired to get up and keep moving. If it was fate's choice that it all end here and now, then so be it; she wouldn't fight it.

Lying still, her breath catching, she rolled onto her back, hoping to reclaim the wind that had been knocked from her. Through the towering bare branches, the large saucer of moon stared down at her, but for all its brightness, it offered little guidance to where the main path was. She was certain they hadn't come this far into the woods. The walk to the clearing had only taken a few minutes so she should have found the entrance by now. Was she running around in circles? With the ground covered in dried branches and decaying leaves, it was impossible to know exactly how straight and level her running had been. What if she never found her way out?

No, that was a silly thought. Daylight would eventually come and at that point she'd be able to figure a way out. The forest couldn't have been much wider than a mile in any direction, so with daylight she'd find a way to the edge, whether it was the side she wanted to be on or not.

Her palms were still stinging, the icy air swirling around her only heightening the warmth of the grazes. She was certain her hands must be bleeding, but even when holding them up to the moonlight it was impossible to distinguish blood from mud.

She should never have let Louise take the torch. Three fourteen-year-old girls, and she – at thirteen, the youngest by four months – was the only one to think a torch would be a good idea.

Bloody Louise! She hadn't always been such a cow to Natalie. Back before Sally Curtis's family had moved onto the base, Louise and Natalie had been best friends. But then Sally, with her blonde mop of curls and rapidly sprouting chest had turned up in September, and suddenly everything had changed.

Not afraid to challenge the rules and push boundaries, Sally soon latched on to Louise, who was only too happy to be led. Jane also welcomed an extra member to the group, especially as Sally had that *je ne sais quoi* that had all the boys tripping over themselves to please her. Jane welcomed Sally

Curtis, because Sally's lack of need of padding somehow elevated the rest of them. Not Natalie, of course, whose chest, she felt, would remain flat as a pancake for all time.

Branches snapping somewhere off to her left had Natalie's head snapping round, her own breathing instantly silenced. Was it possible they weren't the only ones who'd come into the woods on this dark night? Natalie focused on the black hole where she was sure she'd heard the movement, but couldn't make out a thing.

Maybe it was just a wild animal – a squirrel or rabbit of some sort. Yes, that had to be it. Certainly not the ferocious wolf-like creature with blood dripping from its fangs that she was desperately trying not to picture. No, wild beasts like that were things of lame horror movies and books.

Right?

More snapping – this time only yards from Natalie's feet – had her breath puffing out like a steam engine, and she clamped her eyes shut, covering her face with her hands, hoping that whatever bloodthirsty beast it was would simply pass her by.

'I've found her.' Louise's voice carried on the wind, and a moment later, woollen gloves were tearing at Natalie's hands as she screamed and kicked out in desperate survival. 'Natalie, stop, it's us.'

Natalie didn't dare to believe it, and squinting up at the torchlight, she'd never felt so relieved to see Louise and a panting Jane crouching beside her.

'What happened to you?' Louise asked, deliberately shining the torchlight into Natalie's eyes, until she batted it away. 'One minute you were there and the next you were gone.'

Natalie really couldn't explain exactly why she'd started to run, at least not in any coherent manner, so she bit her tongue instead, recognising the warm feeling between her legs and hoping the darkness would hide the patch that had to be forming in the crotch of her black jeans.

'I fell,' Natalie said, pointing her palms towards the torchlight and seeing the grazes, which were far milder than she first feared. They certainly stung more than the dull redness would suggest.

'Yes, well, what did you expect when you raced off without the torch? God knows how far into the forest we are now. Your inner compass was way off, mate. Come on, let's get you up, and then the three of us can go home.'

Louise nodded at Jane, who promptly grabbed one of Natalie's hands, ignoring the grimace as she squashed Natalie's palm and tugged her to her feet. It was only now she was up that Natalie noticed the pain in her right leg, and as her two friends tried to pull her back into the thorn-like branches, she screeched with the pain.

'What is it now?' Louise huffed, stopping and pointing the light into Natalie's eyes; a single tear rolled the length of Natalie's cheek, before dropping from her chin.

Natalie snatched the torch and pointed it down towards her foot. Jane gasped as the beam highlighted the thin stake protruding from Natalie's calf, the tip of it red as blood.

'Oh, Jesus!' the normally silent Jane exclaimed.

'Oh, bloody brilliant!' Louise echoed. 'Look what you've gone and done to yourself now, Natalie. Well done!'

Natalie didn't take well to the sarcastic tone, but was in too much pain and panic to retort. 'I think I should go to the doctor.'

'No,' Louise snapped. 'If you do that, you'll have to explain how it happened, and then they'll want to know exactly what we were all doing here in the woods when everybody else is in bed. No, Natalie. Just pull it out, and clean it up when you get home.'

'I can barely walk, Louise.'

'That's because it's still in there so your leg can't begin to heal. Pull it out and everything will be better.'

'But there might be splinters left inside. It could get infected.'

'Don't be such a wet blouse, Natalie. It'll be fine. Come on, we don't have long. You don't want your parents to find out you snuck out after they'd gone to bed, do you?'

Natalie could easily imagine how angry her dad would get if he even suspected she'd snuck out. 'No, of course I don't.'

'Well then, what are you going to do?' Louise sighed, and her tone was more empathetic when she spoke next. 'Listen, I'm sure it does hurt, but we can't stay here and wait until it gets light. Why don't you pull it out now, then me and Jane can help you get back to the fence, and we can all sneak back through and into our homes. Then, in the morning when we're walking to school, we can pretend like you've done it then and get the nurse at school to look at it.' She paused and checked her watch. 'It's nearly 2am, which means we'll be at school in less than seven hours. Right? Surely it won't get infected in seven hours?'

Natalie had to admit there was some logic in Louise's argument, and she knew that if she didn't agree there was a chance Louise and Jane would just leave her here in the woods to hobble home alone.

'Okay, okay,' she puffed, the winding she'd sustained finally easing. 'Shine the torch at it, will you?'

Louise obliged, and as Natalie reached down to the jagged shard, the second she touched it a burning sensation shot up the length of her leg.

'I can't do it,' Natalie admitted in defeat. 'One of you is going to have to pull it out. Please?'

Louise leaned down and studied the bloody branch before declaring, 'Jane, you pull it out.'

'What?' Jane pleaded. 'Why me?'

'Because I'm holding the torch, obviously,' Louise argued, though it was clear to both of her friends that Louise was as freaked out about the blood as the rest of them.

Not one to cause a fuss, Jane crouched down, coiled her hand around the shard and yanked it out without even warning Natalie.

Natalie yelped in agony, unable to hold back her tears any longer as Jane lifted up the shard of wood, no longer than a cigarette. Up close it didn't look like it could have caused so much pain.

Looping Natalie's arms over their shoulders, the two girls supported their friend back to the main path and ten minutes later they emerged from the all-enveloping forest, back at the perimeter fence through which they'd crawled an hour earlier.

'We'll have to be quick,' Louise warned. 'The security guards will be due to complete their hourly perimeter check soon. Jane, you go through first. Then it's back to our homes, into bed, and then we never speak of this night again.'

'Wait,' Natalie challenged, propping herself against the fence to take the weight off her bloody limb. 'What about Sally?'

Louise's eyes grew dark as she lashed out and slapped Natalie hard across the face, almost sending her tumbling back to the ground. 'Sally was never here. *Is that clear?* We must all swear a pact – here and now – that we were never in these woods tonight. So long as we sneak back into our homes, nobody will be any the wiser.'

'But Sal—' Natalie began to say, before Louise's raised hand cut her off.

'She was never here.'

Chapter Two

NOW

Chalfont St Giles, Buckinghamshire

Jack races around to his side of the car and jumps in, with me following suit. 'If we're lucky we can be in Staffordshire before visiting hours finish at half four. I've got your name down on the list and Turgood knows you're coming... Are you sure you want to meet him?'

Ordinarily, nothing would appal me more than coming face to face with the monster who oversaw a ring of abuse that lasted years in the former St Francis Home for Wayward Boys, but after Jack's revelation minutes earlier, nobody is going to stop me from confronting him today.

'I'm sure,' I tell him, offering what I hope is a reassuring nod.

He stares at my trembling hands as I struggle to engage the seatbelt in its buckle and eventually I feel his warm hands on mine as he helps. I look into his face and see nothing but concern etched across those dark eyes. I nod again, more firmly this time, and he starts the engine.

'You were looking for me,' Jack says. 'Earlier, I mean. When I arrived at the house, you said you needed to speak to me.'

I stare at him blankly, racking my brain for whatever that could have been about. The revelation that Jack has found my sister's face in pornographic material discovered on Arthur Turgood's hard drive has rather ripped the rug from beneath my feet. I try to recall what I was doing in the immediate past before Jack showed up at Fitzhume's country manor.

As Jack races down the long gravel driveway, I catch a glimpse of a man in a dishevelled tuxedo stumbling along the road just beyond the gates and immediately recognise Richard Hilliard, the father of young Cassie, whose return was the reason for today's gathering. I recall the slanging match between Richard and Fitzhume that I observed from the upstairs window of the manor and my subsequent encounter with Fitzhume slaps me between the eyes.

So you admit you were the one who set all this up? You put your granddaughter's life at risk in order to force Richard out of your family?

'Fitzhume is responsible for Cassie Hilliard's abduction,' I blurt out like some paranoid Twitter user.

Jack glances through the windscreen at Richard as we move past him. 'I'm listening.'

I take a deep breath to try and steady my rapidly rising pulse. 'It all makes sense, don't you see? Leroy Denton told us that the group had some rich backer who was calling the shots but he didn't know who that was. I bet if you ask Hank Amos whether he reached out to Lord Fitzhume and demanded more money, I bet he'll admit he did. *That's* what set these wheels in motion. That's why Fitzhume came to me now, not because it happened to be the anniversary of Cassie's abduction, but because he didn't want to pay a second ransom.'

Jack doesn't look convinced by my argument but switches off the car stereo so he can give me what's left of his attention. 'Amos said he didn't know who the rich backer was either. Do you have anything evidential to support your theory? What makes you so certain?'

Her life should never have been in any danger. They were paid enough to take good care of her.

'Fitzhume admitted as much to me,' I say resolutely.

'He did? You got him on the record?'

I again silently curse myself for not having the recorder on my phone running when I confronted him – not that it would necessarily have been strong enough evidence to go to trial.

'Not exactly, but he did admit his involvement to me, and I'm prepared to make an official statement to that effect if that's what it takes.'

I don't know whether Jack realises his entire face has taken a sceptical downward turn, or whether he's just doing a lousy job of covering his doubt.

'Okay, I'll put a call in to DCS Rawani and we'll see if it's enough to make him bite.'

'Make him bite?' I scoff. 'You need to get someone over there right away and haul him out of his fake celebration in cuffs. Wipe that permanent smirk from his face.'

Jack catches my eye apologetically. 'You know it isn't that easy. I wish it were. I wish you making a statement about what he told you would be enough to prosecute but it'll be his word against yours, and whilst your name is one of good standing, his background, links to the Royal Family and unlimited connections trump you.'

This isn't the reaction I expected to hear from Jack. I know we haven't known each other very long, but I thought I understood him.

'Fitzhume is guilty as hell and someone needs to bring about his downfall,' I spit. 'If you won't take action then I'll just bloody well have to do something about it myself.'

I'm already asking myself exactly how I could complete such a course of action when Jack's scepticism returns. But rather than berate me, he reaches for my hand and holds it for a moment.

'I don't doubt what you're telling me, Emma, but I'm just trying to be realistic. We both reviewed the case file and there was nothing to link Fitzhume to the three kidnappers, one of whom is dead, and the other two now behind bars. Even if Amos came clean and pointed the finger at Fitzhume, the CPS would need something physical before even considering charges.'

'So, what? He goes free?'

Jack opens his mouth to speak before thinking better of it.

'Are you seriously telling me that because Fitzhume has money and power he's allowed to get away with his crimes?'

Again, Jack opens his mouth to challenge, but raises his eyebrows in defeat instead. 'As I said, I promise I will discuss it with the DCS once I'm back and if we're lucky he'll allow me to do some discreet digging, but something tells me that Fitzhume won't have left any trail leading back to him – particularly if his military history is anything to go by.'

I pull my hand away and stare out of the window like a petulant teenager. I'm so fed up with people getting away with their crimes because of their so-called power and connections. I know my outlook is naïve, but shouldn't the guilty be punished?

Fitzhume's final words to me rattle in my head. *You dare print a word of this and I will have you brought up on charges of libellous defamation.*

Of course! As far as my publisher and agent Maddie are aware, I will be writing all about Cassie's disappearance and subsequent return for my second book. The idea has been signed off by the publisher and they'll be expecting me to deliver at least a first draft in the coming months. If the police won't take any formal action against Fitzhume then the only recourse is to tell the truth in my manuscript and see where that leads. Right now, I don't care if he does decide to take me to court over it; at least the truth will be in the public domain and people will realise what a snake he is.

I know there's no point continuing the argument with Jack. We have two hours of driving ahead that I don't want to spend in silence and my thoughts now turn back to the reason for our journey.

'You said you've spoken to Turgood already today?'

Jack sighs, and nods. 'As soon as the facial recognition software found a positive match to your sister. I wanted to find out what he knew and hopefully be the one to help your private investigation along. To be clear, the software didn't flag a hundred per cent match. What you need to appreciate is that the footage used to run the check was old and grainy – probably recorded on a handheld camcorder rather than more advanced equipment. The angle of her face in the clips we used wasn't straight-on either, so it's only as good as it can be.'

'Yeah, but you said it was a ninety-two per cent match though, right? That's as good as a hundred in my book.'

He shrugs. 'It's a strong match, which would lead me to conclude it *probably* is your sister.'

My heart strains at the news. For the last twenty years, I've hoped my sister didn't die the day she stomped away from home in the direction of our grandma's before vanishing. A part of me – the part I desperately try to silence and ignore – accepted that she could have died, but from what Jack has said, the footage he's found all but confirms she was alive some four years after she disappeared. That has to give hope that she could still be alive today.

'What did Turgood say when you spoke to him?' I ask now, pins and needles prickling at my thighs and forearms.

'He said he didn't recognise her name and that he hadn't watched all of the videos on his hard drive. He claims not to recall the particular video in question, but admits to sharing such videos with others and said that it could have been inadvertently included in his stock. He was being very vague, and without a solicitor present he was cagey.'

I remember the first time I met Turgood and presented him with Freddie's allegations. He laughed me out of his home, ridiculing the claims as nothing more than spiteful lies. But I'd known he was lying. When I'd first arrived, under the pretence that I was undertaking an investigation into why government cuts were closing valued social care facilities like St Francis, he'd welcomed me with open arms. But the moment I'd mentioned Freddie's name, the atmosphere turned decidedly cold, as if someone had opened a window. He'd crossed his legs, folded his arms, and avoided answering my questions. His reaction had given me all the confirmation I needed to keep digging. That's why I need to look into his eyes today and see what happens when I mention my sister. His body language will tell me whether or not he's lying.

The car grinds to a halt as we join the end of a tailback on the M40. Jack curses quietly as his eyes fall on the long line of brake lights stretching as far as the eye can see.

'What else did he say?' I ask.

Jack sighs. 'He said he wouldn't be surprised to see the faces of a host of missing children appear in those videos. He said there's an entire network operating along the south coast. Your sister might be just the tip of an iceberg that stretches back decades.'

I turn so I can study Jack's face. 'Did you believe him?'

The grimace confirms that he did, even if he didn't want to.

He meets my gaze. 'He didn't offer any specifics, but my next job will be to request the same facial recognition software is run against any other open missing-children cases to see if further matches can be established.'

I catch sight of the ETA on the sat nav display and my heart sinks. It now says we're unlikely to arrive before half past four, and if we don't, my chance to get an answer will certainly end for today.

'Isn't there an alternative route we can take?' I snap.

Jack begins to fiddle with the sat nav. 'Maybe… Once we get to the next junction, we can try to get off the M40 and find a detour, but we're on the slip road, so like it or not, we're trapped on this course for now.'

I sit on my hands as my blood boils with frustration. I don't tell him, but I sense his words may be more prophetic than he realises.

Chapter Three

NOW

HMP Stafford, Staffordshire

We finally make it in through the gates of the prison and into the visitor car park just after four. I'm conscious about how long it may take to get through the sign-in process in the visitors' centre, so as Jack is applying the handbrake, my hand is already on the door handle.

'Hold on a sec, will you?' he cautions, killing the engine. 'Before you go in there, are you sure you want to?'

I frown at the unnecessary delay. 'I wouldn't have come with you if I wasn't.'

'I know, I know, but I kind of put you on the spot when I turned up this afternoon. I didn't give you the opportunity to say no. This will be the first time you've seen Turgood since his trial. Are you sure you're ready? Mentally prepared, I mean.'

My chest tightens as I picture his face in the dock. Even when his whole world was about to come tumbling down, there wasn't an ounce of remorse in his eyes. I wanted to laugh at him, and tell him how good it felt to see justice finally being delivered for Freddie, Mike and Steve. Yet, when the verdict was delivered, I didn't feel any pleasure whatsoever. I have no doubt he finally got what he deserved, but at what cost to Freddie and the others? How many other children suffered at the hands of Turgood and his cohorts but didn't feel brave enough to come forward and have their lives put under the microscope?

I exhale deeply. 'The video on his hard drive is the biggest breakthrough I've had in years. I'd never forgive myself if I didn't see it through.'

Jack nods in reluctant acceptance. 'Very well. The governor is arranging a private room for you to meet him in and I'll be there with you, but as a friend rather than in any formal capacity. I'll hang back so the two of you can speak freely, but I want to warn you to be careful.'

The words catch in my throat. 'Careful?'

Jack momentarily looks out of his window as if summoning the strength to speak again. 'It's going to be weird enough for you coming face to face with him again, but remember it's *his* first time seeing you since the trial too. Since he last saw you, he's been sentenced to spend the rest of his life behind bars. Okay, in a facility specifically used to house sexual offenders, he won't be subjected to the level of violence and recrimination he might have experienced at another Cat-C facility, but it will still be a sharp change to the lifestyle he was used to.' He sighs. 'What I'm trying to say is that he will hold *you* accountable for this change to his circumstances, and he's had weeks to think about what he might say to you in the event your paths ever crossed again.'

'Sticks and stones may break my bones,' I mutter, prising the door open, until he reaches for my arm.

'I'm saying, don't let him get a rise out of you. Right now, you're in shock with what I've told you and you need to keep a clear head in there. Ask him what you want to ask him but don't take whatever he says to heart.'

I fix him with a firm stare and nod. 'I'll be fine. Now, can we get a move on before they say we're too late?'

Exiting the car, we hurry through the car park and into the visitor centre. Jack explains who we are to the guard at the desk, who then asks us both to provide identification. Once he's found us on the computer screen, he makes us sign the register and invites us to deposit any personal items in one of the lockers that line the wall at the side of the building. Once they're satisfied we're not carrying any weapons or contraband, one of the guards escorts us through the gates, along a narrow windowless corridor, and into the beating heart of the facility.

We arrive at a steel door, reminiscent of a cell door in a police station. Outside the room there is a monitor receiving a signal from a camera within the room. It currently displays a table and three chairs but it doesn't appear that Turgood has been brought down yet. The prison guard who escorted us advises that he will wait outside the room and will observe us from the monitor, though won't be able to hear anything said. He tells us he is there for the prisoner's protection as much as our own.

Unlocking the door, he ushers us inside before closing and locking the door behind us. The room itself is brighter than it appeared on the screen. There are high windows, all barred, which let in a surprising volume of light given how narrow they are. Jack selects one of the chairs and carries it towards the back of the room before sitting.

My breathing is shallow and as I drop onto the remaining chair this side of the table, I feel lightheaded. I've been forcing images of Turgood watching Anna out of my mind but now it's all I can imagine, and I want to be sick. Overhead, a fan whirs somewhere out of sight, pumping artificially cooled air into the room, but it is doing little to quell the heat in my face and neck.

There is a crunch and a grinding noise as the door on the opposite side of the room is unlocked, and when it opens a moment later, another uniformed guard steps through and checks Jack and I are both seated before nodding for Turgood to step forward. The prisoner waits for his cuffs to be removed before sauntering into the room, his eyes practically on stalks as he sees me sitting and waiting like an obedient dog.

He doesn't utter a word, merely sliding onto the seat across the table from me and crossing one leg over the other. His almost white hair has grown out more since I last saw him and it looks as though he's made no effort to brush it ahead of this meeting. The pale-blue prison shirt and denim trousers make his face look washed out, and yet he still carries himself with an air of superiority, to the point where it almost feels like he is the one who has come to visit me.

I look to Jack for guidance but see that his head is bent and he is staring at his shoes. Turning back to face Turgood, I'm not sure whether I should speak first or wait for him to engage me. I don't even know how to start, short of demanding answers about my sister.

He doesn't speak either, his tongue poking out to wet his lips but then receding. It's like he's daring me to crack first and break the awkward silence. Unlike him, I don't have time to waste.

'You know why I'm here,' I croak, before clearing my throat. 'I want to know what you can tell me about the video discovered on your hard drive.'

He stretches out one of his hands and considers each nail, as if he's awaiting a manicure, before wetting his lips again and finally meeting my stare. 'What video would that be then?'

He's baiting me, waiting to see my reaction when I mention Anna's name, and I know instantly this is going to be every bit as difficult as Jack has forewarned.

It takes all my strength to summon the words. 'The video featuring my sister, Anna.'

His lips momentarily curl up slightly before he remembers where he is. 'I'm sorry, I don't know to what you're referring. Are you sure it was a video on *my* hard drive?'

I glance back to Jack but he is lost in his own world.

'We both know which video I'm referring to,' I say, biting my tongue.

'I can't say I do. Maybe if you could describe it that would—'

'Cut the crap, Turgood. The only reason I'm here is to appeal to that tiny part of your soul that cannot forgive you for the atrocities you inflicted on others.'

I had hoped it would feel better to blow off steam, but his reaction is one of mirth rather than fear or annoyance.

He leans forwards, crossing one hand over the other, resting them on his pointed knee, as if he's posing for a photograph. 'Have you seen the video?'

I hear Jack's warning echo in my mind: *don't let him get a rise out of you.*

'Where did it come from?' I ask, ignoring his jibe.

He sits back. 'Alas, several years ago, my computer became infected with a malicious virus online, and the result was the downloading of a variety of disturbing videos and images that I tried to delete but which were so embedded that I didn't manage to. That's why the hard drives were in my loft when the authorities discovered them, you see? I'm no technical expert, but I assumed I'd one day find someone who could remove the virus and recover the original content of the drives, but time slips away so easily. I'd forgotten I still had the drives, to be honest, until they were found during the search of my property.'

He's lying, I have no doubt. The way he's framed his posture and the confidence with which he is delivering his lines, there has clearly been some rehearsal involved.

'I wish there was more I could tell you, Miss Hunter, but I'm afraid I can't say what I don't know.'

I've never hated the sound of my own name so much as the way he delivers it with such bitter scorn. I need to find a way to get through to him but short of shaking him by the shoulders, I'm at a loss as to how. It feels like the journey here has been a waste of time. I have no doubt that the only reason he agreed to meet with me was to see how desperate I am, and to lord it over me.

I check my watch. 'Our time is nearly up, so Jack and I had better be going,' I say, loudly enough for Jack to hear.

I'm about to stand when Turgood utters three words that chill me to the bone.

'How is Freddie?'

Our eyes meet and it's all I can do to restrain myself.

'He always did enjoy being the centre of attention,'

Turgood continues, so casually that my skin crawls. 'Such a pity he felt the need to concoct such vicious lies about life at the home. Has he ever admitted to you that he once thanked me for looking out for him? Some of the other boys could be quite rough and ready at times but once I took Freddie under my wing, they left him alone. His life at that home would have been far worse had I not looked out for him.'

Bile builds in the back of my throat. Even now, after the truth has come out and he's been punished for his crimes, he has the nerve to maintain an air of injustice about what has happened.

I won't give him the satisfaction of my outrage. 'Freddie is doing really well, as it goes,' I say proudly. 'He's settled and is using his newfound fame to help others. I've never seen him looking so well, and now he has a rich life to look forward to while you're slowly dying in here.'

I turn to leave, but it appears he isn't done with me yet.

'Do you really want to know the truth about your sister?'

I freeze, but do not dare look into his eyes.

'Because if you're serious about finding out how she ended up on that video, I might be able to tell you something that would help.'

Jack is standing and watching us now and I can see the concern overshadowing his face. I slowly turn back to look at Turgood. He hasn't shifted his position, but he looks poised to deliver the ace he's kept up his sleeve this whole time.

'If you *really* want to know,' he torments, 'then I need to hear you ask for my help.'

I know he's baiting me again, and that I should just leave the room and never look back, but I can see in his eyes that he has been holding back and I would never forgive myself if I turned away from the search for Anna over something as petty as this.

'I see the way you look at me,' Turgood continues, 'with that look of disdain that all younger people seem to carry these days. You hear Freddie's version of events and hold me accountable but you have no clue what it was like being responsible for so many broken lives, dealing with violent outbursts and emotional breakdowns. I did what I believed was in the best interests of those thrust into my care, and whether you believe me or not, I took care of Freddie and the others. They'd be dead if it wasn't for me, so stop hoisting me up as the villain of your piece. There are far worse players out there that you've yet to encounter and trust me, by comparison I'm a saint.'

'I want to know about my sister.'

'Then ask me.'

I grind my teeth, knowing I will regret sinking to his level, but I don't see any way around it. 'Very well. Please help me to understand how my sister ended up on that video.'

His lips curl up fully this time as he claims his simple victory. 'See, that wasn't so difficult, was it?'

I can't bring my eyes to meet Jack's but I can feel them burning a hole into my face.

Turgood rubs his hands together and savours his moment, committing every second of my submission to memory, to play out over and over when he's alone.

'I don't recall ever meeting your sister,' he begins like some great orator, 'but I met many runaways like her – children who couldn't cope with home, or were escaping some revolting upbringing. Being society's most vulnerable, they soon fall in with the wrong crowds and in their moments of desperation they'll take any help offered, even if it comes at a dangerously high cost. At first they'll be reluctant to do what is asked of them, but when the rewards appear and they realise what little is required to bring that element of security, they soon see that there is no way back. If your sister is in one of the videos your police friend over there referred to, then it's safe to assume that she was there by choice. If you want my advice, stop looking for someone who doesn't want to be found.'

I can't contain my rage and I lunge forward, slamming my hands down on the table, growling at the now cowering Turgood. 'You have no idea who my sister is or how far I'm prepared to go to find her.'

I feel Jack's hands on my arms within seconds, and he yanks me away from the table as the bolts on both doors are rapidly undone.

'You'll rot in hell, you son of a bitch!' I manage to shout as Jack drags me from the room, my eyes warm with tears.

Chapter Four

THEN

Bovington Garrison, Dorset

No, that can't be the alarm already, thought Natalie, rolling over to hit the snooze button, but grimacing as the agony of the night's escapades tore up her leg. Although Jane had yanked out the thin branch, Natalie was certain she could feel tiny splinters still firmly embedded beneath her skin, each one waiting to push through into her bloodstream and float around her body for the rest of the day.

'Time to get up, sleepyhead,' her mum called through the closed bedroom door, but thankfully she didn't come in.

Gripping her thigh, Natalie manually lifted and shifted her right leg, holding her breath to fight against the urge to yell out in pain. Her mum would know what to do, how to make it better, but she'd also want to know how Natalie came to have a gaping bloody hole in her calf.

When she'd snuck back in last night, it had taken all her willpower not to knock on her parents' door and tell them exactly what had happened: the woods, the game, Sally... everything. But as she'd hovered by the door, willing her hand to reach up for the handle, she'd remembered the sting of Louise's slap and the warning that they weren't to tell anyone. They'd made a pact, and breaking a pact was a dangerous thing, Natalie knew.

Hitting the snooze button, Natalie propped herself up on her pillows. She leaned back into them and wiped the thin sheen that had pooled on her forehead. The room wasn't overly warm but the effort of moving her leg had taken a lot out of her. Louise had said she was being a wet blouse worrying about the leg, and as an older girl she was surely more knowledgeable about such matters, right? If she said the leg wouldn't get infected, then there really wasn't anything Natalie should be worried about.

Taking a deep breath to settle the bubble of anxiety building in the pit of her stomach, she whipped back the duvet and stared down at the strapping she'd managed to pinch from the bathroom cabinet and wrap around her leg in the pitch black. It was a bulbous and bloody mess, but at least the staining hadn't spread to her bed covers; thank heaven for small mercies. She'd have to dispose of the strapping on the way to school. There was no way it could be reused, and she doubted her mum would be able to get it clean. If anyone asked what had happened to the roll of bandage, she'd just have to plead ignorance.

'I'm going downstairs now,' her mum called through the door again, this time adding a knock to ensure that her daughter was awake. 'Do you want a cup of tea?'

The last thing Natalie needed was for her mum to barge in

right now and see the state of her leg. 'Yes, please. I'm going to shower and then I'll be down.'

There was no response but the tell-tale sound of footfalls on the stairs confirmed her mum was on her way to the kitchen. That just left her dad to sneak past. His routine was like clockwork and, all things being equal, he'd now be sitting in the small toilet reading one of his angling magazines. But he wouldn't remain in there for ever, which only offered Natalie a finite amount of time to get out of bed and into the bathroom without anyone catching her. The trouble was, she didn't think her injured limb would be up to bearing her weight this morning.

What was the alternative?

Delicately swinging her left leg over the edge of the mattress, she lifted and shifted her right leg with her hands again, wincing as the bandage brushed against the bed frame. Then, with another deep breath, she pushed herself off the mattress and planted both feet on the thick pile rug where her slippers, trainers, and pile of school uniform sat. She couldn't help the gasp escaping her mouth, but with her door shut and her parents otherwise engaged, she could only hope neither had heard.

Her grandmother used to say that pain in an injury was the body's way of saying it was healing; Natalie was certain that was a crock, but if there was some truth in the old lady's words, then her body had to be working overtime to heal. Bearing most of her weight on her left leg, Natalie reached out for her chair and rested her right hand on its back, pushing it along as a makeshift Zimmer frame as she made it towards her bedroom door; she wouldn't be able to use it beyond her bedroom without drawing unnecessary attention, but it would do the job for now. Finally, making it to the door, she slowly lowered the handle and peered out, her eyes searching for the figure of her father whilst her ears strained for any hint of where he might be.

Neither sense alerted her to his presence and, venturing forward, she used the wallpapered wall to support her journey forward, only pausing momentarily when the sound of pages being turned confirmed her dad's presence in the toilet. Continuing to the bathroom, she closed and locked the door. relief sweeping through her. Perching on the edge of the bathtub, she raised her nightdress and began very slowly and delicately to unwind the strapping. The bandage crackled and pulled as the congealed bloodstains cracked and tore until she was down to the final wraparound, but she had to stop as the tugging brought tears to her eyes.

The healing process had resulted in the clot binding with the bandage and there was no way to remove it without restarting the bleeding, but Natalie didn't think she had the strength to complete the deed without screaming and wailing.

Her grandmother would have told her just to yank it off like any other Band-Aid, but even the gentlest of pulls was too much to bear. And then she remembered another trick the old lady had taught her when she was younger: it was far easier to remove plasters when they were covered by water, on account of the glue becoming less adhesive. There was no guarantee the same logic applied to a bloodied bandage, but what did she have to lose?

Manoeuvring her injured leg over the side of the bath, she used the large handle her dad had installed for Grandma to pull herself into a standing position, and brought her left leg in to join her right. Then, switching on the shower, she shrieked as a hard spray of cold water hit her upper body like winter's rain. It soon warmed up and, lifting down the shower hose, she targeted the spray onto the stubborn strapping, giving it another gentle tug every few seconds, until the whole thing dropped into the tub with a splosh. The sight of the bloodied hole was still a shock, but as the shower spray continued to work its miraculous magic, the wound began to look less threatening. Her calf muscle was definitely swollen to almost twice the size of its rival but she'd managed to avoid fresh bleeding, and as she switched off the shower and climbed back out of the tub, she would have argued that the leg was slightly less painful than when she'd woken too.

Raiding the medicine cabinet, she located the box of plasters and, selecting the largest square one, she pressed it firmly over the wound and limped back to her bedroom, just as the sound of a flushing toilet signalled her dad's imminent exit.

He didn't speak as he emerged, just closed the door behind him, folding and tucking the magazine beneath his arm and waddling slightly as he returned to his own room, oblivious of the towel-wrapped and dripping girl edging slowly across the landing. Her mum always said he couldn't be relied on for anything until he'd had his first coffee of the day.

Back in her room, Natalie dressed, opting for a thick pair of black tights to cover evidence of the plaster, and, having wrung out the bandage in the bathroom basin, she stuffed it into her school bag, before zipping it up, and hoping that a) her mum wouldn't look inside the bag, and b) the moist bandage wouldn't dampen her books too much.

Arriving in the kitchen, Natalie could hear her mum talking on the phone in the other room, but her dad was already at the breakfast table munching burnt toast with a snarl across his lips. Just a typical breakfast in the Sullivan household. The radio in the background was playing some hit from the 80s – a decade of music Natalie didn't personally care for but which her mum adored. Natalie couldn't understand how grown-ups couldn't appreciate modern music; even the older songs both her parents frequently crooned along to must have been new at one point in time, so they couldn't always have been so stuck in the past. Why couldn't they listen to normal music?

Reaching for the Shreddies, Natalie filled her bowl, before asking her dad to pass the milk. He sighed as he did, as if her request was the most challenging task in the world. He'd obviously got up on the wrong side of bed *again* this morning, but it seemed like he didn't know any other way these days. She knew it was safer just to keep her head down and avoid drawing his attention.

Her mum's voice in the other room grew louder, but Natalie couldn't work out what she was saying, or to whom. Either way, it didn't sound like it was good news she was receiving. A moment later, her mum came into the kitchen, clutching the phone in her hand but pointing it at Natalie.

'I've just got off the phone with Diane Curtis, Sally's mum,' she said, her tone somewhere between anger and concern. 'Seems Sally wasn't in her bed this morning when Diane went to wake her. She's phoning around everyone to see if anyone knows where Sally might be.'

There wasn't an obvious question, but Natalie knew to infer that an answer was expected. Slowly swallowing her mouthful of cereal to buy some time, Natalie opted for ignorance. 'I don't know where Sally is.'

She hated lying to her parents, particularly her mum, but it wasn't exactly a lie; she genuinely didn't know where Sally was. Not now.

Here mum's eyes narrowed. 'I know she's your friend, and the last thing you'd want to do is get your friend into trouble, but her mum is going spare with worry. If you have any idea where she might be, or what might have happened, you need to tell me, Natalie.'

'I told you I don't know, Mum.' The lie felt like a mound of earth she'd just brought up and out of her throat.

'Well, Diane said Sally was tucked up in bed when she checked on her at eleven, and then again at five this morning, but now she's gone.'

Natalie couldn't keep the confused frown from developing, but tried not to give anything away. If her mum had seen her in bed at five this morning, did that mean…?

'What?' her mum asked. 'Do you know where she is? Or where she was planning to go?'

'No, Mum.'

'Swear to me.'

This was the last thing Natalie wanted to do. It would be so much easier just to admit the truth: they'd snuck out, left the safe confines of the garrison, and headed into the woods. She could tell her mum how it had all been Sally's idea, and that Louise and Jane had pressured her into joining them; she could tell her mum how she'd fallen and hurt her leg and then her mum would make everything better. But then Natalie remembered Louise's slap and pact warning, and instead shovelled another mouthful of cereal into her mouth.

'I swear I don't know where Sally Curtis is.'

Chapter Five

NOW

Blackfriars, London

Sitting in the padded chair across the desk from Maddie's latest stack of manuscripts, I can't help but notice the subtle changes she's introduced since my first book, *Monsters Under the Bed*, flew off the shelves. Back when we first met in this very room, the picture reproductions on the walls weren't framed, there was no television or mini-fridge in the corner of the room, and the only luxurious chair was Maddie's own well-worn bright-red faux-leather recliner. I remember her commenting that she preferred to read manuscripts at a forty-five degree angle – caught halfway between rest and the real world. Each to their own, I figured back then.

Choosing the right literary agent is a challenge for all new authors; if you've ever written and tried to publish a book, you'll understand why I say this. I mean, writing a book is a marathon of a challenge, just in terms of putting the words down on paper, but to then give each sentence and paragraph the tender, loving attention they need until what you've produced resembles something nearing literature is far from easy. And then at that point, when you think your part is complete – you've actually written a book for goodness' sake! – that's when the real work begins, because although you believe passionately in the piece of writing you've poured your heart and soul into, convincing a very busy literary agent that it's worth their time to read it is another matter.

I was lucky in that I was introduced to Maddie at a book launch of a friend of a friend. As soon as I explained that I was looking into historical abuse at the St Francis Home for Wayward Boys, with detailed witness accounts from three victims, she was salivating at the prospect. I should explain that *Monsters* is not a work of fiction, and whilst I am proud of the outcome it brought about for the victims – particularly Freddie – it was probably one of the most challenging projects I've taken on.

As an investigative journalist, you're warned that fate can take you down some dark alleys in the search for the truth, but my interviews with Freddie, Mike and Steve were unrelenting; we got through more than one box of tissues along the way. But earlier this year, it all seemed worth it when the men responsible for the vicious abuse were tried and convicted at The Old Bailey. And in the next six months, the documentary about that hellhole will be available for all to stream (keep your own box of tissues to hand).

I can't forget the sneer on Arthur Turgood's face the moment Jack and I went to visit him in his cage three months ago. The gall of the man to see how desperately I needed answers, only to leave me in limbo.

My chest heaves; I'm not going to allow him to spoil my day again.

Maddie's office now bears the tell-tall signs of Christmas approaching. In her defence, Maddie hasn't gone over the top. The tree atop the mini-fridge is barely a metre high and is sparsely decorated with lights and baubles, and there are barely half a dozen festive cards standing on the locked cabinet against the far wall. Maddie once told me she doesn't go into Christmas as much as when she was younger, but I'm the opposite; you can barely move for tinsel, garlands and twinkling lights in my one-bedroom studio flat in Weymouth.

Christmas when I was growing up was always a big occasion; or at least it was until… My chest tightens at the thought of the space on the mantelpiece where two advent calendars had once hung. After Anna's disappearance, it had never felt right to make a big fuss at Christmas. And for a time after I left home, I maintained that status quo of barely even decorating a tree, but that all changed when I met Rachel at university. A city girl through and through, Rachel reminded me of how joyous December can be with a few decorations and festive songs. She also reminded me that Anna might return one day, and would hate to think that her disappearance had robbed us of our Christmas spirit.

The door behind me bursts open and Maddie comes jogging in, panting and flustered, her usual pristine and carefully made-up face red and blotchy, and her mop of chestnut curls sweat-streaked and clinging to her glistening forehead. I don't think I've ever seen her in anything but professional business attire either, and this purple and silver tracksuit is reminiscent of the sort of thing that made shell suits so popular when I was a teenager.

'You're early,' she puffs at me, surprised to find me in her small office with a takeaway cup of tea.

'We said nine,' I say, frowning, as I suddenly question whether *I* am the one in the wrong.

Maddie drops into her new black leather recliner, reaching down to the mini-fridge and withdrawing a chilled bottle of mineral water and drinking half the contents, before looking back to me. 'Are you sure I said nine? I was certain we weren't meeting until ten.'

I'm racking my memory now, certain the invitation in my online calendar said to meet at nine. 'No, I think we were originally going to meet at ten, but then your assistant messaged me and said you had to move it earlier as you have another meeting at ten?'

Maddie snaps her fingers together and screws the lid back onto the bottle. 'That's right, that's right, of course it is. Oh, I'm so sorry, Emma. Yes, now that you've said that it's all coming flooding back. What am I like?'

Maddie is twenty years older than me, but I've never seen her in as big a flap as she is now; usually our roles are reversed with me becoming anxious and stressed about every possible scenario, while she is coolness personified. I don't like being the collected one in this relationship and I'm grateful when she logs in to her laptop and refers back to the agenda for today's meeting.

'I have good news, and not such good news,' she declares, locating a towel from a gym bag squashed down behind her desk and wiping her forehead clean.

Maddie has always been good at managing my expectations and she doesn't hide the truth from me, but she also has a tendency to try and sugar-coat anything that might otherwise feel like a negative. I don't think she does this just for me, but it comes as part and parcel of her role as literary agent and maternal figure to all of her clients. We writers really do have low opinions of ourselves, and it is easy for the tiniest molehill to be blown out of all proportion and enlarged into a menacing ash cloud.

I take a deep breath, determined not to overthink whatever bombshell she's about to drop. 'Okay,' I say, unable to keep the caution from my voice. 'What's the good news?'

'The publisher loves *Ransomed*! They actually think the way it's been written is even better than *Monsters Under the Bed*. They love the dual timeline approach where we learn what was really happening with little Cassie Hilliard's abduction, while in the later timeline we get to follow your investigation. Your editor Bronwen says it reads almost like a piece of gripping fiction, and is even more compelling *because* it's based on a true story.'

'It *is* a true story,' I counter. 'I didn't make up what happened to Cassie Hilliard. It's factual.'

Maddie is pulling a face, her nose wrinkling as she prepares to deliver the not-so-good news. 'Yes, it *is* factual, but... their legal department is challenging some of the conclusions you've drawn at the end of the book. I know we discussed the ending before you wrote it, and I was the one who encouraged you to tell it as you saw it, but the lawyers aren't so sure such conclusions can be drawn without evidence.'

'He as much as admitted to me what he'd done,' I respond, feeling the heat rise to my cheeks. 'He was the one behind it all, and if the lawyers want to see my written notes of that conversation, I'm happy to supply them. They're date- and time-stamped. I jotted them down as soon as we'd finished speaking.'

Her nose wrinkles even more. 'But they say it's still your word against his. He denies any such conversation occurred and that you're just trying to sensationalise your account of Cassie's abduction to sell more books.'

I scoff at the affront. 'Well, of course he's going to say that; he doesn't want the world to know what he did!'

Maddie raises her flat palms in a calming gesture. 'I know he's as guilty as you say, and that you would never dare lie for dramatic effect, but your notes of the conversation are not conclusive proof. I read the first and second drafts of the book, and anyone with half a brain who reads what you've written won't be able to draw any alternative conclusion to the one you've presented. But…'

She leaves the 'but' hanging in the air and I can't say I'm surprised that the publishers are getting nervous. Cassie Hilliard's family have enough money to put the publishers out of business – or at the very least have them tearing through bureaucratic red tape for the next ten years.

'So where does that leave us?' I ask when I've composed myself and remembered that Maddie is merely the messenger.

'They are continuing with the copyedit and you'll have the proposed changes over to you sometime in late January and in the meantime, their legal department will continue to scrutinise the backstory and potential libel implications. The family haven't brought any kind of civil action against them or you yet and they just want to make sure that doesn't happen.'

'Worst-case scenario?'

Maddie lets out a long and fatigued sigh. 'Worst-case scenario, they ask you to reword the final chapter and leave it to the reader to determine guilt. It's not the end of the world to leave the ending open, if you ask me. It will certainly leave your readers with questions, and that in itself will only generate further discussion.'

I'm not convinced, and hate the thought of leaving my readers without the whole picture. 'And best-case scenario?'

'They leave everything as it is and the world gets to see the truth about what really happened. Either way, you look set to have a second bestseller under your belt. Twitter is already hanging on every rumour about the book and its possible publication date. As soon as this wrangle is finished with the lawyers, they've promised to officially reveal the cover and put it up on pre-order.' Maddie pauses and takes another slug from her bottle of mineral water. 'The publishers have talked about an official launch party for the announcement. Now, I know you're not keen on big public displays, but they really think it will help announce the book if you're there to pose for pictures. As much as you hate the term celebrity, *Monsters* put you on the map, and now everyone is desperate to know what's coming next.'

I cringe at the mention of a launch party where I'll be the centre of attention. When did it become necessary for authors to have faces? I'd much prefer to just write and allow all the marketing and publicity to be handled by the experts.

'You're chewing the sleeve of your cardigan again,' Maddie warns.

I yank my arm down, frustrated that I still have that nervous habit. 'They're not expecting me to speak at this event, are they?'

Maddie doesn't have the chance to answer as the phone on the corner of her desk bursts into life. She grabs it on the second ring and adopts her regular telephone voice, but whatever she's being told is clearly not good news as the blood drains instantly from her face. Do I assume this is news from the publisher's legal team?

Maddie hangs up without saying another word, pushes back her chair and charges towards the closed door.

'Maddie, what is it?' I call after her. 'What's going on?'

'There's a woman on the roof,' she replies absently, 'and she's threatening to jump.'

Chapter Six

NOW

Blackfriars, London

The lift takes for ever to arrive and by the time it does, Maddie is white as a sheet. I really don't think it's a good idea for either of us to be going anywhere near the roof, but given Maddie's history, I know there is no way I will be able to talk her out of forcibly getting herself involved. Maddie's father died by suicide when she was at university and she's always blamed herself for not seeing the signs. We've only ever had one conversation about it because she prefers to keep her personal life guarded, but I know she was the last person her dad phoned before he swallowed a handful of painkillers. She told me that, in hindsight, she'd known something was off by the way he ended the call, but she ignored that instinct and has regretted it every day since.

My father didn't reach out to me before he was found hanging by the neck in HMP Portland. I try to think that's because he didn't want to inflict further pain on me, but I wish he had. I wish I could have told him that life without him in it will never be as bright.

I'll be no use in this kind of high-intensity, stressful situation, but Maddie needs a friend more than ever and there's nobody else I can call. How many times has she been there for me when my investigation into Anna's disappearance has stalled, or when my impostor syndrome rears its ugly head and tells me I have no idea how to plot and structure a book? Despite my personal reservations, I will stick to Maddie like glue.

It's a relief when the lift finally arrives on the tenth floor. One of the security guards from reception is standing guard at the door to the roof-access staircase, and he's already told another pair that the scene is out of bounds. What is it with people wanting to gawp at a person threatening to throw themselves from a building? You see it in the movies when someone is teetering on the edge of a rooftop and the crowds gather beneath; if it were me, I'd turn and run. At best, an observer will see the person stand there for a time, until they're talked out of the act; at worst, you'd have to watch as they plummet to the ground and then hear the sickening crunch of bone compacting with concrete before seeing the red puddle spread out from the point of impact.

No, thank you; not an image I want to witness. There's enough evil in this world.

'Roof's out of bounds,' the security guard says to us dismissively.

'You don't understand,' Maddie counters. 'I'm professionally trained for these situations; I've completed the ASIST training.'

He stares at her blankly.

'It stands for Applied Suicide Intervention Skills Training. And I help out on The Samaritans helpline so unless your colleague up there has dealt with a similar situation before, he's going to need my help.'

It's only now that I notice how ill the security guard looks. His name badge identifies him as Clyde, though I don't recognise him, despite my umpteen visits to Maddie's building. Her literary agency takes up a third of the sixth floor – with its view of The Shard – but the remainder of the building is taken up by a wide variety of other businesses. There are also metal detectors and luggage X-ray machines at the entrance so security is pretty high; if this woman has managed to get through all that and up to the roof, she must either work here or have been visiting someone who does.

Clyde now looks at me for some kind of corroboration. I have no idea whether what Maddie has just told him is true or not, though it isn't in her nature to lie about something so serious, particularly when a woman's life is at stake. I choose to nod and back my friend and mentor.

Clyde takes a further second to consider his options, before stepping aside and scanning his security pass at the panel, and opening the door for us. 'Tell my colleague what you told me about The Samaritans stuff, yeah?'

Maddie is straight through the door without another word and whilst I admire her single-handed determination, I do wish we'd stayed put in her office below and waited for news. The stairs up to the next door are large and steep, and lead to a ladder which completes the final part of the journey. The hatch we then have to squeeze through isn't exactly practical, but once on the other side we are immediately on the roof. The wind up here is both gusty and bitter. I close the hatch behind me and take in the immediate surroundings. The roof is largely flat with a number of vent openings, which must feed into the air-conditioning system that pumps through the building all year. It isn't immediately apparent where the woman is – for the briefest moment I can't help thinking we are too late – but then I catch the sound of voices carrying on the wind to our left. Maddie must hear it too as she turns and moves off in that direction without a second's thought.

I hurry after the blur of purple and silver as her tracksuit top flaps in the wind. If I'd have thought about it, I would have suggested we both put on warm coats before making our way up here, but in our blind panic it never even crossed my mind.

Clyde's colleague, who is also dressed in a black polo shirt and trousers, is a couple of metres ahead of us, stooping, arms outstretched in the direction of the woman dressed in brilliant white robes who is standing just short of the edge of the roof. She looks almost angelic.

'Who are they?' she calls out, pointing at us as we approach the security guard. 'I said nobody else was to come up here.'

Keeping his eyes on the woman, the guard turns his head to address us from the side of his mouth. 'This is no place for you. Go back downstairs.'

Maddie ignores the command and stands directly beside him, zipping up her tracksuit top as it continues to flap and float on the wind. 'My name is Maddie Travers,' she calls out to the woman, 'and I work in this building on the sixth floor. What's your name?'

'She doesn't want to give her name,' the guard replies quietly, still talking through the side of his mouth.

'That's okay. You don't need to tell me your name,' Maddie calls out again. 'I'm just here to listen to you.'

'Leave me alone!' the woman fires back.

'I'm afraid I can't do that, sweetheart,' Maddie says, surprisingly calm given the pressure of the situation which I can only watch unfold.

It feels as though I'm not even here, as if I'm sitting alone somewhere watching it play out on a screen, knowing there is nothing I can do to influence proceedings. Maddie, on the other hand, seems intent on taking the bull by the horns.

'Can you tell me what's brought you up to this roof today?'

The woman glances back over her shoulder, her body trembling as she does, though it isn't clear if it's nerves or the chill in the air.

'It's okay, sweetheart,' Maddie calls, 'you don't have to answer my questions. Really, I just want to understand what could have happened to make you think that this is the only way out.'

She turns back to look at Maddie again and I suddenly realise both Maddie and the guard have moved half a step closer to the woman. 'You wouldn't understand!'

'I think you'd be surprised,' Maddie challenges. 'My father felt the same way once – that everything was so bleak that there was nowhere else for him to go. But do you know what? He found a way out.'

It feels like we've reached a stalemate. If Maddie and the guard charged at the woman now, there's no way they'd get to her before she had the chance to hurl herself backwards over the ledge, and yet I can't say for certain that she definitely wants to jump. Having never been faced with a situation like this before, I can't tell whether this is a serious attempt or just a cry for help. Regardless, I'm not sure Maddie is the right person to be trying to talk her down. They have trained professionals for this kind of thing in the police force, who must be on their way by now.

The woman is watching Maddie carefully, but then her gaze falls on me and she stares so intently that I desperately want to look away. It takes all my willpower to hold her gaze.

'There's no way out for me,' she shouts, still staring at me. 'I'm cursed.'

'Tell me about that,' Maddie encourages.

'You wouldn't understand.'

'Try me. I'm a well-educated woman with a vivid imagination. I think you'd be surprised at how much I can understand.'

The woman glances back over her shoulder again as the sound of approaching sirens fills the air. *Oh my God, I think she may actually jump right now.* She is so close that a trip or slip would send her headfirst over the ledge.

Relief floods my body as she turns back to face us again.

'You're not up here by choice, are you?' Maddie tries again. 'Who put this curse on you?'

The woman's eyes are shining in the early morning sunlight. 'We brought it on ourselves. We made a pact not to tell anyone what we did.'

'Was that you and a particular person? A husband? Boyfriend? Girlfriend?'

The woman promptly sits down, her bottom on the ledge; it's impossible to know whether this is a step forwards or backwards. Has she sat to engage, or so it's easier to throw herself back?

'A best friend?' Maddie guesses next. 'What did you and this person make a pact about? I'm assuming it's something you consider bad if you're not prepared to tell me?'

'I can't tell you because then you'll be cursed too.'

'Okay, okay, sweetheart, if you really don't want to tell me, then that's okay, but I won't be able to help if I don't know what help you need. Does your friend know how you feel?'

'They don't care. Nobody does.'

'I care, sweetheart. Even though we've just met, I promise I care about what happens to you. And so does my friend Emma here.'

My eyes widen at the mention of my name. Why drag me into it?

'Emma cares about people who think they've reached the end of the road. She has a special gift for helping them.'

A noise behind us has me turning to look, and now I see a woman clad in black emerge from the hatch. There is a badge and warrant card hanging from a chain around her neck. The trained negotiator. *Thank God.*

'No more people,' the terrified woman calls out, standing up again and pressing her ankles against the ledge.

The police negotiator's hair is silver in colour despite the youthful appearance of her features; I can only assume doing this kind of work, and the stress-level involved, has an aging effect on those who undertake it.

'Natalie, my name is Inspector Marcziesk. I know why you're up here and I've been sent to help you. Is this about Sally? Sally Curtis?'

That name rings a bell but I can't place why it sounds so familiar.

The woman – Natalie, by all accounts – steps back and up onto the ledge. I can't watch and yet cannot take my eyes from her. One sudden gust of wind and she'll be over.

'Steady there, Natalie,' the inspector cautions. 'Nobody

wants to see things end this way. I'm here to listen to anything you want to say. Please don't do something you'll regret.'

Natalie doesn't respond, merely looking from the inspector to me. She's burning a hole into my subconscious again.

'Think about your mum and dad,' the inspector tries once more. 'Think about Louise and Jane. What would they think if they could see you up here now?'

'You're Emma Hunter, aren't you?' Natalie calls out. 'I recognise you from the television. Can you help me?'

I don't know what to say, or how best to answer – not that I have much choice as the words can't get past the lump in my throat.

'You need to find her,' Natalie continues. 'Find Sally. Tell her I'm sorry.'

Before any of us can react, Natalie closes her eyes and falls back off the roof.

Chapter Seven

THEN

Bovington Garrison, Dorset

Natalie had waited for her mum to depart – off to have her hair cut and blow-dried – before venturing from the house, her limp far more pronounced than she would have cared for. Her dad hadn't stuck around after breakfast, and even when her mum was asking questions about Sally, it was as if he was in a world of his own, kissing them both on the head before hurrying away, citing some exercise he had to prepare for. It was the life they lived: army business before all else. Not that Natalie minded living in the confines of the base; there was something reassuring about having a large fence around them.

She winced as she stepped over the threshold and onto the narrow path outside the house. So far the plaster was keeping the blood at bay, but she couldn't be certain it would remain that way for the rest of the day. She'd wanted to bring a spare in her bag in case it started to leak, but there hadn't been any large ones left in the box. No need for anyone to see how much discomfort it was causing her. Later tonight, when she was undertaking homework in her room, she would leave the plaster off and allow air to get to the wound. She felt confident that once it scabbed over, walking would be less painful.

Waiting for her mum to leave the house meant she wouldn't be able to catch the early bus now, but if she could get to the bus stop just after it had left, she'd be first in the queue for the second bus; she definitely didn't think she'd be able to cope with walking the whole way to school. Not today.

Jane emerged from her house, further up the road, but if she'd spotted Natalie then she didn't stop to wave, jumping into the front of her mum's car before they disappeared from sight. It was unusual for Jane to be getting a lift into school, and Natalie was a little put out that they hadn't offered to give her a lift too. It had to be that Jane simply hadn't spotted her, and that Jane's mum had taken pity on her daughter having to carry her violin to school.

That had to be it.

It couldn't be anything else.

Natalie kept her eyes low as the Curtis house came in to view, terrified that Sally's mum Diane might spot her and ask the same painful questions Natalie's mum had asked. Natalie was used to keeping the truth from her own mother, but didn't feel confident she'd survive an interrogation from Diane.

When she dared to glance over at the property, it looked surprisingly quiet. She'd half expected to find some kind of search party on the garden waiting to scour the area, but there wasn't even a car on the driveway.

Did that mean…?

Could Sally have returned?

She was tempted to cross the road and knock on the door to find out, but the prospect that her hope was misplaced was enough to keep her moving forwards, albeit slowly because of the sharp pain in her leg.

Nearing the security hut from where she would exit out to the bus stop, she gasped when she spotted her dad there amongst a small troop of five other men, receiving orders from Lieutenant-Colonel Havvard, the head of base security. Creeping slowly forward, keeping her head bent, Natalie strained to hear what was being said, but the wind was too strong, and the lieutenant-colonel had his back to her. She caught her dad looking over and made to wave but he didn't return the gesture, his eyes turning back on Havvard once more.

The briefing ended just as Natalie reached the security barrier and she waited in line with two boys in the same year group as the guard at the barrier signed them off the base. The troop disbanded, jogging back towards the residences. Her dad remained behind, walking over to Natalie and taking her out of the line.

'What's going on, Dad?' she asked. 'Is Sally back?'

He shook his head solemnly and stooped so his face was at eye level. 'No, and her parents are really worried. Do you know where she's hiding?'

Natalie's cheeks burned. 'No. I told Mum, I have no idea where she is.'

He seemed to accept her response but remained bent over. 'Okay, but do you think one of your other friends might know where she is? Diane and Owen said she was in bed when they locked up last night but wasn't there this morning. Did she mention that she was planning to run away?'

Natalie gulped. 'No, I swear.'

'Okay,' he sighed. 'Listen, do you think you could do me a favour today? Keep your ears open at school, especially with your other friends. If any of them mentions Sally, or they seem to know more than they're letting on, will you tell me? It's very serious and we want to make sure she's back safe and sound. Will you do that for me?'

Natalie forced herself to nod, inwardly cringing for not coming clean to him now.

'That's my good girl. You'd better hurry along now or you'll be late for school.'

He straightened and she moved back to the line at the security barrier, which was now longer.

'Well?' she overheard Lieutenant-Colonel Havvard say.

'No, she doesn't know where Sally is,' Natalie's father replied quietly.

'And you believe her?'

'Of course I do! She wouldn't lie to me.'

'Well, someone knows where she is and we're not going to stop until she's found. Is that clear?'

Her dad grunted. 'The last thing we need is another Denmark debacle.'

'And what the hell is that supposed to mean?' Havvard growled under his breath.

Natalie looked over her shoulder and saw her dad now squirming beneath Havvard's glare.

'Nothing. Forget I said anything. I'd better join the others.'

With that, he saluted and marched back in the direction of the residences.

Chapter Eight

NOW

Blackfriars, London

I don't think I will ever forget that blood-curdling scream for as long as I live.

Even now, an hour later and seated in the warmth and comfort of Maddie's office, I can hear it every time my eyes close: a death's cry as that desperate woman realised that everything she knew of life was about to disappear in the blink of an eye.

Neither Maddie nor I have spoken a word since we were ushered back down here and told to wait for a police officer to come and take our witness statements. I'm about to finish my second cup of hot, sweet tea, feeling no calmer than the moment it occurred. It didn't feel real – like the craziness of a dream that you don't want to quite believe despite what your subconscious is forcing you to accept as reality. One minute she was there, and the next just… thin air.

Inspector Marcziesk and the security guard had rushed to

the edge, as if they'd somehow be able to reverse time and bring her back up, but her blood was apparently already spreading out across the pavement when they looked over. Maddie and I had remained where we were, neither of us willing or able to see what had become of the woman we'd known for less than five minutes. If the scream will haunt me for ever, I dread to think what impact the image of her prone body would have had on the rest of my life.

Watching someone die certainly puts life into perspective; I can't even begin to imagine what must have driven Natalie to plunge ten storeys to the ground, knowing death was the only inevitability. There could be any number of reasons, and she offered little by explanation. I had thought that once the police negotiator arrived the situation would have ended with a positive conclusion – naïve maybe, on my part. Looking around Maddie's office – the stack of unread manuscripts; shelves strewn with her clients' published works; a paltry sum of festive decorations – all of it feels so unimportant in the grand scheme of things. Death can come for any of us just as quickly, and for most we won't even be a footnote in history.

We both start at a knock at Maddie's door. Turning to see who has caused the intrusion, I see a pair of grey eyes, a close-cropped greying beard and a dark uniform. The man removes his hat as he enters, closing the door behind him without a word.

'I'm Sergeant Daggard. Jim. You two are' – he pauses, pushes a pair of half-rimmed spectacles onto his nose and reads from his notebook – 'Emma Hunter and Maddie Travers?'

I nod, standing and offering my hand. 'I'm Emma and this is my agent, Maddie.'

The colour has yet to return to Maddie's cheeks and I've never seen her looking as old as she does right now. Usually, with her makeup applied and her outfit carefully selected, you'd never know there was a twenty-year age gap between us. Right now she looks almost as aged and withering as my own mother.

'I understand the two of you were up on the roof when…' – he takes a moment to choose his words carefully – 'when the incident occurred.'

'That's right,' I confirm. 'Have you come to take our witness statements?'

He offers an empathetic smile. 'That's correct, Miss Hunter, but before I do, how are you both coping? It's vital that we capture an accurate account of what you saw, but it's also important that you both take whatever time and counselling you need to come to terms with what happened. There is a telephone number for confidential counselling that I'll pass to you as soon as we're done, but in the meantime, are you both up to telling me what you saw? If it's easier, I'm happy for you to stay together while I ask you questions.'

There is something about Sergeant Daggard that I instantly warm to. He has one of those voices you hear on late-night radio: relaxed, sincere and capable of putting you instantly at ease. It can't be easy to remain so calm and compassionate in such a situation, and yet there is no trace of impatience or frustration in either his manner or his behaviour. He's placed his hat on the stack of manuscripts and because there isn't a vacant chair, he's instead taken up a position resting on the edge of the filing cabinet.

'I have a detailed statement from Inspector Marcziesk, who informed me that the two of you, and one' – another pause to consult his notebook – 'Sydney Bartholomew were already on the roof when she arrived. Is that correct?'

I wait a moment to see if Maddie wants to engage with him, but she's now rested her head in her hands and is avoiding eye contact with both of us. Knowing Maddie, she's already started the mental inquest into whether she could have handled anything differently. There really was nothing more she could have done though. In fact, thinking back to what I saw, prior to the inspector's arrival, Natalie sitting down on the ledge felt like progress was being made.

'That's right. I mean, if Sydney is the name of the guard,' I answer for the two of us.

'Can I ask what you were both doing on the roof?'

'We wanted to help. Maddie received a call telling her that someone was threatening to jump, and as a trained suicide prevention counsellor, she wanted—'

'A what, sorry?' Daggard interrupted with an apologetic wince.

'Maddie's had training to help talk to people who are contemplating suicide, as part of her work with The Samaritans,' I reply. At least that's what I think she said to Clyde the security guard to convince him to let us up. Oh God, what if that was just bull on Maddie's part? I didn't question it at the time, but is that why she's so quiet now? Surely not.

'Is that right, Miss Travers?'

Maddie doesn't look up, nor respond.

'Miss Travers?'

'Maddie!' I say louder, to snap her out of the trance. 'Sergeant Daggard asked you a question.'

Maddie looks up at both of us; her eyes are red and puffy, and shining with the light from overhead. I reach into my satchel, remove a packet of tissues I always keep in there and pass her one.

'It's all right,' Daggard says to her calmly. 'I'll continue talking with Miss Hunter, and then speak to you afterwards.' He looks back to me. 'You were saying, Miss Hunter...?'

'Um, yeah,' I begin, trying to straighten the memories in my head. 'We climbed up onto the roof and saw the security guard there, maybe five or so metres from the woman, who was standing close to the ledge.'

'Were the two of them in discussion?'

'I–I–I don't really remember... She pointed at Maddie and me, and wanted to know who we were, so Maddie explained.'

'How did the woman – Natalie – how did she seem to you? Was she upset? Angry? Worried?'

'Anxious, I'd say, but yes, there was definitely fear there too. She seemed troubled.'

'And how did she react once you'd identified yourselves?'

I think about the penetrating stare she held on me for what felt like an age, but probably wasn't more than a few seconds. 'Maddie was the one talking to her; I was just observing the scene unfolding. I'm sorry, I really don't remember. I never expected her to actually go through with it.'

'I understand from Inspector Marcziesk that Natalie spoke to you. Can you tell me what she said?'

'She told me she recognised me from the TV.'

'Had you ever met Natalie before today?'

I'm trying to place her face, but I genuinely have no recollection of ever seeing her before being on that roof. She was wearing a cleaner's tabard, and God only knows how many times I must have passed her in this building without noticing her. If only I'd been less wrapped up in my own world, maybe I could have done more.

'No, I don't think so,' I reply. 'Did she work here?'

He shrugs. 'I believe she was working for a cleaning company who recently took over the contract for this building, but I couldn't tell you if she'd ever stepped foot inside the place before today. One of my colleagues is checking that at the moment. Do you recall whether Natalie said anything else to you?'

You need to find her. Find Sally. Tell her I'm sorry.

'She mentioned someone called Sally Curtis, but I don't know who that is. The inspector seemed to know though. When she first arrived, she asked Natalie if her being on the roof had anything to do with Sally.'

Daggard is nodding, scribbling something into his notepad. 'I don't know all the background, but from what I understand, Natalie's friend Sally Curtis disappeared when the two of them were adolescents, some fifteen years ago. Natalie was one of the last people to see Sally alive and blamed herself for Sally disappearing. Been in and out of psychiatric institutions for a number of years, and this isn't the first time Inspector Marcziesk has been called to talk Natalie down from a building.'

I can imagine some of the pain and guilt that must have been coursing through Natalie's mind earlier today. I've felt the exact same thing.

Through it all, there's still a tiny bell ringing at the back of my mind; the name Sally Curtis is definitely gnawing at my subconscious, beckoning me to recall why it seems so familiar.

'Anything else you can remember about what Natalie said before...?' He is desperately trying not to reference the suicide, but I sense it's more for our benefit rather than because he's uncomfortable.

'Nothing at the moment,' I admit reluctantly. 'It all happened so quickly.'

He smiles warmly again before taking my contact details and passing me a business card with his. 'If you do recall anything else, please don't hesitate to call. If I'm unavailable, you can leave a message with a colleague who will ensure it is passed on.'

'What will happen next?'

He narrows his eyes as he looks at me. 'An autopsy will have to be performed to check that she hadn't ingested something that spurred on her decision, but after that the case will be closed. There's no reason to think there was anything untoward, given her history and previous attempts at suicide.'

'How's the inspector coping?'

'She's obviously disappointed that she wasn't able to keep Natalie alive, but she'll receive specialist counselling... which reminds me—' He reaches into a pocket, pulls out a laminated flyer and hands it over. 'I highly recommend the two of you seek some counselling too. PTSD can be a silent killer in its own way.'

I take the flyer, recalling the counselling I was forced to attend after Anna's disappearance, and then my eyes widen in panic. 'Oh God, I just remembered I'm supposed to be meeting Jack.' I look down at Maddie, not wanting to leave her alone.

'Go,' she urges. 'I'll be fine, I promise.'

Chapter Nine

NOW

Hyde Park, London

Hurrying through the bitter drizzle, I'm annoyed at myself for running late. I know how keen Jack Serrovitz has been for today to happen, and I promised I wouldn't allow Maddie's ability to drone on to get in the way of making a good first impression. I'm sure there's probably a more direct route from London Bridge to Marble Arch, but I'm not a Londoner and I'm not yet au fait with how the underground network operates. I know there are different lines and a bazillion stations, but how they all interconnect is still beyond me. In fact, there probably was a quicker pedestrian route I could have taken, rather than relying on a black cab, but given everything that's happened so far this morning, it was the simplest choice – and God knows I could do with some simplicity in my life right now.

I asked the driver to drop me at Marble Arch station, as Rachel had told me that was a short stroll from the entrance of

Winter Wonderland at Hyde Park. Of all the places Jack could have picked for us to meet, this one is certainly picturesque… if not ridiculously overcrowded. Reaching the main entrance, I can see nothing but tourists, wrapped up against the cold, hustling and bustling past me. Checking my phone, I can see Jack has messaged to say they'll wait for me by the ticket booth but I've no clue where that is, and I find myself being swept along and in through the entrance by the crowd. It's only when I feel a firm hand on my shoulder that I realise Jack has located me, and he steers me out of the tide of tourists.

'You made it then,' he declares, though there really isn't any need for the conversation to be awkward.

'Yep,' I reply, equally uncomfortable.

I've known Jack for a little over three months, since he helped me in the hunt for missing seven-year-old Cassie Hilliard. Jack was the police liaison that was organised for me to review the historic casefile, and despite a bumpy start, something like friendship has started to blossom since. He's a nice guy – handsome, funny at times, and I know we wouldn't have successfully located Cassie without his help and support.

But this is the first time Jack and I have seen each other since we visited Turgood at HMP Stafford. I wince as I recall the moment Jack informed me that pictures of my sister had been discovered on the hard drive, and then Turgood's sneer appears behind my eyes again.

'He wanted to rile you,' Jack said afterwards, 'but you shouldn't let him get the better of you.'

Easy for him to say!

All I have left are three facts: my sister went missing twenty years ago, she was still alive when the video was made four years later, and Turgood knows more than he's sharing.

Jack shuffles from one foot to the next as a cold breeze blows between us. He promised he would do whatever he could to make Turgood talk and wouldn't stop until he'd helped me find Anna, but he's not been able to offer anything more than words of encouragement. Turgood's major heart attack eight weeks ago hasn't helped matters. He's currently considered 'too ill to be interviewed', from what Jack has told me. Too convenient if you ask me. At least karma appears to be in play for that belligerent monster.

The reason for today's meeting is because Jack has been begging me to come and meet his daughter Mila. She'll turn seven on Christmas Eve, which is less than a week away now, and I think it's why he's chosen Winter Wonderland as the venue for our introduction.

As we make it through the crowd and to a small clearing just beyond the ticket booths, it's only now that I see Mila is holding his hand. Dressed in a faux-fur coat, leggings and ankle boots, she looks much older than her six years, but when she turns to face me, she is one of the prettiest girls I think I've ever seen. Her long dark hair hangs straight and loose down her back and when she smiles, I can see she has inherited her father's goofy grin.

'This is Mila,' Jack gestures. 'Mila, this is Daddy's friend Emma.'

Mila extends her small hand, and does a half-curtsey as we shake.

'It's lovely to meet you, Mila,' I say, with my most welcoming smile.

'Are you Daddy's girlfriend?' she asks, without a trace of malice.

'Um, well… no,' I reply, thrown by the directness of the question, and glancing at Jack for help.

His cheeks have taken on a beetroot hue too, as he quickly stammers, 'No, we talked about this, Mila. Emma is just a friend. *Remember?*'

'We're just friends,' I concur.

'Emma is that famous writer I was telling you about,' Jack adds. 'Remember? You said you wanted to meet her because you want to be a writer one day too.'

'Oh yeah, I've decided I don't want to be a writer any more,' she corrects. 'Seems like too much hard work.'

'And what do you want to do instead, when you're older?' I ask inquisitively.

'I'm going to ride horses at the Olympics, and then I'm going to be an actress.' She says it so matter-of-factly that you'd think it had been pre-ordained from upon high and etched into a stone tablet.

In fairness, I never thought I'd end up writing professionally. I was a major bookworm when I was younger, but in hindsight I think it was just easier getting lost in a book than having to deal with the fallout of Anna's disappearance. Reading made me want to write stories of my own, where I could control the narrative and the course of the characters; some would say that means I'm a bit of a control freak, but I would counter that I'm just a sucker for a happy ending.

'You can't even ride a horse,' Jack chimes in, still confused by Mila's self-predicted future.

'Not yet, but when Santa brings me a horse for Christmas, then I'll have to learn to ride, won't I?'

I don't know where to look; the expression on Jack's face makes me want to howl with laughter, as he stutters to explain that Santa is highly unlikely to bring Mila a horse for Christmas. He stops short of telling her the truth about the big guy dressed in red.

'Besides,' he concludes, 'a horse won't fit down your mum's chimney, will it? Plus, her garden isn't big enough to accommodate livestock.' He turns to face me, keen to change the subject. 'Shall we go in now?'

I nod, stifling the laugh. Once through the entrance, we find ourselves in a muddy thoroughfare, with market-like stalls on both sides, already encouraging visitors to part with their hard-earned money. There are stalls with bespoke tree decorations, handmade fudge, speciality cheeses, and carved wooden ornaments. I have to be honest, I'm already starting to feel more relaxed and festive, and I have to catch myself before I get swept up in the atmosphere.

I feel awful for leaving Maddie to handle Sergeant Daggard's questions alone, though I was relieved to see her showing him her certificate of training as I was leaving. She definitely didn't do anything wrong in my eyes, and if necessary I'll phone Sergeant Daggard myself and tell him as much. Whipping out my phone, I fire a message of support to Maddie, offering to return after this catch-up with Jack. I'm due to stay at Rachel's flat in Ealing tonight, but we haven't agreed a specific time for me to be home and I'm sure she'd understand my not wanting to leave Maddie alone after what happened. Undoubtedly, the suicide has already made the news headlines across the capital; certainly there were photographers gathered at the entrance to the building when I left. Thankfully, a small tent had been erected over where Natalie must have landed, so hopefully the front pages won't be plastered with a gory shot.

'Are you okay?' Jack asks when we've made it through the stalls. 'You seem distracted.'

I'm conscious that Mila can probably overhear anything we discuss and I don't want to ruin her day. 'I'll tell you later. I'm sorry I was late arriving.'

'You weren't late, not really. Well, maybe by a few minutes, but I'd already taken into account the fact you'd probably get lost on the way from your agent's office,' he chuckles, to show he means no offence. 'Listen, I promised Mila she could go skating on the ice, if you fancy it?'

I shake my head rapidly. 'No, no, no, ice and I are not friends,' I explain. 'I never learned how to do it when I was a child, and then when Rachel and I were at university she said she'd teach me, so we went along to a rink one night, and despite her best efforts I ended up with a ligament strain in my knee and a behind that resembled a bruised banana. Don't let me stop you two though. I don't mind watching from the safety of the perimeter fence.'

'Good heavens, no,' Jack replies. 'I can't skate for toffee either, but Mila's happy going on alone, aren't you, sweetie?'

She nods, totally unfazed by the prospect, so that's where we head, Jack paying for her to hire skates and then helping her strap them on. He joins me at the fence once she's on the ice. I'll admit to feeling pangs of jealousy at how effortlessly she can glide across the temporary rink. If she hopes for an Olympic medal one day, she'd be better off focusing her efforts on skating rather than equestrianism.

'She's a natural,' I say, as Jack snaps some pictures of her on his phone.

'I'd like to take the credit but her mum's been taking her skating since she could first walk.' He puts the phone away.

'I'm glad we've got a moment to talk without her earwigging. I wanted to ask how you're doing?'

'Me? I'm fine.'

Jack turns so he's looking straight at me, and I can see the concern etched around his eyes. 'Are you sure? I know we've spoken a few times on the phone since, and shared emails, but I sense you're still carrying the burden of what Turgood said when we went to see him, and—'

'Turgood is lying,' I say with certainty, 'but short of beating the truth out of him, there isn't a lot more either of us can do about that, is there?'

Jack doesn't respond at first, but continues to stare into my eyes. 'I'm sorry it wasn't the news you were hoping for. Believe me, I've met my fair share of Turgoods, and monsters like him get off on thinking they know more than the rest of us. You have to remember that *you beat him* before. If it wasn't for your extensive research and determination, he would never have been brought to justice for the abuse he oversaw at St Francis. *You're* the reason the police opened an investigation into the home. *You're* the reason he was tried and sentenced at The Old Bailey. And *you're* the reason he will never be able to repeat those abuses.'

But I'm also the reason that Anna stomped off that day.

Jack brushes a stray hair from my face, and gently tucks it behind my ear. 'Have you had any new leads emerge on the website you set up for Anna?'

After the success of *Monsters* and the media attention when Cassie Hilliard was found, there had been a spike in the number of messages I received through the site, but these were words of support rather than clues as to where she might be.

I wish someone could find a bittersweet ending for my story.

'Nothing new,' I say despondently.

'Is that why you're so distracted today?'

I shake my head. 'When I was at Maddie's office, a woman died by suicide after throwing herself from the roof.'

Jack is blinking at me, maybe trying to work out if I'm trying to prank him. 'Seriously?'

I nod. 'Check your phone; I'm sure it's probably trending on Twitter. Her name was Natalie and she must have been about my age, give or take. One minute she was there, and the next…'

Tears bite at my eyes.

Jack puts his arm around my shoulders and pulls me into his fleece coat.

'I'm so sorry. You should have said… We could have postponed today.'

'It was a bit late,' I say, relaxing into his grasp. 'I'll be okay. I was going to ask actually… the woman – Natalie – had something to do with the disappearance of a girl called Sally Curtis. I wondered if it was a case you're familiar with?'

Jack shakes his head. 'Not a name that rings any bells with me, I'm afraid. Certainly not a name that's tied to any of the backlog of cases I'm currently reviewing. Do you have any more detail? Where she disappeared? When?'

'No, just the name unfortunately. It's definitely a name I've come across but I can't quite figure out why. Never mind.'

Jack's giving me a cock-eyed smile.

'What?' I ask.

'That look in your eyes.' He sniggers. 'I've seen it before.

70

When we first met in September you had that look then as well.'

I don't know what *look* he's referring to, but I won't deny that Natalie's final words have piqued my interest.

You need to find her. Find Sally. Tell her I'm sorry.

Chapter Ten

THEN

Wareham, Dorset

The walk to school on Monday morning was a lot more painful than Natalie had anticipated. After the grilling from her mum and dad, she'd ended up leaving late and missing the early bus. She preferred catching the early bus as it was always quieter than the later one. By the time she reached the bus stop, the line was already ten-deep with students of varying ages. On any normal day, she would have had time to bypass the bus stop and walk to school before the morning bell sounded, but with every step such agony, her pace was much slower today.

When the bus had arrived, it had already been packed with teenagers wearing the same dark green blazer and tie as herself. There were no seats available, but at least the bus driver allowed her to squeeze on, perched perilously just behind the yellow line. Three stops later, and she was practically bundled from the bus as the throng of students pushed forwards to get in through the gates to see friends and copy homework before the bell.

Natalie had looked for, but failed to find, either Louise or Jane in their usual hangout at the far side of the playground near the enormous sports centre. When the bell had sounded, she'd hobbled as quickly as she could in through the main doors, up the stairs to the first floor, and along to class 9-E. No sign of Louise or Jane in their seats either, though the space at Sally's desk was almost haunting. Natalie deliberately kept her eyes from looking over at the desk, as if Sally's absence was news to her, as it would have been to most of her other classmates, who were shouting and cooing and gossiping about last night's *Hollyoaks*.

Mrs Engleberry – their registration tutor – arrived two minutes later, and was just wishing everyone a good morning when a knock at the door was followed by Louise and Jane scuttling in and taking their seats on the far side of the class. With heads bowed, they quickly apologised for being late, but neither looked at Sally's desk and both avoided eye contact with Natalie.

When the second bell sounded to announce assembly, Natalie did her best to cut through the flow of classmates to stand beside Louise and Jane, but both were too far ahead and showed no interest in waiting for her.

Louise is probably just feeling guilty about slapping my cheek last night, Natalie tried to reassure herself, though in truth it should have been her avoiding them after what had happened, and she wasn't enjoying this cold-shoulder treatment.

What about the pact? They were supposed to be in this together, weren't they? Didn't that mean banding together and supporting one another through thick and thin?

Assembly was as irrelevant as ever but a real strain for Natalie to remain standing for the entire fifteen minutes of sermons, school hymn and notices. The fact that the canteen was serving spaghetti carbonara was hardly newsworthy; besides, they'd all see the canteen menu when they went in for lunch anyway.

Natalie finally managed to collar the pair of them at mid-morning break, having twice missed them before and after double-science. She didn't want them to know she suspected they'd been avoiding her all morning, but she couldn't keep from checking that they'd both stuck to the plan so far.

'Sally's mum was on the phone to mine first thing,' Natalie bowled out with right away.

Before she could check whether their mums had received similar calls, Louise grabbed Natalie's arm hard, pinching the skin, and yanked her out of earshot of anyone else.

'What the hell is wrong with you?' Louise snapped.

Natalie rubbed her arm gingerly. 'What? All I asked was—'

The spiked glare fired by Louise was enough to stop Natalie repeating her mistake. 'Jane and I were thinking that it's probably best if the three of us just lay low today. Yeah? Don't want to draw unnecessary attention to ourselves. Sally's mum is bound to have phoned the school to say that… *she* won't be coming in today, but it's probably too early for her to phone the police.'

Natalie's eyes widened but she didn't speak.

The police? Natalie hadn't even thought through the full repercussions of what they'd done last night. Would the police really get involved? Natalie had been so concerned with just getting home without her parents discovering she'd snuck out that she hadn't dared to fast forward to possible ramifications.

'So we've just got to stick to our story, yeah? We're all agreed? Last night *didn't* happen. None of us snuck out, none of us went to the woods and we don't know what happened to... *her*.'

But we did sneak out, Natalie wanted to roar, and we *do* know what happened to Sally.

'What's with the face, Nat?' Louise challenged.

Natalie met her gaze but had no idea what shapes her face was pulling.

'Have you already told someone?' Louise continued.

'What? No,' Natalie spat back. 'I wouldn't!'

Louise was eyeing her suspiciously and then something silent passed between Louise and Jane, but Natalie had no idea what the exchange meant.

'I swear to you! I didn't tell anyone.'

'What about your mum and dad?'

'Nobody, I swear.'

'What did they say about your leg?'

Natalie looked down to where both girls were now staring, and saw evidence of the dark patch seeping through the large plaster beneath her dark tights. She'd known the walk to the bus would be too much, and clearly her efforts to clean and treat the wound had failed. She hadn't been able to bring a spare plaster in case the first one failed, and now she'd have to try and snatch one from the medical bay. If she told the school nurse that she needed it for her leg, the nurse would insist on examining the wound, and then alarm bells would sound.

'You'd better get that cleaned up,' Louise said, her words delivered with no empathy.

Louise and Jane began to move away, until Natalie reached out for Jane's arm. It was clear Louise had appointed herself the new leader of the group, but Jane had said nothing to suggest she was in complete agreement with Louise's suggested approach. Jane had always been a bit of a sheep so it was no surprise that she'd yet to speak out against Louise. If Natalie could exert some control of her own, then maybe Jane could be persuaded to her way of thinking instead.

'Jane, would you be able to help me to the nurse's office?'

Jane's eyes widened and she looked to Louise for an answer.

'No,' Louise confirmed. 'We agreed it's best if we all go our separate ways today. If the nurse sees two of you and that leg, she's going to start asking questions – the kind of questions that neither of you are up to answering. Trust me; it's better this way.'

Jane didn't look back, pulling her arm away and following Louise the shepherd.

The day dragged to lunchtime. Natalie had tried to make up a story about a fellow student injuring a hand, but it had been a bad idea to lie to the nurse about the real reason she required a large plaster. She'd eventually relented and pointed at the stain beneath her tights, but had refused to remove her tights to allow the nurse to see the wound. With little other choice, the nurse had handed over the plaster, and Natalie had hurried off to the girls' toilets to swap it over.

She had winced and silently wept as she pulled the old one off. The wound had looked deeper somehow than when she'd cleaned it in the shower this morning, but it was probably just the amount of fresh blood that seemed to be weeping from it.

She did her best to dab it with tissue paper, but even that stung, so she had dabbed for as long as she could before squashing the fresh plaster over the top. Wrapping the old plaster in more tissue, she'd dropped it into the dustbin before she'd hobbled back to class.

When the lunch bell sounded, she hadn't wanted to leave the classroom, such was the burn and ache in the area surrounding the wound, but Mrs Engleberry had insisted *everyone* leave the room so she could go and have her lunch. Natalie had made her way to the lunch hall, sat alone, and eaten the spaghetti carbonara she had ordered. It had tasted cold by the time she'd made it to her seat so she'd only managed half of it before giving up; she didn't have an appetite, what with everything running through her mind.

How different things might have been had she not bowed to Sally's pressure and agreed to meet them at the gap in the perimeter fence. Sally might still be missing, but at least Natalie wouldn't be living with the guilt of her own part in the sticky mess. But then, had she not agreed to go with them, maybe Sally would be here now.

Louise and Jane were the last to return to the class, and for all of Louise's noise about them all staying apart, the two of them had remained suspiciously close. Natalie had never felt as isolated as she did in that moment. She wasn't entirely to blame for what had happened, and if those two were planning to tell the truth, and hang her out to dry, then she would need to be ready with her own version of events. But who could she turn to when the truth had such implications? Once upon a time, she would have trusted Louise with any and all secrets, but a line had been drawn, and even in Sally's absence, it appeared there would be no return to the old ways... to the better times.

Mrs Engleberry was late back to class and when she did enter, there was a tall woman in a business suit alongside her.

'Class 9-E, quiet, please,' Mrs Engleberry told them, and the hum of chatter instantly quietened. 'Good, thank you. Before we get going with our French lesson, a couple of you are needed to speak with Detective Constable Fiona Rimmington. So, Louise Renner, Jane Constantine, and Natalie Sullivan, please go with DC Rimmington now, and wait in Mr Panko's office until she's ready to speak to you. Don't worry, girls, you're not in any trouble.'

Natalie's head snapped from the tall detective to Louise, but her former best friend made no reaction to the news. She was cool as a cucumber, whilst every bone in Natalie's body sensed that the truth of last night was about to spill, and it was only a question of which of them cracked first.

Chapter Eleven

NOW

Ealing, London

The media circus was still in flow when I headed back to Maddie's office to check on her. Vans were strewn on any section of road without a yellow line; cameras were set up on trusted shoulders; overly made-up reporters were scavenging for any titbit of information they could supply to add a fresh angle to the story. I even heard one reporter telling her audience how 'today's incident was a clear sign of the failings in the mental health service of the NHS'.

Thankfully, I managed to keep out of the line of sight as I headed in; the last thing the story of Natalie's final moments required was a sighting of someone with a face as notorious as mine. I was surprised when Maddie's assistant said she'd gone home for the rest of the day; the Maddie I know and cherish wouldn't normally let something like today get the better of her, and now I feel dreadful for not postponing the meeting with Jack and Mila to stay with her.

PS Daggard caught me as I was leaving and confirmed his meeting with her had gone as expected, and he didn't expect the case into Natalie's death to drag on too long, subject to the coroner's and medical examiner's final reports. I tried calling Maddie's mobile from her office but it went unanswered.

With nothing keeping me in Central London, I snuck back out of the building and hurried to the tube station. I'm now exiting at Ealing Broadway, which already feels a million miles away from that tent and the gathered reporters. The way people are hustling and bustling around me here, trying to beat the rapidly approaching rush hour of commuters, it's as if none of them even care that a vulnerable woman took her own life today.

That's probably not fair; half of them may not have even heard about Natalie's suicide, though her name and the search term 'suicide' have been trending for hours on social media. My feed is full of 'RIP' messages, and mental health awareness hashtags. I think it's right that more needs to be done to beat the stigma of poor mental health, but that doesn't necessitate every Tom, Dick and Harry passing comment on a situation they know little about. I'd be willing to bet that ninety-nine per cent of the people passing such sweeping social media commentary wouldn't be able to pick Natalie's face out of a line-up, least of all knew her. I'm sure they mean well but for some, *every* nugget of news is just an opportunity to try and steal a bit more of the limelight for themselves.

I'm grateful when I spot Rachel's flat in the near distance. This will certainly go down as one of the strangest and most desperate days in my life, but I know that speaking to Rachel about it won't result in her staking a claim for a piece of the story, even though she's a journalist at one of the UK's leading broadsheets. I had promised her we'd go out for a few drinks tonight as her model girlfriend Daniella is due back in London today, but a quiet night in would be more appropriate in my view. It was kind of Rachel to let me crash at her place again, even though it does mean sleeping on that rickety old sofa bed, but I'd rather that than the isolation of a hotel room. Plus, it's only for one night. When I'd agreed to come and meet with Maddie today, the thought of a second four-hour train journey in a single day had filled me with dread; better to crash in London for a night and return fresher tomorrow.

Rachel is still desperate for me to buy a more permanent residence here in London, and has even proposed sharing the cost with me, with her living in it all the time, and me staying whenever I'm back meeting Maddie, or publishers, or attending book launches. I can definitely see the advantage for her, and deep down I know it would make sense to have somewhere I could stop over at without feeling like I'm intruding, but it would be another step towards leaving Weymouth, and the small seaside town is too much a part of my life and history to abandon it. I've promised Rachel that we can have a real talk about getting a place together in the New Year, but I don't want to start putting down roots with Christmas so close.

Climbing the stairs to the communal entrance, all I want now is a strong cup of coffee and a chance to get my hands on my laptop. All this time on the tube, alone with my thoughts, my mind has been focused on little else but Natalie and what the name Sally Curtis means to me. I did think about searching for their names on my phone, but the Wi-Fi signal on the tube was intermittent and I hate having to read on my phone; I much prefer the larger screen of my laptop, which is straining my shoulders in the small holdall I brought with me for this overnight stay.

I can hear loud voices just behind Rachel's door, and my first thought is that I must have returned while she and Daniella are having a full-on row; I'm about to beat a hasty retreat when the door flies open and I see Rachel, eyes streaming with tears.

'If you don't like it, then just get out,' she shouts at whoever she's glaring at. 'I really don't need this right now!'

She must catch sight of me in her periphery as she suddenly turns to face me, before grabbing my hand and yanking me in through the door; so much for sneaking away for a coffee and letting the heat die down.

'Emma doesn't have a problem with me and Daniella, so I don't know why you do,' Rachel bellows, and as I look up, I see Rachel's mum is perched on the edge of the sofa bed and her dad is standing by the window, his back to us.

Now this argument makes sense. When Rachel came out to me back in September, I was shocked, but also overwhelmed that I was one of the first people she'd confided in. Naïvely, I hadn't realised she was bi, but I've tried to be supportive ever since. Daniella is lovely, and as I've got to know her better over these last three months, I've seen Rachel blossom as their relationship has developed. But there's always been an elephant in the room: Rachel's parents.

Don't get me wrong, I like Mr and Mrs Leeming; they've always been decent in their dealings with me. I've probably met and spent time with them a dozen times since Rachel and I met at university, and whenever I've encountered them they've been nothing but kind to me. That said, their attitude to modern life and culture is set somewhere pre-1990. They claim to be open-minded, but their views are heavily influenced by what they read in the *Daily Mail* and observe on daytime television. Coming out to them was always going to be a tough journey but I'm surprised it's started so early. I didn't even know they were due to visit.

'I'm not saying we have a problem with it, darling.' Mrs Leeming beckons from the sofa bed. 'But you must understand that it's come as a bit of a shock to your dad and me, that's all. You're a grown woman and you have the right to make whatever choices you want; it's all just a bit surprising.'

Rachel's cheeks are reddening and I can't help but feel I'm intruding, but she wouldn't have dragged me in here if she didn't feel she needed some emotional support.

'Being bisexual isn't a choice, Mum!' she shouts. 'I didn't wake one morning and *choose* to fall in love with another woman. It's not like deciding to become vegan in an effort to save the planet. This is who I am. It's who I've always been. I just wasn't aware of how I truly felt until recently. I had hoped you might both be pleased for me.'

'Oh, darling, we are pleased for you,' Mrs Leeming coos, but even I can hear how false it sounds. 'And I'm sure this woman – whoever she is – is as lovely as you say. I think it will just take your dad and me a few days to adjust to the news, that's all.'

Mr Leeming still hasn't turned to face us, and God knows what he's thinking. Part of me is hoping he's seen something strange beyond the pane of glass, and his attention is fully focused on that rather than silently ruminating on what is a highly emotive subject.

'Hello, Emma, dear,' Mrs Leeming says, as if only just

realising I've stumbled in on this personal family issue. 'And how are you keeping?'

Rachel is panting with fury so I take her hand and gently squeeze it; for her, this debate is not over, but her mother has indicated it is for her.

'I'm very well, Mrs Leeming. How was your journey down from Leamington Spa?'

'Fine, fine,' she says absently. 'I slept most of the way. How's your mum?'

Ah yes, my own personal elephant in the room.

'She's still pretty much the same,' I summarise. They know she's in a nursing home and suffers with Alzheimer's, though they only ever met once, at our graduation. 'You know how it is,' I conclude, 'she has good days and bad.'

'Send her our best, won't you,' Mrs Leeming says, standing and straightening her crease-free knee-length skirt.

I nod, even though I know that telling my mum that the Leemings have passed on their regards will be met with a blank stare; there are some days when Mum doesn't even recognise me. More and more, she mistakes me for one of the nurses or her younger sister, my late aunt.

'George, we should go and check in,' Mrs Leeming says to her husband. 'I think a rest, and a chance for us to freshen up, is just what's required. What do you say?'

He doesn't respond, his attention still focused on the window.

'I don't have to stay,' I mutter to Rachel under my breath. 'I can catch an earlier train home if you need the sofa bed for your parents?'

Rachel shakes her head, and leans closer. 'There's no way they would sleep on a sofa bed in my dingy flat, *believe* me!

Besides, you were here first and *they* didn't even tell me they were coming to visit.' She raises her eyebrows high as she says this last part.

George Leeming turns when his wife takes his hand, and he nods in my direction as he passes by without a word to Rachel.

'Do you want us to give you a lift to the restaurant?' Mrs Leeming says as she pulls the thick woollen wrap around her shoulders, a whiff of her expensive perfume rising into the air as she does.

'No, we'll meet you there,' Rachel confirms, allowing her mum to peck her cheek, but rolling her eyes in my direction as she does.

And then they're gone, and it's just the two of us.

'You fancy a cuppa?' I ask.

Rachel shakes her head, turning and opening the fridge, and removing a fresh bottle of white wine. 'I need something stronger. Grab a glass.'

It's not even four o'clock yet and I'm not much of a drinker, but I know better than to argue either of these points. Rachel opens the bottle and pours a generous measure into two glasses before picking hers up and heading to the sofa bed.

'Sorry you had to witness that,' she offers.

'I'm sorry it didn't go better for you,' I say, joining her on the sofa bed. 'Are you all right?'

'I will be.' She nods. 'Sorry, I had no idea they were suddenly going to turn up today. Daniella was here with me when they arrived and I was just kissing her goodbye when I saw them gawping through the window. She hurried away for a meeting with her agent – bless her – and it's probably just as well given their reaction. Why do they have to be so old-fashioned about things? It's 2020, for pity's sake!'

'You know what they say about choosing your friends but not your family. I'm sure they'll come around though, you'll see.'

'I hope you're right. Anyway,' she sighs, 'how are you? How did your introduction to Mila go? Did you pass the daughter test?'

I playfully slap her arm. 'Jack and I are just friends; you know that.'

She smiles for the first time since I arrived. 'Yes, but I also know that you have a soft spot for him, and I reckon he does for you too. Mark my words, Emma Hunter,' she adds, adopting a Yoda-like voice, 'much romance there is that way I think.'

I'm not so convinced. She's right in as much as I do like Jack; he's a warm and generous individual, and I know how much he dotes on Mila. In a different time, and a different place, then yeah, maybe there could be a romantic attraction between us, but right now I'm happy with things remaining platonic. Given all the effort he's put in to help me go through Anna's case paperwork, I wouldn't want to muddy the waters.

'We're going to have to do a raincheck on tonight's drinks,' Rachel says ruefully. 'Sorry, but the folks have suggested we go for dinner so they can get to know Daniella better.'

'That's something though,' I say positively. 'It's not like they're flat-out denying she exists.' I pat her leg gently. 'Give it time, and I'm sure they'll come around.'

'You're welcome to tag along too if you want? I feel bad for bailing on our pre-arranged plans.'

I take a tentative sip of my wine. 'Thanks, but there's some reading I want to catch up on so if anything, this raincheck is a blessing in disguise. I'll be rooting for you from here though, and then when you're back I'll be waiting to hear how it all went.'

Rachel stands and heads back into the kitchen area to top up her glass, and I can't help but feel that fate has cleared my way this evening because it wants me to take a closer look into Natalie Sullivan's background.

Chapter Twelve

NOW

Ealing, London

After three outfit changes and two more glasses of wine, Rachel left the flat just before six to make the short walk back into Ealing to the local Italian restaurant her parents had chosen. With a fresh cup of coffee and the place to myself, I finally feel like I can relax. I open the laptop and log in.

Having checked my sister's site for any new messages and not finding any, I open a fresh internet window and type in Natalie Sullivan's name. The page fills with links to a variety of newspaper and media sites. I click on the top link for the BBC and an image of Maddie's office block with the erected tent outside fills the screen. I can only presume that the body had already been moved by the time the press was allowed close enough to capture such images, and the thought that Natalie's bloody and twisted body could actually be behind the white flaps makes my stomach turn. To think that she was still alive less than twelve hours ago, and that neither Maddie nor I knew how the day would unfold…

Sergeant Daggard mentioned that this wasn't the first time Inspector Marcziesk had been called to try and talk Natalie out of jumping but when I open a fresh tab and type in her name, there are no relevant hits. Maybe I've misspelled her surname. Closing the tab, I return to reading the BBC journalist's take on the story.

Apparently, Natalie was twenty-eight, single, and had a room at a hostel near Kings Cross, which police are currently examining for clues to explain why she chose to take her life. I've always found the thought of suicide terrifying, especially since Dad. To be in that position where you genuinely can't see any other way out… it must be an odd conversation to hold with yourself – trying to determine the method of how to complete the deed. In this day and age, there are so many different means of doing it.

An image of my mum answering the call that day fizzes into my head. Had she suspected Dad was so close to the end?

I remember when I first interviewed Freddie Mitchell. He told me he'd contemplated suicide on a number of occasions as he'd struggled to deal with everyday life after the abuse he'd suffered at the St Francis Home for Wayward Boys. According to him, three quarters of all successful suicides in the UK are carried out by men, and the most common means was hanging. He said he'd never attempted that but had tried overdosing without success. I shiver just thinking about what would have happened had Freddie been successful. He certainly wouldn't have seen his abusers finally brought to justice, and he wouldn't be bringing valuable insight to the documentary currently being filmed about his and the other victims' lives. And I'm pretty sure I wouldn't be a bestselling writer. Life certainly would have been simpler.

Scrolling back through the search hits, I can't see any mention of Sally Curtis so I re-perform the search but including Sally's name. The first batch of hits still relates to today's story, but then I notice a link to stories from 2005, and as soon as my eyes see the face of Sally Curtis, I suddenly realise why her name sounded so familiar.

Find Sally. Tell her I'm sorry.

I remember reading about Sally's disappearance when I first started to look into what had happened to my sister, and I was trying to find connections. It sparked my interest as I knew the army base well, having visited the tank museum there on school trips. At the time, I remember wondering whether it was possible that there were links between Sally's disappearance and Anna's; given the proximity of the sites of where both girls were last seen, it felt like it warranted further attention. I contacted the PC responsible for reviewing Anna's cold case each year, but a few weeks later he reported that links between their cases had been investigated and dismissed.

Sally was fourteen years old when she disappeared from the army base at Bovington, right on the doorstep of Weymouth. The base – home to close to a thousand military families – is protected by a secured perimeter fence, but from memory, Sally was one of four girls who snuck out one night, left the base through a hole in the fence and went into the nearby wooded area. Sally was reported missing the following day when her frantic mother discovered she was gone. Having phoned the families of Sally's friends, she had reported the incident to the local police, who acted immediately, given Sally's vulnerable state.

The website says Sally was one of four girls who snuck out that night. The other three girls aren't named in the story – presumably for legal reasons – but I don't think I'm jumping to conclusions to assume that Natalie Sullivan may have been one of them. Sergeant Daggard all but confirmed it in Maddie's office.

The question is, who are the other two girls, and how will they be affected by news of Natalie's death? It clearly had a lasting impact on Natalie's life in the aftermath, so there's every chance there's been an impact on them too. Pausing, I pull out my phone and create a draft email; this is the means I use for recording notes, as I always have my phone on me, rather than a pencil and paper.

Uncovering the identities of the two unnamed girls feels like the right first step towards what may or may not be a story.

You need to find her.

It isn't clear why Natalie was so convinced that Sally is still alive. The way this article reads, the police suspected foul play, though Sally's body was never recovered. When questioned, the girls claimed they'd gone to the woods to play some game, that Sally had run off into the darkness, leaving the other girls no choice but to return home. One of the girls' parents claimed her daughter had assumed that Sally had run home and they'd see her at school the following morning. Now that I'm reading the article, I recall why I was so willing to accept the PC's conclusion that Sally's disappearance was unrelated to Anna's: witnesses to the disappearance, the time of day, the proximity of the army base, and the age difference (Anna was nine when she disappeared).

Opening a second article, which seems to regurgitate what I

have already read, I find a link to the Bovington base, and open it to learn it is a British Army military base, comprising two barracks and two forest and heathland training areas. The camp is currently commanded by Colonel William Havvard, who is referenced in the earlier story, but when I try and find an image of him, I'm left disappointed. I add his name to the draft email as another item to follow up on.

I continue to scroll through the search hits until I stumble across a piece written in 2015, on the anniversary of Sally's disappearance. She is barely a footnote in what is primarily a study of children currently missing from the south coast of the UK. There is brief mention of Anna too, along with the photograph that was circulated at the time of her disappearance, but the article is focusing on steps parents should be taking to keep their children safe in modern times. It's rather patronising if you ask me, though the intention is valid. I know from my own research that there are more unsolved missing-children cases than are listed in this article, but these are certainly the best known.

But how many more children have vanished with no mainstream media attention? It just underlines how challenging it is to keep our lost loved ones relevant despite vastly improved communication tools. Ultimately, apart from me, who would really care whether I managed to track down Anna? For so long I've pushed Maddie to agree to me focusing an entire book on my investigation into what happened to Anna, but Maddie has always said that there isn't enough relevant interest in our story. Can the same be said of Sally Curtis? Had it not been for Natalie's nosedive this morning, I wouldn't have even thought about Sally Curtis. Was her suicide more than just giving up? Had it been, in fact, a cry for help? What if her intention had been purely noble: to shed fresh light on her missing childhood friend?

I certainly owe her a few days to poke around and see if I can find closure for those remaining friends and relatives of Sally Curtis. It seems unlikely that she might still be alive; after all, how many fourteen-year-olds could leave home with no money or qualifications and survive? I certainly couldn't have at that age. Closing the laptop, I've already decided that once I get back home, I'm going to make the short journey to the Bovington base and see if any of Sally's friends and relatives are still there, or whether I can find out what happened to them.

Right now, though, I have a more important call to make. Unlocking my phone, I locate Maddie's name and dial.

Chapter Thirteen

THEN

Wareham, Dorset

Just the thought of being sent to the headmaster's office had always made Natalie uncomfortable – not that Mr Panko was a particularly scary disciplinarian, but it was the shame in everyone else knowing that your behaviour had been deemed poor enough to be sent to the head of the school. In her time there, Natalie had only once been threatened with such an act – back in Year 7 – and that had been sufficient for her to keep her nose clean.

Louise and Jane had walked side by side behind the detective, leaving Natalie to bring up the rear. Not a word was spoken, almost as if there were no words left to say as they were led out to the gallows. Once at Mr Panko's office, Louise was invited into the main office with the detective and Mr Panko, leaving Jane and Natalie alone in the secretary's domain just outside the door. This could have been the perfect opportunity for Natalie to try and siphon information from Jane, but unfortunately the only two visitors' chairs in the bay were across the wall from one another, with doddery old Mrs Herrington's desk slap bang in between them. The secretary had worked at the school for longer than most of the faculty and was well known amongst students for sharing titbits of conversations she happened to overhear with the appropriate teacher.

Natalie tried to make eye contact with Jane, even tapping her foot gently, hoping the noise would snap her out of this self-imposed trance she seemed to have adopted, but no amount of glaring and tapping forced Jane to look up at her. At one point, Natalie cleared her throat, but Mrs Herrington was the only one who looked at her, raising an eyebrow in disapproval at the distraction.

Louise had been with Jane for most of the day, but what had they been talking about? The pact between the three of them prohibited discussions about last night, but did that mean Louise and Jane had remained true to the pact? Natalie doubted it very much, so why weren't the two of them as anxious as her at the prospect of being grilled by the police? Louise hadn't batted an eyelid when Mrs Engleberry had announced that the three of them were to go to Mr Panko's office with the detective; it was almost as if Louise had been expecting the announcement to occur... But she couldn't have known, could she?

Natalie's mind raced with unanswerable questions, each sparking fresh worry and concern: if Louise knew the police would be coming in to speak to them, had she already planned what she would say in answer to their questions? Had she coached Jane in what to say? Would they stick to the pre-agreed story? Or had Louise suggested an alternative version of events – a version that would leave Natalie facing all the blame for what had happened? But Louise couldn't know what Natalie had actually done, could she?

'Jane? Can you come in here now, please?'

Natalie's head snapped up at the sound of Mr Panko's voice, his thin frame at the now open door to his office. Louise stepped through the gap and left the secretary's bay without so much as glancing in Natalie's direction. Tall and confident-looking, she strode away and headed back to the classroom, and by the time Natalie turned back to Mr Panko's door, it was already closed with Jane inside.

Louise hadn't looked upset or as if she had been crying; that had to be a good sign. Maybe it was as simple as the detective asking when Louise had last seen Sally, and she'd stuck to the story: the four of them had walked home from school together, and hadn't seen each other again until arriving at school this morning. Nobody had witnessed the four of them sneaking out or gathering at the hole in the perimeter fence. So long as everyone *stuck* to the story, nobody would be any the wiser.

Natalie continued to stare at the door, wondering whether she should swap to the other chair, which was that bit closer to the door; maybe if she was over there she'd be able to overhear a little of what was being said. But to move would draw the unwanted attention of Mrs Herrington.

Jane wasn't as brave as the rest of them – not that Natalie was feeling a single ounce of bravado at this moment. The four of them had once gone to Sally's house to watch a horror film that Sally had pinched from her dad's DVD collection, and Jane had screamed at every tense moment where the killer would appear on screen, and burst into tears at the final encounter between killer and heroine. It had made the rest of them giggle – not that Jane had complained; she knew better than that. She'd always been easily led by the strongest voice in the group, and with Sally gone, that power had been assumed by Louise. If Louise wanted Jane to go off-script then it would happen, and it would explain why Louise had looked so calm and collected as she'd strode from Mr Panko's office.

Natalie rubbed her clammy hands the length of her skirt in an effort to dry them before it would be her turn to face the music. Was it unusually hot in Mrs Herrington's open-plan area, or were her palpitations and sweating just a sign of her guilt? Is that why the detective had decided to leave her inquisition until the end? Had she smelled Natalie's guilt the moment she'd walked into class 9-E? Had she left her to fester, with Mrs Herrington there to record every trickle of sweat that dripped from Natalie's forehead? The stress was unbearable.

She could just tell them the truth. Regardless of whatever Louise had coaxed Jane to say, the truth was always the best policy, wasn't it? Tell the officers about why they'd snuck out to the woods, what had unfolded and why she'd fled in terror, flailing blindly in the dark woods until she'd tripped and stumbled and impaled her leg. Yes, they'd all probably be grounded for months, but at least the burden of the secret wouldn't continue to splice through her every thought. A problem shared is a problem halved according to the axiom, and maybe the same logic could be applied to a confession.

Would the police realise she was telling the truth though?

What if the other two then denied it when confronted? What if they said they had no idea what Natalie was talking about, and that she must have made up the part about the two of them being there? The spotlight would then be firmly planted at Natalie's door, and she would go down in history as the last person to ever see Sally Curtis. If the police then doubted that opening element of her story, they then might question other aspects of it too. They'd assume she was the one who'd made Sally disappear, and then they might lock her up and throw away the key; she could almost hear her dad telling the police how she'd always been such a troubled girl.

The sweat was now causing the collar of Natalie's blouse to stick to her neck, and the wave of nausea currently splashing inside her was not a good sign. Covering her mouth, she attempted to hide the small belch escaping, as bile began to summon at the back of her throat. Did she have time to tell Mrs Herrington she needed to go to the toilet? Would that make her look guiltier? Natalie looked out to the deathly silent corridor; the toilets had to be a good forty-second run from here, and if she stayed, she was almost certain she'd need to reach for the metal wastepaper bin beneath Mrs Herrington's desk. The choice was simple: race to the toilets or reach for the bin.

And that was precisely when the door to Mr Panko's office opened and Jane emerged, teary-eyed, and skulked out into the corridor.

'Natalie, if you could come in now?' Mr Panko said.

Thoughts of throwing up instantly evaporated from her head as Natalie stood, the sweat against her spine surely now showing through her blouse and blazer. This was it: stick to the story or unburden herself of the truth.

When Natalie's eyes next opened, her mind couldn't make head or tail of the beeping sound coming from somewhere behind her, nor why she was lying in a bed, covered by a white sheet. Was it all a dream? Just an intense terror she was now coming around from? Had the whole thing been a nightmare… sneaking to the woods, fleeing in panic, puncturing her leg, the detective at the school?

Natalie rubbed her eyes. Her head was pounding and her body covered in a sweat not dissimilar to the one she'd felt waiting outside Mr Panko's office. Of course it had to have been a nightmare. Why hadn't she spotted the clues sooner? It was almost laughable, and yet the vision had been so intense and so believable.

Allowing her eyes to adjust to the dimness of the room, she now realised that this was not her bedroom, and the white sheet covering her was not the purple duvet she slept with every night. Then her gaze fell on her mother, dozing in a chair beside the bed.

'Mum?'

Cheryl Sullivan's eyes slowly opened and she reached for her daughter's hand. 'Oh, thank God you're awake.'

'W—w—what happened?'

'It's okay, sweetheart, you're in the hospital because you fainted at school and bumped your head on the corner of Mrs Herrington's desk. Because you'd bumped your head and passed out, the school called an ambulance and you were admitted for possible concussion. How are you feeling?'

Natalie felt the blood instantly drain from her face and

before she could stop herself, she leaned over and threw up all over the shiny floor.

All of it was real: the forest, Sally, the detective… All of it.

Mrs Sullivan rushed to the small door in the private room and called for a nurse to come and help clean up. Natalie simply lay back in the bed and allowed them to fuss around her. When they asked her to open her eyes, she did; when they asked her to put the thermometer under her arm, she did; when they told her to take a sip of water, she did. It was as if she was no longer in control of her body; someone else was now pulling the strings.

And when the tall detective appeared at the door and asked her mum if it was okay to come in, Natalie knew the writing was on the wall.

'It's nice to finally meet you, Natalie,' the detective offered warmly, her nose noticeably long and pointing up slightly at the tip. She perched on the end of the bed, notepad in hand, ready to commence the interrogation. 'How's your leg, Natalie?'

Natalie moved her foot beneath the covers and felt the tight bandage around her calf, where the plaster had previously been. They knew about her leg.

'It's fine,' Natalie mustered, her throat unbearably dry.

'Nasty injury that,' the detective continued, 'quite infected from what the nurse told me, but too recent for any real infection to take hold. Did you injure yourself in the woods last night?'

Natalie looked from the detective to her mum: they both knew what had happened. Louise and Jane must have told them everything.

'Don't worry,' the detective continued, shuffling a bit closer, 'you're not in any trouble. Well, certainly not with me, though I'm sure your parents will want to speak to you about sneaking out of the house in the middle of the night. Listen, to cut a long story short, I know that the four of you went down to the woods last night. What I want to know is what happened after the game of truth or dare.'

Chapter Fourteen

NOW

Ealing, London

Maddie's lack of response to my calls has me frantic with worry. I've never had her landline number as she's always been contactable via her mobile night and day. I remember once having a full-on meltdown on the day of publication of *Monsters* and sending her a text message at three in the morning asking if it was too late to cancel the whole thing. Of course it was – the question had been rhetorical and my mind's way of seeking reassurance – but she'd phoned me back immediately to tell me everything was going to be okay. I don't know if talking clients down from the ledge is a common thing for agents to do, but mine does – and so much more.

Scouring the web, I only find the number for her office in central London and I already know she's not there as her assistant said she'd gone home. But that was hours ago; even in the A40's worst tailbacks, she should have made it there by now, which means she's *choosing* not to answer my calls and messages. After what happened on that rooftop, can I really blame her for not wanting to hear from me? To be reminded of what happened?

I can't just leave things alone though, as my anxiety is worsening. The fact that she doesn't want to speak to me – in my head, at least – means that she really *needs* to speak to someone. Maddie doesn't have much by way of family as far as I know. A divorced husband whom she was pleased to see the back of, and no children that she's ever mentioned, so if her mental health is at a low following Natalie's suicide, then she needs someone to talk to. I might not have been on a training course, but I know a cry for help when I see one.

Dialling Maddie's number again, I follow it up with a text message telling her to answer my call or I'll come round and start banging on her door – not that I know exactly where she lives. She took me to her house once, back when I first signed, but it was only a whistle-stop tour to collect something she'd forgotten. I couldn't tell you the name of the road, or the number, so even phoning a taxi won't help. Not that she knows any of that; as far as she's concerned, I've been to her house and could turn up again at any moment.

I'm relieved when she answers. 'Maddie? Oh thank God, what's going on? Why have you been ignoring me?'

There is silence on the line.

'Maddie? Are you there? Can you hear me?'

Her response when it comes is tired and sullen. 'What do you want, Emma?'

It's like I'm speaking to someone else. I know it's Maddie's voice, but there's something wrong with it; she's usually so bubbly and hyperactive, but this Maddie sounds down and out.

'I returned to your office to check on you after seeing Jack, but your assistant said you'd gone home early to work from home instead. I just wanted to check you were okay after what happened.'

She grunts. 'Why would anything be wrong? I'm not the one who threw myself from the building.'

This is definitely not the Maddie I know and love – the woman who sees a silver lining in *every* cloud. Someone leaves a bad review for *Monsters* and Maddie will say it just helps provide some balance; I have a day when I don't manage to add any words to my manuscript, and Maddie says that's just fewer words that will need to be edited or cut. She is the most positive person in my life – to an annoying degree at times – and I don't like that the shoe is now on the other foot.

There can be only one reason her presence has dipped so low.

'It wasn't your fault,' I say quickly, bracing myself for a backlash that doesn't come. 'You did your best, Maddie, but even Sergeant Daggard said this wasn't the first time she'd tried to take her life. With the best will in the world, when someone is adamant about ending their life, there is nothing you can say or do to prevent it. She was a very troubled young woman, and it was only by chance that she ended up on the roof of your building. At least her final moments were filled with your optimism.'

I take a breath to allow Maddie to respond or challenge what I've said, but she remains silent.

'Do you want me to come round? I'm a good listener.'

'No. Thank you, Emma, but no, I'd rather be here on my own. I appreciate you phoning and your concern though.'

For the briefest moment I'm reminded of my first encounter

with Freddie Mitchell. When we first started talking at the homeless shelter he was full of bullish bravado, but I sensed it was all an act he was putting on and after I asked a couple of probing questions, he finally allowed me to see beyond his mask. He spoke of low self-esteem, a lack of reason to keep going, but without the strength to actually commit suicide. He reminded me that it isn't the coward's way out, and actually takes a huge amount of courage. It troubles me that this memory is the one that has chosen to appear while I am speaking to Maddie.

'It wasn't your fault,' I repeat. 'Tell me you don't blame yourself.'

She sniffs loudly, and it's only now that I realise how close to tears she is. 'I just keep wondering whether I should have left it to the professionals. That inspector had managed to talk her down before, but maybe that's because she hadn't had some interfering busybody trying to do her job for her.'

'You did nothing wrong, Maddie. If anything, I thought you were making better progress before Inspector Marcziesk arrived.'

'As soon as I heard someone was up there, I thought it was fate calling me to action. I thought, this is it; this is *my* moment to shine. The work I'd done with The Samaritans, the training course, all of it had been building to *this* moment. That's why I was so keen to get up there and try and talk her down.'

'You gave it your best shot, Maddie. You kept Natalie talking when she could easily have jumped before the inspector arrived. You gave her a chance to save Natalie, but nothing was going to change her mind. Don't you see? I've been reading up on what she told us about. That Sally Curtis thing. Do you remember what she said? She told us to find Sally and to tell her she was sorry.'

'I vaguely remember… what of it?'

I proceed to relay what I've learned this evening about four girls going to the woods to play a game of truth or dare, and only three of them emerging. 'Sally vanished that night,' I conclude, 'never to be seen again. You said you thought fate drove you to that roof, and maybe you were right. Maybe fate wants us to find out what really happened to Sally Curtis.'

She's quiet for a moment. 'Maybe that's the reason *you* were there, but that sort of thing is what you do, not me. My purpose was to keep her alive… and I failed.'

Despite her moving the phone away from her face, I can hear her weeping.

'Why are you so certain that that's why you were there?' I say, allowing my tone to become slightly more aggressive, in an effort to snap her out of self-pity.

'Because I sensed Jordan was there with me.'

Who the hell is Jordan, I want to ask, but settle for 'Jordan?'

'My son,' Maddie says, her voice barely audible down the line.

'I didn't know you have a son.'

'*Had*. He died eight years ago.'

She has never spoken of children before and I'm totally on the back foot. 'Oh God, Maddie, I'm so sorry. I had no idea.'

I hear Maddie blowing her nose and the tears are beginning to sting my own eyes. Of all the things I expected her to say tonight, this was surely the last. I've known Maddie for close to three years now, and I'm certain she's never mentioned being a parent before, certainly not one who had to bury her own son. There are no pictures of family in her office, just the framed artwork she loves to sit and stare at.

'He was at university,' she eventually explains. 'It wasn't long after his father and I divorced, and I think I suspected he wasn't coping with that change. I did encourage him to speak to a counsellor of some sort, but I don't think he ever did. What I didn't realise at the time – none of us did – was that he was suffering from major separation anxiety. Moving to Edinburgh University had been Jordan's choice, but with me working full-time in London and his dad off shagging his way around the Caymans, we had no idea how lonely and isolated he felt. He'd always been such a confident young man, and I hadn't thought he would struggle to make friends, nor that he was crying himself to sleep every night.

'I'd phone and speak to him once a week, and he always sounded so chirpy and full of life… or maybe I was just hearing what I wanted to. I was due to fly up and visit him in a couple of weeks when the call came through. It was a Sunday morning, and they'd located my mobile number in his phone records. I refused to believe it at first. Not my boy. He wouldn't kill himself. There had to be some kind of mistake. It was hard enough when my own father took his life, but my boy wouldn't put me through that again.

'I flew up there immediately, half expecting to be told it was a case of mistaken identity the moment I stepped off the plane, but there was no apology. Two female officers collected me from the airport and took me to the morgue to identify him. The image of his ice-white face beneath that sheet has never left me. It was my son, yet not, somehow. He looked so different without that verve for life I'd always seen in him. People often say that a dead body looks like a relative sleeping, but not Jordan; I barely recognised him. He'd lost a lot of weight – a symptom of his separation anxiety – and when they took me to his room at the hall of residence, he hadn't even unpacked any of his things. He'd started skipping lectures near the end, developing agoraphobia, until it became too much, and he...'

Maddie's words trail off, and I don't feel the urge to push her to finish the most painful sentence she's ever thought to say.

'Oh gosh, Maddie, I'm so sorry. I wish you'd told me sooner.'

'It's not something I talk about very much,' she says, and I'm relieved that a fraction of the old Maddie is back in her voice. 'I don't want people to feel they constantly have to walk on eggshells when I'm around.'

'So that's why you were so desperate to help Natalie.'

'Yep. I thought it's what Jordan would have wanted. I wasn't there when he needed me, but I hoped I might be able to save another naïve parent from the pain I've suffered.'

'You tried your best, and I'm sure Natalie's parents would be grateful for that.' I take a deep breath, considering my next words. 'Do I need to be worried about you tonight, Maddie?'

A small laugh. 'No, you don't need to be worried, Emma. I've felt the pain suicide causes, and I'm not at a point where I feel all is lost. I just need some time to get my head together. Okay? I might take a few days off work if that's okay with you? It's practically Christmas anyway, and the legal team at your publishers are still dragging their feet over *Ransomed*, and that won't get resolved until January. You should take a few days off too. Go and spend some time with your mum before it's too late.'

Overwhelming guilt floods my mind in a split second. Here I am talking with a woman who would give anything to spend one more second with her child, whilst I haven't been to speak to my own mother in over a week. The call of home echoes louder than ever in my ears.

Chapter Fifteen

NOW

Kings Cross, London

I'm not expecting to be woken by the sound of my phone ringing, nor the urgency in Jack's voice when he tells me he needs to see me immediately. I ask him what it's regarding, and whether we should meet somewhere for breakfast, but he simply says it's probably best if my stomach is empty. He refuses to go into specifics over the phone. Even when he collects me from Rachel's flat and starts heading along the A40 into Central London, all he'll tell me is he's received a call from Sergeant Daggard, the officer who took mine and Maddie's statements after Natalie jumped, and that it was Daggard who thought I should take a look inside Natalie's room at the hostel in Kings Cross.

Abandoning his car in an overpriced NCP car park, he leads me to the opening of the hostel. I'm surprised there is no police tape, nor any kind of guard preventing entrance to the building. We head in past the bald guy in reception, who doesn't bat an eyelid when he sees Jack leading me through. We head up two flights of stairs, and then I spot Sergeant Daggard standing at the entrance of a room at the end of the corridor. He takes off his cap and smiles as we approach.

'Thank you for coming, Miss Hunter. I hope you didn't mind me asking Jack here to call you?'

In the bright light of the corridor, I can now see Jack better and his face is as pale as milk.

'That's fine,' I respond, 'though I'm a little confused as to why I'm here.'

Daggard runs a hand through his bright white hair. 'To be honest, I didn't know who else to contact. I came here as per procedure to check for any kind of suicide note, or to find anything that might shed light on exactly why Natalie Sullivan took her life yesterday morning. I didn't expect... it's all a bit beyond my experience, to be honest. I remembered us talking yesterday, and I'm obviously aware of the work you did to support the Met's investigation into the disappearance of Cassie Hilliard earlier this year. I know Jack from years ago, and so I phoned him and asked if this might be more akin to your work and he agreed to fetch you.'

Neither of them is making much sense and both seem to be avoiding stating why they felt there would be some benefit in me coming to see Natalie's room in the hostel, which in itself must be breaching all manner of police procedures.

'What exactly am I here to look at?' I ask when I can take the suspense no longer.

'It might be best just to show you,' Daggard begins to say.

'But we should probably warn you first,' Jack interrupts, 'that what lies beyond this door is not easy to take in.'

My imagination is now racing with all manner of evils: a dead body, a dead animal, something worse?

Jack nods and Daggard returns the hat to his head before twisting the handle and pushing the door open. The first thing I notice is the faint smell of incense, reminding me of the years when Mum would force us to attend Catholic Church every Sunday. The room is pitch-black, and as I allow my eyes to adjust, I can see that the curtains are closed and there is no trace of the streetlights we passed outside the hostel.

'Mind your step,' Daggard says, holding the door open with an outstretched arm, but not actually entering the room himself. Jack isn't making any effort to move forwards either.

'Can you switch on the light?' I ask, as I peer into the darkness, and my hand begins to feel along the wall immediately to my right. I stop as I touch some kind of sheet of paper on the wall. As I begin to pull my hand away, my finger brushes against something tight – a cord of some kind.

'The light fitting has been disabled,' Daggard whispers beside me. 'You'll need a torch.'

Reaching into my pocket, I remove my phone and switch on the torch app; at the same moment Daggard flicks on his larger torch and cascades the beam across the far wall. I gasp at what I see.

I don't know what I was expecting to find in the room, but the dead eyes of the pig's face staring back at me never entered my imagination. The head is crudely secured to the wall approximately five feet from the floor using large nails which protrude from the skin of the neck that remains in place.

'This is how I found the room when I arrived,' Daggard winces.

A large, thick-rimmed black circle has been etched around

the pig's head, but from this distance it's impossible to tell whether it's paint or some other unknown substance. For the briefest of moments, the positioning of the head reminds me of the kind of crude reverence commonly associated with devil worship, but I instantly dismiss the thought.

Daggard continues to shine the torch around the room and I see now that the cord my fingers brushed against is in fact coarse red string that has been pinned to the walls using drawing pins. There are loads of strands criss-crossing from one wall to another, like the sort of laser maze you'd find protecting priceless works of art.

'What is all this?' I ask rhetorically, not sure anyone bar Natalie would actually be able to answer me.

Stepping further into the room, I use my phone's torch to scan the walls, starting immediately to my right, and slowly tracing the origins of each strand. Where I was searching for a light switch, there are pages taped to the wall, each bearing unfamiliar scripting. There must be a dozen or so A5 sheets, crudely torn from some kind of book, and each numbered chronologically. Ducking beneath the cords and leaning closer, I see the writing is in Middle English, the kind of words I recall reading in Chaucer's *Canterbury Tales* when I was at university.

There is a large map of the UK next to these sheets stretching the length of the wall and pinned in place. It too is dated, with city names more common to the early nineteenth century, though some are still recognisable, including Winchester. There are also small red circles drawn around certain locations, but at a first look, there is no rhyme nor reason for them. Each circle has its own cord stretching to another part of the room.

It truly is like nothing I've ever seen before.

Selecting one of the red circles, I gently press the string between my thumb and forefinger, and follow it across the room, almost stumbling on a sealed cardboard box in the middle of the floor. Jack catches my arm as I teeter backwards and corrects my balance. Continuing to follow the string, I come to a printed cutting from a newspaper. The paper is brown from age, and the ink is difficult to read because it's so blotchy, but it appears to relate to a story about frogs poisoned near a druid site in North Devon. There are more newspaper cuttings taped at various points around the walls, some older than others, all relating to strange goings-on. As well as the frog story, I find a cutting about goats being mysteriously dyed blue during a turbulent storm.

My head is spinning as I continue to look at each cutting, clearly collected over a significant period of time, but I find myself gasping again when I see Sally Curtis's eyes staring back at me from behind the door Daggard is still holding open. It isn't Sally herself, rather the image I've seen plenty of in the last two days – the image supplied by the family for use in stories relating to her disappearance. There are a number of red strings attached to this particular cutting from a broadsheet which disappear to the far corners of the room.

The overwhelming nausea suddenly coursing through my body forces me to dart out of the room and drop to the floor.

'It's okay,' I hear Jack saying to me as I feel his hand rubbing circle patterns on my back. 'You lasted in there longer than either of us. Take a minute and get your breath back.'

He's right. I hadn't realised at first but I hadn't taken a single breath from the moment I laid eyes on that pig's head. No wonder I feel so lightheaded now.

I nod as I focus on taking as many deep breaths as I can manage.

'You should probably get some fresh air,' Jack encourages.

'I'll be fine,' I reassure him, pushing myself back up to my feet but avoiding looking at the pig's head.

'Is this what I think it is?' I say to Daggard and Jack at the same time, but neither meets my gaze. 'Was Natalie Sullivan a practising witch?'

Jack is the first to speak. 'I don't know. It looks like she was mixed up in something and because of the large sheet about Sally Curtis…' His words trail off and he finishes with a shrug.

I picture Natalie on top of that roof, dressed in those brilliant white robes, and how I'd thought she looked almost angelic.

You need to find her. Find Sally. Tell her I'm sorry.

I don't want to believe what's in that room, but I don't think the image will ever leave my memory. The pig's head is there every time I close my eyes, and I now desperately wish I'd never laid eyes on Natalie, nor heard her final words. I'm not usually squeamish, but I now understand why Jack sounded so terrified on the phone.

'There's something else you should see,' Daggard says, moving his torch to a particular area on the floor.

Following the beam, I see the cardboard box I stumbled into, but it's what's written on the lid of the box that has my legs turning to jelly.

A name.

My name.

Chapter Sixteen

THEN

Dorchester, Dorset

Question after question tumbled from the detective's mouth as Natalie's mother watched on, an ever-increasing scowl forming on her face. By the time DC Rimmington had closed her notebook, Natalie was pretty sure she would never be allowed out of her parents' sight again.

'If you do think of anything else I should know about,' she finalised, proffering a card in the direction of Cheryl Sullivan, 'don't hesitate to get in touch.' She turned back to stare directly at Natalie. 'Sally's parents are frantic with worry, Natalie, and I'm sure you're just as keen as they are to see her return safely. If you do have any method for contacting Sally – whatever that may be – please use it, and tell her to at least phone and confirm she is alive and well. It's hard enough sleeping rough in the height of summer, without these wintry breezes to deal with.'

Natalie's mum's glare had reached its peak at that point,

and as soon as the detective was gone, Cheryl was at her daughter's bedside, threatening to clip her around the ear. 'If you know where Sally is, you need to tell the police – or me – *now.*'

Natalie genuinely wished she did have some method for communicating with Sally, but unless Currys was now designing walkie-talkies that reached other worlds, they were already beyond that point.

'I–I–I don't know, Mum, I told you! I have no idea where Sally is.'

'But you have means to contact her, right? That's what the detective suggested. What about Louise? She's good friends with Sally. Would she know how to get hold of her?'

It was a fair question, and despite Louise's protestations to the contrary, if *any* of them would have a secret method of communication with Sally it would be Louise. Natalie simply shrugged at her mother's question.

'And what about your bloody leg?' Mum continued. 'What the hell did you do to that?'

'I tripped and fell, that's all.'

'Have you never heard of disinfectant? You're lucky it hasn't blown into a full infection. Had that leg been left untreated for any longer they might not have been able to save it.'

Natalie hadn't heard the doctor or nurse mention anything about amputating her leg and it would be typical of her mum to exaggerate the situation to make Natalie feel worse.

'I'm sorry, Mum.'

'Are you? Are you, Natalie? Wait till your father hears about this—'

'No, Mum,' she interrupted. 'Please, don't tell Dad I snuck out.'

'It's too late for all that, young lady. The school phoned your dad when they couldn't get hold of me. Just count yourself lucky that he was away on an exercise and couldn't get back.'

Natalie could almost picture her father's thunder-like face as he received the news that his precious daughter had gone behind his back and snuck out of the house.

An hour later, and following a car journey of enforced silence, Natalie snuggled beneath her duvet on the end of her bed. None of them understood how difficult it was to be the youngest in the group, having to bow to every demand just so the others wouldn't omit her from future activities. It hadn't been Natalie's idea to go to the woods in the middle of the night, nor had she wanted any part of it, but then Sally had said she wouldn't be 'one of the sisters' if she didn't come, and the thought of being ignored by the rest of them at school had changed her mind. She'd made the ultimate sacrifice: risking everything just to keep in their good books... and now it had cost her everything.

Pushing her hand beneath her mattress, Natalie felt around until her fingers brushed against the spine of the book she was looking for. Carefully sliding it out of its hidden position between the bedframe slats, she opened the diary to a fresh page, and poured out her darkest secrets. She couldn't write what had really happened beneath those claw-like branches in case anyone else discovered the journal, so instead she wrote about the same fantasy version she'd rehearsed, before relaying it to the detective while her Mum listened on.

A knock at the door had Natalie scrambling to hide the

diary beneath the duvet. She had it hidden a second before her mum appeared in the doorway carrying a cup of tea and a packet of ginger nut biscuits.

Her mum plonked herself down on the duvet, directly over the diary, and handed Natalie the steaming mug. 'There's something I need to ask you, Nat, and I want you to be totally honest with me. Okay? You won't get into any trouble; I just want to make sure that you're not being forced into anything you don't want to be.

Natalie kept her gaze straight while her pulse performed somersaults and her mind raced with frantic worry. *Oh God, she knows!*

'This trip into the woods last night,' her mum began, 'was it just you girls there? I know that's what you've all said to the police, but there's still time to change your stories. I'm not sure I believe that the four of you snuck out of the base to play some childish game. Why go to the woods to play it? What was wrong with the playground down the road? At that time of night it would have been deserted, and nobody would have seen you there. It's where the four of you go most of the flaming time anyway, so why *not* there? It just doesn't make any sense in my head, unless the four of you were up to something you couldn't risk getting seen doing.'

She knows! She must do. Why else all these questions?

Natalie's fringe was soaked through with sweat as she watched on, waiting for the moment her Mum would ask the most pertinent question and her face would reveal the dark secret they'd yet to tell a living soul.

'Were there boys in the woods with you?' her mum asked.

Natalie almost gasped with the surprise of the question – not one she'd expected.

'No, of course not,' she managed as her pulse spiked.

Her mum was looking at her strangely. 'You're at that age when your body is going through all kinds of changes. I know what it's like, having been through the same change back in the day. You probably have all manner of strange pains and sensations as your body transforms from girl to woman, and it's understandable that you might be curious about certain aspects of that…'

Natalie's panic had swiftly reverted to awkward cringing. The last thing she needed was to talk about sex with her mother. Hadn't she been through enough already today?

'Mum, we didn't go to the woods to have sex with boys,' Natalie said sharply, hoping to end the conversation there.

'No? If not boys, then… were you… I mean, did the four of you…?'

From the way her mum was now squirming awkwardly on the bed, Natalie knew exactly what she was picturing, and was almost as horrified at the image. 'Ooh, no, Mum, we weren't having sex with each other. I'm not a lesbian.'

'There's nothing wrong with being a lesbian, Natalie. I read about it in *Cosmopolitan*. It's actually quite trendy, and apparently one in five women these days has experimented with lesbianism in one form or another.' Despite trying to sound comfortable with the prospect of her daughter coming out, Cheryl Sullivan's body language suggested the opposite.

'Seriously, Mum, I don't have any problem with girls fancying girls, and boys fancying boys, but I'm not gay.'

Her mum did a lousy job at hiding her relief, but it was still tinged with concern. 'If not that, then what were the four of you doing in them woods? The only other conclusion I can draw is that you were taking drugs, but I thought we raised you better than that.'

That should have been the story they concocted; the punishment might have been greater, but it would have been a far more believable story than the game of truth or dare. Natalie was certain DC Rimmington hadn't bought the lie either, as she'd focused the majority of her questions on the game: who'd been asked what and what dares had been completed.

'We weren't taking drugs, Mum.'

'No?' her mum sniffed the air, as if half expecting the whiff of marijuana to prove Natalie wrong. 'You would tell me if you were being pressured into taking drugs, wouldn't you?'

Natalie lowered her mug of tea, and fixed her mum with a sincere look. 'I'm not taking drugs, Mum. I'm only thirteen.'

With the lecture complete, Cheryl stood, leaving the ginger nut biscuits on the mattress. 'Would you do me a favour? I have some letters that need posting. Would you be a love and take them to the postbox while I have a shower? Considering your dad will probably ground you when he gets back later, this might be the last time you get a break for freedom.'

Natalie agreed and pushed herself from the bed, securing the diary back beneath the mattress when she heard the shower burst into life. Locating the envelopes on the kitchen table, Natalie scooped them up and headed out into the faint drizzle, the grey sky overhead threatening greater showers in the imminent future. Natalie half hobbled, half limped the hundred-metre distance to the tall round red letterbox, desperately hoping her mum would manage to calm her dad down before he began his angry interrogation of last night's fable.

Turning back for home, the last thing Natalie expected was to be confronted by a red-faced Louise. 'What the fuck did you say to that detective?'

'I told her what you told me to say. I told her about the game of truth or dare.'

Natalie couldn't understand why Louise looked so hot and flustered; after all, it wasn't Natalie who'd let slip that the three of them had snuck out to the woods. Thanks to Louise and Jane's mini-confessions in Mr Panko's office, it was Natalie who'd been caught on the back foot when DC Rimmington had turned up at the hospital.

'The detective knew all about us being at the woods,' Natalie continued. 'Why didn't you warn me you were going to tell her?'

Louise looked offended by the slight and quickly scanned the immediate vicinity for any beady eyes poking out from behind curtains. 'Not here,' she said. 'Meet me at the hut.' She turned to leave.

'Wait,' Natalie tried. 'I'm grounded and my mum will be expecting me home straightaway.'

Louise fixed her with a hard stare. 'The hut. Two minutes.'

Natalie watched her walk away, knowing that Louise would head down the next alleyway that ran behind the hut and the nearby houses before coming out the other side, closer to the entrance. It wouldn't really matter if Natalie used the same route, but she sensed Louise would be angry if she did, so Natalie headed back down the road, towards her own house, but hurried past as she got near. With any luck, her mum would still be in the shower and wouldn't notice if Natalie was a few minutes late back.

The hut – an outbuilding of sorts, intended to host after-school activities – was set back from the main road, and was where Louise, Natalie, Jane and Sally would usually congregate after school for the drama club run by Pete, one of the servicemen. Natalie was surprised to find the hut unlocked, and as she proceeded through the double doors, soon found Louise huddling close to the small electric fire, the only source of heat in the large yet quiet building. Natalie headed over, and stretched her hands out over the warm orange light.

'They still haven't found her,' Louise began, rubbing her arms for warmth. 'That's despite me telling them where we snuck through the fence and approximately how far we went into those woods.'

'Why did you tell them anything, Louise? The plan was to only tell them we'd snuck out once they knew.'

She smiled wryly. 'Because I knew one of you two would freak out inside Panko's office and let it all slip anyway. It was safer just to admit it. Worse to have been caught in a lie.'

There was some logic to Louise's thought processes, if indeed that was the real reason she'd spoken out. It was just as likely that Louise would have been the one to have buckled under the glare of Rimmington's interrogation.

'I wouldn't have told her anything,' Natalie said defensively. 'I can keep a secret. If anything, Jane probably would have caved first.'

Natalie felt bad throwing their other friend under the bus, but Jane had done little to support Natalie earlier at school, so she was fair game.

'Yeah, you're probably right,' Louise snickered, and the tension in the room lifted a fraction.

'Do you think they'll find her?' Natalie asked, instantly

regretting it when Louise's face turned a dark shade of crimson.

'Why would you ask me that? How the hell do I know? It wasn't my idea to… to go through with it. It was all Sally's idea, *remember*? She wanted us to do… *that*. I agreed with you that it was a bad idea, but you know how difficult it could be to go against Sally.'

Natalie wanted to correct Louise and tell her that she was as much to blame for last night's tryst as Sally, but knew there was little point. If Louise had now convinced herself that she'd been sceptical, no amount of argument would change her mind back.

'But what if they find evidence of what we did?'

Louise pulled a face. 'And how are they going to do that?' She paused, studying Natalie's face. 'Wait, did you tell them? Did you tell the detective why we were really there?'

It was Natalie's turn to look hurt. 'Of course I didn't! Do you really think I'm capable of betraying my friends like that? It's bad enough that my dad is going to yell and scream at me when he gets back tonight, without them knowing anything about *that*.'

Louise continued to consider her, until her face softened again. 'Good. Well don't be forgetting what will happen if any of us admit the truth.'

'What if Jane lets something slip?'

'She won't! I've dealt with Jane; she'll keep her gob shut. You're the only loose end I'm now worried about.'

'Fuck you, Louise!' Natalie snapped. 'I said I won't snitch and I mean it!'

Louise took a step back from the fire. 'All right, calm down. I just had to be sure. No need to go all menstrual on me.'

Natalie didn't share the smirk, but took a deep breath to calm herself down.

They both started as the doors to the hut opened, maybe both expecting to see a half-dead Sally emerge – that or DC Rimmington ready to haul them away for what they'd done. Both sighed with relief as they spotted the freshly shaved chin of their drama tutor Corporal Pete Havvard, the son of the lieutenant-colonel.

'I came as soon as I heard the news,' he said, hurrying over to the two of them and hugging each in turn. 'How are you both?'

'Holding up,' Louise replied first, rubbing her shoulder up against his green, woollen sweater, until he wrapped his arm around her again, holding her.

Natalie wanted to slap her for using Sally's disappearance to make her move on Pete. He'd been strictly off limits for all four of them; they'd sworn a pact at the start of the year that none of them would try to win his heart, as it wouldn't be fair on the others. Even now though, Natalie could smell the scent of his cologne and wanted to be as close to him as Louise was. Presumably, in Louise's eyes, the earlier promise was now off with Sally out of the picture.

'They sent us home from school early,' Louise continued, making puppy dog eyes at him. 'Poor Natalie here fainted when she heard the news.'

If Pete hadn't been there, Natalie was certain she would have slapped Louise for that comment. It was typical of her to make Natalie look like the weakest link.

'Gosh, are you okay?' Pete asked, and Natalie revelled in his concern as Louise silently squirmed at the backfiring of her plan.

'I bumped my head, but the doctors said any concussion would be minor.'

Pete's emerald eyes matched his jumper so well, and the buzz cut to his naturally dark locks complemented his chiselled cheek bones and well-groomed torso. He was a walking, talking action figure so it was no wonder all the girls on the base swooned whenever he passed. Not that he'd ever been anything but professional and gentlemanly – having the lieutenant-colonel for a father meant he had to live above and beyond the minimum expectations, and he did so with aplomb.

'If either of you ever need to talk about… stuff, I'm a really good listener. Yeah? I can't even begin to imagine how worried you both are about Sally, but I'm sure we'll find her and bring her back safe and sound. Knowing what this place is like, no stone will be left unturned.'

Natalie shuddered at the thought of the stones being lifted in the woods, and the truth of their crime being unveiled. If they'd stuck to the original plan, maintaining that none of them had snuck to the woods, they wouldn't now be under the suspicion of DC Rimmington and Sally's parents. Only time would tell if they would all live to regret Louise's recklessness.

Natalie's eyes widened as she remembered her mum in the shower. 'I need to go. Are you coming, Louise?'

Louise didn't move. 'Actually, I could do with talking through my feelings with someone, if you can spare a few minutes, Pete?'

'I don't mind talking to you, Lou,' Natalie tried, but her friend didn't even look round to acknowledge the offer.

'You run along, Nat. Don't want your parents telling you off for staying out past your bedtime.'

It was another dig that Natalie couldn't respond to without sounding even more childish. Giving them one final look as Pete lifted down two chairs from the tall stack in the corner, Natalie could only hope that he rebuffed Louise's advances and stayed true to his professionalism.

Chapter Seventeen

NOW

Kings Cross, London

My eyes haven't left the lid of the box since Daggard first drew my attention to it. *So that's why he contacted Jack to get me here this morning.*

'When we met yesterday,' Daggard says, his voice still calm yet somehow graver now, 'you told me you'd never met Natalie Sullivan prior to the encounter on the roof.'

'I hadn't,' I say, a little too defensively. 'I swear to you, I had no idea who she was until that inspector turned up and used her name for the first time.'

'Well, it would appear she knew who you were. How else can you explain the box with your name on it?'

In truth, I can't, and that's what troubles me the most. She can't have known we would run into each other on that roof. The only people who knew I was coming to visit Maddie were Rachel, Jack, Maddie and Maddie's assistant. I didn't share on social media that I was going to be in London for the night, nor did I check in when I arrived at Maddie's office. I don't want to consider the possibility that Natalie somehow hacked through Maddie's security walls and caught sight of her calendar, but even if she did, she couldn't have known Maddie would come up onto the roof to try and talk her down... nor that I would tag along.

'Maybe someone left the box here after Natalie jumped,' I suggest, as the only logical explanation. 'Like an accomplice or something?'

Daggard shakes his head. 'I've checked the security footage for this floor and nobody entered Natalie's room from the moment she left on Friday morning to my arrival here last night.'

I don't like how the pig's head is still staring at me, watching my every move. It feels like it's laughing at me, knowing all the secrets but not willing to give any of them up, even in death.

'Maybe it was only a coincidence that she happened to see you on the roof, having left this box for you,' Jack tries, now back inside the room and following the links between some of the red strings, but steering clear of the pig's head.

It's the most logical theory we have for now, but why leave a box for me at all? What would make her think I'd have any interest in following up on Sally's disappearance? There must be hundreds of other Emma Hunters in the UK, so leaving a box here with my name on was no guarantee I'd get to see it.

'You're certain that the two of you never met before?' Daggard tries again. 'She was working in the same building as your agent, so is it not possible you could have passed on the stairs or in a lift?'

I asked myself the same question right after she'd jumped but I still didn't recognise her face. 'I'm certain,' I conclude.

'All of this must have taken months to piece together,' Jack says, drawing our attention back to the maze of string in the room. 'It's like a cat's cradle, and without knowing where it begins or what she was searching for, it's like trying to piece together a jigsaw puzzle without the final image on the box.'

You need to find her. Find Sally. Tell her I'm sorry.

'Maybe she was looking for Sally,' I suggest. 'Those were her final words to me, so maybe that's what she'd been doing, and had given up hope. I suppose it's not unreasonable to hope that the police would come here after she'd jumped and would link me to Maddie, and therefore to this box. It relies on dozens of ifs, buts and maybes, but it certainly beats the alternative.'

'Which is?' Jack asks, raising his eyebrows.

'That she came back from the dead and wrote my name on the box afterwards.' I almost laugh as the words tumble from my mouth, but as Daggard's torch catches the pig's eyes again, I'd be willing to believe almost anything right now.

I look back to the cardboard box. 'Hey, it's open.'

'We had to be sure it wasn't a bomb, or something sinister,' Daggard explains, his face cloaked in regret. 'To be honest, I'd thought it might be the rest of Porky Pig up there, but it's just some books and other bits and pieces. Go ahead,' he encourages, 'take a look.'

I don't move. Part of me doesn't want to know what a woman going to her death chose to leave for me, a perfect stranger.

Jack is poised and ready so I nod for him to lift the flaps and take a look. Daggard remains by the door, shining his torch beams down on the box as Jack begins to remove each book in turn, holding it into the light and reading the title.

'*The Secrets of Wicca*,' he says of the first one, a hardback with no dust cover, resembling the order of service books I used to see at church. '*Wicca and its Pagan Origins*,' he says of the next, this time pausing and opening the inside cover to skim-read the blurb. His eyes widen as he meets my gaze. 'Maybe you should be the one...' His words trail off as I shake my head.

'Very well,' he continues, 'the next four, five... no, *six* books all appear to be journals or diaries belonging to Natalie. There's a couple of books on someone called Gerald Gardner, and one on a woman called Sybil Leek. Those names mean anything to you?'

I shake my head. 'Should they?'

Jack studies the blurbs of both books before meeting my gaze again. 'Well, Gerald here,' he says, waggling the book in his left hand, 'was the founder of the pagan religion Gardnerian Wicca, whilst Sybil Leek was a practising witch living in Burley on the edge of Hampshire's New Forest in the 1950s. She had a shop there and everything.' He takes a deep breath, 'Jesus! What have we stumbled into?'

The air in the corridor suddenly tastes as dry as it had in the room, and all I know is that I need to get outside as quickly as possible. I don't hesitate to explain my actions, turning and sprinting to the end of the corridor, down both flights of stairs, through the main doors, and back into the pollution-filled air of Central London. I am sucking in lungfuls of air when Jack appears at my side.

'Are you okay?' he asks, concern etched across his goofy features.

I'm not even sure where to begin answering that question. 'I–I–I don't know. I just had to get out. Sorry.'

'Forget about it,' Jack says, anxiety hanging from his attempted smile. 'It's a lot to take in. I nearly threw up when I first saw the pig's head. Had Daggard not been there, I probably would have.'

'I don't understand what it is she's expecting of me. I didn't even realise witchcraft was still a thing. It's the stuff in children's stories, and horrific tales of witch-hunts from the seventeenth century.'

My head is spinning. Witches to me are old women dressed in black with pointy hats, sooty cats, broomsticks and cauldrons. They're fantastical characters in books and television shows I've watched down the years, but they are firmly *not* set in the real world.

I still feel lightheaded as I try and straighten. 'What are we saying? Natalie Sullivan was a witch? If so, for how long? Was it just a recent thing she'd taken up in her desperation to locate her missing friend, or…?'

I can't complete the thought aloud.

Those woods… it's been troubling me since I first read about how Sally Curtis disappeared. Rachel even mentioned it yesterday afternoon. What were the girls really doing in those woods at such a late hour?

Is it really possible that three fourteen-year-olds and one thirteen-year-old went into those woods to cast spells and perform rituals? It sounds ludicrous to even think about it, but that's what the scene in her room in the hostel is suggesting.

'This is uncharted territory even for you,' Jack comments, and I don't think he's ever spoken a truer word.

Daggard appears at the entrance carrying the large

135

cardboard box. 'I've requested the room to be photographed for posterity,' he explains, 'but as far as Natalie's suicide goes, the body is set to be released back to the family, ahead of cremation in the next day or so. I thought you might want to take this with you, seeing as it was addressed to you. Of course, if you do come across anything incriminating about what happened to that other girl – that Sally Curtis – I'd urge you to contact your local police force and report it. Okay?'

Jack accepts the box and agrees to carry it back to his car. Once it's in the boot he asks, 'Where do you go from here?'

'I guess I should read through some of this stuff,' I tell him. 'Though given how close the Bovington Garrison is to home, it probably makes more sense for me to return to Weymouth. The last thing Rachel needs is me getting under her feet.'

'Well, if you get stuck, or just want a sounding board, you know where I am.'

I thank him as we get back into the car. I really don't know what I would have done without him here today. Despite the craziness of what we just witnessed, his cool head made it more bearable.

'Are you sure you're okay? You're pale as a bedsheet.'

I try and offer a more reassuring smile. 'Just not used to dealing with the supernatural, that's all.'

His eyes meet mine, and the atmosphere is electric. He opens his mouth to say something but my ringing phone cuts him off.

I'm tempted to ignore the call but then I see Rachel's name in the display and I cave. I start as I hear her sobbing.

'Em, I n–n–need you to come home.'

Chapter Eighteen

NOW

Ealing, London

I was unable to get much else out of Rachel, as her attempts at speaking became lost in her painful sobs. She's never been one for dramatising so I'm already fearing the worst as Jack drops me outside her flat.

'Do you want me to come in with you?' he asks, his anxiety reflecting my own.

I look out of the window and see Rachel appear at the window. Even from here I can see her eyes are red raw and it doesn't look as though her life is any danger. Remembering the dinner she was due to have last night with Daniella and her parents, I fear the worst.

I turn back to Jack, and manage something resembling a reassuring smile. 'I've got this, but thanks for the lift back.'

The tension in his cheeks eases. 'Okay, but call me if you need anything. *Anything*.'

I try the smile again, grateful to have him so close, before exiting the car with the box of books and hurrying up the steps and through the communal entrance to Rachel's building. As soon as I'm in the door, she's on me, burying her head in my shoulder.

'D–D–Daniella… l–l–left me.'

All I can do is set down the box, embrace her and let the torrent of her tears blot into my t-shirt. Her fists are clenched behind my back, as if not knowing whether to be mad or to give up hope all together. She is silently screaming, suffocating with each breath she takes, holding onto her pride. I know there is nothing I can say to ease her trauma in this moment; I also know she doesn't want to hear words, not yet.

I hold her until I hear the sobs start to ease, and this is the moment I suggest she move to the sofa while I put on the kettle. She nods and moves towards the lounge part of the open-plan room. Heading into the kitchen area, I spot the open bottle of wine on the counter and quickly transfer it back to the fridge before filling the kettle. When the tea is made, I carry the mugs over and join Rachel on the sofa.

'Do you want to tell me what happened?' I say, offering her my hand.

She pulls a tissue from the sleeve of her mustard-coloured woollen jumper, and dabs her eyes with it. 'Sh–sh–she said it was because sh–she's mega busy with work, but I know it's because of how my parents were at dinner last night.'

I'd assumed the meal had been a success because she'd stayed over at Daniella's hotel, but of course there could have been a different reason Rachel hadn't come home.

'Dad started it all off when he asked Daniella how long

she'd been a lesbian for, like it's some decision she made one morning. They just don't get it. I felt so embarrassed as they wheeled out one idiotic question after another. He followed it up with, *I suppose there must be lots of you in your industry*. What the hell is that supposed to mean? The fact that she is a fashion model *and* a lesbian are coincidental, for pity's sake! One did not cause the other.'

I can hear her dad's voice in those words and find myself cringing for Rachel's sake. 'I'm so sorry, Rachel. What did Daniella say?'

There is a momentary glint of a smile but it's quickly replaced by sorrow again. 'She was dignified and didn't show any trace of anger. I have no idea how she stayed so calm. She held my hand beneath the table the entire time and if she hadn't been with me, I think I would have laid into Dad and told him exactly what I thought of his bullshit. Daniella stayed composed and tried to explain that she'd always known deep-down who she was and had tackled her confusion head-on. She tried to educate him but he wasn't listening, not really.'

'And your mum?'

'She was no better! She'd quickly try and change the subject whenever the waiter was passing, as if we were talking about something so steeped in shame that we'd be lynched on the way out of the restaurant. And to make matters worse, when Daniella told them she was vegan, Mum launched into a tirade about how eating meat and dairy had never done our ancestors any harm, and how the world had gone bonkers if it thought switching to a plant-based diet would save the planet. It was like we'd stepped back in time! Suffice to say, we made it through the main meal but excused ourselves before dessert.

I then spent the rest of the evening grovelling to Daniella and trying to convince her that I don't share my parents' petty-minded ignorance.'

'I'm so sorry, Rach. I'm sure they'll come around. In fact, I bet after a good night's sleep they'll both realise how silly they are being, and beg you for forgiveness.'

She shakes her head slowly. 'I think you give them way too much credit. Last night was a real eye-opener for me. I'd almost convinced myself that I was the one being silly to be scared about coming out to them, but clearly my fears were warranted.'

'But you've told them now; you must be a little relieved to have it out in the open, to no longer have to hide who you are.'

She dabs her eyes again. 'Quite frankly, after last night, I don't think I ever want to see either of them again.' Her words are laced with bitterness and disappointment, and whilst she might think she means them, I can see how much hurt it is causing her to even contemplate it.

'Daniella was so quiet when we got back to her room. She said it wasn't my fault that the evening had been ruined. We stayed together, but we both tossed and turned most of the night, and then at dawn she told me she thought it best if we take some time apart to consider things. I told her I didn't need any time, that I'm in love with her, and that I don't care what anyone else thinks, but she told me she didn't know that she felt the same way about me...' Her words trail off as her eyes shine once more.

I've seen Rachel break up with boys before – usually she did most of the breaking off – but I've never seen her as upset as this.

She wipes her eyes and takes a deep breath. 'She said she

was going to LA for two weeks over Christmas, as her agent has got her an audition for some film over there, and she's hoping to take some acting lessons before she does it. I told her I had some time off work, which I was originally going to spend with my parents, but could fly out with her instead... but she told me not to. She said I should give her some space to get her head straight, and then we could talk again when she's next back in the UK.'

I squeeze her hand again. 'I'm sure last night came as quite a shock to her too, and maybe her head is a bit all over the place if she's feeling stressed out about this audition. Maybe a break could be exactly what you both need, and who knows what might happen while she's over there? It might be the jolt she needs to realise that she feels exactly the same way about you. Take the time you need. I think you should call your parents and see how they are after last night, and if you really don't want to visit them for Christmas, then you're obviously more than welcome to come back to Weymouth with me. It would be fun – just like uni.'

She smiles, and it's great to see a glimpse of the old Rachel returning already.

'Where were you when I phoned? The signal was terrible.'

I explain Jack's frantic call, and then what we discovered inside the room at the hostel. She pulls a sickened face but I know she isn't as easily phased as I am by such horrors.

'I didn't even realise witchcraft was still a thing,' I conclude, echoing what I said earlier to Jack.

'Oh no,' Rachel corrects, 'it's never been more popular than it is right now. I co-wrote a piece on some university students last year who believed in the practice of love potions and spells. It was written with tongue firmly in cheek, but according to the last census, there's something like twelve thousand people who claim to be followers of pagan religions steeped in witchcraft. One of the writers you mentioned, Gerald Gardner, was the founder of the largest movement, Gardnerian Wicca. I remember doing some research on him at the time, which I can try and pull up if you fancy a read?'

She reaches down and pulls up her laptop. The last thing I really want is to delve into the occult, but I'm relieved to see my tale is serving as a welcome distraction to her broken heart.

'In fact,' Rachel continues, 'from memory, the south coast of England was prime ground for covens and practising witches, Actually, now that I think of it, part of our article touched upon the New Forest coven, which was formed by that Sybil Leek woman you mentioned. It's not what you think though. They practised chants and incantations, but I don't know that there's any tangible evidence that such spells and the like have ever worked.

'We read one story from the 1940s of a group in Hampshire who walked naked into the woods and performed a ritual where they essentially sent a telepathic communication across the water to the Nazis in Germany to tell them they'd never manage to cross the Channel. This was during the height of World War Two, but was largely dismissed as coincidental when the war was won. The only reason the story retained any notoriety was that several members of the group died after the incantation, though given their age, and how cold a night it was, they could just as easily have contracted pneumonia or died of hypothermia.'

I still can't bring myself to believe that Natalie was a practising witch, despite Rachel's efforts to convince me otherwise. There's only one place I'm going to find any answers, and that's to speak to Natalie's mum directly.

'Rach,' I say, drawing out the vowel, 'I don't suppose you fancy driving us to Weymouth now, do you?'

I'm ready for her to argue against the idea but she takes one look around the room and nods firmly. 'I'll pack a bag.'

Chapter Nineteen

THEN

Bovington Garrison, Dorset

Two nights had passed since Sally had vanished and yet Natalie was still not able to sleep – not properly anyway. Last night, she had spent hours staring at the blue digits of the bedside clock, willing them to change quicker so she could start to put distance between herself and what they'd done. Sleep had come in patches, but ended every time her subconscious returned her to the enveloping darkness of those woods. As much as she wanted to forget, her mind wouldn't allow it.

She'd woken at dawn this morning, screaming and crying. Her mum had come in and pressed a cold hand against her forehead, trying to quieten her before she woke her dad. Natalie had welcomed the rocking embrace her mum had wrapped her in, so desperate to tell her what they'd done that night, but knowing she wouldn't understand and would be horrified to have such a despicable daughter. Her mum had made her a warm mug of cocoa to try and settle her back down but Natalie hadn't wanted to return to anything resembling slumber.

'I think we should keep her off school for a little longer,' she'd overheard her mum's hushed tones from the breakfast table. 'She's definitely not right; her bed sheets were soaked through when I went to her this morning. I think she wet the bed; she's thirteen, for crying out loud! I thought those days were behind us.'

Natalie would have welcomed the distraction of schoolwork, but Sally's empty desk would have served as a constant reminder of why she wasn't there. The school wouldn't be so understanding if Natalie didn't return at some point, but what good would she be in this sleep-deprived, zombie-like state?

'I'm sorry about wetting the bed,' she said glumly as she joined her mum at the breakfast table once her father had left for the day.

Cheryl gave her a concerned look. 'Was it a nightmare?'

Natalie nodded.

'What was it about?'

Natalie couldn't remember exactly what had triggered her absolute terror on this occasion, though all the dreams she'd been having followed a similar theme. 'I can't remember.'

'Last night wasn't the first nightmare either, was it?'

Natalie shook her head.

'Are you still worried about Sally? I'm sure she'll turn up soon; you can't let it worry you so much.'

That was easy for her to say. Her mum hadn't been there; she didn't know what they'd done.

'You can't blame yourself for Sally running away, Nat.

Whatever happened – an argument or whatever – *she* chose not to return home when the rest of you did; you can't hold yourself accountable for her choices.' She paused. 'I'm worried about you. It isn't right for a girl of your age to… to be wetting the bed,' she mouthed the last part, unable to make eye contact. 'Here, have some cornflakes.'

Natalie didn't accept the cardboard box being waved before her. She hadn't felt like eating since that night, and right now she didn't care if she never ate again. 'I'm not hungry.'

Cheryl frowned at her. 'You need to keep your strength up, Nat. You're stick-thin as it is; no boy is ever going to want to go out with you if he can't see you.'

Natalie sneered at the comment. Who cared whether or not a boy ever fancied her again? Was that really all her mum was worried about? Missing out on grandchildren?

'Listen, I saw Mr Panko on the base yesterday and he said he thought it would be a good idea to organise some counselling for you and the others. Seems you're not the only one struggling to deal with Sally's sudden absence; half the class have been off since the news broke, apparently.'

Natalie could already picture those who would use Sally's disappearance as an excuse to get a couple of days off school with their supposed stress; most of the class couldn't give two hoots about Sally – or the rest of them.

'So,' Cheryl continued, 'Mr Panko has arranged for a specialist to come to the base today and talk to the lot of you about your feelings; it's important not to bottle these things up. It's voluntary, but I really think you'd benefit from going along. What do you say?'

Typical of Panko to assume the quickest way to get everyone back to school was to organise some kook doctor to talk to them. It would take more than talking to save Natalie and the others.

'You should go along and listen to what the counsellor has to say, and then maybe we could ask if you can have a private session with him at the end. It might stop your nightmares and bladder weakness to talk through how you're feeling, and what might be causing your strange behaviour.'

'Fine, whatever,' Natalie commented, pouring cereal into her bowl.

Her mum looked so relieved, quickly standing and reaching for her packet of cigarettes. 'Wonderful!' She beamed, clearly pleased by what she would consider top-notch parenting. 'I'm going to jump in the shower and get ready, and then we can walk to the hut together.'

Natalie didn't answer, as her mum left the room and headed up the stairs to the bathroom. Natalie reached for the box of cornflakes and tipped the contents of her bowl back into the plastic packet. At least her mum would think she'd eaten.

———

Natalie's mum hadn't returned for lunch as she'd promised, and Natalie could easily have left the house and got up to all kinds of mischief, with neither of her parents aware of what she was doing. She hadn't; instead she'd wandered round the house, occasionally watching television, occasionally reading, and occasionally listening to music. Eventually, boredom had got the better of her and she'd gone up to bed, willing death to take her during her sleep. She hadn't slept – or at least it felt like she hadn't. She'd tossed and turned, diving through each memory of that night, trying to make sense of what had happened... of what they'd done.

'The best way to tackle a problem is head-on,' her grandma would have said if she were still alive today.

For so many hours, Natalie had tried to ignore and not relive those memories, but how else was she going to understand what had happened to Sally? She thought about the real reason they'd agreed to meet in that particular clearing, on that particular night. The moon had looked so large as she'd watched it slowly rising from her window, in unison with the day's light source setting through the frosted glass of the bathroom window behind her. A perfect balance: night and day, darkness and light, good and evil.

Guided by that enormous ball of white in the dark sky, she'd waited until she could hear the gentle rumble of her mum's snoring and the grunt-grunt-rattle of her dad's drunken slumber. She'd dressed quietly, using her collection of stuffed toys to shape an outline beneath the empty duvet cover, in case one of her parents did stir and come and check on her. They never came close enough to physically check, so the outline would be enough to convince them she was still there; she'd hoped so at least. Then she'd very carefully lowered her bedroom door handle, pulling it towards her slowly to offset the creak in the hinge that always sounded the moment the door reached a forty-five degree angle. She stopped it just before and squeezed through the gap.

She'd slid down the stairs on her bottom, as many an early Christmas-morning raid had taught her that this was the quietest way to avoid creaking floorboards. She'd stopped still at the front door, hearing movement above her. Terror had instantly flooded her body when the upstairs bathroom light had flashed on, and she was certain she had been caught in the act. All it would take was for her mum or dad to look down the staircase and see her framed in the moon's spotlight through the glass panel in the front door. Ducking into the living room would have required her to open that door, which would have made even more noise and definitely awakened whoever it was to her presence down here. Holding her breath, she stayed perfectly still, silently willing them to return to bed without a second thought. It was the longest two minutes of her life, but finally the bathroom light was switched off and footsteps marched back to the bedroom, and then the bed sighed under the weight of its occupants once again.

Natalie had remained crouched where she was for a further five minutes before using her keys to unlock the front door and slip through, locking it behind her. Even as she made it to the bottom of the driveway, she'd expected one of her parents to suddenly realise she'd gone and come tearing after her, but the upstairs bedroom light remained off. That hadn't meant she was home free though. There was every chance one of the neighbours could be outside, or just happen to be looking out of their window as Natalie passed, so she pulled the hood of her black coat around her ears, bent her head, and hurried along the road before eventually arriving at the gap in the perimeter fence.

Her paranoid self had known it was a mistake to climb through the gap. She had half expected the others not to be there in the clearing waiting for her... like the whole thing had just been a cruel trick they were playing on her. Did they know she didn't deserve her place in the circle? Did they know she'd lied when they'd asked if she was ready? Could they tell she hadn't reached that level of maturity yet? It hadn't mattered though. The others had giggled with giddy excitement when she'd stumbled through, torch in hand.

A raised voice snatched Natalie back to the present.

'You don't understand the pressure I'm under,' her dad was growling. 'She was the last person to see her and that must mean she knows what happened.'

They were arguing about her; they must have assumed she was either out or fast asleep. Natalie lay still, listening to every word, desperately hoping they wouldn't come up and realise she was faking.

'She says she doesn't know and I'm inclined to believe her,' her mum retorted. 'That policewoman interviewed all three of the girls and seemed happy enough with their explanations.'

'But how can she not know where Sally went? She was there, Cheryl. They all were. One of them must know where Sally went, or how she got off the base.'

'Not necessarily, Geoff. Natalie said Sally ran off while they were playing their game and you know better than anyone how dark those woods are. It would have been impossible to know whether she ran in a straight line or doubled back.'

'I got dragged in before Lieutenant-Colonel Havvard again today. He isn't happy that Sally still hasn't been traced and has ordered all personnel to double their efforts. But he spoke to me in private and told me I need to do whatever it takes to get through to Natalie. I need her to tell me everything.'

The sound of a foot hitting the first stair sent a shiver through Natalie's entire body. He was going to come up and interrogate her right now. Would she be able to stick to the script?

'Wait, Geoff. She's asleep up there. I'm telling you that she doesn't know anything more. I'm her mother and I know when my daughter is lying to me.'

Natalie only released her breath when no further footfalls followed and she heard the living room door being opened and closed. Their argument continued, but their voices were barely more than a rumble through the floorboards. Pushing back her duvet, Natalie slipped out of bed and slid down the stairs on her bottom, hovering on the last step as she listened in at the door.

'Havvard says he can't afford another Margaret Kilpatrick disaster.'

'But that was all resolved. She sent that postcard from Denmark, I thought?'

'Yes, but… that's two girls who managed to sneak off the base. He's head of security and it doesn't reflect well on him.'

'Better that than her being found dead, surely?'

'He's convinced she's still on the base hiding. Reckons one of the families has taken her in and is keeping her hidden.'

'Who?'

'That's just it; he doesn't know. That's why we're all getting the tenth degree every morning. Part of me thinks he believes *we're* harbouring her… Wait, Cheryl, tell me she's not here.'

'Of course she's not! What do you take me for? Diane is one of my best friends. I wouldn't do that to her.'

'What about what she told you about Owen and his moods?'

'What about it?'

'It lends motive as to why she ran away, if you ask me. If he's really as violent as Diane let on—'

'No, Geoff, you can't tell Havvard about that; Diane told

me in the strictest confidence. Besides, she never said he'd struck Sally.'

'Maybe not, but that doesn't mean he hasn't. Or maybe she's witnessed him hitting her mum and couldn't stand for it any longer.'

'Keep your voice down, will you? I don't want Natalie knowing about any of that, and you swore you wouldn't tell.'

'I need to give him something, Cheryl,' he said, his tone more pained now. 'He's the sort of man who can make life very difficult if he thinks I'm holding out on him.'

'I don't want you questioning Natalie about it any more. She's told us what she knows and that's an end to it. She's in a fragile state. Don't forget, she's just lost a close friend and it's a very confusing time for her. I… I found tampon wrappers in the bathroom wastepaper bin. She hasn't told me her periods have started yet, but she's the right age.'

'I thought they handled all that stuff – sex education – in schools these days.'

'They do, but that doesn't make it any less confusing. Her body is going through all sorts of changes and I just don't think she needs any more pressure from you, or the likes of Havvard. *I* will work on her for you, okay? But I'll do it *my* way, and in my own time. For now, you'll just have to try and keep Havvard at bay.'

Natalie had heard enough. It was bad enough that what they'd done had resulted in Sally disappearing, but now it was affecting her family life as well. No longer caring about any noise, she leaped out of bed, ran downstairs, yanked open the front door and tore off down the drive, not even stopping to look back to see if her mum or dad were chasing; she didn't care. Too much hurt and pain had come from their actions and she needed to put a stop to it by any means necessary.

She hadn't expected it to be raining and, wearing only her slippers and with the bandage tight around her calf, her pace wasn't as fast as it had been on that night, but she ploughed on past the hut, past the playground, almost slipping as she made it to the patch of darkening grass. It wasn't even four o'clock and yet the sky was barely light enough to guide her way.

Collapsing against the perimeter fence, she wailed when she saw that their hole had been sealed up with a series of cable ties, and a new sign had been erected warning that the perimeter was out of bounds to unauthorised personnel. She couldn't do what she needed to from here. This wasn't where they'd acted it out; the ground she was now on wasn't sacred.

Sucking in huge lungfuls of breath, she gripped the wire fence and pressed her mouth through one of the hexagonal shapes. 'Give her back! You weren't supposed to take her! Take me instead. I don't care. I will swap myself for her. Listen to me!'

Something heavy barging into her back caused Natalie to release her grip of the fence and slump to the ground.

'What the hell are you doing?' Louise hissed at her. 'Everyone will hear you.'

'I don't care,' Natalie grizzled back, panting heavily and still trying to get her breath. 'We did this, but maybe we can undo it. If we could just get back through the fence to that clearing, then—'

Natalie couldn't complete the sentence as Louise kicked out, catching her square in the midriff. All the air instantly left Natalie's body.

'You say another word and I swear to God I will kill you myself. Do you understand?'

Natalie couldn't argue, protecting her gut with both arms and praying that a second blow wouldn't be forthcoming.

Louise was now leaning over her, pointing. 'Just keep your fucking mouth shut, Nat. That's all you've got to do. Keep quiet, and all of this will go away. Don't forget who you're messing with. If the truth gets out, he won't just stop at Sally; he'll come for all of us, and our families. Is that really what you want?'

Chapter Twenty

NOW

Weymouth, Dorset

The trip back to Weymouth has passed without incident, with Rachel belting out every word of every song on the *Bridget Jones's Diary* soundtrack and me trying my best to hum along. There are hardly any cars parked along the seafront so Rachel doesn't struggle to find a space outside my flat. The journey down here hasn't been totally wasted as it's given me the chance to read more about Sally Curtis's disappearance on my phone. I've managed to learn the name and current address of Natalie's mum, Cheryl, though there's very little information about her dad, Geoff.

I'm keen to speak to them both about that time in their lives when Sally Curtis disappeared, to try and understand why that particular incident still haunted Natalie some fifteen years later. My first thought was that she must have somehow been involved in Sally's disappearance. Ultimately, Natalie and the other two girls were the last to see Sally, so does that mean they were lying about what really happened? When the four girls went into the woods, did something more than a game of truth or dare occur? Could Sally have died in those woods, never to be seen again? I'm sure the police at the time would have scoured those woods for disturbances in the ground, and Natalie's final words to me also wouldn't make sense if Sally had died at her hand.

You need to find her. Find Sally. Tell her I'm sorry.

'Are you sure you don't want me to give you a lift to the holiday park?' Rachel asks, as I open the front door and let her in.

'Probably best if I go on my own,' I suggest, though I'm grateful for the offer. 'The last thing Natalie's grieving mum will want is an avalanche of questions. I'm only really going to pay my respects, and to try and get a sense of who she was. I shouldn't be too long, but feel free to start looking through the books in the box she left for me.'

She mock-salutes me and then bursts into a fit of giggles. 'Aye aye, skipper.' She pauses and spots the carefully wrapped package on the unit beside the door. 'Ah! Is this for me? You shouldn't have.'

The gift, wrapped in scented tissue paper, is a beautiful floral scarf that I bought for Mum for Christmas. I've been meaning to take it up to the home and give it to her, but I haven't been a good daughter in recent weeks. We officially stopped exchanging presents when she first went into the home, as she doesn't get to go for days out that often and it didn't feel right accepting her financial gifts; money in an envelope can be beneficial at Christmas, but is not really in keeping with the spirit of the season.

I really should make more of an effort to spend some

quality time with Mum. She seems to be having more and more 'bad days', and most of the time when I'm with her, I'm sure she doesn't have a clue who I am. I did moot the idea of asking the nursing home whether they'd be happy for her to come to mine on Christmas Day, but the steps up to my front door are steep and I'd worry that she'd become anxious at not knowing where she is or who I am.

'No, it's for my mum,' I explain, suddenly conscious of the fact that my gift to Rachel – a diamante photo frame with a picture of me, her and Daniella – will need replacing unless things change for the better.

'Oh, I see,' she says, continuing through to the kitchen. 'I suppose I'd better go and buy you something in town if I'm going to be down here for the big day,' she calls back over her shoulder.

'There's really no need,' I call back. 'Just the pleasure of your company is gift enough.'

This has her in hysterics as she mimes sticking her fingers down her throat. 'You'd better get going before I throw up for real.'

My phone vibrates as I'm closing the front door, and I smile when I see it's a picture message from Freddie. He's snapped a selfie with a handsome guy in, presumably, his early twenties, with a mop of strawberry-blond hair. Both are smiling at the camera but it's Freddie's message beneath the image that makes me chuckle:

Is it wrong to fancy the actor playing me in the series? Does that make me a narcissist?

I send a laughing emoji and confirm his suspicions. Typical

Freddie to fall in love with himself. At least it looks like he's having a good time on the set of the documentary based on the crimes in *Monsters*. The producers don't want to use the book's title, and instead have chosen the title *Care of the State* to underline the failings in the system that allowed Turgood and his cohorts to continue their abuses for years unstopped. It also allows the producers to mark the disparity between my book and the actual series: whilst both focus on the crimes and the cover-up, they've chosen a different structure to the show, using actors to play the main characters with added soundbites from psychology experts and Freddie himself.

For a long time, I didn't think Freddie would be keen to see that time of his life played out for the world to see, but he told me that he hopes it will give others the courage to speak up, or the impetus to listen when victims do speak up. I couldn't be prouder of how much Freddie has grown in the few years I've known him.

My phone vibrates again.

Will you be around later? There's something I've been meaning to discuss with you.

I reply to tell him I'll let him know when I'm home. My internet search for Natalie's mum, Cheryl Sullivan, listed her as a permanent resident in one of the local holiday parks a little way along the coast, and so with my usual satchel over my shoulder, I head out into the blustery wind. Despite the proximity to Christmas, it is mild outside, and though the paving slabs are wet, there is no moisture in the air, save for the crashing sea.

Following the incline up to the private residences, I spot

Cheryl's home almost immediately. A woman with short grey hair is sitting on the balcony, chain-smoking, her eyes bereft of any hope and the ashtray on the floor beside her spilling over.

'Mrs Sullivan?' I ask as I approach. 'My name is Emma Hunter, and I want to offer my condolences for your loss.'

She breaks free of her trance-like state long enough to look me up and down, stub out her cigarette and light a fresh one. She makes no effort to invite me up, or shoo me away.

'I was with Natalie on the roof when… when it happened,' I say quietly.

This catches her attention and when her gaze meets mine again, her eyes are shining. 'You was with our Natalie?'

I nod. 'It was my friend who was trying to talk her down. I wanted to come and pay my respects to you.'

She stands suddenly and nervously checks the horizon, even though there isn't another soul in sight. 'You'd better come in,' she says absently, turning and heading in through the open door. I make my way up the stairs and join her inside. It's a mid-size static home, probably enough room for four to sleep comfortably, and it is so clean that if I didn't know better, I'd say it was more of a show home than anyone's permanent residence. There is the odd homely touch – a photograph of Cheryl laughing somewhere, a pair of brass candlesticks with no candles, and three matching patterned cushions on the sofa – but not a thing is out of place. She invites me to sit at the table while she makes us tea, before she makes a deliberate effort to shut the door through which we entered. I'm relieved when she extinguishes her cigarette too.

'You looking to do a story on my Natalie then, are you?' she asks, when she's joined me at the table.

'Oh no, that's not the reason I came here,' I try, not entirely believing the words as they tumble from my mouth.

'Oh, I thought you was here to offer to do one of them book things you do… about her like.'

'What makes you think that's why I would come here?'

'Well, you're a journalist, aren't you? You're the woman who brought justice for them boys at that home; you found that missing kiddie a few months back, right?'

My notoriety precedes me once more.

'I'm sorry, Mrs Sullivan, but my interest here is really just to offer my apologies that we couldn't do more to stop Natalie's death.'

Cheryl shrugs. 'She's been trying to do it for years. Don't get me wrong, I'm devastated that she's gone, but in many ways I'm relieved she's finally at peace. She was always such a troubled girl after what happened.'

'Are you referring to the disappearance of Sally Curtis?'

She nods. 'It all seemed to go pear-shaped after that. Natalie was never the same, and when her dad died overseas a year later, it felt like a blessing that we was getting out of that place.'

'The Bovington Barracks?'

'Yeah. Things are different in a place like that. Everyone knows everyone's business, you know?'

'Natalie mentioned Sally to me just before… she told me to find Sally and to apologise to her. I wondered what she wanted to apologise for.'

Cheryl doesn't immediately respond, but reaches for her packet of cigarettes and lighting one.

'The stories I could tell you about that place would set your hairs on end. Running away was the best thing that Sally

Curtis could have done, even if it did cost the rest of us everything.'

The pig's head appears in my mind until I shake it away. 'What makes you so certain she ran away?'

'Her body was never found, was it? And them girls swore they were the last ones to see her alive, so what other answer is there? They checked their clothing and what-not, you know. From that night, I mean. It was a couple of days after she'd vanished, but they rocked up – that DC Rimmington and her cronies – with some kind of warrant saying they could confiscate the clothes Natalie and the others had been wearing in the woods. Took it all away for forensic examination – not that they found anything, other than Nat's own blood from where that branch punctured her leg. No trace of Sally's blood on any of them, and the police reckoned they'd have found some trace of her if the girls had killed her.'

'What did Natalie say happened in those woods? I read a news article that said the girls had gone to the woods to play truth or dare.'

'Ha!' she exclaims. 'If you believe that tosh you'll believe anything!'

I don't want to ask her outright about witchcraft, but I can't stop thinking about the printed sheets pinned to the walls of the room at the hostel. 'There was another reason the girls were in the woods then?'

'Isn't it obvious? Boys!' she crows. 'All them young, fresh recruits coming to the base for training, away from home for the first time, and being put through their paces by rigorous routines, led by bullies. Is it any wonder they'd go with any girl who fluttered her eyelashes at them?'

She sounds so sure of herself, and yet nothing I've read

online suggested that the girls were doing anything other than playing a game.

'Did Natalie tell you they'd met up with soldiers in those woods?'

Cheryl pauses, as if listening for intruders in her home, before leaning closer. The stale tar on her breath is nauseating. 'She never admitted it to my face, but Nat used to keep a diary. She didn't know I knew about it, and from time to time I'd take a look. I wasn't prying; I just wanted to check that she was doing okay, and not being bullied.'

Her expression is firm as she states this lie, and maybe after all this time she genuinely believes that reading her daughter's private thoughts isn't prying, but I'm pretty sure thirteen-year-old Natalie wouldn't have felt that way.

'It was as if she wanted me to find it,' Cheryl continues, now staring blankly at the wall as if the memory is being projected before her eyes. 'She must have known I'd find it. I think deep down she wanted me to find it. Anyway, I looked at the entry for the days before and after the woods, and although she didn't specifically say they were meeting boys, there were enough clues to hint that they were up to no good.'

'Like what?' I ask, opening the draft email on my phone, poised to type my notes.

Her brow furrows in annoyance at the question. 'I can't remember exactly what she'd written, but I remember thinking at the time that the clues were hinting at boys and sex.'

I make a note to check the journals when I'm home. Having been a teenager who kept a diary of my own, I know that half of what I wrote was in code, in case my parents ever got hold of it.

'She took all that stuff with her when she left home,' Cheryl continues with disappointment. 'I know when we moved off the base a lot of stuff got thrown into boxes as we moved in a hurry, and to this day there are still things we never managed to recover. Couldn't wait to get us out of that house and wave goodbye.'

'Wait, the army threw you off the base because Sally went missing?'

Cheryl's mouth curls into a snarl. 'No, don't be ridiculous! It was when Geoff – Nat's dad – died overseas a year later. They promise to look after the families of fallen soldiers, but we was living in a three-bedroom house with only Geoff's military pension to live off. It was prime market space, that house, and so we were asked to leave and start over outside the barracks. They had a new family moved in by the night we were out.'

'Did you share your suspicions with the police?'

'Not gonna do their job for them, was I? Besides, they wasn't all that interested in what had happened to Sally Curtis anyway. I mean, at the start they came in and tried to do things their way, but there wasn't a lot they could do when that Colonel Havvard stamped his authority.'

I jot the name down. 'Colonel who, sorry?'

'Colonel William Havvard – well, he was Lieutenant-Colonel Havvard back then – was in charge of barracks security. He didn't like the police interfering with what he saw as military matters. The forest was part of the land used for training purposes, therefore it was an extension of the barracks – and as such, under his watch when Sally ran away. He took it as a personal affront when the police suggested Sally could have been killed in the woods.

'Most people don't understand what a closed community it

is for army families. Back then there must have been a couple of hundred families living in the barracks, but everyone knew everyone else. Most of our kids attended the same schools, we attended the same army parties, we babysat for one another when our partners were home on leave. Secrets don't remain secret in a place like that, and when outside influences try to interfere with that lifestyle, the pack gathers close to defend itself. Don't get me wrong, when you're on the inside of that pack, you feel safe and secure, but go against the grain and you're soon pulled back into line.

'Before Geoff died, I'd wondered whether life would be easier if we could run away and put the whole place behind us. After Sally went, Nat was never the same; her school work was affected, and she seemed unable to smile or laugh anymore. I was sure she'd probably try and run away too at some point, but then news of her dad's death put paid to that. We left and moved in here, and the rest is history.'

It feels like quite a blasé conclusion to draw considering what I witnessed on the rooftop yesterday. Natalie might have physically escaped the confines of that army base, but mentally it was clear she had stayed trapped there, still thinking about the friend she lost.

'Sally's parents can't have been happy with the police being prevented from carrying out a full investigation?' I ask, thumb poised on the screen.

'I wouldn't know. After the truth came out about the girls sneaking off to the woods, our families became ostracised; we were guilty by association. We'd allowed our children to go behind our backs and sneak out, therefore we were just as culpable for Sally disappearing. Sally's parents were swallowed up in the community spirit: families going out at all hours to search for Sally and hanging posters on every available lamppost and nearby shop window. Imagine what it would be like if an army was sent out to scour for a missing child, and you'll have a good idea about what happened to the towns in and around the base – only it was the wives and children of the army who were set to the task.'

'Where are Sally's parents now?'

'Still on the base, the last I heard. Sally's dad is a captain there now, I think. I haven't spoken to either of them since Nat and I left. I've moved on with my life since then, and I expect they probably have as well.'

'Do you have a number for them at all? I'd like to speak to them if I can. Natalie was adamant that I try and get hold of Sally, and if she did run away as you suspect, then maybe she has reached out and made contact with her parents latterly.'

Cheryl stands, opens the bedroom door, marches back to the main room and collects her jacket and handbag from the hook near the main door. 'We'll go together. I need some more ciggies anyway.'

Chapter Twenty-One

NOW

Bovington Garrison, Dorset

When the bus pulls up outside the base, I start as the armed soldier emerges from the hut beside the security barrier. Despite how Cheryl had described the place to me, I hadn't expected to see such a heightened level of security. The window at the security barrier is closed, and I now see an instruction board affixed to the side of the guard's hut, detailing that all approved visitors must sign in before being escorted to their chosen location on the base. As far as I'm aware, we have no such permission, so I'm not sure how Cheryl thinks we're going to get in. However, rather than approaching the barrier, she promptly turns and begins to cross the road away from the base.

'Are we not going inside?' I ask, hurrying after her.

'Too many eyes and ears in there. I messaged Diane and she'll meet us in here.'

I now see a small pub with a thatched roof just around the

next corner, out of sight of the base – and yet barely a stone's throw away. Cheryl pushes the door open just as the first spots of rain splash against my cheeks.

The pub is a bit of a dive – grime-stained windows, flashing lights from the out-of-date fruit machines, and the ancient staining of cigarette smoke darkening the once white ceiling. At least it's quiet, though I can just about make out the sound of a television voice commentating on a horse race somewhere nearby. Approaching the bar, I scan the refrigerators for something non-alcoholic to drink, as it's barely eleven o'clock. Cheryl is less conscientious and orders a pint of Guinness and a bag of dry roasted peanuts.

'I'll grab us a table,' she says, as the old man behind the bar sets her glass on the thin towel on the bar.

He looks at me, his eyes asking what I want, without his lips uttering a word.

'Do you serve tea or coffee?'

He shakes his head.

'I'll have an orange juice then, please.'

He stoops to the fridge and removes a glass bottle, twisting off the cap, as he places it in front of me. 'Seven-fifty.'

Once I have my change, I carry my bottle to the table where Cheryl has already devoured the bag of nuts.

'Used to come in here all the time,' Cheryl tells me, looking around the carpeted room. 'Especially when Geoff was overseas on short-term assignments. It's nothing special, but at least it's quiet.'

A gust of wind blows through the bar as the door is opened a minute or so later. A woman with blonde curls stands in the doorway, wearing a huskie-coloured faux-fur coat, and in the brightest ruby slippers that would make even Dorothy jealous. Her lipstick is the same shade, and as she brushes raindrops from the coat, she winks at the bartender.

'I'll have a large G&T, Ray,'

Her high-pitched accent certainly isn't local and, based on experience, I'd guess she was raised closer to Essex than this neck of the woods.

She joins us at the table a moment later and Cheryl introduces us.

'Emma Hunter, let me introduce you to Diane Curtis. Diane, this is the writer I messaged you about.'

I extend my hand, which she shakes, before removing the coat and hanging it from a stand in the corner.

'I was so sorry to hear about your Nat,' Diane says, sitting down and immediately squeezing Cheryl's hand. 'I always thought she seemed to take our Sal's disappearance the worst.'

'Thank you,' Cheryl replies, raising her glass in silent toast to her daughter's memory. 'Hopefully she'll find some peace after all this time.'

Diane turns to face me as the barman carries over her large G&T and I hand him more cash. 'You're much prettier in person,' she tells me, before covering her mouth with her hand. 'Not that I mean you don't look pretty when I've seen your face on the telly, I just mean you're even prettier in person.'

The heat rushes to my cheeks and I just about manage to thank her for the compliment.

'So, you're planning on writing a book about my Sally, are you?' she says next, causing me to nearly spit out a mouthful of juice.

'No, I never said that.'

Diane looks to Cheryl for confirmation, who nods. 'No, but

you said you weren't doing a story on our Nat, and then you started asking all those questions about Sally. I just assumed…'

Both women are now staring me down, suddenly questioning why I have so dramatically appeared in their lives. I can't say I'm even certain how we've ended up here.

You need to find her. Find Sally. Tell her I'm sorry.

Diane now leans in closer, talking in a loud whisper. 'I know my daughter didn't just run away, Miss Hunter. *They* know what happened to her, and they've been covering it up for years. Once you understand what Gestapo-like rule that place is under, you'll see why we have to be so careful when speaking.' She pauses and takes a sip of her drink.

'As far as the army is concerned, Diane and I lost touch after Geoff's death,' Cheryl picks up. 'Meeting up became trickier, but then Diane started using Facebook to let me know where she'd be. She'd post something casual about going to the hair salon, or the supermarket, and I'd know that was my cue to see her there. We're not friends on Facebook, but her privacy settings are open so I'm able to see her posts when I need to. Similarly, if I need to speak to her urgently about something, I'll send a cryptic text message, which appears on her phone as the name of an old friend of hers from college. She can't message me direct in case her bill gets checked. It doesn't always run so smoothly, but they've left us little other choice.'

'Isn't it a bit risky meeting *here* though?' I ask. 'We can see the base from the window.'

'Clever, isn't it?' Diane beams. 'Because this place is right under their noses, it's the last place they'd assume we'd meet. Hiding in broad daylight, so to speak.'

The two women paint the army as some kind of clandestine

organisation hell-bent on keeping them apart, though they've offered little evidence to support such an allegation.

'Tell them why you're convinced your Sal is still alive,' Cheryl urges her.

Diane's eyes widen and she takes an enormous breath. 'Well, there were so many things about that time that just didn't make sense: whispered conversations, knowing glances exchanged between men in uniform whose faces I didn't recognise. I raised my concerns with my husband Owen, but he told me not to worry, and that the army looked after its own. That was how he phrased it. In the early days, I presumed he was right, and the way in which all the wives, husbands and partners flocked to us, it really did feel like we were part of some enormous machine. The entire operation was managed from the moment we reported Sally missing, but I just wanted her home, safe and sound, and I allowed myself to get swept up in all the plans to post her picture and scour the local towns for any sight of her.

'I remember about six weeks after her disappearance, the local police thought they'd found a sighting of her at the train station in Dorchester. CCTV from the station a week after she'd vanished showed a girl of a similar height and build waiting on the platform for a train to arrive. It was raining on the night in question, and so the girl had the hood pulled up and over her head, so it was impossible to make a positive identification from the video, but it was the first tangible clue that DC Rimmington had managed to find. The image was shared on social media, and in the local news, and it was the first positive news we'd received. What we didn't know at the time – what Rimmington and her colleagues had failed to share – was that when the CCTV footage rolled on, the girl didn't board a train as everyone had assumed, but in fact left the station and climbed into a car in the car park. This car was eventually traced back to a local builder who'd been called out late by his own daughter, who admitted to being the girl on the station. It was Colonel Havvard's influence that finally revealed the truth, and from that moment onwards, we were discouraged from relying on Rimmington and the civilian police force.'

She pauses for another drink and Cheryl excuses herself, heading out to the shelter in the beer garden to light up.

'What do *you* think happened to Sally?' I ask Diane.

'I honestly don't know,' she replies evenly. 'I wasn't surprised that she'd snuck out of our house that night, as she was the sort of girl who liked to push the boundaries. She wasn't a minx like some of the newspapers suggested. I know that Nat and the others briefly came under suspicion, but if you met the three of them you'd know none of them could hurt a fly, and having spoken to them individually, I have no doubt in my mind that they don't know where she went either. They said they were playing truth or dare, and Sally was dared to go and find some sort of implement that could be used as a sex toy – a fallen branch or whatever – and never returned. They assumed she'd run off home, leaving them in the woods, and were just as shocked when she didn't show up at school the next day.'

'So, where did she go then?'

'That's the thing, you see. Those woods form part of the base, but there is still a fence that marks the outer boundary – and it's barbed-wired. There are signs everywhere warning the public not to enter because there are always military exercises being carried out. And the army themselves checked that outer perimeter fence and there was no sign of a breach, so the only way our Sal could have left the woods was back through the hole through which the four of them had used. Unless she's been living in those woods for the last fifteen years, she had to have snuck back onto the base, but then where did she go? Back then, the base didn't have the level of security cameras that it does now, so there wasn't any footage of her emerging from the woods, but there are plenty of houses she could have snuck into. But that still doesn't explain what happened to her afterwards. It's impossible to sneak off the base without someone helping you.'

'So, is that what you think happened? Sally had help getting away?'

Diane shakes her head as Cheryl returns from the beer garden. 'She was fourteen years old, and whilst she might have passed for sixteen, there's no way she would have been able to secure a home and a job. As much as I want to believe that someone helped Sally to escape, I simply don't believe it. For one thing, no vehicles were reported as leaving the base that night. That kind of scenario would require weeks of planning and organisation, which wasn't one of Sally's strengths. She was too impulsive. She took after me in that way.'

I take a moment to choose my next words carefully. 'Was there any reason Sally might have wanted to run away? Was she happy at school? Um… was there anything troubling her at the time? Was she being bullied? You mentioned boyfriends earlier, so is it possible she ran off with one of the new recruits staying on the base?'

'Oh no, nothing like that as far as I'm aware. She was a nice girl, very popular at school, and if anything, *she'd* be the bully rather than the victim. That detective asked all these questions at the time.'

Cheryl is now sitting back between us, and Diane's responses sound so well rehearsed that it's starting to bother me.

'Which returns me to my original question, Mrs Curtis. What happened to Sally? On the one hand you say that you don't think she ran away, yet on the other hand you're suggesting that the army is covering up the truth. I'm at a loss as to what you believe really happened.'

She's about to respond when she suddenly closes her mouth and her eyes dart to something over my left shoulder. Turning, I see that a man in camouflage attire has entered the pub and is now staring at the three of us at the table. Ray, the barman, has mysteriously disappeared.

The man must be in his mid-fifties with greying hair that I would guess was once ginger, and with a puffy face that has enjoyed more than the occasional fine meal. There is a wry smile gripping his features as he moves slowly towards us.

'What's all this then?' he asks, his voice a deep Welsh baritone.

Neither Diane nor Cheryl respond, and for some reason childhood memories of being caught doing something naughty flicker to the forefront of my mind.

Cheryl and Diane are avoiding eye contact, and before he even turns to me, I sense I already know who he is.

'You're Emma Hunter,' he declares, meeting my gaze. 'It's a genuine pleasure to make your acquaintance. I'm Colonel William Havvard, and I've been told your novel makes quite the interesting read.'

So much for hiding in broad daylight!

'What a cosy meeting this is,' he says, reaching for a stool at a vacant table and pulling it over, before sitting on it. 'You don't mind if I join you, do you?' he asks rhetorically.

There is still no response from Diane or Cheryl, and as I see Havvard staring at my mobile phone on the table, I feel compelled to end the recording and quickly hide the phone back in my satchel.

'I presume you're all discussing the anniversary of Sally's disappearance?' Havvard continues. 'I wish you'd let me know as we've been meaning to do something fresh to see if we can't throw some fresh light on what happened to her. We like to look after our own. And I don't mind admitting it's never sat easy with me, her disappearing like that. So, how far had you got in the story of what happened to Sally?'

The mood at the table has become suddenly icier. Cheryl and Diane's reactions to Colonel Havvard's appearance tells me they either fear or respect him; maybe it's a little of both. In fairness, he is an imposing figure. Though we've never met, even I feel like I'm doing something wrong just being here.

I'm about to answer his question when Diane suddenly looks up with tear-stained eyes and beats me to it. 'Just a chance encounter, that's all this is. Emma here's an old friend of Cheryl's, aren't you, Emma?'

I feel compelled to nod out of courtesy, but decide to throw the spotlight back onto him.

'Colonel Havvard, you said something about wishing to throw some fresh light on Sally's disappearance. What did you have in mind?'

He gives me a curious look. Maybe he's not used to women who aren't afraid to stand up to him.

'I'm intrigued to know how you fit into this conversation, Miss Hunter. Are you hoping to find the hidden clue that finally brings closure to this truly horrific set of circumstances?'

I don't appreciate his tone, but then, I also think he's trying to get a rise out of me so I don't react. 'You think too highly of me, Colonel Havvard. Yes, I'm an investigative journalist, but I can only follow clues that are there to be found. I haven't actually decided whether or not I can add anything to this situation. And if you're already planning some kind of fresh campaign to try and shine new light on the case, then there's probably little else I can offer.'

I deliberately haven't mentioned Natalie's dying words to me, as I don't feel it is my place to do so. And I don't understand why I'm feeling so guilty about talking to Cheryl and Diane; we're not breaking any laws here.

'I'm sure having a famous writer in our midst wouldn't be a hindrance to our plans. If anything, it might help uncover the truth of what happened that night.'

There isn't a trace of concern in his manner, and in spite of the awkward silence that has now descended over Cheryl and Diane, he looks relaxed… almost like he's enjoying himself.

'So what exactly have you got planned, Colonel Havvard?' I say, keen to upset the tables.

'Well,' he begins, suddenly leaning forwards and interlocking his fingers beneath his chin, 'I have a meeting booked in with Mr Panko, who was head teacher at the school Sally attended. He's also keen to remind the public of Sally's disappearance, and even mooted the idea of organising a televised reconstruction of Sally's final known movements.'

'They did a reconstruction fifteen years ago and it didn't help,' Cheryl snaps.

'But technology has moved on since then, and maybe fresh

interviews with her friends could also help. It's common for the human species to repress memories at times of conflict and trouble, and who knows what one of them might now recall all these years later?' He turns to face Cheryl. 'What do you say, Cheryl? Would your Natalie be willing to go in front of a camera and answer questions about that night?'

She quickly wipes her eyes with the back of her hand. It's clear Havvard isn't aware of Natalie's suicide, or if he is, it was a particularly snide remark to make.

'I have contacts in the media now,' I interrupt, 'and might be able to put you in touch with someone who could help organise that.'

Havvard is still staring at Cheryl and Diane, but nods. 'Great.' He looks at his watch. 'I should probably be getting back to the base now. I'll walk you back if you'd like, Diane?'

She stands without comment and pulls the faux-fur coat over her shoulders before following him out into the rain like some obedient canine.

Cheryl reaches for her stout and downs the pint before wiping her mouth with her sleeve. 'What a knobhead!'

I assume she's referring to the colonel. 'I'm sorry if he upset you. I keep forgetting how much you must be grieving right now.'

She suddenly grabs my wrist. 'You're going to investigate, aren't you? Don't be put off by Havvard's assurances of a televised reconstruction. He's been promising to do something to bring the case back to life for years without ever delivering. Diane would have told you as much if he hadn't been there.'

'What's the situation between her and him? It can't just be his rank surely?'

'Diane's husband Owen reports to Havvard directly so he

has the power to keep Owen close by or send him off for more dangerous assignments; Diane daren't go against him, out of fear of losing Owen. She saw the pain and trouble I went through when Geoff died and I don't blame her for clinging to him for dear life. We need you, Emma. Diane and I don't necessarily agree on what happened to Sally that night, but it's clear that *something* happened. Whether she actually ran away and made it out of the camp, or whether something worse befell her and she's buried in those woods, it's been fifteen years and Diane deserves to know the truth.'

I don't want to disappoint her but it wouldn't be fair to mislead her either. 'I'm actually in the middle of a project already,' I tell her. 'The Cassie Hilliard manuscript is being heavily scrutinised and may require major rewrites depending on what my publisher's legal department concludes.'

Her face has dropped, though she doesn't want me to see how disappointed she is. 'Hey, no worries. Of course I understand.'

'I'm not saying I won't continue to dig around in Sally's case, but I just want to manage your expectations a bit. If Colonel Havvard can organise the televised reconstruction, it could give the case the attention and spotlight it requires, and who knows who might remember seeing a young girl sneaking out of the base that night?'

She stands, either bored of the conversation or keen to get out before a fresh tear appears in her eyes. 'Sure, of course, fingers crossed it all works out. I'm gonna go now as I need a cigarette. You all right to find your way home? The bus should be along in a bit anyway.'

'Yes, of course, and I'm sorry again about Natalie. I hope she has found the peace you were so keen for her to receive. If there's anything I can do in the meantime, I'll leave you my number.'

I remove one of the colourful business cards Maddie insisted I carry on me at all times, and hand it to her. Cheryl takes one look at the card before burying it in the pocket of her fleece top, and then she heads back out to the beer garden. Ray the barman appears at my table and collects the glasses before shuffling back to his post at the bar.

Moving across to the window, I see the rain is still bouncing on the slick surface of the road and the ground beneath the bus shelter is soaked through too. There's no obvious sign of an imminent bus so I call a local taxi firm and order a driver. He promises he'll be with me in a few minutes.

'Terrible business all that,' Ray pipes up, his voice gravellier than when he'd been gushing over Diane in that polka-dot dress.

'What, sorry?' I ask.

'That girl going missing like that. It was in all the local newspapers and we had news vans parked up on the street for days. Did a roaring trade in sausage and egg breakfasts, I can tell you. Still, it's not right, is it? Young kid like that disappearing into thin air. If you ask me, them soldiers know a lot more than they're letting on.'

I can't tell if this is all conjecture or whether Ray knows a lot more about life over the road than he's letting on. I move across to the bar so I don't have to shout to him. 'What makes you say that?'

'Well, it stands to reason,' he muses. 'Folk like that... Some of the shit they must have seen overseas... it's bound to mess with your mind, isn't it? What do they call it? Post-traumatic stress and all that. If you ask me, the police should have dragged every one of them soldiers who were there that night in for questioning. At least one of them must have seen or heard something. And it's not like it's the first time a girl has gone missing from the base.'

This nugget garners my attention but before I can question him further, my taxi pulls up outside and he moves away to serve a new customer.

Chapter Twenty-Two

THEN

Bovington Garrison, Dorset

The rain was falling more heavily now and the patch of ground around where Natalie was cowering under the death-like stare of Louise was becoming increasingly soft and slippery.

'But they won't stop until they find out what happened,' Natalie tried to say over the noise of the heavy splashes. 'The truth will come out eventually, Lou, and then it will be so much worse for all of us. If we come clean now, maybe… I don't know, maybe they can reverse what we did.'

'Ha!' Louise crowed. 'It's not like anyone can turn back time.'

'You know that's not what I meant!' Natalie spat back, though she would give anything for a spell with the true magic to control time. 'We didn't know what we were doing – *clearly* – but I'd bet we could find someone with more experience who could work out what went wrong and fix things.'

'This isn't some dumb fucking Disney movie! Nobody can fix what we did and the sooner we all move on the better.'

Why wouldn't she listen? They hadn't meant for things to get so out of control. What had happened was an accident and there had to be a way back. Natalie was certain something could be done but she had neither the knowledge nor the experience to fix it. But maybe Jane would know of something or someone who could help; after all, it had been because of what Jane had said that Sally had convened the meeting in the woods to begin with.

Louise leaned closer. 'We made a pact – you, me and Jane – practically on this very spot. We said we wouldn't mention a word of what happened and we need to stay true to the pact. Now, swear you won't tell anyone what we did. Swear it, Nat, or I promise you, you *will* regret it.'

Natalie closed her eyes and wished that this was all some elaborate dream from which she could wake if only she could realise how crazy it was. Jane had told her all about lucid dreaming and how it was possible – with enough willpower of course – to control what your subconscious projected. Natalie thought about her favourite memory: a holiday to the Seychelles with her parents when she was five; they'd played on the beach and in the warm sea, and eaten chocolate ice cream after dinner every day. Back then, it had been everything she'd wanted from a holiday, and right now she would have given anything to be back there, with the sun on her cheeks and the grainy sand between her fingers.

'Swear it, Nat,' Louise's voice cut through the memory. 'Swear on your parents' lives that you won't tell anyone.'

Natalie kept her eyes closed. What did it matter what she

told Louise? She could say she swore on their lives, without actually meaning it; they were only words after all.

'Do you swear on their lives that you won't tell anyone what we did, Nat?'

'Yes,' she finally screamed, opening her eyes and hoping the shine of tears wasn't evident to Louise.

'Shake on it,' Louise added, thrusting out a hand.

Natalie grabbed the hand and pulled herself to her feet. 'I told you I'll keep quiet, but—'

Louise's finger in her face cut Natalie off mid-sentence. It was no use; Louise wouldn't listen to any kind of challenge. Jane on the other hand… If Natalie could just get Jane alone for ten minutes, maybe she could convince her to help. Jane's mum had books all about ancient practices and traditions. Maybe if they read them, they'd find out where it had all gone so wrong. Getting Jane alone would be difficult as Louise's house was directly across the road, so any kind of social visit would be carefully observed and undoubtedly interrupted. School was also out, and when the three of them returned in the morning, Natalie had no doubt that Louise would keep Jane compliant at her side.

'I'll be watching,' Louise taunted, pointing two fingers at her eyes and then at Natalie. 'Remember that. I'm always watching.'

With that, Louise pulled the hood up over her head and hurried away; it wouldn't surprise Natalie if Louise ran straight to Jane's house and told her all about this little encounter.

There has to be some other way of getting a message to Jane, she thought, as she slowly made her way home. But who could she trust to deliver such a message? It seemed as though her prayers had been answered as she saw Corporal Pete Havvard parking his car at the hut and diving in for cover. He clearly hadn't seen her moving through the shadows, otherwise he might have waved or asked if she wanted to shelter from the rain inside the hut.

Could Pete be trusted? He'd always been pretty decent to all of them, though she knew it was only his good looks that had first attracted Sally and Natalie to his after-school drama club. As far as Natalie was aware, he'd never encouraged their flirtatious behaviour and hadn't shown any favouritism, actively encouraging all of his students to search their souls for the right performance.

She didn't have to tell him about what they'd done; all she needed was for him to slip a message to Jane telling her what Natalie wanted to try. No, a letter would be too dangerous. It was too easy for Pete to read it – or, worse, for Louise to intercept it. No, it had to be simpler than that. She could ask him to ask Jane to meet her in secret at the playground. Maybe then Louise wouldn't see what was going on. It had to be worth a chance; if there was any way to undo what they'd done and get Sally back, it had to be pursued.

Cutting across the wet and muddy grass, she made a beeline for the hut entrance through which Pete had just entered, but as she opened the door she heard voices inside. Pete was talking to someone. Was it Louise? Had he come here for a secret rendezvous with her?

Natalie opened the door a fraction wider and stepped inside, closing it behind her. The hut was freezing as usual, though the cold atmosphere probably wasn't helped by her dripping wet trousers and hoodie. At least she would dry off slightly before having to continue the journey home. If she ran flat out she'd be there within five minutes, but she'd reached the point of wetness at which she wasn't sure it was possible for her to get any wetter. Even as she shuffled closer to the double doors into the large hallway, she could feel the splodge of puddles in her slippers. Her mum would probably go ballistic but it wasn't something a night on the radiator wouldn't cure.

As she drew closer to the inner doors, she was relieved to hear that the other voice belonged to a man, and not Louise. That had to be a positive sign; she'd yet to coil Pete around her little finger, which meant he might be willing to pass Natalie's message to Jane. Natalie crept closer, wincing every time her toes felt the cold splash of rain water and hoping the noise couldn't be heard from inside the hall. Raising herself onto tiptoes, Natalie could just about see over the bottom edge of the glass in the large double doors. She spotted Pete straightaway, framed by the light emanating through this small pane of glass, but the lights remained off in the hall. Whoever he was talking to was off to the right, hidden by the shadows.

Only, as Natalie strained to hear what they were discussing, and who the mystery figure might be, she realised that it wasn't a conversation they were holding, rather an argument. Whilst she couldn't make out what the shadowy figure was saying, Pete's responses were delivered with a raised and angry voice.

'You can't do this! It isn't fair. I have commitments here.'

The low rumble carried across the air.

'I'll put in a complaint with the colonel. You wouldn't like that, would you?'

There were further rumblings that Natalie still couldn't quite distinguish from her hidden position outside the door.

'You can't send me to Germany! People will ask questions. They'll want to know why you've banished me.'

Natalie gasped silently. They were sending Pete away? But why?

'Oh, I see now,' Pete continued. 'That's what this is, isn't it? You can't stand to look at me so you figure, out of sight, out of mind.'

Natalie's eyes widened as the large figure of Lieutenant-Colonel Havvard stepped out of the shadows and stood directly in front of his son. 'You can't blame me for reacting this way.'

'But I'm your son. Doesn't that count for anything?'

'No son of mine would allow himself to get mixed up in something so… so sordid.'

Natalie frowned, pressing her ear closer to the edge of the window pane and hoping the vibrations carried through the glass.

'Sordid? There is nothing *sordid* about it. It's part of who I am, Dad, but it doesn't change the fact that I am your son, and I love you.'

'It's heresy! That's what it is! Sneaking about in dark places, cavorting with the devil himself!'

Natalie pushed herself back from the door. Was it true? Was Pete familiar with the myths and legends in the books Jane had told them about? She'd mentioned something about a local coven but Natalie hadn't realised there would be members on the base. Clearly Pete's father wasn't happy to have learned this about his son if his reaction was to have him transferred from the base, but Natalie never would have realised Pete was in a coven. Did Jane know? Is that how her mum had become involved in those practices? Did that mean Pete might be able to help?

Natalie instantly dismissed the idea. When Sally had first suggested their trip to the woods, Jane had told them it was a big mistake to try things they weren't trained to do. She told them that the Wicca religion was top secret, and to reveal members was a punishable crime. Jane had warned that if her mum found out what they were doing, she would be in serious trouble.

'Please, Dad?' Natalie heard Pete scream from the hall, swiftly followed by the sound of heavy footsteps marching towards the door.

Natalie just about managed to dive for cover as the door she'd been cowering behind swung open and the lieutenant-colonel stormed out, causing the main door to the hut to crash into the wall as he threw it open.

Pete hurried after him. 'Is that it? You've washed your hands of me? I'm no longer your son?'

Their voices trailed off into the distance as they disappeared into the night, leaving Natalie in a heap on the floor, her arms drawn around her legs, and her chin pressed into her knees. She'd never felt so isolated, so alone. And the worst part was that she'd brought it all on herself. She never should have lied to the others when they'd asked if she'd had her first period. She hadn't wanted them to think of her as the baby of the group any longer, so she'd even boasted about having regular periods for ten months, knowing Sally's had only started six months before. As far as they were concerned, she was as much a woman as they were, but when they'd gathered in the clearing and Jane had started the incantations, guilt had coursed through her veins, and when Sally had then disappeared, she'd known instantly that *she* was the reason. Natalie shouldn't have lied to them, and now Sally would be lost for ever because she had.

Chapter Twenty-Three

NOW

Burley, Hampshire

By the time I've finished recounting Cheryl and Diane's accounts to Rachel, our mugs are finished and she is staring wide-eyed at me.

'What do you think happened to her then, this Sally Curtis girl?'

I shrug, because I still haven't made up my own mind about whose version of events I believe. 'Natalie's mum Cheryl is adamant that Sally died on the base that night. Sally's mum Diane believes that her daughter simply ran away, though she can't provide any explanation of how Sally left the base unseen by anyone. I suppose, given a mother's wish to always want the best for her children, it makes sense that she'd choose the ending that brings least pain. But if that is what happened, where has Sally been for the last fifteen years? She was fourteen, with no money, qualifications or family to rely on. How does someone like that survive?'

'More often than not they don't.' Rachel expresses what we're both thinking. 'If she did manage to get away from the base, where would she go? Are there any homeless shelters nearby? Surely that would have been the first place the police would have checked for her?'

I nod my agreement. 'Homelessness isn't just a problem in bigger cities, and there are shelters scattered along the south coast, but none within walking distance of the base that I'm aware of.'

'What about boyfriends? Did the police ever investigate whether she was being groomed online? Maybe she arranged with someone to collect her from the base?'

'I honestly don't know, but I would have assumed that would have been one of their first thoughts. Neither Cheryl nor Diane mentioned it though, so I can only assume it turned out to be a dead end, but worth following up on nonetheless.'

Rachel raises her eyebrows. 'You're planning this to be your next investigation then?'

'No,' I say at first, but who am I trying to kid? The idea of a girl who disappeared into thin air has too many touchpoints with Anna's disappearance that I can't just ignore it. As unlikely an outcome as it is, I can't ignore the prospect that whoever took Anna twenty years ago also could have taken Sally.

'So, what then?' Rachel pushes.

'I don't know,' I reply, collecting the mugs, and carrying them over to the counter by the sink. 'It's been fifteen years since she vanished. I'm not going to manage to uncover some sparkly new piece of evidence from that long ago. Besides, both the local police *and* the military branch pored over every witness account from the time and turned over every stone. I don't want to give Sally's parents false hope by agreeing to start looking into what happened.'

Rachel moves across to me and rests a palm on each of my arms. 'You're a damned fine investigator, Emma. You have a way of looking at things without bias or prejudice, and seeing them for what they are. You have a great bullshit-detector, which allows you to see when people are hiding the truth, and if your gut is telling you to have a dig around then we both know you won't be able to rest until you've done that.'

I know she's right and I appreciate the pep talk, but I don't know where to begin. 'How would you tackle the story?' I ask after a moment. 'Let's say she'd only just gone missing in the last day or so and your editor sent you here to see what you could find out. Where would you start?'

Rachel turns and begins to pace the small floor space in the kitchen – certainly not the most conducive of places for creative thought. 'I suppose I would try and rule out the least likely possibilities first. Ultimately, there are only two options for what actually happened: either she left the base or she didn't. Unfortunately, the routes go in opposite directions so of the two, which is most likely?'

'The police scoured those woods and didn't find a body, so the most logical conclusion is that she escaped somehow.'

'Right, I agree. Remind me, what did Natalie say about her before she jumped?

You need to find her. Find Sally. Tell her I'm sorry.

'She told me to find Sally and apologise.'

'So, logically that would suggest Natalie still believed Sally to be alive, right?'

I shake my head. 'Not necessarily. The apology could have been figurative. She might have meant for me to find Sally's body and lay her to rest. And given what I found in her room at the hostel, my gut is screaming that something bad happened to Sally that night.'

'How old were Sally's friends?'

I open the draft email in my phone and consult my notes. 'Louise Renner, Jane Constantine and Sally Curtis were all fourteen, and Natalie was thirteen. They were all in the same class, but Natalie was four months younger than the other three.'

'How many fourteen-year-old killers are there?'

'Does it matter? There's been at least one, so we can't rule them out as suspects just because of their age.'

'You're right,' Rachel concedes. 'But if they did kill her in those woods, what happened to the body? It's one thing to kill, but quite another to dispose of a body. Burial is the easiest option, but it would have taken them hours to dig a hole and bury the body, and police dogs would have picked up on her scent if that were the case. What did the girls say they were doing in the woods?'

'Playing truth or dare.'

'In the middle of the night, in some dark woods? I don't believe that for a second. Come on, Emma, don't ignore what's right in front of your nose.'

She raises her eyebrows but I'm not prepared to accept that Sally's disappearance had anything to do with incantations.

'With the exception of Natalie's room, I've seen nothing to suggest Sally or the others were involved in witchcraft. For all we know, Natalie took up the religion years later... Maybe to try and find closure for whatever has haunted her for so long.'

'Okay, let's put that to one side for a moment. What did the girls claim had happened to Sally?'

'They said she just ran off during this game.'

Rachel snaps her fingers. 'Then that is probably where I would start with the investigation, to be honest. In order to determine whether Sally left the base or remained there, you need to understand *exactly* what those girls were doing in those woods and why Sally ran off in the first place. What more do we know about Sally's home life?'

'I didn't get the chance to ask Diane why she was so adamant that Sally must have run away and I'm not sure she'd be willing to say if asked directly. Maybe I can speak to Cheryl again and see if she can shed any light on matters.'

'Good, yes, you do that, and see what else you can find out about life on the base. Do you have contact details for the other girls… this Louise and Jane you mentioned?'

I shake my head. 'No, but again, I can ask Cheryl. What are you thinking?'

Rachel has moved through to the hallway and laid her suitcase down flat. She lifts the lid, pulls out her laptop, switches it on and carries it back through to the kitchen. 'Fifteen years is a long time. There are plenty of things I wouldn't have dared admit to my parents when I was their age, but as yesterday has shown, I'm prepared to tell them almost anything now. Maybe Louise and Jane will be more open to admitting what the four of them were doing in the woods.'

I jot the note down.

'Stop me if I'm taking too much control,' Rachel says. 'My editor tells me I do that sometimes.'

To be honest, I'm just grateful for the help. 'Nope, I appreciate your thought processes. I'm not sure how easy it will be to speak to other people who were on the base at the time though. That Colonel Havvard was quite an imposing presence, and from the way Cheryl and Diane quietened when he caught us in the pub, I sense it's still quite a closed community. I'm not sure how well our digging will go down.'

The memory of the atmosphere in that small pub triggers another flashback. 'The barman,' I suddenly recall, 'right before I left, he said something about Sally not being the first girl to go missing from the army base.'

'Did he say anything else?'

I try to recall his exact words, but they're lost. 'He said something about not trusting the soldiers, or that suffering with PTSD could cause them to snap, or something. I'm not sure, but he definitely said Sally wasn't the first girl to go missing. Can you have a search and see what you can find?'

Rachel is already hammering at the keys of the laptop and scrolls through article after article referencing Sally Curtis.

'Can you filter the results to show only hits before Sally's disappearance in 2005?' I ask as I lean over Rachel's shoulder to look at the screen.

Rachel applies the filter, and the first hit practically leaps from the page:

MISSING MARGARET LOCATED IN DENMARK

Rachel clicks on the link and a story from a local Dorset newspaper appears, bearing a picture of a spectacle-wearing teenager with a mop of blonde curls, squinting at the camera. She's wearing a Manchester United football shirt and jeans, and the bright sky in the background suggests the image was snapped somewhere abroad.

According to the article, Margaret Kilpatrick, aged fifteen, had been missing from home for nearly three weeks, before a postcard mailed from a fishing village near Copenhagen had arrived at the home of her father and stepmother. The postcard revealed that she had left because she did not like her stepmother and would not be returning to the UK. The card said she was enrolling at a nunnery, where she would complete her education before dedicating her life to God. The family – living on the army base near Bovington – had been relieved, and not surprised by their daughter's choice, as she had often spoken about a life of service after school. The police in Denmark had confirmed that they had seen Margaret and that they would leave it up to the UK authorities to determine whether extradition would be required.

'Is there anything else about Margaret Kilpatrick later on?' I ask, something stirring in the back of my mind, but unable to quite glimpse what.

'Nothing obvious,' Rachel confirms. 'I don't imagine Danish nuns are allowed to have Facebook accounts, but I can do a search if you want?'

My mind won't settle and I start pacing. 'Who on earth runs away from home to join a convent?' I say aloud.

'Maybe she heard God's call?'

I frown at Rachel's attempt to lighten the mood.

'And at such a young age too,' I continue. 'I don't know about you, but I had no idea what I wanted to do with the rest of my life when I was fifteen. It takes some faith to decide to commit the rest of your life to religious orders.'

'You're assuming she stayed a nun. She might have left the convent, for all we know, and settled down with a Danish pig farmer.'

I scowl at the reference and she quickly apologises.

'Did either Cheryl or Diane mention Margaret Kilpatrick?'

I shake my head.

'Well then, the two situations are probably unrelated. Sally hasn't been seen since, but it says Margaret sent a postcard from the convent *and* that local police were able to verify she was there. Besides, Margaret escaped the base years before Sally disappeared, so the chances are the two girls didn't even know one another.'

I hear the barman's words in my head again: *them soldiers know a lot more than they're letting on.*

The article doesn't specify how Margaret left the base, but I suppose it is possible Sally would have been aware of this story, and maybe had planned a similar escape. It would certainly explain why Diane was so prepared to cling on to the theory that her daughter simply ran away from home. What it doesn't explain is why Natalie was so keen for me to pass on her apology.

'I have an idea,' Rachel says, running to the front door and grabbing her coat. 'All I ask is that you keep an open mind.'

I don't know where I was expecting Rachel to drive us to, but a cosy-looking cottage on the outskirts of Burley in Hampshire's New Forest probably wasn't it. On what is a seasonally mild day, the cottage resembles something you might find on a postcard – quintessentially British, and were it not for the festive time of year, ordinarily I would have expected to see the garden overgrown with daisies and buttercups. Instead, we find a recently mown lawn, a small rockery and fountain in one corner, and two beautifully decorated fern trees either side of the entrance.

I had assumed witches didn't celebrate Christmas and as Rachel parks up, I'm wondering what other gothic clichés and suppositions will be dispelled today.

'What's with the face?' Rachel asks, as she kills the engine.

I catch a glimpse of my frown in the side mirror. 'Is this really it?'

Rachel stares out at the cottage. 'Beautiful, isn't it? You can't see it from the main road, on account of all the trees surrounding it, but it's the kind of place I always pictured you retiring to one day. I could just imagine Jack chopping logs for the fire, while you rummage in the beehives making honey.'

She laughs hysterically as I glare at her. 'For the hundredth time, there is nothing going on between me and Jack, okay? We're just friends.'

Her grin widens. 'Yeah, yeah, sure. Keep telling yourself that. But if you were to ask me—'

'Which I'm not,' I interrupt.

'But if you *were* to ask me, I'd say he fancies the pants off you, and if you don't make a move soon, you'll be permanently stuck in the friendzone.'

'What makes you think *I'd* want anything more than that?'

She fires a sardonic look. 'Oh pur-lease, it's written all over your face whenever you catch a whiff of his cologne. It's okay to admit that you fancy him, Emma. He's cute – in a goofy kind of way – but the two of you would make a sweet couple.' She holds her hands up in mock surrender, as I glare harder at her, feeling the heat rising to my cheeks. 'I'm just saying, that's all. You like him. He likes you. What are you waiting for?'

I know what she's trying to do. Her love life has gone up in smoke and so she's hoping to temporarily live vicariously through mine. I don't want to discourage her if it's helping keep her mind off her breakup with Daniella and the fallout with her parents, but I hate being the focus of her attention.

'If you want a real challenge,' I muse, 'you should try setting up Maddie with someone.'

Rachel rolls her eyes. I do find it frustrating that my best friend and agent-confidante don't get on. They're both wonderfully caring people and both have been so supportive of my writing journey, but they can barely stand to be in the same room together and I've never really understood why.

'You should give her a break,' I reason. 'She's going through a bit of a bad time at the moment. Seeing Natalie jump from the roof stirred up old memories of her own son who died by suicide while at university. If anyone could do with cheering up, it's Maddie.'

'But I don't love Maddie like I love you, and besides, I don't know *who* she's interested in.'

'Wait, you think Maddie's gay?'

It's Rachel's turn to frown. 'How would I know?'

I shake my head. 'It was just the way you said… Oh, never mind, forget I said anything. I take it you haven't heard any more from Daniella?'

The drop of her head answers the question.

'Oh well, not to worry. Maybe you'll grow up to be an elderly spinster like me. Hey, maybe we should put an offer in on this place in preparation. We could move in, grow old, get some cats and knit.'

Rachel rolls her eyes again but a small smile breaks through the gloom. 'Fine! If you don't want to admit your attraction to Jack, who am I to judge? Shall we go in?'

My hand is actually trembling as it reaches for the door handle, as my mind swiftly returns to the present and the real reason we've come here. I wouldn't have said I fear the occult, but I guess I'm definitely wary of forces I don't understand… and maybe it's the simple brainwashing that we've all endured down the years that instantly makes us recoil at talk of witchcraft and paganism. As a species, we naturally fear what we don't understand and tend to act defensively, but who's to say whether one belief system is more correct than any other?

Rachel certainly doesn't appear to be nervous and so I suppose I can take some comfort from that. She approaches the front door with abandon and pulls the cord of the rusty bell that hangs outside. It chimes untunefully, and a moment later the sound of a heavy lock being twisted is followed by the opening of the door. For a split second, I picture a craggy old woman with green skin, warts on the end of her pointy nose, and a cone-shaped black hat, but the woman who greets us has none of those things.

'Rachel!' she declares excitedly, delicately placing a hand on each arm and pecking each of Rachel's cheeks as if they are models catching up in Paris or Milan or somewhere. She must be in her late fifties; her closely cropped hair is a light grey colour and complemented by the pastel shades of her peach-coloured jumper and white cotton trousers.

'Hi, Imogen. Thanks so much for agreeing to see us at such short notice.'

'That's okay. I didn't have much on this morning anyway, and my tealeaves did suggest an important visitor would be coming my way this week. Please do come in, both of you.'

She disappears into the cottage followed by Rachel. I close the door once inside. The smell of freshly cut flowers and herbs hits me instantly, and it reminds me of one of those high-street shops that sell perfumed soaps. The mixture of fragrances is quite overpowering and I have to pause to steady my breathing before continuing along the hallway and into a large living space. The room is so bright, aided by a large window in the middle of the ceiling. Imogen is across the room and closing the door on what looks like a cross between a conservatory and a greenhouse.

'I'm sorry about the smell,' she offers, turning back to face us both. 'My nostrils have become accustomed to it after all these years but I know it can be a bit toxic for others. It should die down in a moment or so, with the doors closed.'

'Imogen is a botanist,' Rachel explains, 'specialising in rare flowers with mystic properties. Would that be a fair description, Imogen?'

Imogen smiles. 'That's a kinder way to explain what I do than I'm used to, but yes, it's a close enough approximation. Please do sit, both of you. Can I fix you some tea?'

'Tea would be lovely, thank you,' Rachel replies for both of us, ushering me over to the two-seat sofa when Imogen has left the room.

'What are we doing here, Rachel?' I ask, as I perch on the edge of the sofa.

'Imogen is one of the world's leading authorities on the rejuvenating powers of plants and herbs. She has hundreds of different species in her laboratory there, as well as in her garden, and she studies their physiology, ecology, genetics and structure. She regularly publishes articles online about what she's discovered.'

'So she's like one of those traditional Chinese medicine

specialists who would prescribe root extract for backache, and that kind of thing?'

Rachel tilts her head. 'Not exactly, but I suppose your analogy isn't a million miles away. She doesn't prescribe anything to anyone, rather she experiments with different species of plants to better understand how they can benefit other species, whether that's humans, animals or other plants.'

'I thought you said we were coming to meet a witch?'

'Not exactly. Listen, as well as being this leading authority, Imogen is also a practising Wiccan – you know, like that book Natalie left in the box for you?'

'The tea won't be too long,' Imogen says, returning to the room, and sitting across from us in an armchair. 'I must say it is a great honour to have the famous Emma Hunter in my house. I came across your book at a local fete and couldn't put it down once I started reading it.'

'That's very kind of you to say,' I reply, averting my eyes.

'I'm sorry,' Imogen says quickly, 'I didn't mean to make you blush, Emma. I'm a firm believer in expressing positivity whenever possible; there's far too much negativity in the world at the moment, so I send out positive vibes from my tiny corner of the world, and hope to brighten some of the gloom.'

She pauses until I return her stare to show that my minor embarrassment has passed.

'How exactly can I help the two of you today?' she starts again, this time looking at both Rachel and me.

'We wondered if you'd mind telling us a little more about Wicca and what it means to be considered a Wiccan witch,' Rachel replies.

Imogen smiles and stands. 'I'd be happy to. I'll just fetch the tea and then we can begin.' She heads out of the room, returning less than a minute later with three transparent glass cups and saucers with a yellowy broth in them.

'It's my own recipe,' she explains as we each take a cup and saucer, 'a mixture of lemon rind, valerian, chamomile, passionflower and a dash of honey for sweetness. It's quite citrusy, but very good for calming the nervous system and encouraging endorphins.'

She nods at both of us to try the tea and I have to admit I'm nervous as I put the broth to my lips but it is quite pleasant and fragrant.

Imogen lowers her cup to the floor before resting her palms on her knees. 'I presume you've both heard of a man called Gerald Gardner, the founder of modern Wicca?'

Rachel nods. 'We have a book about him, but I was hoping you might be able to provide a more succinct account.'

'Okay, I'll do my best,' she says before starting in on a full rundown of Gerald Gardner's life – how he encountered and was indoctrinated into the New Forest coven in the 1930s and how he set up his own coven in Bricket Wood, from where he initiated many other witches. 'Becoming Wiccan isn't something you just decide,' she continues. 'You need to be formally welcomed and taught the laws of the religion. Those who think it is a quick way to cast spells and magic are usually left sorely disappointed and go off and find other religions to follow. Whilst there are some Wiccan witches who choose to engage in the darker nature of the mystic world, most of us don't as such practices come back to haunt the crafter of the spell threefold. That's one of the doctrines, you see.

'For me, the worship of one omnipotent and omniscient god never sat right. Wiccans, by contrast, worship both the horned god and the moon goddess; that's why so many incantations are delivered when the moon is at its fullest. The majority of spells and incantations cast are seeking to fulfil good work, not the hexing and curses popularised in television and film. It does make me laugh whenever I catch sight of an image of a loner in a black cape and pointy hat, waving a wand over a stone cauldron. Whilst there is some historic imagery that supports such stereotypes, modern Wicca isn't so dark and devious.'

I'm reminded of the poem *Incantation* by Elinor Wylie, one of Anna's favourite poets. In it the poet explores how even in the darkest situation, light can still be found.

'The horned god,' I say, taking another sip of the delicious tea, and feeling my shoulders gently relaxing. 'Do you mean the devil?'

'Good heavens, no,' Imogen corrects. 'We're not satanic worshippers. It's a common misconception that witches are carrying out Satan's work, but that really isn't the case. Do I look like someone in league with the devil?' She adds a light chuckle to show I haven't offended her. 'A lot of the misconceptions are simply rumours spread by those who have been so brainwashed that they refuse to believe what we say. There was a famous Wiccan witch by the name of Sybil Leek who lived here in Burley back in the Sixties, before emigrating to the US. She ran a shop in the village and tried to educate her neighbours, but fear resonates.'

I sit forward as a fresh thought stirs my mind. 'What if a non-Wiccan tried to carry out a spell or incantation, but it went wrong somehow. What could the repercussions be?'

Imogen ponders the question. 'It's so hard to say. I suppose it would depend on what spell was being cast.'

You need to find her. Find Sally. Tell her I'm sorry.

'Are there any kinds of spells that could cause someone to disappear?'

Imogen frowns. 'I'm really not sure. I wouldn't have said so, no. Again, it would depend if the caster was on their own or part of a coven. Wiccans can be solitary practitioners, or part of a coven, you see?'

'Well, what if four non-Wiccans gathered in a forest to incant something, and one of them vanished into thin air? Is that possible?'

Imogen finishes her tea. 'I really wouldn't have said so, but I'm not overly familiar with the darker side of magic. It would all depend on what they were trying to do, but I've never heard of anyone vanishing into thin air. As I said, most Wiccans only cast positive spells out of fear of the threefold law.'

Which leads me to only one conclusion: I need to find out exactly what those girls were trying to incant in those woods, who knew about it and who else might have been there.

Chapter Twenty-Four

NOW

Weymouth, Dorset

I'm already feeling sombre as I rise from bed. I didn't know Natalie, but I accept that seeing those who knew and loved her weeping at the crematorium is going to make today a tough one. I was surprised to receive Cheryl's call last night, inviting me to attend, but once she'd asked, I didn't have it in me to decline. So, having showered, I'm now staring at the black suit I reserve for these occasions.

'Are you sure you don't want me to come with you?' Rachel asks, as she climbs back into bed, and pulls the duvet up to her chin.

I had thought about asking Cheryl whether it would be okay for me to drag Rachel along, but it felt weird, and I don't want to put my best friend through an emotionally charged cremation for no reason.

'I'm sure,' I reply absently, dressing quickly, 'but I appreciate the offer.'

'Fair enough. Hey, listen, I was thinking I could continue having a look through Natalie's journals while you're out? Maybe we'll find a clue about their spell-casting in there.'

When we got back from Imogen's place yesterday afternoon, I had set about reading through the diaries Natalie had left in the box for me, in an effort to get to know her better and maybe unlock the truth about what happened, and why she felt so compelled to end her life. I left Rachel reading up on Gerald Gardner and Sybil Leek.

'That's a good idea,' I confirm, checking my reflection in the mirror, 'but bear in mind that these were written by a thirteen-year-old who may well have been aware that her mother could stumble across them, so look for any hidden or double meanings in the language used. I tried putting myself back in my thirteen-year-old head as I was reading them last night, but didn't glean anything useful. I tried reading them from the time of Sally's disappearance, but there might be greater benefit going back even further. Maybe there will be clues as to what led them to even consider spell-casting.'

Rachel puts her thumb up and says goodbye as I head out of the flat where the taxi is waiting for me. The Weymouth Crematorium is situated up the road in Westham and is therefore walkable, but it's blowing a gale out here this morning and I don't want to arrive looking like I've been dragged backwards through a hedge. It's not vanity; it's a show of respect to Natalie, Cheryl and the other mourners. It's an odd place for a crematorium, when you consider that it's surrounded by residential homes, two schools, and a couple of playgrounds. It isn't the first time I've attended the crematorium, and as the taxi driver drops me at the main entrance, memories of my dad's service come flooding to the front of my mind.

It was much sunnier that day – hardly surprising given that Dad died in late spring. He used to joke that he would never want to be buried and become worm food – far more efficient to cremate and scatter. When Mum would challenge him on the subject, he'd joke, 'I've always loved a big barbecue. Seems a fitting end.' I try not to think about that time in my life. Mum and Dad had been separated for several years by that point, following Anna's disappearance, but it didn't make his death any less sudden. I'd been due to stay with him the same weekend we ended up attending the crematorium; it was *that* sudden. I still know so little about what really happened to him. He was working at HMP Portland, that much I *do* know, but the rest has come from overheard whisperings and throwaway lines. Mum was adamant she didn't wish to discuss it before, and now I'm not sure I'd want to make her remember it.

I should really find out whether Mum would prefer to be buried or cremated, but it isn't an easy conversation starter, particularly given her current health concerns and the Alzheimer's. It's difficult to know whether I'm getting a response from Mum now, or the much younger woman she sometimes still thinks she is. I'm just hopeful her final wishes will be included in her will.

The crematorium is part of the larger estate of Weymouth Cemetery, and so I follow the signs to the crematorium, soon finding Cheryl, in a long black dress, outside the entrance. I was expecting to see a flurry of mourners hovering outside or just inside the building, considering the service is due to start in the next ten minutes, but there is only one other person – a man in his early thirties, puffing on a cigarette – leaning against the building.

'Thank you for coming, Emma,' Cheryl says, clutching my hand.

'You're very welcome. Are you expecting a big turnout?'

Cheryl shakes her head. 'Nat didn't have too many friends and apart from me, not much by way of family left. Both Geoff and I were only children, like Natalie, so no big slew of uncles, aunts and cousins to choose from.'

Maybe I should have dragged Rachel along to make up the numbers. I know from experience that the crematorium can hold about a hundred mourners and in fact for Dad's cremation it was standing room only, with a large number of his prison guard colleagues turning out to say goodbye.

A long black car with tinted windows pulls up in front of us and as the rear door opens, a blonde woman with long legs exits, quickly joined by a tall man with a closely cropped beard. The blonde straightens her dark suit before donning a large round hat. She offers her condolences to Cheryl, and it's only through eavesdropping on their conversation that I realise who is speaking.

'I'm so sorry for your loss, Mrs Sullivan. I was so sorry to hear about Nat's passing. It's been years since I last saw you, and I'm sorry we're not meeting under different circumstances.'

'Thank you, Louise. How's your mum?'

Louise Renner gives me a curious glance, as if trying to work out who I am, or perhaps why she might recognise my face.

'Mum's very well,' Louise replies, focusing her attention back on Cheryl.

'Is she still living at the base?'

'Good heavens, no! They left that life when Dad had his stroke; they retired to Torquay where she was from, and so Dad can be close to the sea. My uncle still works at the base though. You should give Mum a call some time; I'm sure she'd love to hear from you.'

Louise Renner clearly hasn't been affected by all that went on with Sally's disappearance – at least not in the same way that Natalie was. Where Natalie's head was all over the place and she had reached a point where she could no longer continue, Louise, by contrast, seems very much switched-on and together. The man at her side – presumably her husband – is wearing a tailored suit and has the well-toned physique of someone who hits the gym at least a couple of times a week. They move on and head into the building.

The guy who'd been smoking is next to approach, leaning in and kissing Cheryl's cheek before passing on his condolences. I should take my leave so that I'm not intruding on their private conversation, but Cheryl has hold of my hand and I don't want to upset her by extracting it brusquely.

'I wish there was more I could have done,' the man now says. 'I sometimes wonder what might have been had the IVF not failed. That seemed to be the beginning of the end for us.'

'You were always my favourite of her boyfriends, Sam. I really wish things had worked out better between the two of you. I appreciate you coming today.'

'To be honest, Mrs Sullivan, I never stopped loving Natalie, and when you called the other day to tell me what had happened, my heart broke in two all over again.' He breaks off as his eyes fill and he apologises, heading back to his smoking post.

'The one that got away,' Cheryl leans in and whispers. 'He was like the light at the end of her tunnel. Brought her back from the brink, and for the two years when they were together, I actually thought she would settle down and find happiness. They were engaged when they decided to start trying for a baby, but it wasn't to be. Caused a strain between them, it did, and eventually the relationship crumbled, and that's when she moved to London to start afresh. I should never have let her go off by herself like that, but what can a mother do when her adult daughter makes up her mind about something like that?'

I wonder if my mum ever had similar thoughts when I told her I was moving to Bournemouth for university. I tell myself she didn't because her mind was always so focused on the child she lost, rather than the one she still had, but maybe there were moments when she wished I hadn't decided to go into further education.

Cheryl squeezes my hand. 'We should probably head in now. Would you mind sitting with me? I had hoped Diane would be able to come along, but she can't get away from the base undetected.'

'Of course,' I say, leading her into the building, the memories of Dad again bubbling at the surface of my mind.

Thankfully, I haven't had to attend too many funeral services, but they're never easy, even when you barely know the person. The administrator moves to the front of the room when Cheryl and I take our seats in the front row. Louise and her husband are about three rows behind us, and when Sam enters he comes and sits the other side of Cheryl. Is this really all Natalie has to show for twenty-eight years of life? Five people to say goodbye, two of whom she didn't even know.

The straw coffin looms in front of us all, and the irony that they used to burn witches to death in mediaeval England isn't lost on me. Did Cheryl know about her daughter's dabbling in the Wiccan religion? The administrator leading the service doesn't appear to be from any specific denomination, but it isn't clear if that was Natalie's choice or her mother's.

The door clattering at the back of the room causes us all to turn and stare at the commotion. A black woman dressed in a figure-hugging skirt and satin top has entered and is doing a terrible job of moving quietly forward; her stilettos are clip-clopping in rhythm until she finally darts into the fifth row from the back and sits.

'Ah, I'm glad she managed to make it,' I hear Cheryl mutter.

'Who is that?' I whisper back.

'One of Natalie and Louise's old friends: Jane Constantine.'

The missing piece of the jigsaw. So, the small coven is reunited, here in a place of religious significance. I watch her as she composes herself, before nodding towards Louise who is staring back at her. What secrets the two of them must hold… and I'd be fascinated to know whether they've maintained contact down the years, and whether either or both were in touch with Natalie. There's no guarantee that either will speak to me, but I won't have a better chance than after the service.

Chapter Twenty-Five

THEN

Bovington Garrison, Dorset

Natalie's dad hadn't been home when she'd returned, and her mum hadn't kicked up too much of a fuss when a sodden Natalie had walked back through the door, quickly stripping her and running a hot bath, carefully preventing the leg bandage getting any wetter by tying a polythene bag around it.

Natalie had allowed herself to be mothered and tended to, even though she didn't feel like she deserved any of her mother's affection. If Sally's disappearance was her fault, then so was Pete's imminent departure to Germany. What would happen to drama club with Pete gone?

He mum had fixed her a cheese and pickle sandwich and a cup of hot chocolate while Natalie had bathed, and as she devoured both, her mum brushed the knots from her matted hair.

'I do wish you'd talk to me about what's going on in that

head of yours,' Cheryl had begun. 'You're such a pretty girl when you smile, but I can't remember the last time I saw you smile and laugh. I know puberty can be tough, and I'm sure they offer better counselling and guidance at school than I could provide, but I am here for you, sweetheart, if you ever want to talk. Okay?'

Natalie had forced a smile in an effort to pacify her mother, but had opted against opening up, Louise's threat still stinging in her ears. What if Louise was right, and spilling the beans brought trouble for her parents too? They didn't deserve to suffer as a consequence of her actions.

'I heard you and Dad arguing,' Natalie had offered by way of explanation for running out of the house in the pouring rain.

'Oh, you don't need to worry about your dad and me. It's healthy to have some friction in a marriage. Stops things getting boring. What did you overhear?'

'Oh, nothing specific, I just heard your raised voices. I assumed it was about me.'

Her mum had stared at her for a long time, maybe trying to read her mind. 'Why would we be arguing about you? Don't worry your pretty little head about any of that grown-up stuff. Just know that we both love you very much, and want you to know you can talk to us both about anything. Okay? *Absolutely anything*.'

At nine o'clock, unable to stifle her yawns anymore, Natalie had said goodnight and headed up to bed, relieved when her mum hadn't put up any argument.

But something had disturbed that slumber five minutes ago, and now she couldn't stop thinking about all the lies she'd told her mum in the last week. If Lieutenant-Colonel Havvard was putting pressure on her dad, didn't they deserve to know the truth? Well, not the actual truth, but a version of it? She could easily tell them that Sally had secretly told her that she intended to run away. At least that would bring everyone some closure. At least they'd stop looking for a girl they would never be able to find. If her dad then revealed that news to his superior, it would take the heat off. Louise and Jane would be angry, but she could say that Sally had confided in her in secret, and that neither of them knew what she was secretly planning.

There was that noise again – like glass breaking, or crashing. She definitely hadn't imagined it. Pushing back the duvet, she moved across and opened her bedroom door, peering out and down the stairs. Creeping to the bathroom, she could hear the rumble of her mum's snoring in their bedroom, but as she looked in through the gap in the doorway, she couldn't see the outline of her dad's body beneath the duvet.

The sound of low voices from beneath the floor told Natalie that it was likely her dad had fallen asleep in front of the television again, and probably the sound of glass was emanating from the television set. Sitting on the top step, she gently lowered herself down the staircase on her bottom as she had done earlier, but stopped just as she was about to open the door to the living room.

'I know all that, Bill,' her dad's voice carried, 'but I've tried, and she really doesn't know where Sally ran to.'

'One of them must know,' Lieutenant-Colonel Havvard's voice boomed. 'Let me speak to Natalie directly. I need to know where she's gone, Geoff.'

'With all due respect, Bill, I will handle my daughter.'

'Do you think she knows where Sally went? She's your

daughter; you must have an idea if she's lying or telling the truth.'

'Cheryl says she's telling the truth. That she really doesn't know where Sally ran off to.'

'But you have doubts, don't you? I knew it! Just let me have five minutes alone with her and I'll have her singing like an angel.'

'No, Bill! *I* will speak to her.'

Natalie had no doubt they were discussing her, and wondered whether Louise and Jane's parents were receiving the same level of pressure.

'Do you want a refill?' her dad asked next, followed by the clinking of the decanter against two glasses. That must have been the sound that had woken her – they were drinking whiskey – but Natalie hadn't even realised they were on first-name terms.

'I don't know what I'm going to do if we don't find her,' Havvard continued, now sounding further away from the door. 'The secrets that girl could spill would be… well, it could be the end for all of us.'

Natalie froze. What *secrets* could Sally possibly know to jeopardise someone as important as the Lieutenant-Colonel Havvard? Could Sally have overheard him discussing top military strategy with her dad Owen? What possible motive would Sally have to share that with anyone?

'What's Owen said about it?' Natalie's dad said next. 'Has he given any reason why she would run away?'

There was a momentary silence before Havvard spoke again. 'He says he doesn't know, but there have been rumours before – all hearsay as far as I'm aware – but I don't believe things were quite as cosy at home as he would like the rest of us to think.'

'I know the rumours you're referring to, Bill, and I raised my own concerns with you about Owen and his violent temper, and you assured me you had dealt with it.'

'I had. I mean, I *have* dealt with it. He was given a final warning about his behaviour and ordered to attend anger management classes.'

'Where was he on the night she disappeared though?'

'At home in bed with Diane of course.'

There was anxiety in her dad's voice when he spoke again. 'But how do we know she didn't make it home that night? What if Owen did hear her return and confronted her about sneaking out? I know from my reaction to finding out about Nat's trip to the woods how incensed I was. What if Owen had been drinking and things turned violent?'

'Owen couldn't kill his own daughter. Don't be absurd, man!'

'It could have been an accident. They do happen, *remember*?'

Natalie stirred at the tone her father was now using.

'This isn't like that, Geoff.'

'No? How can you be so sure? Listen, I know you didn't mean what happened, which is why I helped you sort it out. How can you be so sure history isn't repeating itself now?'

Natalie started at the sound of a tumbler being slammed down against a table. 'That is a very serious allegation to be making about a friend of ours, Geoff, and unless you have a shedload of evidence to back up your theory, I wouldn't go mentioning it again.'

'Okay, Bill, I'm sorry. You're right, I know you are. Owen

couldn't kill Sally and then cover it up. I'm sorry. I didn't mean any offence.'

'And the less you say about that other thing, the better,' Havvard growled. 'You don't want to get on my bad side, Geoff. You know what I'm capable of.'

Natalie couldn't stand the suspense any longer, and hurried back up the stairs on her bottom, making it up barely seconds before Havvard emerged from the living room, slamming the front door as he left.

Natalie had seen the bruises on Sally's torso when she'd been changing for PE once. Natalie had even asked her what had caused such patches of yellow and purple. Sally had laughed it off and said she'd missed a step and fallen down the stairs the week before, but there had been something in her voice that had made the memory stick in Natalie's mind. What if her dad was right? What if Sally *had* made it out of the woods and back home? What if all her worrying about the spell going wrong was just teenage angst?

There was only one way to find out. Waiting until her dad had gone to bed, she snuck back out of her room and down the stairs, finding the empty decanter and two empty glasses still on the small coffee table next to the sofa. Reaching for the phone, she covered the mouthpiece with her sleeve, and dialled 999.

'I'd like to report a murder,' she whispered into her sleeve.

Chapter Twenty-Six

NOW

Weymouth, Dorset

My attention is drawn back to proceedings by Cheryl's whimpering when the administrator invites Sam up to the stage to say a few words about Natalie. He squeezes Cheryl's arm, before heading to the small podium and microphone.

'What can I say about the brilliant and beautiful Natalie Sullivan that will adequately summarise who she was and what she meant to all of us? The woman I met was shy and vulnerable, and kept a high defensive wall, but once that was scaled she was funny, and smart, and had so much love to offer. But there were problems in her life too; I'm sure that will come as no surprise to any of you here. She struggled with her mental health, and whilst for a time she found balance, trouble was never too far away.'

Cheryl sobs quietly beside me and I place an arm around her shoulders in an effort to provide some level of comfort. I really wish Rachel was here now; she's so much better with emotive situations like this.

'When Cheryl called and told me how Natalie had died, I have to be honest, I wasn't surprised. Devastated, but not surprised. Sometimes those who appear strongest and most able to cope with anything are just putting on a show, and I think that was definitely the case with Natalie when we were together. I wish, when she reached the point where she knew she couldn't go on, she'd just picked up the phone and called me. I don't think I will ever forgive myself for not being there when she needed me most. I…' He stops and squeezes the bridge of his nose. 'I'm sorry, Cheryl, I can't do this… not with *them* here.'

He is now staring directly at Louise and Jane and there is a definite sudden chill in the room.

'How the two of you have the audacity to come here and mourn the woman that you broke as a girl is beyond me. How dare you sit there and pretend to weep at her passing!'

I glance over my shoulder and can see that Louise has buried her face in her hands, but Jane is staring directly back at Sam, who now leaves his post at the podium and returns to Cheryl's side.

'I'm sorry,' he whispers. 'I know I promised I wouldn't say anything, but they shouldn't be here. Natalie would never tell me what happened when she was younger, but she would occasionally mention their names and it would make her so upset.'

'It's okay, Sam, it's okay,' she whispers back, resting her head on his arm.

The shuffling behind me is confirmation that Louise and her husband are leaving, and I so desperately want to go after them and confront Louise about that night fifteen years ago, but I can't abandon Cheryl like this either.

The administrator returns to the podium and does his best to return to the order of service, which continues in a more abrupt fashion, ending with Natalie's favourite song as the coffin is lowered into the hatch beneath it, ready for the fire. Both Sam and Cheryl sob while this happens, and even I feel my eyes tearing up, even though I only spent a couple of minutes in Natalie's presence. Crematoriums can be like that though – so heavily charged with emotion that it's difficult not to get sucked into the maelstrom.

As we stand to leave, I'm surprised to see Jane Constantine is still sitting towards the back of the room. Despite Louise's early exit, she has remained and, as we pass, she makes a beeline for Cheryl.

'I'm so sorry for your loss, Mrs Sullivan.'

'You shouldn't even be here,' Sam says, stepping between them, clearly not one who cowers at confrontation.

'I know I don't deserve to mourn her, but despite what you may think, Natalie did mean a lot to me and I genuinely feel the world has lost a great spirit in her.'

Sam leads Cheryl out of the large room but I hang back and nod at Jane. 'It's Jane Constantine, isn't it?'

Jane considers me before nodding briefly. 'Sorry, have we met?'

'No,' I quickly reassure her. 'I'm...' – how best to describe my role here today? – 'I'm a friend of the family. Are you in a hurry to get away, or would you be able to spare me a few minutes to talk about Natalie?'

She crooks her arm and the sleeve of her jacket rolls up,

revealing a diamante-encrusted watch. 'I've got time. It's not like I'll be very welcome at the wake.'

I usher myself past Jane and sit down on the seat beside her. 'You went to school with Natalie, right?'

Jane smiles briefly, nodding. 'Supposed to be the best time of our lives, right? It was for a while, but growing up on that base was so stifling. I didn't realise it at the time, but since I've moved away, I now see it was suffocating me.'

'Did you remain on the base for a long time after Natalie left?'

'I was there until I turned eighteen, and then I left to go to university. My mum retired from active service shortly after, and she and my dad relocated to Norfolk to be closer to where I was studying.'

'Have you managed to remain in touch with Louise Renner? I saw her here earlier, but I think she rushed off.'

Jane looks around the large, empty room, as if searching for something. 'I haven't seen her since I left for university. The last I heard she was planning on taking a gap year, and then we just lost touch. I didn't even realise she'd be here today, but I suppose it shouldn't be such a surprise.'

'How come?'

'We were good friends once upon a time – me, Louise, Natalie and… Quite the little crew on that base. I thought we'd be friends for life and that nothing would separate us.'

'You were there in the woods the night Sally Curtis disappeared, weren't you?'

Her eyes widen in sudden panic, and this time she checks over her shoulder as she takes in the entire room. 'Who did you say you were again?'

'My name's Emma Hunter and Cheryl asked me if I would attend today.'

Her eyes are practically on stalks as her brain makes the connection. 'I know you! You're that writer who's always on the television. You wrote that book about them kids in the boys' home.'

'Yes, I am, but that isn't why—'

'Sorry, luv,' she says, hoisting herself up, 'I ain't talking to no reporters about any of that business.'

'Please,' I say loudly enough for her to look back. 'I was with Natalie when she took her life.'

'You some kind of sicko then, or what? Like one of them killers returning to the scene of the crime?'

Something has her rattled and despite my best efforts to calm her down, she's only growing tenser. 'I'm sorry, luv, but I have nothing further to say to you.'

She's moving towards the door. I can't keep beating about the bush: directness is the only answer. 'Before she died, Natalie made me promise I'd find Sally and tell her she was sorry. You were there in those woods when Sally died, and I know the four of you were practising some kind of witchcraft, Jane.'

She stops, but doesn't turn.

'I think Natalie was under the impression that the spell you all cast somehow caused Sally to vanish, and she's spent the last few years trying to unravel whatever it was you did. You should have seen her room. It was a shrine to Sally – maps and clippings of other mystical events from the years littered the walls. I'm not here to expose your secrets, Jane, I just want to live up to the promise Natalie demanded. I need to find Sally.'

This last statement has Jane turning back to face me. A line of saltwater is barely clinging to her false eyelashes, but she's not the only one. My own vision is misting as that's the first time I've admitted that I *need* to find Sally. Despite trying to convince myself that it would be impossible, and that I didn't want to offer Cheryl and Diane false hope, the truth is I now *need* to find Sally. My mind and soul won't allow me to rest until I do.

'Natalie wasn't right in the head in those later years,' Jane says coldly. 'What we did… the reason we were there was kids' stuff. It had nothing to do with Sally disappearing.'

I shake my head. 'No, there's more to it than that. Natalie blamed herself for what happened… to the point where her only out was death. You can't belittle what happened when it caused such pain and hurt to one of your coven.'

Her mouth drops. 'We weren't a coven!' she shouts. 'We were four stupid girls who got mixed up in something none of us could comprehend. Yeah, we made that clearing look proper with oats and chalk, and stones and tree decorations… I probably went over the top with all that shit, but all we did was say some words. It wasn't real; none of it was.'

A small gale blows in as Louise Renner opens the door to the hall; she's frowning. 'What's going on in here? I heard shouting. Jane, are you all right?'

Jane wipes the tears from her eyes, her acrylic nails catching and almost tearing off the false eyelash. 'Louise, I… I didn't say anything.'

Louise holds her hand up to cut her off. 'I recognise you, don't I? You're someone famous?'

'Not exactly,' I say, the introvert in me taking over.

'What were you two arguing about?'

'We weren't arguing,' I say defensively, uncertain why I

suddenly feel so intimidated to be in this woman's presence. Is this what it was like for Natalie all those years ago? Is that what Sam meant when he verbally attacked Louise and Jane at the podium?

'I heard raised voices. Jane is my friend and if anyone comes after her, I will put myself forward to help her.'

Jane is nodding now, almost gloating at me as she cowers behind the other woman. I wish I had my own guardian to come to my aid. Why didn't I bring Rachel with me?

'I was asking Jane about the night Sally Curtis disappeared,' I say, channelling my inner Maddie. 'You were there, Louise, along with Jane and Natalie. I am trying to find out the truth about what happened to Sally that night. I mean, what *really* happened to Sally.'

Louise looks from me to Jane, glaring at her friend before returning my gaze. 'That's all ancient history. What gives you the right to go dragging all of that up, especially on a day like today?'

'Natalie's last words were to ask me to find Sally, and to tell her she was sorry. You tell me why she would say that.'

'How would I know what was going through that woman's twisted psyche? She was mentally unwell. You do know that, right? She'd been sectioned in a psychiatric hospital.'

'She was a troubled young woman,' I counter, 'and I believe her troubles stemmed from whatever the four of you did that night. All I'm trying to establish is what happened, so that maybe I can find her and bring her home to her mum and dad.'

Louise scoffs. 'You wouldn't want to if you knew what they were really like.'

This is a new angle. The only accounts I've had of Sally's home life have been from Cheryl and Diane herself.

'Why? What was life like at home for Sally?'

Louise scoffs again but doesn't immediately answer.

'What do you mean, Louise?' I try again.

'What I'm saying is that you should get your facts straight before you start coming after three naïve schoolgirls. If you really want to know why Sally took off that night, you need to look for what she was running from.'

'So, if nothing happened in those woods, and Sally left of her own volition, why all the secrecy? Why all the lies about playing truth or dare that the three of you clung to all these years? If you knew Sally had run away, why not tell the authorities that?'

Louise shakes her head. 'Come on, Jane, let's get out of here. We should probably make some kind of appearance at the wake. Despite all her flaws, Natalie was a good friend once upon a time.'

Jane doesn't take a second look at me before interlocking her arm with Louise's and the two saunter off like they are somehow above my questions. I'm about to chase after them when I feel my phone vibrating in my pocket. Answering it, I head out of the room so I won't lose sight of Louise and Jane.

'Miss Hunter? It's Pam Ratchett, one of the nurses from your mum's home.'

I freeze, a tight ball of dread inflating in my gut and rising through my ribcage.

'Is she…?' I can't finish the sentence.

'Your mum's had a fall, Miss Hunter. She's conscious, but she's in a bit of a bad way. We thought you should know, in case you wanted to see her.'

'I'll come straightaway,' I say without hesitation.

Chapter Twenty-Seven

NOW

Weymouth, Dorset

Having made my excuses and apologised to Cheryl for not attending the wake, I hop into a taxi and head straight for the nursing home on the other side of Weymouth. I often try to walk to the home but I desperately need to check on Mum. I've been meaning to call in on her but have kept making excuses, and now the guilt is overwhelming. Maybe if I'd gone to see her today instead of to a stranger's funeral she wouldn't have fallen. I'm being irrational but it's only because I know that recently I haven't been the daughter she needs.

Maybe it's because of the time of year, or because it's the middle of the day, but for once the road leading up to the nursing home is bare of cars. Usually, there isn't a single spot to park in, but today there is plenty of choice, and so the taxi driver can park quite near to the large wrought-iron gates, which I've never seen closed. Paying him, I dive out of the car and hurry in through the gates. Ginger, the overweight tomcat, is asleep on the wide stone steps that lead up to the large painted door. He's a regular feature and on any normal day I'd stop to pet him, but not today.

The front door is locked as it always is, and so I jab my finger against the buzzer on the sidewall. The door whirs as it unlocks, and I yank it open, not giving my nostrils the time they need to adjust to the insipid pong that clings to every molecule of air inside the place. I know it's a potent cocktail of urine and body odour, and a signal that death lurks nearby. Signing in at the reception window, I tell the young woman in the purple tabard who I am – not that I need to; my fame precedes me here.

'Hello, Emma,' she says chirpily, as if she hasn't a care in the world. 'Pam asked if you would go to her office before you see your mum. It's down the hall, second door on the left.'

I look towards the hallway to see where she means, before turning back. 'Is Mum… is she okay?'

The woman nods, and smiles. 'Nasty fall, and she's going to have a ghastly shiner on her face come morning, but otherwise okay, I think. There's a doctor in with her at the moment just checking nothing is broken.'

Thanking her, I head to Pam's office as instructed, knocking sharply. Pam comes to the door and opens it, beckoning me in.

'You weren't joking when you said you'd be right over,' she says. 'I didn't know if you were local today or with your agent in London.'

If you ask me, the nurses here are heroes who don't receive the recognition they deserve for the work they do caring for our infirm. They're also incredibly supportive of my career. Shortly after *Monsters* hit the number one spot on the *Sunday Times* Bestsellers List, they asked me if I would come and speak to the residents about my writing career, which I was only too happy to do. Ever since, they always ask how I'm getting on, maybe living their own dreams vicariously through me. The publishing industry isn't all parties and quaffing champagne, which I'm sure is how some of them imagine it.

'I hope my phone call didn't worry you unnecessarily,' she continues. 'It doesn't look like there's anything more than a bit of bruising, and of course the shock of the fall.'

'Can you tell me what happened? Where was she when she fell?'

Pam retakes her seat across the desk from me and I sit in the vacant chair.

'It was shortly after breakfast. The residents had returned to their rooms, ahead of what would have been wash time for those who require help, including your mum. From speaking to the staff on duty on your mum's floor, they were due to call on her next when they heard an almighty thump. Hurrying to her room, they found her sprawled on the bathroom floor, having seemingly slipped when getting out of the shower. They managed to get her up and over to the bed, and we called for a GP to come and examine her immediately, though we're pretty sure she's managed to avoid breaking any bones. Very lucky, all things considered.'

'What was she doing trying to shower herself? She knows she needs help doing it now. We've both had that conversation with her.'

Pam nods. 'And she's reminded as breakfast finishes every day too. That's what I wanted to speak to you about.' She pauses, almost as if trying to choose her words carefully. 'I know you don't get here to see her as much as you'd like, so it may be that you haven't noticed, but her short-term memory is getting a lot worse. I remember when you first brought her in here she'd forget some names and words, but it's becoming more frequent now. She often wakes screaming and crying because she doesn't realise where she is. She isn't the only one this affects; we've had plenty of residents who wake so disorientated that they fall into blind panic. You can imagine how scary that would be, right? To wake in a bed and room you don't recognise when as far as you're concerned you should be at home, surrounded by all the things you know and love.'

I can't say I haven't noticed her memory worsening. When she first moved in – against her will, I might add – she would occasionally call me by the wrong name, but for every bad day she'd have five or six good days. More recently, the balance has shifted and the bad days outweigh the good. I've been waiting for someone like Pam to break the news so we can discuss the extra care she's going to require from here on in. I had hoped I was just unfortunate to see her on the bad days, and that she was thriving when I wasn't here. So much for wishful thinking.

'As you know, the temperature on the taps in all of our rooms is carefully controlled to prevent anyone scalding themselves, so I'm not worried about that, but today has shown it may be time to move her to one of the bedrooms without shower facilities, and have her washed in the specialist rooms that our staff would take her to.'

I can't agree more. The thought of Mum being disorientated and slipping in the shower again isn't one I care to dwell on.

'Whatever you think is for the best,' I say. 'You tell me what's going to be best for her, and I'll happily agree to it. After all, you're more experienced with this kind of thing.'

'There are additional costs involved with the level of care your mother may now require; that's why I thought it best we talk about it in private. Not all of our clients can afford the additional payments required...'

'Please, Pam, money isn't the issue. I just want Mum well looked after.'

Pam smiles. 'Good, as it should be. I do so hate discussing money – it's the worst part of this job – but that went a lot more smoothly than I was expecting. How is the writing going? Have you got a new project on the go?'

I'm keen to go and see Mum now that I've established what happened. 'My next book is with the publishers as we speak, and I should know more about release dates in the coming weeks.'

'I do envy you,' Pam says, as she stands and moves to the door. 'I always enjoyed writing stories at school – fiction though, not the sort of thing you write. It's a real skill you have, Emma. I wish you the best of luck with it.'

Pam opens the door and a young man is standing there with his hand raised, as if he was about to knock.

'Ah, Dr Benjamin, what perfect timing. This here is Emma Hunter, Bronwyn's daughter. Dr Benjamin was the doctor examining your mother.'

I stand and shake the hand he offers. He's much younger than I was picturing when Pam said a GP had been called to check on Mum. He has fair hair and a close-cropped beard, but I'd swear he's even younger than I am. He certainly looks it.

'Your mum is in her room,' he says, not returning my smile. 'I left her shouting at the television.' He fixes Pam with a stare. 'Pam, would you mind if I had a word with you?'

I take my cue to leave, thanking Pam again for her help,

before heading back along the corridor to the winding staircase. Mum's current room is on the second floor, where the more physically able reside. That will probably change in the coming weeks, as the less-abled are all on the ground floor. Presumably there is a room available, as Pam didn't suggest there would be any kind of delay in rehoming her, once the finances are in place.

I arrive outside her room and press my ear to the door to see if she's moving about inside. The gentle hum of the television suggests she is exactly where Dr Benjamin left her. Knocking once, I open the door and head inside.

'Hi, Mum, how are you doing?'

Her room is the size of a hotel room in a budget chain and she is tucked into bed, but I can't help gasping as I close the door and see the purple and yellowish bruising covering her left cheek.

'Emma, what are you doing here?'

My mouth drops at the question. I can't remember the last time she used my name to address me. I'd assumed that today was another of the bad days on account of her attempt to shower herself, but maybe that was naïve of me – or maybe the shock of the fall has her synapses firing again.

'I heard you had a fall,' I reply, moving across and kissing her good cheek, before perching on the side of her bed. 'How are you feeling now?'

She frowns at me. 'Like a fool! I felt full of energy this morning and thought I'd surprise the nurses by washing myself before they arrived. I had a lovely shower, and as I was getting out, my leg turned to jelly and next thing I knew I was lying flat out on the cold bathroom floor. Before I could call out, they came rushing in, talking down to me like I was a naughty schoolgirl. You look like you've lost weight, Emma. Are you eating enough?'

A single tear escapes my eyes. I have longed for this moment, to have a conversation with the old mum whom I haven't seen for so long. Before she moved in here, she'd always tell me I'd lost weight and needed fattening up, like some prize calf.

'I'm fine, Mum,' I say, taking her hand in mine, and noticing the bruising isn't confined to her face. Her whole right hand and wrist is turning a darker shade, which is presumably why Dr Benjamin was called to examine her.

'Shall I make us a cup of tea?'

She presses her left hand to my cheek. 'I'd like that, sweetheart.'

Chapter Twenty-Eight

THEN

Bovington Garrison, Dorset

Staring out of the upstairs bathroom window on what was a grey and drizzly scene, Natalie watched as swarms of men and women in military fatigues and dark uniforms moved from one property to the next. They'd yet to knock on their door, but it would only be a matter of time. She hadn't realised her late-night call would cause this level of activity. She'd assumed that Detective Rimmington would be back and would maybe focus her attention on searching the woods, but she hadn't expected this kind of intrusion.

'Come away from the window,' her mum said, appearing in a dressing gown from her bedroom. 'What are you looking at anyway?'

It wasn't much after eight and the noise clearly hadn't disturbed her mum's sleep.

'Looks like police,' Natalie said, as casually as she could. 'There's loads of them.'

Cheryl came forward and peered out over her daughter's shoulder. 'Wonder what that's all about,' she muttered rhetorically. 'Nothing to do with us, I'm sure. Shouldn't you be getting your uniform on for school?'

Natalie was still in her pyjamas, having barely slept since she'd placed the phone call. What if the police were able to trace where the call had come from? She hadn't thought about that last night when she'd covered the mouthpiece with her sleeve. What was the point in trying to disguise her voice, if they still knew the call originated from this address? She should have snuck out and used the phone box down near the hut. At least then it wouldn't have been so obvious who'd placed the call.

'I'm not feeling well,' Natalie said, not needing to make her voice sound any croakier than it already was.

Cheryl placed a warm hand against her daughter's forehead. 'Doesn't feel like you have a temperature. In what way do you feel sick? Are we talking a simple cold, or like you might vomit?'

Her mum… pragmatic as ever.

'I don't know,' Natalie feigned. 'My tummy hurts, and my head aches, and it hurts to swallow. I think I might be coming down with something.'

Cheryl gripped Natalie's face in both hands, pulling her eyelids down a fraction. 'You do look a little peaky, I suppose. If you stay off again, I won't be here to look after you, though. I'm expected at Mrs Roberts's to do some cleaning and ironing. Do you think you're well enough to look after yourself?'

Natalie nodded slowly, hoping to confirm her weariness.

'Very well then. I'm sure one more missed day won't do you any harm. Do you feel like you can eat any breakfast?'

Natalie gripped her gut and shook her head.

'Very well. Why don't you head back to bed and I'll call the school? I'll bring you up a cup of tea when I've eaten.'

With that, Cheryl headed out of the room and down the stairs, leaving Natalie to hobble back to bed. She wasn't faking the nausea; that part was real – probably brought on by the imminent arrival of that Detective Rimmington demanding to know why Natalie had phoned 999 to report Sally murdered.

When the telephone operator had asked for more detail, Natalie had only given as much as she dared: Sally Curtis had been murdered the night she disappeared and that she'd been seen leaving the woods and returning home. She'd stopped before naming Owen Curtis as the potential suspect, but figured Rimmington was probably smart enough to connect the dots. Natalie had seen Sally's bruises first hand, and her father should have to face the consequences of that at the very least. His bad temper was clearly a known factor, so why hadn't anyone thought to question Owen Curtis as a suspect in his daughter's disappearance? It didn't explain what he'd done with Sally's body, but if the police could tie it to him, then they'd be sure to find Sally once and for all.

Natalie had just clambered back into bed when she heard the doorbell sound, swiftly followed by the sound of her mum's voice saying, 'She's upstairs in bed. She's not feeling very well.'

Oh God, they'd come for her! They had to know Natalie had placed the call, and now they would demand to know why she'd called last night and why she hadn't mentioned anything when the detective had interviewed her at the hospital the day Sally was reported missing. She'd been too scared back then, and certain that the spell-casting had caused it – not that she could tell the detective any of that. The four of them were already in enough trouble without dragging up the *real* reason they'd gone to the woods when the moon was full. She'd just have to say she'd thought about it, and it was the only logical explanation for what had happened to Sally. Hadn't Sherlock Holmes coined the expression *when you eliminate the impossible, whatever remains, no matter how improbable, must be the truth*? Sally's dad must have been the one to kill her, accidentally or not.

A knock on Natalie's bedroom door was followed by her mum entering. 'The police are here, and they've asked to take your clothes away for forensic examination. You know, the ones you were wearing on Sunday night when you were in the woods with Sally.'

'They want *my* clothes? What for?'

Cheryl looked too flustered to offer an accurate explanation. 'I don't know about that. What were you wearing and where is it now?'

Natalie had hidden the jeans she'd been wearing on account of the puncture hole in the leg, and the blood from her wound, as she hadn't wanted her mum to see them and question what had happened. Since the truth had been exposed in the hospital, Sally hadn't even thought about getting them cleaned and repaired.

'My jeans are in the bottom of my wardrobe, along with the t-shirt and hoodie I was wearing.'

Her mum moved straight to the wardrobe and dug out the items. 'What about your pants, shoes and socks?'

Natalie furrowed her brow. 'What do they need all that for?'

'I told you, Natalie, I don't know,' her mum replied sharply. 'Just tell me where they are.'

'I was wearing my black trainers, but pants and socks would be in the washing basket; I can't remember which ones I was wearing.'

Cheryl disappeared out of the room and headed back downstairs, stopping at the shoe cupboard to collect the trainers. Natalie had moved to her door and was peering down the stairs, watching as a uniformed officer held open a bag for her mum to drop the clothes into. He sealed the bag with tape, and wrote something on it before turning to leave.

'Good morning, Natalie,' Detective Rimmington's voice carried up the stairs.

Natalie hadn't noticed her standing at the entrance to the living room and knew it was too late to duck out of sight.

'Would you mind coming downstairs to answer a few questions for me?' Rimmington asked, so casually it would be impossible to disagree,

Natalie felt bile building at the back of her throat as a cold sweat instantly soaked through the back of her pyjamas, but she stepped out of the room and slowly made her way down the stairs. Pulse racing, and heart thundering in her chest, Natalie followed Rimmington through the living room and out to the kitchen. She froze when she saw Lieutenant-Colonel William Havvard already seated at the table.

'I hope you don't mind,' Rimmington explained as she took the seat adjacent to him, 'but the lieutenant-colonel has asked to sit in on the interview.'

His eyes didn't leave Natalie's as she continued into the room. He was like a lion waiting to pounce and tear her limb from limb.

'As the police are so insistent on causing a disturbance here on the base today, I want to make sure that they aren't taking advantage. We are a family, after all. Isn't that right, Natalie?'

Did he know she'd placed the call? Had he heard her eavesdropping on his conversation with her dad, and now he'd come to make sure she didn't go blabbing about what she'd heard?

'Please take a seat, Natalie. Because of your age, you're required to have an appropriate adult present with you whilst I undertake the interview. Usually that would be a parent, so are you happy for your mum to stay in the room?'

Natalie's eyes were still fixed on Havvard's as she nodded.

'Good, then why don't you sit down next to your mum and we can begin?'

Natalie pulled out the chair beside her mum and sat.

'This interview is going to be undertaken under caution, Natalie, in accordance with the Police and Criminal Evidence Act. What that means is, I will be formally recording your answers to my questions, and the document will become a legal document which could later be referred to in court if appropriate. It's nothing for you to be scared about, but the reason we require an appropriate adult to attend the interview is so that they can ask any questions on your behalf, to ensure you fully understand what is being asked and what it means. Okay?'

Natalie nodded, wishing she could wake from the developing nightmare.

'Okay,' Rimmington continued, 'you do not have to say anything, but it may harm your defence if you do not mention something which you later rely on in court. Anything you do say may be given in evidence.'

Natalie blinked as the words settled in her mind. A police caution? A court trial? Did they think she'd done something wrong? She'd reported Sally's murder in good faith. She hadn't anticipated getting into trouble for it.

'Do you have any initial questions, Natalie? Or do you require me to explain the caution any further?'

Natalie shook her head under the heavy stare of Havvard.

'Good, then can we start with what happened on Sunday night when you last saw Sally Curtis? I know I've asked you about it before but in your own words, can you explain where you were, and what you were doing when you last saw Sally?'

Natalie proceeded to recount the story she'd delivered in the hospital room, how the four of them had gone to the woods to play truth or dare. At no point did she mention the spell, nor the fact it had been Sally's idea that they meet at the clearing and lay it out as Jane's mum's book dictated. She could feel Havvard's stare burrowing deeper and deeper into her soul as she spoke. Did he know about the Wiccan spell they'd cast? Was he here purely to stop her mentioning Pete's possible involvement in the practice?

Rimmington allowed her to speak without interruption, asking additional questions until she heard the answers she was expecting.

'Someone phoned the police last night and reported that Sally was murdered on Sunday night, which is why our officers and Lieutenant-Colonel Havvard's people are asking your neighbours whether they can remember hearing or seeing anything unusual on Sunday night. Now, I need you to remember that you are under caution, Natalie, and what I want to know is whether you saw Sally leave the woods after your game on Sunday night. I know the three of you have said she ran off, but did you see where she went, or whether she ran towards the hole in the fence through which you'd all snuck?'

This was the moment, the chance to tell the detective about the bruises on Sally's torso and about the conversation she'd overheard last night about Owen Curtis's bad temper.

Natalie remained silent, looking from the detective to Havvard and then back again. She finally shook her head. 'I told you, I didn't see where Sally went after she ran off. It was so dark and she didn't have a torch. I don't know how she could have found her way back out.'

The detective closed her notebook and placed the lid back on her pen, offering Natalie a warm smile. 'Thank you for answering those questions, Natalie. I appreciate you taking the time to speak with me, and I hope nothing I've said today has upset you. Despite last night's phone call, we are still treating Sally as a missing person, as there is currently no evidence to suggest anything bad has happened to her. I would ask, however, if you do recall anything else about that night – no matter how insignificant – that you ask your mum or dad to contact me. Okay?'

Natalie nodded and watched the detective and Havvard stand and be shown to the door by her mum.

Chapter Twenty-Nine

NOW

Weymouth, Dorset

All those days when Mum thought I was just another of the 'interfering nurses', as she calls them, or when she thought I was an eight-year-old version of myself, and even when she had no clue who I was or what I was doing in her room, they melt into memory after the last twenty minutes, when Mum and I have *just talked*. She's asked questions about my writing – I wasn't even sure she remembered I wrote books – and so I have told her all about *Monsters* and *Ransomed*, and I was close to tears when she told me how proud she was to see how my career is flourishing.

I know not all visits will be like this; that she will forget who I am again in the next hours, days or weeks, and it shines a light on just how cruel an illness Alzheimer's is. I'm trying not to think about those future visits filled with my own tears and frustration. I'm just concentrating on being with her here in the moment. It's the perfect Christmas present.

'I bet you've already got your next book planned out, haven't you?' she asks, extending the cup in her hand towards me for a refill from the pot.

Accepting the cup, I fill it with the dregs of the pot on the side and pass it back to her. 'I'm working on a story at the moment. It's about a fourteen-year-old girl who disappeared mysteriously about fifteen years ago.'

Mum stares at me. 'Can I ask a blunt question?'

I nod. 'Of course.'

Her brow furrows. 'Do you think... I mean, if *your* sister hadn't gone missing, do you think this is what you would be doing with your life? Writing books, I mean?'

The question catches me off guard. The truth is that I never pictured myself as a writer when I was younger. Yes, I enjoyed making up stories at school and always had a penchant for language, but I've kind of stumbled into what I'm now doing. I only took the job at the local newspaper because I didn't want to be stuck working in a nine-to-five office. I liked that I could set my own hours; I liked chasing down stories and trying to get to the heart and essence of the truth. Had Freddie Mitchell not opened up to me that first night we met, I'd probably still be freelancing for the *Dorset Echo*.

'I've never thought about it, Mum. Why do you ask?'

She sips from her cup. 'I know life wasn't easy at home when you were growing up... your dad and I splitting up, and me so focused on trying to get Anna back... It must have been very tough for you at times.'

My eyes are filling and I can't prevent them from doing so. This is not only the most candid she's been in months, but it's also the most honest conversation we've ever had. Never before has she admitted prioritising Anna over me after she wandered off that day. I can only imagine how long these thoughts have been bubbling beneath the surface of her troubled mind, waiting to be released.

'I understood that you wanted to find her,' I say, dabbing my eyes with the sleeve of my cardigan.

'Well, I'm sorry that I haven't been there enough for you. It's funny, after they got me up off the bathroom floor, I caught a glimpse of that photograph on the side there.' She waves at the frame she means, beckoning me to go and collect it for her, which I do. 'Yes, this one. Do you remember where it was taken?'

I look at the picture of me, Anna, Dad and Mum. We are all beaming, and in the background I can see what looks like a seafront, pier and some amusement arcades. I don't even recall the picture being taken, though I have seen it here a number of times.

'I don't know, Mum.'

She accepts the frame and turns it over in her hands, but fails to swivel the clasps keeping the felt-covered back of the frame in place. I take it from her and turn the clasps, lifting off the back. She pulls out the image and pushes it close to her nose, trying to read something on the upper corner of the back.

'Brighton, May 1998,' she tells me, before showing me the pencil-scrawled date. 'Your dad had won us a weekend break away at a fancy hotel along the seafront. We arrived Friday night after school and left on Monday morning. I remember we all had to share a room, and you and your sister moaned about your dad's snoring.' She smiles at the memory and I just want to cuddle her, to commit this passage to my long-term memory. 'I remember your dad devouring the fried breakfast each morning, but you and Anna were just excited that you were allowed Coco Pops, because I wouldn't let you have them at home.'

I don't remember this particular incident, but I do recall Anna and me always busting a gut to get to the breakfast bar on those rare occasions we'd be on holiday, desperate to see whether the hotel stocked Coco Pops.

'Sounds like us,' I say warmly.

'You'd have been... ooh, what... four or five? I think Anna would have been...?'

'Seven,' I answer for her, doing the calculation in my head.

'Yes, that's right. The two of you kept on and on and on at your dad to let you go on the arcades along the seafront. God knows how much money was wasted on those machines where you can scoop out teddy bears. Do you remember those? They probably don't have them anymore.'

'They do,' I advise her. 'All the old amusement arcades are still going, though they've added some newer, more violent games since then.'

She nods but is staring wistfully into the distance. 'I think that was my favourite holiday. It wasn't long, but it was perfect... surrounded by the people I loved most in the world, and before all that nasty business with your dad and your sister.'

It's an interesting way to summarise her daughter going missing and her husband's suicide, but I don't question her on it, instead squeezing her hand.

'We had other holidays,' I counter. 'I remember we spent a week in South Devon. A week at Butlins in Bognor Regis. We even flew to Jersey at one point, I think?'

'Did we...? I really don't remember.' She tries to sit up in bed but her arm slips, the cup tips, and suddenly there is tea all down her nightdress. 'Oh gosh, I'm sorry,' she quickly whimpers.

'It's okay, Mum,' I try to reassure as she suddenly starts crying. 'I can get you cleaned up.' I take the cup from her and put it on the side. 'There's no need to cry over spilled milk, even when it also includes tea,' I say, trying to ease her obvious concern.

'Oh no, I'm sorry, I'm so sorry, it was an accident.'

'Mum, it's okay, it really is. No need to make a fuss. Come on, I can get you out of this nightdress and into a clean one. The good news is you didn't get any on the bedspread.'

I pull back the duvet before the excess liquid leeks down onto it, and take her frail hand. She's trembling as she swings her legs out, her voice still little more than a whisper.

'I'm so sorry, please don't be cross.'

I lift her chin slightly so I can look straight into her eyes. 'I'm not cross, Mum. Okay? This is nothing. I'm sure you had to clear up much bigger messes when I was younger.' I smile at her, until her worry softens, and then I lift the nightdress up and over her head.

The fact that she isn't wearing a bra doesn't come as a shock, but it is her chamois-like wrinkled skin, black and blue down her left side which causes me to gasp. The colouring is much deeper than the bruising on her face, and as I study it closer, it doesn't look as recent as the yellowing of her cheeks.

'You look like you've been in the wars, Mum. Tell me again how you fell in the shower.'

'I told you, I slipped and fell.'

'Yes, but how?' I look closer at the right side of her torso which looks almost jaundiced, such is the intensity of the golden colour, similar in shading to the bruises on that side of her face. 'Mum, the bruising on this side of your body… was today not the first time you've fallen?'

'I can be so clumsy at times. Please just fetch me a new nightie.'

I move to the chest of drawers and locate a new nightdress in the second drawer down, carry it over and help her slip it over her head. Then I help her to her feet, so the gown will slide down and over her bottom, before getting her back into bed, but as I do I find further latent bruising along the back of both calves.

The home hasn't phoned me before to say that she'd fallen and injured herself. Today was definitely the first time, but clearly Mum's bruises are telling a different story. Either she fell but managed to get herself back up without any trouble, or these injuries were caused in another way.

I pass her a tissue so she can wipe her eyes. 'That was the last of the tea. Do you want me to ask the staff to make you a fresh pot?'

'Probably best not to,' she says, blowing her nose and composing herself once more.

'The bruises on the backs of your legs, Mum… how did they happen?'

She stares blankly back at me. 'What bruises are those, dear?'

Oh no. When she refers to me as 'dear' it usually means she can't place my name, which means those firing neurons are starting to burn out again.

'Mum? Look at me, please. Your legs are covered in bruises which can't have been caused by your fall today. Can you tell me how you got them? Did you fall before?'

'I don't know what you're talking about, dear. What fall?'

My heart is breaking as the confusion descends on her face. 'You fell getting out of the shower this morning. Do you remember?'

'Did I?' She half laughs. 'I can be so clumsy at times. Oh well, no harm done.'

I'm not cold enough to show her the outcome of the fall by holding a mirror to her face. Tucking her into bed, I kiss her cheek and promise I'll come back and visit her again soon, but I can see from her face that she's struggling to recall why my face looks familiar. How is it that so many strangers can recognise me instantly, and yet the one person I want to know every contour of my face doesn't?

She is happily humming along to the theme tune of *Bargain Hunt* as I close the door behind me and hurry back along the corridor, willing the tears not to break free of my eyes. I take the stairs down two at a time until I'm outside Pam Ratchett's office door once again. Knocking, I hear her stand and move to the door. Dr Benjamin is sitting in the chair I vacated as the door opens.

'Ah, Emma, I'm glad you've stopped by. There's something we'd like to speak to you about.'

I don't wait to be invited in, pushing through the gap between Pam and the door. 'There's something I want to speak to you about too.'

Pam closes the door and encourages me to sit in the remaining vacant chair, but I don't want to sit. My mind is whirling with questions and irrational conclusions… and I want answers.

'I've just had to change Mum's nightdress and she looks like she's been in a boxing match. Have you seen how battered and bruised she is?'

Pam fires a silent look at Dr Benjamin. 'That's what we were hoping to speak to you about, Emma. Please do sit.'

I huff, but relent and pull the chair over, plonking myself down on it.

'Dr Benjamin has just brought your mum's condition to my attention,' Pam says, before Dr Benjamin clears his throat and leans forward in his chair.

'Today's the first time I've been called here to treat your mum,' he begins, his voice deeper than I was expecting for someone his age. 'And I was shocked to see how bad a state she is in. The good news is, I don't have reason to believe she has suffered anything more than bruises as a result of her fall today. I have carefully examined her face, ribcage and left wrist, and all have the normal range of motion for someone her age. I was, however, concerned about the bruising I discovered on the right-hand side of her torso, the bruising behind her knees, and a swelling on her right shoulder.'

I didn't see any swelling on her right shoulder, but then I didn't give her a full body examination.

'Having spoken with Pam, here,' he continues, 'she's said your mum hasn't reported falling before to any of the nursing staff, and we wanted to check whether she's mentioned anything to you. All falls and injuries have to be recorded in the home's log as they are primary healthcare practitioners for all their patients and are subject to oversight by both the NHS and local council authority.'

I feel my eyes filling again. 'I'm not aware of any previous falls, and when I asked her just now she had no idea what I was talking about.'

A silent look is exchanged between the two of them again. What is it they're keeping from me?

'I asked her about the bruises too,' Dr Benjamin continues, turning back to face me. 'She clammed up as soon as I mentioned them, kept trying to distract me with what she was watching on the television. She was evasive the more I pressed, but she was also growing more upset as I asked about specific bruises.'

'She spilled her tea,' I say, 'and it was when I changed her that I saw the bruises. She dismissed my concerns as her just being clumsy, but I think it's more than that. When she spilled the tea, her mood totally changed, like some cold shadow fell across her. She became overly apologetic and upset, despite my trying to calm her down and reassure her that it was just an accident. It was almost as if...'

The penny drops. *Oh good God, no.*

'She was terrified she would be in trouble,' I continue, now understanding the silent exchanges between Pam and the GP. My eyes widen as my mind processes why they specifically wanted to speak to me. 'Oh God, you don't think... Oh God, you do... You think *I* could do that to her? How could you?'

'Nobody is accusing anyone of anything,' Pam quickly pipes up.

'*I* didn't cause those bruises!' I say raising my voice in defiance. 'I *couldn't*; she's my mum.'

'We're not accusing you of abuse, Miss Hunter,' Dr Benjamin chimes in, 'but I have reason to suspect that *someone* may have done this to your mum. That's why I was keen to speak to Pam at the earliest opportunity.'

'So, what are you saying?' I ask, wiping my eyes with the tissue again. 'One of the staff has been...' – I can barely get the words off my tongue – 'beating my mother?'

'We don't know anything yet,' Pam interjects as defensively

as I was a moment ago. 'We will need to carry out an internal investigation to better understand what has occurred. Our home has always had a perfect track record with our staff and there's no reason to assume that standards have slipped.'

'How else do you explain the state of my mother's body? And how the hell wasn't the bruising identified before Dr Benjamin here examined her?'

Pam is blushing. I know I shouldn't be targeting all my anger at her but she represents the home and its employees so she has no choice but to take it.

'I assure you, Emma, that I will get to the bottom of whatever has happened here. I will speak to all my staff to find out why this bruising hasn't previously been brought to my attention, and will speak to the staff and other residents about whether they're aware of how the injuries might have been sustained. I know it doesn't make up for what has gone on, but I assure you it will be stopped forthwith.'

'You think I'm going to allow her to stay somewhere that puts her health in danger?' I say rhetorically, but I know it's an empty threat as soon as the words leave my lips. This is the highest-regarded nursing home in the town, and the most convenient for me to reach without having to drive... and I certainly can't have Mum move in with me.

'Your mum has a good quality of life here, and I would discourage you from jumping to rash decisions,' Pam says. 'I assure you I will keep a personal watch over her while I carry out my investigation and I will update you as soon as I have got to the bottom of it. I assure you that your mother's and the other residents' welfare is my primary concern here.'

It isn't ideal, but what other choice do I have for now? Most nursing homes have waiting lists and I'm not going to be able to get her transferred overnight.

Dr Benjamin leans towards me. 'If it's any consolation, I've only ever heard good stories about the level of care afforded to the patients here. I think your mum will be perfectly safe with Pam keeping a closer eye on her wellbeing.'

It is the merest of comforts but I nod my agreement. 'Very well. Carry out your investigation, but in the meantime I will be considering her future here.'

Pam nods in resigned acknowledgement. 'Thank you, Emma, and please do accept my deepest apologies that this has happened. Believe me when I say I am just as angry as you that this has happened to one of our residents.'

Standing, I compose myself and head for the door, sign out at the reception window and exit into the cool breeze, which is welcome relief to the fire burning behind my cheeks.

Chapter Thirty

NOW

Weymouth, Dorset

The walk home is long and unyielding, but it has given me the opportunity to put things into perspective. I was ready to lynch Pam for not noticing the abuse Mum has suffered sooner, but I am just as guilty of not knowing what's been going on. Had I been a more attentive daughter and visited her more over the last few weeks, maybe I would have spotted the signs sooner. It still doesn't tell me how best I should proceed. Prior to this afternoon's news, I would have recommended the nursing home to anyone and everyone, so should I allow this one issue to tarnish my otherwise high opinion? Is Dr Benjamin right and I should trust Pam to undertake an impartial investigation and get to the truth?

My mind is still on this dilemma when I arrive home and I can't help smiling when I see a familiar face on my doorstep.

'Hello, stranger,' Freddie Mitchell says, quickly coming over and giving me a big hug. 'How've you been?'

'I've been better,' I admit.

He stands back, concern instantly gripping his aging face. 'Whatever is the matter?'

'Nothing to worry about,' I say, waving away his concern, 'just something with my mum. Forget about it. How are you? I'm surprised you're back here so soon. I thought the film company were putting you up in a plush hotel while you were busy consulting on the project.'

Freddie is grinning and fluttering his eyelashes. 'Yes, I have to admit I'm becoming rather accustomed to this grand lifestyle fate has thrust upon me. I now only bathe in the best champagne France has to offer – might as well bathe in the stuff, as I'm not going to drink it.' He bursts into laughter. 'On a serious note, life is… well, grand, I suppose. Never in a million years did I think I'd be rubbing shoulders with media darlings all falling over themselves to be nice and ask about my experience. You did that for me, Emma Hunter, and I'll be eternally grateful until my dying day.'

I've missed effervescent Freddie. On his day, when his mood is high, he has the ability to soar, and you just want to hold onto his hand and let him carry you with him. When I think about all he went through, he deserves every bit of happiness he can wring out of that story. Good luck to him!

'What are you doing on my doorstep anyway?' I ask. 'Didn't Rachel let you in?'

He gives me a confused stare. 'I rang the bell but there was no answer. I was about to message you and check you were still back here when I saw you coming along the street.'

'Rachel must have gone out,' I say, before explaining that she's staying with me for a few days over Christmas.

'That'll be nice for you,' he says, following me in through

the front door. 'I do worry about you living here on your own. It's about time we found you a big strong man – or woman – to take care of you. I know plenty of lesbians who'd gobble you up for breakfast.'

'Thanks, but I'm doing fine on my own. What is it with you and Rachel constantly trying to set me up on dates? It's my choice to be single and I'm happy as I am. I don't need a man – or a woman – to define who I am.'

'You go, girlfriend,' he teases, emphasising his naturally effeminate voice, which is something he does when he's nervous of his surroundings, a defence mechanism he's been employing since he was a child.

'Everything okay with you, Freddie? Your message the other day said you had something you wanted to talk about?'

Freddie doesn't answer, instead heading straight through to the kitchen and picking up the pair of washing-up gloves that live on the draining board. He puts the plug in the sink and begins to fill it with soapy water. This is another of Freddie's defence mechanisms; whenever he has something troubling him, he feels the need to wash and clean until he's figured a way through the fog in his mind.

I'm so used to seeing him dressed in a flannel shirt and sleeveless denim jacket that the Christmas jumper he's wearing is particularly eye-catching. Overall it is a cream colour, but it has candy canes, bells, gingerbread and fir trees stitched into the fabric. I join him in the kitchen and lower my bag to the table.

'I like your jumper,' I tell him, as he sets to work on the plates neither Rachel nor I washed after last night's takeaway.

'Thanks. It was a present from the actor who's playing my younger self in the show. I definitely think he fancies me and, well, you know me… What about you anyway? You look like you've just come from a funeral.'

'I have, of sorts. A new story I'm working on.' I pause. 'What is it you wanted to talk to me about, Freddie? Is everything okay? Are you all right for money?'

He fires a hurt look at me. 'Is that what you think I came here for? Money? Oh please, I just wanted to see how my friend is doing, that's all.'

Now I know he's lying, particularly as he's cleaning the plate he's already scrubbed three times. I know better than to push him, as Freddie is one who needs to speak at his own pace.

'I am very well, thank you, Freddie, and it really is great to see you again. Can you stay for dinner? I'm sure Rachel will be disappointed she missed you if you have to rush off.'

'Yes, I can stay. Filming has finished until next year, so I'm at something of a loose end anyway.'

'Great! What are your plans for Christmas Day? You're more than welcome to come round here and spend it with me and Rachel.'

He places the last of the crockery on the draining board. 'That's kind of you, but I'm planning to spend the day at the shelter, serving soup and bread to the regulars.'

I first met Freddie in the homeless shelter here in Weymouth and since he's got himself back on his feet, he's felt duty-bound to give back to those still in need and spends more time there than away from the place. I'm not surprised he plans to volunteer over Christmas.

'If you two find yourselves bored after the Queen's speech, you'd be more than welcome to come along and support too.'

'We might just do that,' I say, knowing I definitely will and hoping I can convince Rachel to join me.

Freddie removes the gloves and joins me at the table, wiping his hands on his navy jeans. 'How are things going with that dashing policeman friend of yours?'

Not this *again*!

'I've told you, Freddie, Jack is just a friend.'

'Have you spoken to him recently?'

'I saw him briefly yesterday, why?'

'Has he spoken to you about me?'

I frown. 'Nothing specific springs to mind. Why?'

He looks fractionally relieved but his shoulders have strained, as if he's somehow bearing the weight of the world. 'Good, then he kept to his word.'

'His word? What's going on, Freddie? Whatever it is, you can tell me, you know that.'

He looks away and as he does, I now see the afternoon sunlight reflecting in his shining eyes. He takes a deep breath but continues to look towards the kitchen window. 'Okay, here goes… He – Jack, that is – he contacted me a couple of weeks ago and told me something that I hadn't really thought about for some years. It wasn't easy to hear and I asked him not to mention it to you until I'd had the chance to speak to you first.'

I can't think why Jack would contact Freddie directly, and not through me, particularly if it relates to Freddie's history. Jack had no involvement in Freddie's case and as the prosecution is now finalised, there's no way it should have come back across Jack's pile of cold cases.

Stretching out my fingers, I take his hand in mine. 'Jack hasn't mentioned you to me, I promise.'

He squeezes my knuckles as tears drip from his eyes. 'H–h–

he phoned me because he discovered something in the course of a case he was looking at. Videos of me from years ago; videos where I'm not fully clothed, and where men are… doing bad things.'

A lump forms in my throat, seeing how difficult he's finding it to tell me.

'I'd forgotten Turgood and the others would sometimes make us… perform on camera. It wasn't something any of us were comfortable with but they'd always offer an incentive if we agreed to go along with it. It could be cigarettes, or chocolate, or the latest chart-topping record. I think I reasoned with myself that the abuse would occur regardless and it was better if I at least got something out of it.

'I never mentioned it to you when you interviewed me, as I'd forgotten all about it… repressed it from my memory or something. And then your Jack phoned and it all came flooding back.'

I still don't understand what any of this has to do with Jack and I can't deny I'm a little put out that he's been keeping this from me. So much for being friends!

'Freddie, that sounds horrific, and I'm so sorry. I swear Jack hasn't mentioned it to me at all.'

'Then he's definitely a keeper.' He smiles, but it doesn't last. 'The thing is, Emma, the videos he came across were on the same hard drive as the one where he found videos of your sister Anna.'

Suddenly it makes sense! But if Anna's video was in the same collection as Freddie's, then that must mean…

'The videos were always incentivised,' Freddie says as if reading my mind, 'so if your sister was also forced to be in them, the chances are she was also bribed in some way.'

Is it possible that Freddie's abuse is somehow linked to Anna's disappearance? It doesn't make any sense in my head. What happened to Freddie and the others occurred because they were at the St Francis Home for Wayward Boys. No girls were ever resident at the home.

Freddie is squeezing my hand tighter. 'I thought it was better you hear it from me rather than Jack. I didn't want you thinking I'd deliberately not told you about them. I'd genuinely forgotten until he phoned. Don't be cross with him for not telling you; I swore him to secrecy.' He pauses. 'I understand if you want me to go now. I wouldn't blame you if you never wanted to see me again.'

'Don't be silly, Freddie. I don't blame you for whatever fate befell Anna. I'm glad you felt able to tell me. Please stay.'

Freddie wipes his eyes with the sleeve of his jumper. 'It's at times like this I wish I wasn't on the wagon!'

I can't disagree that a drink would take the edge off but it wouldn't be fair to open wine while Freddie is here.

'That Jack is definitely a good-un. He told me he wouldn't stop until he finds out how Turgood came into possession of all the other videos they found on his hard drive. He definitely fancies you, you know. How else can you explain him going out of his way?'

I can't answer that question, and I don't like the feelings of mistrust currently coursing through my mind. Jack knows how important finding my sister is, yet he was willing to sit on new information that could have helped. I smile encouragingly at Freddie as I don't want him to see how disappointed I am on the inside.

Chapter Thirty-One

THEN

Wareham, Dorset

It had been more than a year since Natalie had been called out of class and asked to attend the headmaster's office. Mr Panko's secretary, Mrs Herrington, looked ashen as she asked Natalie to take a seat while she went through to his office to announce Natalie's arrival. Mr Panko also looked in shock as he emerged from his office and invited Natalie through.

The memories of being here when they'd formally announced that Sally had been reported missing flooded Natalie's mind as she tentatively stood up and willed one foot to follow the other. They hadn't asked Louise or Jane to leave the class, only Natalie. Had Sally been found and revealed that she'd been taken because Natalie had lied about starting her period?

And then she saw her mum sitting in one of the chairs across from Mr Panko's desk, her head buried in her hands. It was clear she'd been crying. No, it was worse than that; she'd been sobbing. Her eyes when they met Natalie's were red raw and puffy, her makeup a mess of colour in all the wrong places, and the tissue in her hand soaked through.

'Please take a seat, Natalie,' Mr Panko said, as he closed the door on the goggle-eyed secretary.

Natalie ignored him and immediately went to her mother's side, dropping to her knees and seeking reassurance that everything would be okay. 'Mum? What's happened? Why are you crying?'

Seeing someone she cared about so much looking so devastated triggered Natalie's paranoia. Something *really* bad must have happened. Was her mother dying? Had the cat been run over? Her grandparents had all died years ago, so it couldn't be that.

'Mum, what's going on?'

Cheryl looked to Mr Panko, unable to say the words herself.

'Natalie, it's about your dad,' Panko's voice carried across the desk. But the moment he said 'dad' it was as if Natalie had been sucked into a vacuum where sound struggled to penetrate.

'What did you say?' Natalie asked, as the words refused to break through her cerebral cortex.

'I'm so sorry, Natalie. Your dad has been killed while on duty. He saved two of his unit in the process; he died a hero.'

Her mum was wailing again as if hearing the outcome for the first time, but Natalie's brain had yet to process the news. It had to be a mistake, a cruel joke being played out. Her dad couldn't be dead. The soldiers from Bovington didn't die while serving in other countries; that was just those soldiers from other bases in parts of the country she'd never heard of. None of her friends' dads had died while serving, so it couldn't have happened to her dad. That wouldn't be fair.

'We thought it best if you head home with your mum,' Panko said quietly. 'I know you're preparing for your GCSEs, but I can arrange for your homework to be sent home while you come to terms with this news. I truly am sorry, Natalie.'

Her mum was still sobbing and Panko had yet to burst into laughter, which could only mean they weren't joking. But if this wasn't an elaborate ruse, then that meant…

The tears streamed from Natalie's eyes in less than a second, and an enormous burst of emotion erupted from her throat. Images of her dad filled her mind: him dancing, him laughing and him picking her up and twirling her around; him tossing pancakes and him saluting in his uniform; him opening Christmas presents in his dressing gown and him diving into the swimming pool; him kissing her good night and telling her that monsters didn't live under her bed.

The drive back to the base was muted, both Natalie and her mum lost in memories of the man they wouldn't make any fresh memories with. By the time they reached the house, Natalie felt as though she was cried out, but her mind still refused to accept that this was now a reality. At fifteen, she wasn't ready to say goodbye to her dad. He was supposed to live long into her adulthood. He was supposed to give her away on her wedding day years from now, supposed to sing lullabies to his grandchildren as he had done with her. He was only forty-three; that was no age to be dying. He couldn't have completed all the things he wanted to in his life. What a waste!

'I'll put the kettle on,' her mum said once they were inside, though instinctively she moved to the fridge and pulled out the open bottle of wine. 'You want tea?'

Natalie shook her head. What good was tea? It wouldn't bring him back. It wouldn't paper over the gargantuan crevice that had opened in her heart. It wouldn't ease the anger and pain now coursing through every cell in her body.

Stomping upstairs, Natalie slammed her door in protest, almost hoping her mum would come up and tell her off, just to give Natalie an excuse to lay into someone. She needed to let it out, to shout and fight, to scratch and claw, to unleash the pure hatred at someone, anyone. She collapsed on her bed, thumping her fists into her pillow, roaring as she did so until eventually, and breathlessly, she crumpled into it.

'I love you, Dad,' she said silently. 'I'm sorry I wasn't a better daughter.'

Fresh tears came and as they fell she replayed as many happy memories of him as she could think of: trips away, the mess he'd made when they'd tried to make Mum a birthday cake, the way he'd always sing song lyrics wrong.

She must have fallen asleep still thinking of him, because when her eyes opened, the sky outside was darker than when they'd left school just before lunchtime. Changing out of her uniform, she decided she'd go and check on her mum. It was hard enough losing a dad, but for her mum it didn't just mean losing the man she'd loved and married, it meant losing a co-parent.

Natalie stopped outside her room as the voices from the living room carried up the stairs. It was her mum and someone bickering about something… a man's voice.

Was it possible? Had there been a mistake? Had her dad returned to prove that they'd misidentified his body? Is that why her mum was shouting? Natalie tiptoed down the stairs, certain she had to be dreaming, but wanting to enjoy every exciting moment of it. She could picture walking into the room and seeing him there, his arms open wide and beckoning her to him. Imagine the look on Mr Panko's face when he realised he'd broken the news to the wrong child!

Natalie paused at the door, desperately wanting to hear the familiar echo of her dad's voice to confirm his identity before she burst in through the door.

'Please,' her mum was saying. 'You can't do this to us. After everything he did for you – and I don't just mean his civil duty – you owe us! You owe him!'

'I'm sorry, it's out of my hands. It's army policy. You have sixty days.'

'Please, I'll do *anything*. Don't throw us out. Not now. Not yet. Nat has her exams next year. Can't we stay until then?'

'I'm sorry, the wheels are already in motion.'

'Bill, you're more powerful than that. You could stop the wheels turning if you wanted to. I'd make it worth your while, you know. Sandra wouldn't have to know; it could be *our* little secret. I remember the way you used to look at me when Geoff's back was turned.'

'No, Cheryl. Don't degrade yourself like this.'

'Fine! Well, I suppose I'm no longer your type anyway, am I, Bill? You like them much younger than me, don't you?'

'Stop it, Cheryl! Don't say something we'll both regret.'

'Oh no, don't worry, Bill, your secret is safe with me. I vowed to Geoff I'd never tell, and I won't, but if you don't want Sandra to know how you get your kicks, you should think twice about that sixty-day eviction notice.'

'I don't know what you're talking about and you'd do best to think twice before spreading malicious filth about me.'

The lounge door flew open and Lieutenant-Colonel Havvard almost barged into Natalie, stopping himself at the last moment. He considered her before saying, 'I'm sorry for your loss, Natalie.' With that, he opened the main door and headed out.

Natalie continued into the room, sickened by her mother's attempts to seduce Havvard, but refusing to make eye contact. 'What was all that about?' she asked.

'Nothing,' Cheryl replied, reaching for the nearly empty bottle of wine. 'Just grown-up stuff. We're going out for dinner tonight; get your shoes and coat on.'

Cheryl disappeared through to the kitchen, carrying the bottle of wine, her glass clunking as it was slammed against the kitchen table, the sound jolting another memory to the forefront of Natalie's mind. This time it was a voice – her dad's voice – from this very room. *I know you didn't mean what happened, which is why I helped you sort it out.*

And then a second voice – Havvard's voice – growling angrily. *You don't want to get on my bad side, Geoff. You know what I'm capable of.*

That had been a year ago, on the night Natalie had reported Sally's murder. The call made from this house. Could Havvard have found out and assumed it was Geoff who'd called 999? Was he really as powerful as everyone claimed? Natalie's mind continued to make leaps and bounds, following no rational logic, until they arrived at one concrete conclusion that she couldn't shake: *she* was the reason her dad had died.

Chapter Thirty-Two

NOW

Weymouth, Dorset

I'm glad when I hear seagulls announcing the end of the night, after what has been a barrage of painful dreams all featuring Anna in some capacity or another. I don't need to be an expert in understanding dreams to know that Freddie's revelation is what caused the onslaught. Not his fault, but I could have done without it last night. I feel drained now as I lie in bed, feeling as though I've spent the entire night battling evil demons; I shouldn't feel this tired after a solid six and a half hours of sleep.

Freddie, Rachel and I toured the pubs of Weymouth before ending up in an Indian restaurant where Rachel proceeded to recount embarrassing tale after embarrassing tale about my love-life failures while at Bournemouth University. It genuinely felt like they'd conspired to shame me into asking them to help alleviate my current single status. They were doing it in a kind way though, and I know they only have my best intentions when they tell me I should ask Jack out on a date. My hands feel clammy at the very thought. Despite their assertions to the contrary, I can't see that Jack has any interest in anyone but his daughter Mila. Rachel and Freddie haven't seen how he is when she's around; there's nothing he wouldn't do for her, and I have no doubt that is the reason why he isn't currently seeing anyone. That, and the fact that his job isn't exactly conducive to starting new relationships, not without the aid of dating apps.

At least the conversation – as cringeworthy as it was – distracted me from what Freddie had said about the videos Jack had found of him on Arthur Turgood's hard drive. I didn't mention it to Rachel when she returned from the library where she'd been looking at newspaper archives; I'm sure the fewer people who know about it, the better for Freddie. It's certainly not something I'd want the world to know about Anna.

That still leaves the question of how a video of Anna wound up on Turgood's hard drive. If Turgood's health continues to deteriorate, there's a chance we will never find out how and why he had a video of my sister being abused in his possession at the time of his incarceration.

I saw a version of Anna's video in my dreams last night, even though I've only seen the still frames that Jack was able to share. In my head, the video was in full high-definition Technicolor detail. Only, in my dream, she wasn't the four-year-older version from the still shots, but the nine-year-old girl I still remembering leaving our front garden and walking innocently down the road towards our grandmother's house. I've never hated having an overactive imagination as much as I did when I woke screaming and crying at four this morning.

Poor Rachel was scared half to death by the outburst and it took longer to calm her down than myself. She'd offered to stay awake and talk to me about the dream but I hadn't wanted to share the horror of what I'd been forced to see. The only silver lining I can draw – and it really is scraping the bottom of the barrel – is that Anna's appearance on that video means she wasn't killed the day she went missing. All manner of horrible things might have befallen her from that moment onwards, but death wasn't one of them.

I can't decide if that is a blessing or a curse.

A gentle knocking at my door is followed by Rachel returning to the room, carrying a tray on which is a glass of juice, a mug of coffee and two slices of buttered toast. 'I thought you would benefit from a little TLC this morning,' she says, waiting for me to prop up my pillows, before resting the tray on my lap. 'How are you feeling?'

'I'm okay,' I say, biting into the toast. 'Thanks for this; I can't remember the last time I had someone bring me breakfast in bed.'

'Well, don't go thinking it will become a habit,' she chuckles. 'I'll be expecting you to return the favour in the coming days.' She pauses. 'Your nightmare last night was about Anna, wasn't it?'

I swallow the toast.

'You were saying her name while you were asleep, right before the screaming started,' she explains. 'I didn't want to push you on it last night because you seemed so upset, but I'm here if you want to talk about her or the dreams.'

'Thank you. Jack found a video of her on Arthur Turgood's hard drive, of all places. In it, she's approximately thirteen years old… and being forced to do some pretty horrific things.'

The look of shock on Rachel's face is what I was hoping to avoid but she deserves to know what caused her to be woken so abruptly during the night. Given she's the co-trustee of the Anna Hunter Foundation, a charitable organisation we set up to support the families of missing people, it seems only right she understand what she's now involved in.

'I'm so sorry, Emma. That's truly awful. Has Jack managed to speak to Turgood and find out where the video came from?'

I shake my head. 'We tried; we even visited him in prison, but he kept his mouth shut. He probably sees it as the best way he can get revenge on me for exposing his abuses at the home.'

'What about his co-defendants? Could they shed any light on it?'

I shake my head again. 'The hard drive was Turgood's personal property and not purchased until long after the St Francis Home had been closed down. Right now, he's the only one who knows how and where he got it from.'

Rachel moves to the window before turning back to face me. 'There is another thought of course, though I'm sure it's one you don't *want* to consider.'

I stay silent, waiting for her to elaborate.

'Assuming Turgood didn't make the video of Anna – which seems realistic given his penchant for young boys – then there's every chance he isn't the only one who has a copy of it. Now, I know you won't want to think about any more perverts viewing the film, but it stands to reason that there would be multiple copies, and if that's the case, it's not an unreasonable leap to assume somebody supplied the videos, and if so—'

'Then Anna could be mixed up in something much larger,' I finish for her.

'Yes, exactly! What if Turgood's hard drive is merely the tip of the iceberg? Can you speak to Jack about it? The Metropolitan Police have an entire department that investigates that kind of behaviour, right? I'm sure they must do.'

I'm already reaching for my phone before she's finished. 'Jack? I need to speak to you about something urgently,' I say, when the answerphone cuts in. 'It's about the video of Anna. Freddie told me what you also found and it got me thinking. Give me a call back when you get a moment, will you?' I hang up, the cogs still turning in my head.

'I'm going to jump in the shower while you wait for him to phone back,' Rachel says.

'Wait,' I catch her, 'before you do, how did you get on at the library yesterday? We never got the chance to talk about it before dinner.'

She stops and sits down on the end of the bed. 'Oh yeah, so I was reading the journals Natalie left for you from the time of Sally's disappearance and most of it is pretty standard pre-menstrual teenage girl stuff. There's no mention of Sally until about a week after she disappeared, but even then the only reference is acknowledgement that a whole week has passed. There's no mention of witchcraft or spells that I can deduce, unless she's writing in some kind of code, but one thing I did find of interest is reference to someone called Pete. I assumed boyfriend at first because of the way she writes about how handsome he is, but then she wrote something about him leaving the base and how life would never be the same again, and that got me thinking that maybe he was a soldier at the time. I went to the base to try and see if I could take a look at their recruit records, but they wouldn't let me beyond the security barrier, stating that I'd need to put my request in writing to the colonel in charge, but even then the guy I spoke to didn't sound confident that my request would be granted. That's what then led me to the library, in case the records were public access, but they weren't. So while I was there I asked to have a look at archived copies of local newspapers, which might have carried more granular detail of the investigation into Sally's disappearance.'

'And?'

'*And*, I found a picture from an article a month after the disappearance. It was midway in the edition, and was only confirming that the search for Sally continues, *but* the picture they'd used was of Sally and some friends – including Natalie – at some kind of drama club, and one of the names beneath the image was a Corporal Pete Havvard.'

Rachel leans over the edge of the bed and fishes into her handbag, extracting a sheet of printed paper and handing it over to me. It's a photocopy of the newspaper article she's just referred to, and in the grainy image I can see a young Natalie and the familiar face of Sally Curtis. Beside the two girls is a youngish man, with close-cropped hair and a stern jaw that I recognise from my meeting with Cheryl and Diane when the imposing Colonel William Havvard disturbed our private conversation.

'He's the son of the guy who runs the base,' I say, studying the pixels closely. 'He looks very cosy with the girls in this image.'

'That's what I was thinking.' Rachel smiles, her eyes widening. 'Apparently, he ran this drama club as an after-school activity at the time when Sally went missing. So, I reached out to the local police, and was given the name of one Detective Fiona Rimmington. She's Detective Inspector now, but was just a DC when she headed up the initial investigation into Sally's reported disappearance. She was only too happy to speak to me about the case. Apparently it riles her that they never found Sally. I asked her whether this Pete had ever been formally interviewed in the wake of the disappearance and having consulted her notes she said he wasn't but that it had been a struggle to get the cooperation of the base to speak to any of their personnel.'

I recall something Cheryl told me when I first met her at her static caravan. *Secrets don't remain secret in a place like that, and when outside influences try to interfere with that lifestyle, the pack gathers close to defend itself.*

'You think this Pete Havvard was somehow involved in Sally's disappearance… and his dad covered it up?'

Rachel shrugs. 'It's not the most outlandish theory. Definitely worth pursuing, even if it does turn out to be a dead end.'

I can't forget the way Cheryl and Diane clammed up when Havvard joined us at the table in the pub near the base. It was like he had some kind of invisible control over them.

'Okay,' I say. 'You have a shower, and then we'll see if we can't go and visit Colonel Havvard for ourselves, and ask him a few awkward questions, see how he reacts.'

Rachel is gushing as she stands and races to the bathroom. I finish my toast and juice before carrying the tray through to the kitchen when I hear my phone ringing. Assuming it's Jack, I pick it up, though my phone doesn't recognise the number calling.

'Hello? Emma Hunter here.'

'Hi, Emma, it's Sam Johnson. We met yesterday at Natalie's cremation. I hope you don't mind, but I got your number from the business card you left with Cheryl. I'd really like to talk to you about Nat, and why I think she killed herself.'

Chapter Thirty-Three

NOW

Weymouth, Dorset

I'm grateful when Rachel insists on accompanying me to meet Sam at the seaside café along the waterfront. We take a deliberately scenic route to reach the venue so it won't be obvious from where we originated. Precautions, Rachel calls it.

'You don't know this guy from Adam,' she repeats as we near the café. 'For all you know he could be some serial stalker and rapist. You can never be too careful these days, Emma.'

I've already tried to explain that I did briefly meet him at the crematorium yesterday, and that I'm sure Cheryl wouldn't have given my number to a psychopath, but she's not having any of it.

'Doesn't mean he isn't a weirdo too, you know. This one woman I know went on a blind date with a friend of a friend – they'd been set up – and the friends had described him as a really great guy. Apparently he worked in a dog shelter and voluntarily did the collection basket at his local church every

Sunday. Well, when they went back to her place after the date to… you know, she went into the bathroom to get changed and when she emerged, he was lying in bed dressed in her bra, pants and stockings!'

I'm not sure how much of this story is true, and how much is Rachel's imagination trying to justify her point. What *is* clear is how much London has changed her outlook on life. She never used to be so fearful of strangers, and whilst she's right about women needing to be more careful in this day and age, not *every* stranger is a pervert or deviant.

Sam is already sitting at a table in the window as we enter. He has a bottle of mineral water in front of him, but no mugs of tea or coffee.

'Hi Sam, this is my friend Rachel. She's a journalist too. I hope it's okay that she's here as well?'

He looks at Rachel before nodding. 'It's fine.'

'Do you want a cup of tea or coffee?' I ask pleasantly, as Rachel hangs her coat on the back of one of the chairs.

'No thanks,' he replies, lifting the bottle. 'I'm on a detox.'

Who on earth does a detox in the run up to the festive period? I totally understand why so many people cut out toxins and try to start the year with better fitness plans, but Christmas is a time for over-indulging, surely?

I order a gingerbread latte for me and a frothy cappuccino for Rachel, and carry the drinks over to the table.

'Thanks so much for agreeing to meet with me,' Sam launches, before I've even had a chance to remove my coat. 'Cheryl said you may or may not be investigating the disappearance of Sally Curtis, and that you believe it has direct links to Nat's suicide.'

'That's not exactly the situation,' I say cautiously, 'but it was Natalie's suicide that led me to Sally's disappearance. What exactly did you want to tell me?'

'That you're spot on. Nat's suicide has *everything* to do with the disappearance of Sally Curtis.'

I won't deny my interest is piqued and I'm already switching on the recorder on my phone as I sit. 'You don't mind, do you? It means I don't have to make notes and can fully concentrate on what you're saying. So, where do you want to start?'

He unscrews the cap on the water and takes a small sip. 'Nat was obsessed with Sally's disappearance – to a dangerous degree, I'd say. Not when we were going out – back then I had no real idea about any of that history – but after we broke up, it quickly became clear that that period in her life was still having a profound effect on her present.'

'In what way?'

'She blamed herself for Sally vanishing and the subsequent fallout at the base.'

I look at Rachel and mouth the word 'fallout' at her, but she shrugs.

'At the service yesterday,' I continue, 'you made reference to two of Natalie's friends causing her trouble when they were all younger. Can you elaborate?'

He nods. 'Yeah, that Louise and Jane. I wish I could remember half the stories Nat told me about the two of them. Always conspiring against her, from all accounts – especially that Louise. I still can't believe they had the gall to rock up at the crematorium yesterday.'

'They bullied her?' I question.'

'Not physically, but definitely mentally. They'd sworn this pact not to speak about what happened in those woods when

Sally disappeared, and no matter how many times Nat wanted to come clean, she was terrified about what would happen if she broke the pact. She blamed herself for her dad dying. Did you know that? Even though it happened overseas and was bad luck in terms of how his unit was attacked, she held herself accountable. Said it all stemmed back to what happened that night and how she broke the rules. None of this came out until… until after she failed to conceive through IVF. She claimed it was all her fault because of her role in that night.'

'Did she tell *you* what happened in those woods? From what we've managed to deduce it could be something to do with the Wicca religion. Did she ever mention that to you?'

He shakes his head. 'I don't know what that is. Nat didn't like to talk about that period in her life prior to the IVF failure, but afterwards, she wouldn't stop talking about it… without saying very much. I remember waking one night and finding she wasn't in bed. I got up and went looking for her, discovering her on the floor in our kitchen, her back to the fridge. She was soaked through with sweat and rocking backwards and forwards. I tried to lift her but it was like she was in some kind of a trance or something, and when I tried to carry her back to bed – assuming she was sleepwalking or something – she lashed out at me with a shard of broken glass I hadn't realised she was holding.'

He stops and rubs a thin scar above his right eye. 'That was the beginning of the end. I found she'd dragged the shard across her abdomen and that's when I had to ask the GP to have her taken into a psychiatric unit for a couple of weeks. She was so disturbed – no, traumatised – that I didn't even recognise her. I wanted to help her but when she was released, she said she was a danger to me and didn't want to see me die as her dad had. I refused to leave and then one day I returned from work and found she'd cut up all my clothes with scissors and moved out. I found her at her mum's, but she said she'd never loved me and that the IVF failure was fate's way of saving us both from a lifetime of heartache. I thought if I gave her some space she'd realise she was unwell and get the treatment she clearly needed, and that we'd eventually get back together... but that's never going to happen now.'

The version of Natalie that Sam is painting is much more in keeping with the one I met on the rooftop of Maddie's office building; the version that Cheryl described is of an angel who wouldn't harm a fly, let alone herself.

'You said she blamed herself for Sally disappearing but do you know why?'

He shakes his head. 'Not exactly. It definitely had something to do with the night she vanished, but whenever I'd press her for more detail, she'd clam up and tell me I wasn't part of the inner circle, and that punishment would come if she broke the pact. That Louise and Jane did such a job on her; I swear they broke her at such a vulnerable age and that's why I hold them responsible for what's happened.'

'Did she ever mention someone called Pete to you?' Rachel interjects.

Sam considers the name. 'No, I don't think so. Why, who is he?'

'We think he was a friend of some sort at the base, but we also wondered whether he had anything to do with Sally's disappearance.'

Sam's eyes widen. 'She did mention a figure in the woods with them that night but she never gave a name. The way she spoke of him, I always…' His words trail off as he thinks better about finishing the sentence.

'Go on, please,' I urge.

'Well, it sounds so silly saying it aloud but… the way she spoke of this figure was like he was… a mythical type of character – a demon or the like – but that could have just been her imagination running away with her.'

Imogen Amperstock's words run through my mind: *Wiccans, by contrast, worship both the horned god and the moon goddess.*

I try to choose my words carefully but there's no easy way to ask my next question. 'To the best of your knowledge, did Natalie ever mention the practice of witchcraft?'

His cheeks redden. 'What are you suggesting?'

'When we went to Natalie's room at the hostel where she was staying at the end, we found what was essentially a shrine to Sally, but there were also a variety of Wiccan symbols and ideograms scattered around the room, including a couple of books left in a box with my name on. I think Natalie was trying to tell me that Sally's disappearance involved some kind of witchcraft in those woods, but proving that theory is becoming a struggle.'

'Nat wasn't a witch!' he declares, raising his voice. 'Is that why you're doing this? Does Cheryl realise that's what you intend to print?'

Rachel has eased back in her chair but I can understand his anger.

'I'm not saying Natalie was practising witchcraft at the end, but I do believe she may have been cajoled into something when she was young and vulnerable by the group of girls she thought were her friends. You said yourself this all happened at such an impressionable age for Natalie and I don't think it's too big a leap to suggest that living with that guilt and regret – and it manifesting over time with a series of unfortunate events, including her dad's sudden death – could have an extreme effect on her mental health. You said she blamed herself for Sally's disappearance, but how could she be to blame unless she killed Sally herself?'

His eyes widen and he's about to jump to his ex-fiancée's defence again before I raise my hand to cut him off.

'I don't believe Natalie or the other two killed Sally, but what's the alternative? Why would Natalie be so troubled by the events of that night unless it involved something she didn't feel she could live with? Why push away the one man she loved?'

His eyes are watering as he looks out of the window, his mind trying to process the suggestion. 'She phoned me two weeks ago. I haven't told Cheryl because I feel guilty about not realising it was a cry for help. She said she wanted to apologise to me for any hurt or pain our breakup had caused and that it was important I moved on with my life. I didn't see it for what it was; I naively thought she was trying to lay the groundwork for a potential reconciliation at some point in the future. She said she thought she'd finally found a solution to her problems and was back on speaking terms with Jane, and that it had really helped clarify what they'd all been through back then.' He tears a napkin from the box on the table and wipes his eyes. 'I thought I was getting the old Nat back. I even took her old engagement ring to the jeweller's to have it cleaned up in preparation. I never stopped loving her and I don't think I ever will. I should have realised she was phoning to make her peace before the end. I was so stupid.'

I lean forward so I can fix his eyes with my own. 'No, you weren't. I was up on that roof when she jumped and I didn't think she was going to do it. She was threatening to but I thought the police were going to talk her down... and then the next second she was gone. There was no way you could have known what she was planning to do. Please don't blame yourself. If anything – and from what Cheryl told me – you were the only good thing going in Natalie's life. I know it doesn't make it any easier but I truly don't believe any of this is your fault.'

He looks at his watch. 'I should probably be going. I told Cheryl I would help her scatter Nat's ashes today. Please don't paint Nat as some kind of witch or monster. She was so much more than that.'

'I won't, I promise,' I say as he stands and heads out into the bitter wind.

'What next?' Rachel asks, when he's gone. 'You still want to go to the base and ask about that Corporal Pete Havvard?'

I shake my head. 'No. I think we need to go and pay Jane Constantine a visit. If Natalie did get back in touch with her, I want to know exactly what they discussed.'

Chapter Thirty-Four

THEN

Blackfriars, London

Pushing the cleaning cart into the lift, Natalie was relieved to find the carriage empty. Had she had to make eye contact with a perfect stranger and give that nod of acknowledgement, pretending that everything was okay – as she had done countless times before – she wouldn't have been able to keep her mask raised. She'd probably have broken down there and then and confessed what she was planning to do. They'd probably have thought her crazy but it was unlikely they would have allowed her to continue without reporting it to someone. At best, they would have left her to her own devices, probably reporting the incident to the security guards in the main reception hall; at worst, they'd have insisted on staying with her until help arrived. Neither outcome would have been satisfactory.

As the lift doors began to slide closed, she thought back to the morning's events, trying to recall the list of activities she'd memorised late into the night. There were so many things she'd wanted to do to ensure all her affairs were in order. To miss just one of the tasks from the list would be to ruin everything she'd spent weeks planning.

She'd sat and re-read each of her diaries late into the night, trying to recall what had motivated her to write each line. Back then, she'd been deliberately ambiguous in her use of language, knowing her mum wouldn't have taken the time to truly think about what could be hidden between the lines – not that she was even certain her mum *had* ever snuck a glance at the diaries. Maybe all that pretence and secrecy had been a waste of time; it certainly hadn't helped her own need to decipher last night. Her personal memories of that time in her life – thirteen going on seventeen – were now heavily clouded by a lifetime of regrets and what ifs. What if she hadn't gone to the woods that night, would they have cast the incantation without her? Jane had said they needed a minimum of four people, which is why she'd forced herself to sneak out that night. If she'd been braver and stayed in her bed, maybe they would have had to bail out and then Sally would have survived. But she'd been weak – she'd always been weak – and now she could only dream about a lifetime where she'd not caved.

She thought there were enough references to that time that an educated adult would be able to read the hidden messages, but she'd decided to pack the books about Gerald Gardner and Wicca in the box to be safe. If the recipient knew enough about Wiccan practices, then actually a lot of what she'd scrawled in her pre-pubescent handwriting would be decipherable enough. And if her plan worked, then Sally would return anyway and everyone else's lives would make sense once again.

That night really had been pivotal in the lives of so many. Things had never been the same between her, Jane and Louise afterwards. Louise had clearly seen Natalie as the weakest link – she was probably right – and had sought to detach herself from the chain, putting as much distance between herself and Natalie as she could. If only Natalie had found it easier to turn her back on what they'd done and ignore the overwhelming guilt. For a time, she thought she'd managed it. Time had numbed some of the pain, and then Sam had served as sufficient distraction that thoughts about those woods only ever returned in the deepest of sleeps on the darkest of nights.

It had felt like a second chance, meeting Sam. He hadn't known anything of her history and had loved her for who she was, rather than who she'd been. For two blissful years, anything had seemed possible, but then she'd realised she was kidding herself to believe happiness would ever brighten her door again. His proposal had been the highlight of their relationship, and him having come from an adopted family of siblings, he'd been keen on them starting a brood of their own. She'd wanted children too – children she could imbue with the wisdom of her own mistakes, children she could teach to be stronger and braver than her. They would have been born in memory of Sally, but after a series of pre-IVF tests, it had soon become clear that things weren't right. She'd never told Sam that the doctors had warned her that IVF would be expensive and in all probability a waste of time.

'It's not that you're unable to conceive,' the gynaecologist had said, 'but the landscape inside your womb doesn't lend itself readily to conception.'

What had that even meant? Sam hadn't been able to attend that appointment due to work, but she'd known that even if she'd told him what the doctor had said, he'd have insisted on them trying. He was always able to find a silver lining to every cloud, and that's what she'd loved most about him. She should never have allowed things to develop to that point though. When the doctors broke the bad news, she hadn't been surprised.

'I'm sorry, but none of the eggs took,' he'd offered sympathetically.

Sam had remained upbeat – as he always did – and told her they would simply save up and try again. It wouldn't have been fair on him to allow the illusion to continue any longer. He deserved to be with someone who wasn't carrying the devil's curse with her, someone who would be able to give him the life and family he so desperately craved, someone who hadn't caused her own barrenness fifteen years ago.

The lift pinged as it reached the top floor. From here it was a short walk to the rooftop access door, through which a ladder would take her to her final destination. Pushing out the cleaning cart, she parked it near the door, not in anyone's way, and hopefully it wouldn't be spotted until the deed was complete. Swiping the security pass she'd pinched from the guard's desk when she arrived at dawn, she was pleased when the LED changed from red to green and then she pushed through.

She'd thought about phoning Sam to say goodbye but when they'd last spoken a couple of weeks back, she'd heard the unmistakeable sound of hope in his voice. He'd asked to meet her for a drink and she'd agreed, not wanting to let him down, but hadn't messaged to confirm a date and time, like she'd promised to do. If she'd phoned last night, it would only have added to that false hope, and the last thing she wanted was to hurt him any more than she already had.

She'd also considered phoning her mum, but knew she wouldn't have been able to keep her true intentions a secret. She'd left a letter to her mum hidden in the back of one of her diaries, and hopefully it would eventually be passed to her. It wasn't anything too gushy, simply an apology for not being a better daughter. Better to keep it simple.

The final action before leaving her room in the hostel had been to scrawl Emma Hunter's name on the lid of the box. Originally, she'd planned to put Jane's name on the box; after all, some of Jane's recent advice had been invaluable in helping Natalie find the solution to their problems, but a part of her was still reluctant to trust the Jane who had been so willing to abandon Sally and toe Louise's ever-changing line. Would she have done the same this time? Would she keep their biggest lie a secret, so nobody would be any the wiser?

Natalie had stolen a copy of Emma Hunter's book *Monsters Under the Bed* from one of the agent's offices on the sixth floor, just to see what all the fuss was about. By the second chapter she'd been glued to it, re-reading the entire book the moment she finished the final word, keen to understand exactly how the author's mind worked. *Like a dog with a bone*, she'd overheard one of the agents saying once when describing Emma Hunter's approach, and Natalie could well imagine she would be a formidable force – assuming the box was passed to her, of course.

Placing her foot on the first rung of the ladder, Natalie now questioned whether she should have mailed the box to Emma directly. What if the police didn't go to the room in the hostel? What if they didn't care and the hostel manager eventually threw away all of her stuff? If the box never got to Emma then there was every chance the truth would never be discovered.

What if her own sacrifice wasn't enough to bring Sally back? The idea had come to her during a phone call with Jane last month, and everything in her head had suddenly aligned. Sally's unexplained disappearance – her being taken – because the incantation had been ruined by Natalie's own lie: that was their punishment, and because Natalie was to blame, it would have to be she who made the sacrifice in order to get Sally back. It made perfect sense.

The wind whipped at her face as she pushed up the lid and clambered out onto the roof, feeling surprisingly calm as her final seconds rapidly approached. She felt at peace; all fear and worry had evaporated from her mind the second she stepped out. All she had to do now was keep walking, reach the edge, close her eyes and let death claim her soul for its own. Would Sally ever know that Natalie had made up for her previous mistake? Would she ever be able to forgive Natalie for all the pain and hurt she caused?

Looking to the edge of the roof, Natalie smiled when she saw the image of her dad waiting for her. His arm was outstretched, beckoning her to take his hand; he would guide her on her final journey.

She wasn't expecting to hear the man's voice calling from behind her, and as she turned to face him, for the briefest of moments she wondered why he had been sent to try and talk her out of it. And as the minutes passed, and he continued to speak and beg her not to go through with it, she questioned whether it had all been a big mistake. Then her eyes had fallen on Emma Hunter's face, and in that moment, she realised that the guard's interference was her final test. She'd passed with flying colours, and now, as she backed up to the roof's edge, she was ready for the final step.

Her new life would begin, and Sally would return.

Chapter Thirty-Five

NOW

Swanage, Dorset

Jane Constantine's name and address are listed in the online directory and the trip to Swanage where she now lives takes under an hour in Rachel's car. My father always wanted to retire to Swanage one day; it still maintains some of the older ways of the world and Dad liked the fact it hadn't been spoiled by the need for shopping centres and multi-storey car parks. Mum was never so keen on the idea, but it soon became forgotten about after Anna's disappearance. Still, the small fishing town holds a warm place in my heart. Even as we park up and head down towards the shoreline, I'm reminded of the times we would come here for fish and chips on a Sunday afternoon, and Dad would always end up buying Anna and me a 99 with a flake.

Turning right at the bottom of the hill, we head towards the town centre, passing the brightly coloured beach huts, abandoned on account of the season and blustery wind. I imagine most of the few people we can see moving about on the street ahead are locals. Passing the amusement arcade, I can see Rachel's eyes widening at the flashing bulbs of the interior; maybe she's reliving childhood memories as well. For all her claims about being a city girl and never wanting to vacate the smog of London, I think there's a seaside girl buried deep and she could yet be convinced to give up city life.

'Oh my God,' she suddenly exclaims as we cross the road. 'Is that a Wimpy? I haven't seen one of those in forever! Did we just go back in time?'

Looping my arm through hers, I push us onwards without answering. Dad was right; this place is unspoiled.

We eventually arrive at the shop we're looking for. It sits in the middle of the town, fronted with tall single-pane windows and with the painted frames in dire need of resuscitation. I must have been into this shop a dozen times and never did I realise it was owned by Jane Constantine. The windows are full of trinkets, aimed at catching tourists' eyes. There are the usual array of keyrings and bracelets with the most popular children's names, along with a host of fridge magnets, some with picturesque shots of the town, others with humorous slogans. But stepping into the shop is almost like going through the wardrobe into Narnia. A bell rings as we push the door open and take our first tentative step inside.

The pungent aroma of burning incense hits the senses first. It's different to the smell encountered in Natalie's room at the hostel, but it wouldn't surprise me to learn that Natalie had purchased hers from here, particularly if Sam was right and they were back in touch. The central heating must be on maximum too as both Rachel and I feel the need to unzip and remove our coats, such is the climate change compared to outside. Above our heads, mirrored decorations catch the daylight as they twirl, and there isn't room for the two of us to walk side by side, such is the sheer volume of merchandise crammed into the place. It really is a shop of curiosities. In fact, it's not Narnia we've wandered into, rather, like Alice, we've tumbled into Wonderland.

'Are you looking for something in particular?' a woman's voice calls out from somewhere near the back of the shop.

Looking around, we appear to be the only two in here so I conclude she must be talking to us. Pushing onwards into the shop, past a collection of goblin statuettes, I find Jane Constantine slumped over a glass counter, deep in study of paperwork spread out across the counter. There is an old-fashioned register beside her. She's not dressed in the figure-hugging business suit and heels from yesterday's service. Instead, she's wearing a long purple and gold robe, which might appear odd in any other setting, but seems to perfectly fit the peculiar nature of the shop in which we find ourselves.

She looks up from her papers as we approach and it takes a moment for her to realise who I am.

'You!' she exclaims.

'Hi, Jane,' I say, stepping forwards and offering my most placatory expression. 'I'm sorry to come and see you at work, but—'

'I told you yesterday I'm not speaking to the press,' she interrupts. 'Please leave my shop.'

I take another step forward. 'I understand why you might be worried about speaking to me, Jane, but Natalie trusted me and I'm hoping that will be enough to convince you that you can trust me too. Natalie *chose* to throw herself from the building where my agent works. I don't know if she knew I would be there or not, but I do know that she left a box in her room with my name on it. Inside it were her private journals from the time you were all living on the base, as well as books about Wicca.'

I pause but she makes no effort to cut me off again. 'I'm not trying to sensationalise what happened to Sally but Natalie begged me to find her and that's what I'm trying to do. Unless I'm very much mistaken, the four of you went to those woods to carry out some kind of enchantment or incantation, but something went wrong and Sally vanished. Having spoken to Natalie's fiancé and her mum, I now know that Natalie blamed herself for what happened. But I don't understand why. You're the missing piece of the jigsaw, Jane. Please don't shut us out.'

I'm not entirely sure where that earlier anger came from but now she seems to be considering the request. At least, I thought she was, but now she's come out from behind the counter and moved to the front door. Is she about to kick us out? No, she's actually locking the door and has spun the 'open' sign to 'closed'. She moves back through the shop and ushers us towards a closed door at the back.

'Do either of you want a cup of tea? I'm due a break anyway.'

Jane leads us into what is little more than a boxroom with two chairs and a small square table. There is a small basin and crudely shaped countertop on which stands a stainless-steel kettle and an open box of herbal tea bags. She encourages us both to sit while she leans against the basin.

'If I'd known this is how things would end up, I never would have suggested the spell in the first place,' she eventually says when the kettle has boiled. 'Two friends gone, and for what?'

'Can you tell us about that night?' I ask softly, silently switching on the recorder on my phone, and resting it on the table. 'What led the four of you there, and what actually happened?'

She fixes the drinks without asking either of us whether we're happy drinking herbal tea. 'It was a very confusing time for all of us, as I'm sure you can imagine. Puberty, the stress of exams, parents being sent abroad and never knowing whether we'd see them again. That's what drew the four of us together, I think. When I look back on that time, it was our shared apathy about life that bonded us as a group. When we were together, it felt like nothing in the world could stop us; we were formidable. At least, I thought we were.'

Her face is cloaked in sadness as she speaks, and I have no doubt in my mind that she isn't trying to deceive us. She is speaking from the heart, despite the obvious pain it's causing.

'Although the four of us were good friends, Sally and Louise were their own little clique. As the elder two, they both received the most attention from boys and I think they both thought themselves slightly elevated from the group. Which is why it was odd when Sally came and spoke to me about her little problem, rather than Louise.' Her lips curl up a fraction at the memory. 'At first I thought she was joking but then she showed me the stick and I realised how terrified she was.' She pauses to allow the suggestion to sink in, before adding, 'Sally was pregnant.'

'Pregnant?' I echo, snatching a glance at Rachel who is equally captivated. 'Who was the father?'

Jane shrugs. 'She never told me. When I asked, she said it was better if I didn't know; she didn't want to get him into trouble, I think. Bearing in mind she was underage, whoever had slept with her would be facing serious consequences.'

I recall Cheryl's suggestion that the four girls had snuck to the woods to meet the latest batch of recruits at the base. 'Do you have any idea who it might have been? A name or anything? Getting an underage girl pregnant is motive for killing her.'

She considers it for a moment. 'If I had to guess – and it would solely be a guess – then I'd say possibly Pete Havvard. He was a soldier on the base who led a drama group we all attended.'

Rachel fires me a knowing look but I put a finger up before she says anything. 'Why would you suggest him?' I ask.

'I don't know…' She smiles again. 'He was always super friendly and encouraging to all of us. I know that both Sally and Louise fancied him and had sworn some pact that neither would pursue him to save the other's feelings, but that might also be why Sally came to me instead of Louise. Maybe she knew that Louise would connect the dots and they'd fall out. I don't know. Anyway,' she sighs, 'Sally knew my mum was into Wicca and casting occasional enchantments when our dads would go overseas, and she asked whether there might be something that could be done to take the baby away. She didn't want to tell her parents and she couldn't face going to her GP, as she was sure the truth would get back to her parents. She was adamant she couldn't keep the baby as she had school and plans for her future. I told her I would see what I could find and I came across a purifying spell. It was designed to help prevent the plague or something, from what I recall, but some of the side effects included cleansing the body and soul, so I figured it might work.

'The spell required there to be at least four of us, and Sally was adamant that I couldn't tell anyone about the pregnancy, and so we came up with this plan to tell the others that the spell would help ease period pains, as we were all then having our periods. I rummaged through my mum's things to find what we needed – candles, oats, pig's blood – and then we headed to the woods. Sally was the one who chose the clearing and she led us there. We drew a large circle on the ground using the porridge oats and placed six lit candles at key points within the circle. I forgot to bring the pig's blood from the fridge so Sally suggested we use our own. She took out a small chopping knife, and ran it across one of her fingers, encouraging us to do the same, and then we joined bloody hands and began the enchantment.

'I remember how cold and windy it was that night and after a few minutes of dancing around in the circle, I was certainly feeling dizzy, but then a sudden gust blew out the candles and we found ourselves in total darkness. Sally became frantic and kept saying she could hear someone nearby. Louise reckoned it was just the creaking of tree branches but Sally was petrified and started screaming, breaking free of our hands and vanishing. I'd have said she ran off but I couldn't see and I didn't hear the sound of running. She literally vanished.'

It's a lot to take in: the pregnancy, the incantation, the account of Sally's disappearance. I'm not prone to believing in the supernatural, as in my experience there is always a rational explanation for strange events, but even I'm stumped.

'Is it possible someone saw you enter the woods or could have been watching?' I ask.

'I don't really remember. Sally certainly thought there was someone there, and Nat later told me she was sure we'd inadvertently conjured some dark spirit who had taken Sally as his prize.'

'Why didn't you tell any of this to the police at the time?' Rachel asks bluntly. 'If Sally's boyfriend could have been responsible, don't you think the police should have been given the opportunity to speak to him?'

'That's just it. When I look back on it now, I can't believe how stupid I was… we all were. I was a dumb fourteen-year-old messing with powers I didn't understand and I was terrified that I would be locked up for causing Sally to disappear like that. I didn't dare tell my mum. Louise told me we had to keep it quiet or risk being sent to prison. I believed her because it was easier to keep quiet than come clean. Not a day goes by when I don't regret our actions.'

Rachel leans forward. 'With the benefit of hindsight, and given what you know now, what do you think really happened to Sally that night?'

Jane chews on the tip of one of her acrylic nails. 'I just don't know. Surely, if she'd died, the police or the army would have found a body. They searched all over those woods but came up with nothing.'

'Not if it was covered up by those running the base,' Rachel counters. 'If Pete did get Sally pregnant, who else would he turn to in his hour of need? His dad was in charge of security on the base at the time, and he was also instrumental in having the police investigation handed over and essentially wound up.'

'But Pete wasn't violent. I just can't see that he could have hurt Sally.'

'Desperate people do desperate things, Jane,' I warn. 'Just look at Natalie's reaction to it all.'

Jane bites harder on the nail to the point where I'm sure I can hear it splintering. 'When she phoned me last week, I had no idea what she was planning to do, I swear. She kept asking me about the power of sacrifice but I didn't realise she planned to exchange her life for Sally's.'

'What makes you say that?' I ask.

She looks from Rachel to me. 'As soon as I got Cheryl's call, it dawned on me why Natalie had been asking so many questions about undoing spells and the use of blood sacrifices. To be honest, it's all a bit beyond my understanding and relates to the darker side of the practice that I choose not to indulge in. There are some witches out there who do, but not me, nor my mum in her day.'

'You're a practising witch now?' I ask, suddenly aware we're on unfamiliar turf.

'I prefer to call myself a practising Wiccan, but yes, to all intents and purposes, my religion is based on the belief in powers beyond everyday notions.'

I stand and move closer to Jane, fixing her with an empathetic stare. 'Tell me the truth: do you believe the spell you cast in those woods resulted in Sally's disappearance?'

She looks uncertain for a moment before shaking her head. 'I don't see how it could have.'

'Then you need to contact the police and tell them everything you've just told us,' I say earnestly. 'I know it's been years, but let's not allow Natalie's death to be in vain. She wanted the truth to come out, and now you need to pick up the mantle for her. With modern equipment, it might be possible for them to scan those woods looking for evidence of disturbed ground. If Sally *is* buried there, they'll be able to find her.'

'But the police combed those woods with sniffer dogs and they didn't find her.'

'She may not have been buried until after the police search,' Rachel challenges, and it's a valid argument.

'I know this won't be easy for you,' I say, taking her hands in mine, 'but I'll stay here with you while you make a statement to the police. In fact, I know exactly who you should speak to, someone who won't laugh at the story and will know how best to take things forwards.'

Tears fill her eyes. 'Do you really think that's what Nat would want?'

I nod. 'There's been no trace of Sally since that night and for me the only logical conclusion is that she didn't make it off that base alive. At the very least, it warrants consideration by the police. Your witness statement would formulate new evidence – maybe enough to entail a review of the casefile. Natalie was prepared to give everything to bring Sally back. Will you help me find her?'

The blood drains from Jane's face but she doesn't fight, just moves back into the shop and fishes the mobile phone from her handbag.

Chapter Thirty-Six

NOW

Swanage, Dorset

Waiting for the arrival of Detective Inspector Fiona Rimmington takes an inordinate amount of time. In the interim, Jane has reopened her shop – although only three customers have actually been through in the last hour, and I can't say I recall hearing the till ring once; it must be tough for shopkeepers out of season.

Rachel and I agreed to wait with her, partly to offer her our support, but also to make sure she sticks to the script and doesn't leave out any details. I know it's all just supposition, and there is nothing concrete to conclude that the father of Sally's baby killed her to silence allegations of abuse, but I'd rather believe that than some fantastical theory involving witchcraft and spells gone wrong.

Sitting in the tiny boxroom with the kettle and microwave doesn't exactly stimulate the mind, and so whilst I am once again searching for any references to Pete Havvard on my phone, Rachel is busy reading the latest of Natalie's journals, which she was carrying in her handbag. So far it isn't clear why the diaries were left to us, as most of the writing appears to be about little more than the average teenager's angst. We've all been that age, trying to understand our changing bodies and mind-sets. They could simply be any teenager's depiction of coming-of-age.

I once again stumble across that image of Pete Havvard and the girls that Rachel found in one of the local newspapers the other day. He doesn't look like what I imagine as the sort of person who could assault an underage girl, but then, is that because my view of such monsters has been tarnished by what I've encountered in recent years? Those abusers arrested through Operation Yewtree were all of a certain age, though most of them would have been younger when the acts were undertaken. And most fictionalised dramas portray paedophiles as grizzly old men who need to break the law to get their kicks, but is it so far-fetched to think that all those older paedophiles still had similar urges when they were younger?

If Corporal Pete Havvard had inadvertently impregnated Sally, wouldn't he see her as a threat to his future? He'd have been facing dishonourable discharge from the career he'd chosen, not to mention imprisonment and a requirement to sign the sex offenders register. Rachel said it herself: desperate people are capable of desperate acts... even murder.

Detective Inspector Rimmington isn't what I expect when she does arrive. Given it's been fifteen years since she was heading up the investigation into Sally's disappearance, I would have thought she'd bear the battle scars of a hardened detective's face, but she doesn't look much older than me. Her hair is cut into a bob, bleached and dyed a shade of cherry red, but there is little sign of wrinkles around her eyes. She must be at least forty, but you wouldn't know it.

'It's been a long time,' she says to Jane, before looking from me to Rachel. 'And I'm sorry, you two are?'

'Just here to support,' I confirm. 'We're… friends of the families.'

If she recognises my face, she doesn't give anything away. 'Right, Jane, is there somewhere we can sit and talk?'

Jane leads her into the boxroom that Rachel and I have recently vacated and the two of them sit at the table, leaving Rachel and me to hover near the door. Jane proceeds to explain what she told us of the night in question, about the reasons they went to the woods and the shock as Sally vanished into thin air. Tears prick at my eyes as Jane speaks about Sally's secret pregnancy and how she had a boyfriend on the base that she'd told none of the girls about. I can't imagine how painful it must be to finally reveal a secret held onto for so long, and I can't help thinking that had it been revealed sooner, Natalie might still be around.

'Oh my God, you need to read this,' Rachel whispers, pulling on my arm and leading me away from the conversation.

'What is it?' I ask, as she thrusts the diary beneath my nose.

'It's the last entry she wrote in her journal, from the day before she died, but it's different to the previous entries. It looks like she'd stopped writing in her diary when she reached eighteen. Up until this point, there was nothing jumping out as relevant, but then there are these two blank pages, and the next date was the day before she died. I think she knew it was all going to end on that rooftop, and she left this message for someone to find.'

There is an urgency to the scrawl and it isn't immediately easy to read, as some seems to have been written in shorthand, for which I don't have an eye.

'I can't read this,' I tell her, passing it back.

Rachel accepts the book and her eyes dance across the page. 'It starts with her offering an apology to her mother, saying that had she been stronger then none of the pain that followed the night in the woods would have occurred. She says she believes it was her attempts to tell her mum the truth about that night that caused her father to be taken from them. It then gets a bit darker. She talks about going to those woods, and how the four of them dabbled with evil spirits, making a pact with them to ease their period pains, but that her own lack of development at that age led to her becoming barren. She apologises to Sam for not telling him the truth about her condition. She talks about wanting to do the only thing that will undo all the hurt and pain. She says those spirits will only accept an eye for an eye, and she hopes her own sacrifice will finally allow Sally to return and continue her life.'

I try and swallow the lump in my throat. It is clear that Natalie genuinely believed that the incantation delivered in the woods was real, but that just shows how damaged she was by those events at such an impressionable age. I would give anything to have been able to hear that passage the day before I met her on that rooftop, to dispel the myth. Rachel's Wiccan witch friend Imogen already told us that the horned god and moon goddess are not akin to the devil, but for whatever reason, Natalie believed they were. Despite Jane's revelation about Sally vanishing into thin air, and this latest passage from

Natalie's diary, in my mind I have no doubt that Sally's disappearance had little to do with witchcraft and everything to do with an abusive adult who should have known better… and his father who helped cover the crime.

'What happens now?' I ask Rimmington, as she emerges from the room with a tearful Jane following.

'I will take this statement to my superiors and ask whether there is any appetite to review the Sally Curtis casefile. If they agree, then we'll have to make contact with the lieutenant-colonel at the base and make arrangements.'

Natalie's final words echo in my mind again. *You need to find her. Find Sally. Tell her I'm sorry.*

It finally feels like we're getting closer, and whilst I'm sure Colonel Havvard will do whatever he can to protect his wayward son, a secret this big can't stay buried for ever.

Chapter Thirty-Seven

NOW

Weymouth, Dorset

As the ringing phone wakes me, I sense that today is not going to be a good day. Just as I was dropping off last night, Cheryl phoned to say she'd heard through Diane that Sally's case is to receive a full review, starting imminently. I felt pleased at the time, hopeful that when Rimmington and her team go to the base, they'll finally manage to find Sally and bring her parents and friends the closure they deserve. Yet, as I'm rubbing my eyes this morning, something just isn't sitting right in my head. I know I was dreaming before the ringing started but for the life of me I can't recall what the dream was about.

I immediately answer the call when I see it has originated from Mum's nursing home. Pam Ratchett's voice sounds low and sincere as she confirms the purpose of the call.

'I'm afraid to tell you that your mother isn't the only resident here on whom we've found bruises. I want to assure you that I am as shocked as you that this kind of thing has been going on under my nose.'

It's a relief that I'm no longer under suspicion, though I knew I was innocent of the blows clearly inflicted on Mum's frail body. Of course it doesn't make it any easier to hear the truth about what has been going on while I've been avoiding visiting in case it's another 'bad day' for her.

'After you left the other day,' Pam begins, 'I requested Dr Benjamin examine all of our other residents to check their health. As I've said to you many times before, our residents' health is my primary concern. I don't want to go into too many specifics with you, Emma, for the sake of those affected, but I can confirm that your mum is one of half a dozen with suspicious bruising. My initial step was to look for any patterns in the care of those six residents, but there wasn't anything obvious. I didn't want to believe that any of our staff here could be capable of such cruelty, and I'm relieved to confirm to you that my belief has been rewarded. Having spoken to each of those affected, several have confirmed the culprit's name and I have now instigated steps to have him removed from the home.'

It's not even eight o'clock and my brain isn't yet tuned to the ways of the world, so I'm not sure what she's trying to say. 'You're saying it wasn't one of the nurses?' I ask, stifling a yawn.

'That's right. We heavily vet all of our care staff before offering positions and each receives regular observations of their duties as part of staff appraisals. It's a bit of micro-managing on my part, but I prefer to know everything that's going on here and don't like to leave any stone unturned. Regrettably, it appears I took my eye off the ball with what has happened, and I want to offer you the sincerest apology for that.'

Rachel rolls over next to me as the conversation has woken her too, and she rubs her eyes as she yawns at me. 'Is that the police?'

I shake my head and leave the bedroom, so as not to disturb her sleep any further. 'I'm confused,' I tell Pam, 'if it wasn't one of your nurses responsible, then who?'

'I'm afraid I'm not at liberty to say exactly who, but it appears one of our other residents was the cause of the assaults.'

'One of the other patients?'

'I'm afraid so. He was named by two of the six and when questioned, admitted what had been going on. I have now spoken to his daughter, who brought him here in September, and she has said that this is not the first time he has become overly aggressive in a facility such as ours. She says it's something to do with the time he spent overseas in the army – not that there is any excuse for that kind of behaviour.'

I recall the barman's words again after I first met Diane: *some of the shit they must have seen overseas – it's bound to mess with your mind, isn't it?*

Pam sighs painfully. 'Suffice to say, we are arranging for him to be transferred to somewhere more specialist, so I wanted to personally phone you and let you know that your mum isn't in any danger of repeat behaviour.'

'She should never have been in harm's way to begin with,' I say bitterly, though the aggression is aimed at myself as much as it is Pam.

'I understand your disappointment, and that's why I wanted to take the opportunity to speak to you personally and reassure you that nothing like this will occur again. We are tightening our local controls to spot any warning signs in future and to ensure that each staff member is looking for any signs of mistreatment.'

I think about Cheryl's desire to see Natalie just one last time and Diane's wish to know what really happened to her daughter. Mothers never stop loving their children and needing to mother them.

'What if I don't feel comfortable leaving Mum in your care any longer?' I ask, without really considering the consequences of such a question.

'Well, by all means you are more than welcome to move her to an alternative home if you think that's the right thing to do, but I would urge you to consider the implications for your mother's health. It may not be in her best interests to be moved, given the known issues with her memory loss, and the early onset of Alzheimer's.'

Rachel moves through to the kitchen and holds the kettle up towards me. I nod as caffeine is exactly what I need, though this call certainly has made me more alert than before.

'I need to consider my options,' I tell her with a sigh. 'I don't think I could live with myself if I thought my inaction was putting her health at risk.'

'I absolutely understand your concerns, Emma, but I can assure you that problem has now been eliminated.'

'Eliminated? It should never have been a problem in the first place.'

Rachel cocks an eyebrow at my raised voice.

'I agree wholeheartedly, and I wish you could see how much I regret this situation ever developing.'

'Not as much as I regret it, Pam. Maybe it was wrong of me

to turn my back on her and put her in a home to begin with. She was my primary carer for so many years and at the first sign of trouble, I shuffled her off to a home to wash my hands of responsibility.'

Rachel is shaking her head at me, and mouthing the word 'No.'

'Your mother's health requires professional help, Emma, and you shouldn't feel guilty about that.'

If that's the case, why do I feel so guilty? I think, but don't say.

The truth is, as soon as the GP confirmed my suspicions about Mum's fading memory, my initial reaction was to find her the best place where she would receive the level of care she required. It wasn't easy and it's not cheap, but I allowed myself to believe it was for her own good. Now, though, in light of what has happened, I can't help feeling I opted for the easy route.

'Given the proximity to Christmas,' Pam continues, 'what I would urge is that you don't make any rash decisions. She is perfectly safe here now and we have moved her down to the ground floor as I promised we would, so she is receiving additional oversight and support. Take some time to consider your options, as you suggested, and if you still don't feel comfortable entrusting her care to us, then I certainly won't bear a grudge if you choose to move her to an alternative facility. The only caveat I would add is to consider what is best for your mum. She has friends here. She has nurses who understand her condition and her background. She knows the layout of the home and where to go at meal times and who to ask for help. Adjusting all those parameters right now may not be the best thing for her.'

I agree to her staying while I take the time to weigh up my

ptions, before hanging up the call.

'I presume that was the home?' Rachel asks, as she hands me a cup of tea.

'Turns out it was one of the patients who assaulted Mum, apparently.'

Rachel gasps. 'One of the patients? Jeez.'

'Exactly. What if it happens again? They missed that this guy was violent, not to mention the fact that she was covered in bruises so they're just as capable of making the same mistake again, aren't they?'

Rachel sips her coffee. 'What's the alternative? You can't have her back here with you.'

'Why not? Isn't it my responsibility to take care of her?'

'Not if you're incapable of doing so. Look at this place, Emma. It's tiny. It's fine for your purposes but you'd have to make so many alterations to make it safe for someone with your mum's health issues. Plus, you're not always here. Who would look after her when you have to go to London, or when you're neck-deep in another story?'

'I could hire a private nurse to monitor her here.'

'Unless you're planning on paying someone to be here twenty-four seven, that's not practical. Besides, you're twenty-seven years old; it's time you started living *your* life. At some point you might meet someone you *do* want to settle down with. Maybe you decide you want to put down roots and start a family of your own. None of that will be possible if you have your mum living with you.'

I know Rachel is trying to be pragmatic and I'm grateful for her opposing view, but it doesn't ease the guilt that I have all but abandoned Mum in that home.

'Trust me, if the shoe was on the other foot, and it was me

316

questioning whether to invite my mum or dad to live with me, I wouldn't give it a second's thought. You have done the right thing in getting her into that home. While she's there she gets close to twenty-four-hour supervision, but is able to live independently. I really wish you'd stop beating yourself up about this. You've done far more than many others; yes, this incident was unfortunate, but could have happened at any nursing home. Don't forget how convenient it is for you to go and visit her when you need. If you moved her somewhere else, that might require more travelling, and mean you see even less of her.'

I can't concentrate on this right now. I know that Rachel and Pam are right, and that it's only my own guilt that's forcing me to even consider moving her in with me, but that doesn't make it any easier. Despite their valid arguments, she's my mum and she *is* my responsibility. Things might be different if Anna was still around, and we could reach the decision together, but right now I'm all she's got and that burden feels so heavy to carry alone.

'You want some breakfast?' Rachel asks, switching on the toaster.

I'm about to respond when my phone starts ringing again, though the number isn't familiar.

'Emma? I can't believe you managed to do it.'

'Cheryl? Do what, sorry?'

'They're at the base now – the police – and they've got sniffer dogs and a whole army of personnel. Diane just phoned me and said they've got a warrant to search the woods for traces of Sally's body. They're going in now. Diane told me to phone you and say she's put our names on the visitor list. She wants us there with her.'

Chapter Thirty-Eight

NOW

Bovington Garrison, Dorset

Having showered and dressed, I haul myself to the base, arriving within the hour, but the scene I witness is far crazier than the last time I was here. It's clear there is a wave of activity inside the base just from the number of vehicles parked just inside the confines. The poor guard at the security post is sweating profusely, probably getting it in the neck from both his superiors as well as the officers and CSI technicians who appear to be swarming the place like flies sensing death nearby.

I show him my identification and explain Diane should have put my name on the list. I'm expecting him to kick up some fuss as he did the last time I was here, but he barely checks before signalling me through. There's no obvious sign of press outside the base, save for one van that pulls up just as I've gone through the barrier. Again, I don't imagine it will be long before more moths gather close to the flame, particularly once it gets out that the police are once again hunting for Sally Curtis.

I'm surprised by the level of activity inside the perimeter. God only knows how many favours Rimmington needed to call in but it feels like she's pulled every available resource. It seems a bit much based solely on Jane's statement yesterday afternoon, but there was something about the look in Rimmington's eyes that told me she had unfinished business at this base. It's a cliché to suggest that this is the one unsolved case that has haunted her for the last fifteen years, but I've no other way to explain it.

Following the instructions in the text message Cheryl sent, I'm unable to get beyond the second roundabout, as this is where the police outer cordon begins. I phone Cheryl and she tells me that they are at Diane's house and that she will come and meet me at the tape. It takes ten minutes, but then I spot the cigarette-chomping Cheryl in a leopard-print tracksuit coming towards us. She is in stark contrast to the men and women in uniforms and blue overalls buzzing about inside.

'This is what they should have been doing fifteen years ago,' Cheryl comments loudly enough for the officer at the cordon to hear. She explains who I am, and once my ID has been checked and I've signed in, I'm granted entry, though he warns us both that we won't be allowed past the next cordon. As Cheryl leads me towards Diane's house, I suppose I'm surprised at just how normal the street looks. I could be on any average residential road in any average town in the south of England: the houses are a string of semi-detached three-bedroom properties, each with a small lawn at the front, bordering a concrete driveway; there are ordinary-looking cars parked on most of the driveways and you'd never know we are in the heart of a working armed-forces area. I can just make out the outer cordon about a hundred metres from Diane's house.

'Our house was along there,' Cheryl comments when she sees me looking. 'Of the four families, we lived closest to those bloody woods, but all were within a five to ten-minute walk.'

There are pairs of eyes at every window of every house, watching the activity. If they don't already know, it won't be long until they figure out why the police are here. I hurry after Cheryl, hoping my presence here hasn't been noted. Diane has enough going on today without me adding to the distraction.

A uniformed officer answers the door but allows us through when he sees Cheryl.

'That's PC Plod,' Cheryl jokes, before leaning closer to me. 'That's not his actual name but he's been posted here to keep us informed of progress, or something. Not very talkative but I love his deep and brooding eyes.'

He doesn't respond, simply closes the door behind us and remains on guard on the doormat. Presumably he's some kind of family liaison or close equivalent.

Diane's eyes are bloodshot and her cheeks are red and puffy when we find her hunched over on the sofa in her otherwise well-maintained living room. She is wearing a thick dressing gown, despite the stifling warmth of the room, and I quickly relieve myself of my coat before sitting at the dining table in the corner

Cheryl squats down next to her friend and rests a hand on hers. 'I take it there's been no news whilst I was out?'

Diane has a lost look in her eyes; they're open but they're not focused on the present. She shakes her head but doesn't speak. I can only imagine what she must be going through. When I last met her, she was so convinced that Sally must have run away. It's probably easier than admitting the possibility that she died all those years ago. The human mind can be cruel in that way: if you believe in something for long enough, it becomes the truth in your mind. To then have that truth whipped from beneath you like a rug must have her in serious turmoil.

She's probably trying to recall the last time she saw Sally… what they spoke about, whether she could have said or done anything differently to stop the inevitable occurring. I know, as I have asked myself those questions thousands of times before when thinking about Anna. There is nothing I can say or do in this moment to bring her any relief. All we can do is listen and offer words of encouragement, though they're worth nothing. For Diane Curtis, it is just a waiting game.

Cheryl stands, announcing that she's going to put the kettle on, but nods for me to follow her through to the kitchen. Once inside, she closes the door to, so we won't be overheard by Diane. 'Who do you reckon did it then?'

It isn't clear whether she's just after a bit of salacious gossip or is asking me before bowling out with an opinion of her own. I don't have to wait long to find out.

'Sam said you was asking questions about Bill Havvard's son, the drama teacher? You reckon it was him then, do you?'

Something still doesn't sit right with me about that possibility but I can't put my finger on what.

'I don't think we should be making assumptions about anything yet, Cheryl,' I casually chastise. 'Let's just wait and see what the police find. You never know, they might come away empty-handed.'

She scoffs. 'I doubt it. That Rimmington was here first thing, telling Diane that they'd got hold of some specialist equipment that can search underground for levels of disturbance. Apparently builders use it for checking foundations. She reckoned that if Sally is buried in the woods, it's only a matter of time until they find out where. They sent sniffer dogs in to try and narrow down where to search, and based on some witness statement, they now know where our girls were right before it happened.'

I choose not to mention that the witness statement came from Jane.

'Once they find the location,' Cheryl continues, 'Rimmington said it would take several hours to recover the body, depending on how far down she's buried. They have to be careful to preserve the evidence, or so she said.'

'Even so, there's nothing to say for certain that Sally is buried in those woods,' I challenge. 'Even if she was killed that night, her body could be buried anywhere.'

Cheryl's eyes widen. 'You mean under a patio, like in that old TV show?'

This was not the reaction I was hoping for.

'Not necessarily, but yes, within reason. We're assuming a killer would choose to bury her in the woods where they could work undisturbed and out of sight, but that's not to say for certain that she's there.'

Natalie's words are there in my head again. *You need to find her. Find Sally. Tell her I'm sorry.*

Natalie was so certain that they'd caused Sally's disappearance that she was prepared to end her own life to make amends. I can't help wondering whether we'd all be here now had Natalie not committed suicide, so in some way her wish is coming true.

The sound of the front door opening is followed by footsteps stomping through the hallway towards the living room. Cheryl whips the door open and we catch a glimpse of a man in army fatigues dropping to his knees at Diane's feet. He buries his head in her lap and she strokes the back of his dark grey hair.

'Owen's home,' Cheryl says, surging forwards, but he turns his head at the sound of her voice.

His face is a rage of red pain and anger. 'What the hell is *she* doing here?'

Cheryl stops still, a rabbit in the headlights.

'I called her,' Diane soothes, rubbing her hand over the back of his head once again, forcing him to face her. 'I don't care what you say, Owen, she's my friend and with you away, I needed someone here with me.'

'I came back as soon as I heard,' he says, meeting her gaze, brushing his fingers over her raw cheek. 'I'm so sorry I wasn't here sooner.'

There is obviously love still between these two. After Anna disappeared, my parents' marriage swiftly followed suit. They both outwardly blamed the other but I'm sure that deep down neither could forgive themselves for not being more cautious. Tragedy has the ability to break a marriage but it can equally forge the bond in steel; it appears the latter happened for these two.

'Have the police said whether…?' Owen tries to ask, unable to complete the sentence.

Diane shakes her head, fighting the urge to cry again. 'Not yet.'

'But they think…?'

This time Diane nods and tears do break free of her eyes.

Owen leaps back to his feet. 'I need to be there; I need to see with my own eyes. Stay here and I'll tell you as soon as I hear.'

Diane reaches for her husband's hand but he is already too far away.

'I want you to escort me to the scene,' we hear him bark at the PC at the door. 'I want to speak to whoever is in charge. If you believe my daughter's remains are nearby, then I want to be there when she's recovered.'

The PC is doing his best to pacify him but eventually relents and the two men leave the property. It's an odd reaction to the news that his missing daughter may have been so near for so long. I understand the anger and the desire to want to do something, but there is no advantage to him being any closer to the woods than in his own house. Once something – if anything – is found, I'm sure the Curtis family will be the first to hear about it.

Diane reaches out for Cheryl who takes her hand and joins her back on the sofa. With nothing else I can do, I return to the kitchen to make the drinks, quickly locating the pots of tea and coffee in one of the cupboards. The fridge is covered in postcards, each attached with magnets with locations written on them. Removing one, I skim read the back and see that it was sent to Diane by Owen while he was away working in Stuttgart. Checking another – this one from Washington DC – it appears there is a pattern to the cards. Each time he goes abroad he must send Diane a card of wherever he is. There's one in particular that catches my eye but before I can look at it properly, I hear the front door opening again and this time Owen Curtis is joined by the familiar face of DI Rimmington.

She doesn't acknowledge me, merely marches past the kitchen door and into the living room. Her next words send a shiver the length of my spine.

'We will need to run checks to confirm, but we believe we have located the skeleton of a young woman.'

Chapter Thirty-Nine

NOW

Bovington Garrison, Dorset

The last hour has simply flown by. After Rimmington's announcement, the Curtis household has been overtaken by a variety of different men and women, to the point where names and purposes of visits have become a blur. It reminds me of the days that followed Anna's disappearance all those years ago. I must have met dozens of people – interviewed by so many different faces – all wanting to know what I could recall about the exact moment Anna had left the garden. Could I remember if there were any unusual vehicles in the road, did Anna give any hint that she might not be going to our grandma's house, had she sworn me to secrecy, was this just part of some idiotic children's prank, did I see any figures following Anna? Question after question, asked a dozen different ways to try and make me trip over my own memory of what really happened.

I'm not blaming the police for these methods of

interrogation. Ultimately, their goal is the same as the family's, but it is an inordinate amount of pressure in what is already a tense situation. Technicians in protective overalls have been in to collect samples of Sally's clothes in order to establish whether there is any link to the rags remaining with the decomposed cadaver. Other technicians have asked for photographs of Sally's face so that bone structures can be compared. Someone else wanted a sample of DNA for comparison. Another wanted name and address details of Sally's dentist. So many people all charged with following up on a different angle and all making their own demands.

I feel like a spare part, hunkering down and allowing all this interference to go on around me. I wanted to leave them to it – the last thing they need is extra people in the way – but when I offered to leave the house, Rimmington told me she wanted to speak to me about Natalie before I left. So, here I am, sitting next to Cheryl, forcing down more tea and desperately hoping I can use the facilities at some point soon.

Cheryl has never looked so relaxed. It's as if she's drawing some kind of entertainment from all this hoo-ha, as if she's picturing the unfolding scene like a live-action version of one of the crime dramas she loves watching so much on television. I'm certain she'd accept if someone came round offering popcorn.

'Miss Hunter, could we have that word now?' Rimmington asks, coming into the room and targeting me directly.

I glance at Diane who is lost in a trance as her husband Owen answers questions beside her; I can only imagine the types of questions going through her own mind.

Following Rimmington upstairs, we pass a cloaked technician who confirms they've finished with Sally's room and that the photographs will be available to view within the hour.

'Please take a seat,' Rimmington directs, as we head into what must be a guest room, on account of the limited furniture and mementoes on display.

Rimmington is much more formidable than I think I gave her credit for. The way Cheryl and Diane had described her to me is not what I'm now facing. This isn't some timid DC being undermined by the head of base security and forced to backtrack on her investigation. This is a woman who has learned from her mistakes and experiences and is all the stronger for it.

'I didn't realise who you were when we met yesterday,' she says, offering me a stick of gum which I decline. 'When I got back to the station, I was telling one of my team about Jane Constantine's statement and about you and your friend being there, and he thought it was hilarious that I hadn't realised who I was speaking to. I apologise for my ignorance.'

I wave away the apology. 'There's really no need. I'm nobody in the grand scheme of things.'

'Not from what I've subsequently been told. I don't get much time to read these days – demands of the job, you know.'

I nod, though I can only imagine just how much of a strain the role puts on her ability to unwind. I've met plenty of detectives in my time, yet never once one who manages to maintain any kind of work-life balance. It certainly isn't a role for everyone.

'And from what I now hear, you were also the last person to see Natalie Sullivan alive, meaning that you are now my focus for the next twenty minutes at least.'

I think back to the moment Maddie and I stepped out onto

that rooftop, how the cold wind clawed at my face, feeling as though it could suck us up into its grasp at any moment.

'It was Natalie's final words to me that seemed to start all of this off,' I admit, 'though I think Natalie had more of a hand in me becoming involved than I'd initially believed. It feels like she chose me to go down this route and I'm just following the trail of breadcrumbs she left.'

'Why do you think she chose you?'

It's a good question and one I'm not sure I'll ever get to the bottom of. 'I don't know,' I reply. 'My name's been in the news a lot this past year so maybe she just figured I might sniff out a story and run with it.'

'I don't think it's that,' she says, popping the gum into her mouth and disposing of the foil wrapper in a pocket of her suit jacket. 'Yes, you're somewhat famous now, and maybe that's how she first came across your name, but I think if Natalie were looking for some kind of fame through you, she wouldn't have jumped. I think, in her hour of need, she needed someone relentless, someone who wouldn't stop until they'd found out the truth.'

I can't tell if she's just trying to butter me up, or if there is some other ulterior motive to the ego massage.

I smile in acknowledgement. 'Her final words to me were to find Sally and apologise to her. At the time I didn't know who Sally Curtis was, nor what Natalie might want to apologise for. I think now... she was a muddled young lady. She set me off on some trail of modern witches and I think she did genuinely believe that she and her friends *were* in fact responsible for what happened, when they probably did little more than freak themselves out.'

'I agree. As soon as I heard Jane Constantine's version of

what really happened in those woods, it only confirmed what I've thought for so many years.' She joins me on the bed. 'I never bought into the idea that she had run away from the base – there were too many people who would have seen her making her escape – and so something else must have happened. I was petitioning my own DI at the time to let me bring in every one of the soldiers on the base and systematically interview each. In fairness, had we known about Sally's pregnancy fifteen years ago, I probably would have had the backing of my DI. Instead, he bowed to the pressure coming from the military and allowed them to assume unofficial control of the investigation. I don't blame him as we were under such work pressures that any help would have been gratefully accepted.'

I'm surprised she's being so open with me but I can't help feeling there's some other reason she's being so candid.

'You're confident you've finally found Sally then?'

She offers a non-committal shrug. 'Time will tell, but I've no reason to be doubtful at this stage. Our teams will work through the night to carefully extract the bones and begin their verification checks. My chief superintendent has given a hundred per cent support for the next forty-eight hours and that means it's all hands to the pump until the clock stops. That still won't necessarily turn up what really happened to Sally, nor who robbed her of her young life, but my initial priority is to bring Owen and Diane some closure after failing fifteen years ago.'

I wish someone could do the same for me and Mum.

'I presume you made a statement to my colleagues in the Met after Natalie jumped?'

'Yes, it was a PS Daggard I spoke to.'

'Great, well, I'll ask if they can send a copy down for our files here. Tell me one thing before I go and speak to Owen and Diane again. Why did you tell Jane to phone me yesterday? I would have thought, given your chosen profession and contractual obligations, that you would have taken more of the credit.'

'I never got into writing for the credit,' I say sombrely. 'There must be a million damaged lives out there with nobody looking to help set the course straight. For me, it's about doing what little I can to help those who need it. I'm a firm believer in karma and it's my hope that one day someone might return the favour. Until then, as you said, it's about reuniting a missing girl with her grieving parents.'

She laughs at the response. 'You ought to go into politics with that level of diplomacy! One last question: assuming it is Sally we've found, who do *you* think killed her?'

'I wouldn't like to guess.'

She laughs again. 'That's the right answer.'

I follow Rimmington down the stairs but there is a commotion in the living room that has erupted in our absence. Opening the door, Rimmington steps in, demanding to know what's going on. And as my eyes meet those of Louise Renner, I think I already know the answer.

Chapter Forty

NOW

Bovington Garrison, Dorset

Louise Renner stands out like a sore thumb in the landscape of army fatigues, police uniforms, baggy tracksuits, and Diane's dressing gown. Her perfectly pressed business suit and skirt shimmer in their decadence and there isn't a single hair that has escaped the cosmetic straightening or the platinum-blonde bleaching. This is a woman who takes great pride in her appearance and from the way she is staring down her nose at DI Rimmingon and at me, we clearly don't match up to her impossibly high standard.

'We haven't been properly introduced,' Rimmington says, striding forward and cutting the ice. 'I'm Detective Inspector Fiona Rimmington, and you are?'

'Actually, we met fifteen years ago, though in fairness I've done a lot of growing up since then.'

I can see the image click behind Rimmington's eyes. 'Louise Renner?'

'Well, it's Baker now, but yes, I was Renner before I got married.'

'I'm pleased you're here, Louise, as you were on my list to speak with this morning, so you've saved me a job of coming to you. Out of curiosity, what exactly are you doing here?'

Louise looks around the room, taking us all in, maybe trying to decide whether she is comfortable sharing in front of everyone. 'It's all over the news,' she says. 'The police are on the base and speculation is that you've reopened the investigation into Sally's disappearance. Judging by the hive of activity at the woods, and the number of police coming and going from this house, I'd say the press are spot on.'

'That doesn't answer my question, Louise,' Rimmington says, moving further into the room, and closing the door behind us. As far as she is concerned, the trap is sprung and Louise won't be making a swift exit.

I don't know why Rimmington is so worried. If you ask me, Louise has no intention of disappearing anytime soon. The pieces are all starting to slot together in my mind, but the image I'm seeing is so ludicrous that I'm not prepared to believe it until I hear it for myself.

'I was visiting my uncle at the barracks and when I saw all the activity, I came for a closer look. You can check with security if you don't believe me. My name's been on the guest list for at least a week.' She briefly looks down at her Louboutins and when she next looks up, her eyes are shining in the midmorning light streaming through the window.

Rimmington takes another step closer, nodding her head. 'Why don't you tell us what you recall of that night fifteen years ago, Louise?'

Louise reaches into her Dior clutch bag, removes a fresh

tissue, and dabs at her eyes and nose. 'I didn't know Sally was pregnant – at least, not at the time. I knew she'd started having her periods – we all had – and I'd told her how painful I'd found the whole experience. Sally said her last had been agony and that was why Jane suggested we go to the woods to try and do something about them. I'm not sure any of us thought it would make a difference but Nat was so enthralled by the possibility. No, wait, she was terrified, certain that we'd inadvertently conjure some mythical demon who would steal our souls or something. She was being ridiculous but she refused to listen to reason. I knew that whatever Jane was planning wouldn't make an ounce of difference, but the thought of us all sneaking out and congregating in the woods felt exciting. It was us against the world.

'I knew Jane didn't know what she was doing. At school she'd been bigging herself up, claiming she'd witnessed some of her mum's incantations and saying how easy it would be to cast something that would take away our monthly pain. The look on her face when we all agreed to go along with it confirmed she'd been bluffing but she wouldn't admit as much. Yet, as soon as we reached the clearing, it was obvious she didn't have a clue what she was doing. She drew this circle on the ground using porridge oats, for heaven's sake, and then she lit some candles, which wasn't practical given how windy it was that night. It was just harmless teenage fun as far as I was concerned.

'Then the chanting began. I can still hear the low rumble of Jane's voice and how I desperately had to fight the urge not to erupt into a fit of giggles. She told us we had to close our eyes in order for the spell to work properly but I had my eyes open the entire time. I saw Sally slip off her shoes and begin to sneak away into the darkness of the woods. I thought she was just doing it as part of a practical joke so we'd all think she really had been taken by some wicked spirit, but then I caught the look of panic in her eyes, right before the final candle flame extinguished. There was a rumbling in the distance – thunder I think – and when Nat then flicked on her torch, she screamed hysterically because Sally had vanished.

'I played along, thinking Sally would leap out at any moment, but then Nat dropped the torch and raced off into the woods herself, leaving Jane and me to hurry after her, knowing she was bound to get herself lost – which of course she did, falling and impaling her leg on a branch. We helped her back to the hole in the fence and I formulated the premise that Sally had been taken. It was cruel on my part, and I only said it because I was annoyed at how Nat was overreacting. I believed we'd all see Sally at school in the morning and everything would go back to normal. When she wasn't there and then you showed up and started asking questions, I couldn't get my head around it.

'I knew Sally hadn't been taken by some spirit, which is why I swore the other two to secrecy, but I didn't believe Sally would have had the guts to actually sneak off the base. I was convinced she must have fallen in the darkness and bumped her head, but when I went back to the fence so I could go and look for her, the hole had been sealed up. They sent teams of people in to look for her, and I'm sure there were dogs too at one point, but there was no sign. She had actually vanished.'

We're all watching Louise. I consider myself a good judge of character and, whilst I don't approve of some of the things she has said so far, I don't doubt a single word of her story.

Looking over to Cheryl and Diane huddled on the sofa, they too are hanging on every word.

'Then I ran into her at the hut a day or so later,' Louise continues. 'I'd gone there to try and speak to Pete – sorry, Corporal Pete Havvard, our drama teacher – about it. I was livid when I saw him with his arm around her shoulders. We'd both fancied him, you see, but we'd made a pact that neither of us would pursue him and it looked as though Sally had broken that. I can't remember what we said but I recall lots of shouting and screaming and Pete had to forcibly drag me off her. That's when he said I was to be careful because she was pregnant. That tipped me over the edge. Not only had she broken our pact, she'd actually slept with him too, and got herself knocked up. I knew instantly that would be the end for Pete; he'd be arrested and sent to prison and Sally would probably have to drop out of school or move off the base and I'd lose my best friend. Sally said she was still trying to process what was happening and couldn't bear to face her parents, fearing they'd be so ashamed of her.'

She looks at Owen and Diane at this point, who are both in floods of tears. Having met Diane, I would have said she'd look to comfort her distraught daughter, but then maybe she's mellowed over the years.

'They swore me to secrecy,' Louise continues, her voice calm and even, 'and then when Pete was told he was being transferred to Germany, they saw it as the perfect way out of their troubles. Sally arranged to meet me in secret one more time and said she was going to move to Germany with Pete and raise her child. I so desperately wanted to tell someone so that she'd be stopped from going, but I also didn't want to see Pete get into trouble. I was so torn but I kept my mouth shut. I so desperately wanted to tell you that Sally was still alive, Mr and Mrs Curtis, I really did, but the longer it dragged on, the more difficult it became.'

Diane has stopped crying, as the news slowly sinks in, though it must be hard to contemplate exactly what Louise is saying over the stress and anxiety the day has already thrown at her.

'Y–y–you mean, she's alive?' Diane whispers, unable to get the possibility into words. 'Our Sally is alive?'

All eyes are on Louise and as she nods, the first tear breaks free of her carefully applied eyeliner. 'Yes. I spoke to her two days ago, after Nat's service. I figured she should know what had happened.'

Nobody moves, nor speaks.

It's the strangest feeling, like we're all trapped in some kind of lucid dream. There's a bubble around us and nobody wants to risk it popping and the dream to end.

Rimmington is the first to speak. 'So that I'm clear, you're saying Sally Curtis is very much alive?'

Louise nods again, her face crumpling in emotion as she watches Diane and Owen come to terms with the pain she's helped cultivate for the past fifteen years. Neither is bursting with joy at the news that their missing daughter has not only been found, but is alive and kicking. It must be the greatest news they have ever received and yet it is tarnished by the fact that Sally has effectively avoided them for such a period. No parent wants to acknowledge that their child could even contemplate such an idea.

'And you said you spoke to her two days ago?' Rimmington clarifies. 'How?'

'FaceTime,' Louise replies absently. 'She's still living in

Germany – in Alsace, on the border with France – with Pete, who is now teaching English as a foreign language in a primary school.'

'Can you get her on the line now? I'll need to verify what you've told us.'

'I can try,' she whispers, before moving towards Diane and Owen and falling at their feet. 'I am *so* sorry I never told you the truth. I'm a mum myself now, and it's only since my daughter was born that I've really been able to contemplate exactly what you must have been through. I've been encouraging Sally to reach out to you and end this sham for months. She was already getting to the point where she was planning to make contact, I'm sure of it.'

Rimmington now has a phone to her ear and exits the room to carry out her conversation in private.

This news really is overwhelming and at no point from the moment I first encountered Natalie Sullivan did I ever believe that Sally actually did survive that night, let alone that she's been thriving overseas with everyone oblivious to her existence. But as I look at the space Rimmington has just vacated, I realise that nobody has yet addressed the enormous elephant in the room: if Sally Curtis didn't die that night fifteen years ago, whose skeleton is currently being extracted from those woods?

Chapter Forty-One

NOW

Bovington Garrison, Dorset

Louise's hands are trembling as she holds her mobile out, trying to stream the screen to the large television hanging from the wall. Rimmington is now back in the room and we've all been given a fresh cup of tea in the ten minutes that has passed since Louise dropped the bombshell. The television flickers momentarily and then Louise's phone wallpaper and apps fill the screen.

'I sent her a WhatsApp, so she should be expecting our call,' Louise tempers, remaining near the television so she can control the camera on her phone. She presses the FaceTime app and clicks on a contact called Alsace and the familiar whirring fills the room via the television speakers.

A woman's face fills the screen and at first I can see no resemblance to the images of Sally Curtis I have poured over in online news articles this past week, but then she moves back from the camera, and her muddy brown eyes come into focus, along with the slight crook in the bridge of her nose and I instantly know that this is Sally, albeit fifteen years older. Her hair – once a mess of curls – is now closely cropped and has been dyed almost coal-black. It's easy to see why no aging software would be able to predict the face before us and why she's managed to disappear into the background for so long.

It makes me think of Anna once again. Last year, I spent a lot of money to have a company age some of the images of Anna I have in order to see if anyone would recognise this older, more rigid face, but there's only so much such software can reproduce. If someone doesn't want to be found – as has been the case with Sally – then maybe it's possible to simply vanish and never be heard from again.

The Sally before us now looks quite taken aback by all the faces staring at her from a living room she once knew to be her own. Rimmington has only allowed a bare minimum of individuals to observe this call. Diane and Owen are here of course, as are Cheryl and Louise, Rimmington herself, and for some reason Diane insisted I remain too. The other officers have been banished to the kitchen.

'Mamma?' Sally's voice now carries through the speakers. 'Is it really you?'

Sally's eyes are already watering, as her larger-than-life-size face continues to dominate the screen. I feel tears stinging my own eyes as Diane's sobs come breathlessly, making it sound like she's having an asthma attack.

'S–S–Sally?' Diane stammers. 'Is it r–r–really you?'

'Yes, Mamma, it's me,' Sally cries out, no longer able to keep her emotion at bay.

Owen has yet to speak, but I can see from the tautness of

his cheeks that it's taking all his strength to remain strong for his wife.

'Hey, Sal,' Louise now says, far more composed than earlier. She has shed her tears for today and I doubt we will witness any more from her – certainly not in public. I imagine she will not allow her mask to slip again until she is back in the darkness of her own bedroom.

'Hey, Lou,' Sally says, her face contorted between joy and agonised pain. 'Did you tell them about what we discussed?'

There is the slightest Bavarian twang to Sally's accent. Years of living in Germany have clearly had an effect. Otherwise, she looks like any normal, healthy twenty-nine-year-old woman. She is two years older than me, and I am envious of her clear complexion and the healthy colour of her skin. Every time I've pictured Anna out there somewhere in the world, waiting to be found, I've always imagined her in a worse-for-wear state, yet Sally is the polar opposite. She isn't someone who is struggling; she is blossoming, thriving, even. As painful a decision as it must have been to turn her back on her friends and family and start over, it clearly agrees with her.

'I've only told them how Pete helped you get away,' Louise replies to Sally's earlier question. 'I figured you'd be the best person to share the rest. Is that okay?'

Sally nods, and now balances her phone on some kind of table near her legs. As she sits back in the armchair, we get the tiniest glimpse into her world. Immediately behind the sofa are large glass windows, and golden sunshine is pouring in all around her. Beyond the windows there is a huge plantation of green lawn, with several leafless trees waving daintily as if wishing us a welcome. I would guess we're in a conservatory of some kind, given the wicker frame of the armchair.

'Mamma, Dad, I'm so sorry,' Sally begins. 'I know I will never be able to make you understand what I did, nor why, but I am sorry for any hurt I have caused you. I wanted to phone you so many times but I didn't know how to start, and then it was like everybody simply forgot I had gone and that made it easier for me to move on. I want you to know that my choice wasn't made because I don't love you, but in that moment, I had to do what was best for me and for... my son.'

A hush falls over the room. Jane and Louise had confirmed that Sally had been pregnant on the night she disappeared, but neither said whether Sally had kept the baby.

Sally stands and disappears from the screen, returning a moment later, clutching a silver-framed image of herself and a young man at least a foot taller than her. His likeness to the image of Pete Havvard that Rachel found online is uncanny. He is dressed in a shirt and tie – a school uniform, I would presume – and he has such a shock of ginger, curly hair. He stands tall and proud, with one arm draped around his mother's shoulders. This is not a young man who has been dragged up under the judgemental eyes of those around him.

'This is Joshua, Mamma. He's at school right now, but I can't wait for you to meet him.' Sally wipes her eyes. 'He is such a special boy and I am so proud of the young man he is turning into. He is so smart, and funny, and caring. You would be so proud of him too.'

I glance back at Diane's face. Her mouth continues to open and close as she sobs mutely, her eyes transfixed on the screen before her, soaking in every pixel of her lost daughter and the grandson she's never met.

Sally lowers the framed photograph, positioning it so it fills the bottom quarter of the image on the television. She then beckons to someone off screen and a moment later, an older, but unmistakeable, Pete Havvard joins Sally, perching on the arm of her chair. His cheeks are already reddening as he lifts a hand in a wave, like a man standing before a firing squad.

'I want to make something clear,' Sally continues, taking Pete's hand in hers and squeezing it tightly. 'None of this is Pete's fault. I don't want him to be held accountable for the decision I made. He has been the greatest friend and support to me for these last fifteen years, taking care of me and Joshua as his own, putting a roof over our heads and food on the table, and asking nothing in return.'

Owen isn't buying the act though, and leaps to his feet, tottering unsteadily as he snatches the phone from Louise's grasp. 'You filthy bastard! You defiled my little girl and then you absconded with her. You ought to be strung up from the nearest yardarm.'

'No, Dad,' Sally fires back, no longer intimidated. 'This isn't Pete's fault! He isn't the monster here.'

'Don't be ridiculous,' Owen fires back. 'Years of being trapped in his company, he's probably brainwashed you into thinking it was *your* idea. Don't you see, Sal?'

Louise reaches to take control of the phone but Owen's grip is too tight.

'Please, Dad, you're not listening. You don't understand,' Sally implores. 'Pete isn't the man who did this to me. Pete isn't Joshua's father.'

Owen is staring into the phone, probably far too close for Sally and Pete to be able to see anything but his brooding and bloodshot eyes. The rest of us are staring at the television, watching the silent exchanges and knowing looks between the two of them, as if they're waiting to deliver a well-rehearsed performance.

'Please, Dad, give the phone back to Lou, so I can see the rest of you. Please?'

He throws it in Louise's direction, but doesn't return to his space on the sofa beside Diane, instead pressing an arm against the closed living room door and resting his head on his forearm.

'Thank you. Now, I know what I'm about to say won't be easy to hear – God knows it isn't easy to say – but it's the truth. Pete was never interested in me or Louise – not like that. He wanted to help us learn skills, which is why he taught the drama class, but sexually we never would have been compatible.' She pauses and looks to Pete for confirmation, which he provides in a simple nod. 'Pete is gay; he always has been.'

Our eyes all focus on Pete, whose face reddens even further. 'It's true,' he confirms. 'I love Sally, and I love Joshua, but as a sister and brother. I wasn't out-out back then; I was confused and wanted to deny how I really felt, but once I came to Germany, away from certain pressures, I was able to embrace who I want to be. And Sally has been as much of a rock for me as I have been for her.' He smiles at Sally and the kinship between them is apparent. Pete turns back to the camera. 'When my dad caught me in town with my arm around another guy, he flew off the handle. I remember him dragging me to that old shack of a hut and berating me. He accused me of being sordid, told me that I was committing heresy. He even accused me of sneaking about in dark places, cavorting with the devil himself! Can you believe the nerve of the guy, when he—'

Sally puts a hand up to stop him. 'Things are a lot more relaxed over here and Pete left the military after a year. We rented a flat for a bit while I nursed Joshua and he got a job teaching. It hasn't been easy – for either of us – but we made the right decision to come here. You only have to look at how well Joshua is doing to see that.'

I'm about to ask the obvious question when Rimmington beats me to it. 'So if Pete isn't the father of your son, who is?'

The two of them exchange glances again, before Sally takes a deep breath. 'Pete's dad, Bill Havvard, was the one I slept with.'

Diane screams and Owen bangs his arm against the door, turning as angry tears blot on his cheeks.

'What?' Owen demands. 'N–n–no, it couldn't be.'

Sally has fresh tears as she nods. 'I swear to you, Dad, it was him. It only happened the once. He caught me after I snuck out of that very house one night and offered to walk me back home. I was terrified he would tell you and Mamma that he'd caught me drinking in the park and I begged him not to. He said he would keep my secret, if…' She swallows audibly. 'If I would let him kiss me.' She scoffs now. 'I thought it was a small price to pay and I was picturing Pete as it happened, which is probably something I should see a therapist about.' She laughs insincerely. 'I knew that what he was doing was wrong but Louise and I were always so competitive at school that I thought this would give me the edge. I knew what he was doing and I didn't ask him to stop, but I regretted it as soon as it had happened. He promised he wouldn't tell you two about seeing me out late and I knew he'd have to keep it quiet because I now had something over him. I was naïve enough to think I couldn't get pregnant, so I didn't tell anyone until it was too late.

'I have so many regrets about that time in my life, but without them I wouldn't now have Joshua and so, despite everything, I wouldn't change a single thing about my life. I've learned to forgive and forget.'

Rimmington already has the phone to her ear once more. 'Get Colonel William Havvard to the Curtis house, *now*. I don't care if he's busy! Oh, and get a transport vehicle ready too.'

Chapter Forty-Two

NOW

Bovington Garrison, Dorset

DI Rimmington and I have excused ourselves from the living room to allow Sally a little time to reconnect with her parents without us gawping. I'm not going to lie; this is certainly not how I expected today to go, and yet it wasn't a total surprise to hear Sally accusing Colonel William Havvard of assaulting her. From my first encounter with him – when Cheryl and Diane were with me in the pub across the street from the base – it was clear that he likes to dominate proceedings. I've known bullies in my time and I had a similar feeling when I first interviewed Arthur Turgood back before I was ever able to prove the abuse that he'd mercilessly inflicted on Freddie Mitchell and the other boys. I've seen that malevolent look that feeds on holding power over others, and both Turgood and Colonel Havvard have it in spades.

A commotion at the front door signals that the colonel has

arrived and as his booming voice carries into the kitchen, it's clear he's rattled.

'What the bloody hell is this circus you've got going on here?' he yells at the poor officer assigned to open the door and verify guests. 'First of all, you come onto my base while we're setting up for the day then you wave that ridiculous piece of paper in front of my face saying you have the right to search the training woods, and now I find you here harassing one of our families. Your chief superintendent will be hearing about all this, I can assure you!'

Rimmington has been lurking just behind the kitchen door, eagerly listening to every word. Our eyes meet and, from the look of glee now crossing her face, I don't think it's fear holding her back. This moment has been a long time coming for her and I can't blame her for wanting to revel for a moment.

She emerges from her place and looks at Havvard for a long moment but when she speaks there is no sound of gloating. 'Colonel Havvard, thank you for making the time to come and see me. I promise you we won't keep you for any longer than is absolutely necessary to clear up a few minor details.'

I want to applaud her calmness, as even I'm chomping at the bit to scratch his eyes out. Yet the delivery of her words has done exactly what she intended. All the bluster and fuss has gone out of him, like a balloon deflating before my very eyes. Offering him that element of submissiveness has lulled him into thinking that he's still in control, when I sense he is anything but.

'Perhaps you'd like to step into the kitchen?' Rimmington suggests, and that's my cue to leave.

Havvard pushes past me as I scuttle out of the room and makes his way to the kitchen sink by the front window, away from the door. With the lounge door closed, there isn't anywhere for me to go, so I perch on the stairs instead. Rimmington nods at me but leaves the kitchen door wide open. I would have expected her to close it to give them some privacy, but maybe there is an element within her that doesn't feel wholly safe being alone with this bully.

'Have you been made aware that the remains of a body have been located in the woods where we were searching this morning?' Rimmington begins.

'Yes. And?' His tone is short and untrusting.

'Based on a witness statement we received yesterday, we had reason to believe that the remains might belong to Sally Curtis, which is why I am in this house right now. It will take several hours for samples of earth to be collected, and for the bones to be recovered intact, but we are hopeful of making a positive identification in the coming days.'

'Well, that's good, isn't it?

'Yes, and we located them much sooner than we'd anticipated, which will hopefully mean we'll be out of your hair soon.'

'Good. With Christmas around the corner, I don't want your lot interfering with what our families have planned. It's a pain in the arse that you've closed half this road off as it is.'

She's nodding with false understanding. 'All very necessary though, I'm afraid. You must understand that we have processes and procedures to follow.'

He grunts.

'Anyway,' Rimmington presses on, 'that isn't the reason I asked you to meet me here, Colonel Havvard.'

'It isn't?'

'No.' A pause. 'The truth is that a very serious accusation has been levied at you and I wanted to bring it to your attention informally like this to give you the opportunity to answer the charge.'

'An accusation against me? By whom?' His mood has definitely changed, and in my head I'm picturing a tiger circling its cage, waiting to lash out at the buffoon who dared to enter it.

'By your son, Colonel.'

'Pete? What's he got to do with any of this? When did you speak to him?'

'This morning, via video call, as it happens. Have you spoken to him recently?'

'No, not for a while… We don't really speak anymore… It's complicated.'

'Oh, I see, well, um, your son has made a statement accusing you of impregnating Sally Curtis in the weeks prior to her disappearance.'

The silence is deafening and I can't take my eyes from them.

'He said what?' Havvard's voice booms.

Rimmington remains where she is. 'You can understand why I wanted to bring this to your attention as a matter of urgency,' she replies calmly, with an air of bogus submissiveness. He might be a tiger waiting to pounce but she is a spider, carefully building a web to trap her prey. I think I'm really starting to like DI Rimmington.

Havvard can see his world unravelling before his eyes. 'Well, he's lying of course. I never… I don't know why he'd say such a thing!'

'But you understand that when such an accusation is made, I'm obliged to investigate it. Are you saying that it isn't true?'

'Of course it isn't bloody true!' he bellows again. 'What do you take me for?'

'So you *didn't* have sexual intercourse with Sally Curtis in 2005?'

'No, I did not!' he replies evenly.

'Thank you for confirming that, Colonel. There is something else I neglected to mention. Your son Pete wasn't the only witness to come forward and levy this accusation at you. Sally herself has confirmed the timeline of events too. She says you caught her out late one night and blackmailed her into having sex with you, sex which resulted in her falling pregnant.'

Rimmington has stopped speaking and as I watch her, I see she is doing a wonderful job of keeping the smug look from her face.

'You've spoken to Sally?' His voice is quieter now, almost reluctantly accepting his fate.

'Oh, yes. Turns out she's alive and well, and living with Pete in Germany.'

His face reddens by the second as he realises he is now tangled in the carefully laid web.

'And she says I had sex with her and got her pregnant?'

Rimmington nods as if she's casually confirming a meal choice.

'She's lying!' Havvard yells. 'Simple as that. I am a decorated war hero. I'm set to receive a CBE in the Queen's New Year's Honours List in just over a week. You see what they're trying to do here, don't you? They're trying to smear my name to embarrass me and take the sheen off my deserved recognition.'

Rimmington feigns confusion. 'Why would they want to do that exactly, Colonel?'

'Oh, because that boy is a deviant, of course. I didn't want to bring it up – because I know it isn't politically correct in this day and age – but the two of us had a falling out some years ago when I found out he likes… well, he's gay. That's what this will be about now. It's his attempt at revenge when things are finally going right for me.'

He's reaching; a desperate man will do desperate things when pushed.

'Still,' Rimmington muses, 'it is a serious accusation and I will need to formally investigate the allegation, if only to prove your innocence of the charge, you understand?'

'If I'm supposed to have… *done* what they've said, why is she only coming forward now? Why didn't she accuse me when it happened or tell someone about it? I mean, fifteen years ago? There won't be any evidence to prove anything one way or another. It's her word against mine and how can you put any credence in the words of a girl who's pretended to be dead for the last fifteen years? It's nonsense.'

'I understand, Colonel, I really do. However, there is one way you can one hundred per cent discredit this allegation.'

'And that is?'

'Consent to a DNA test. The thing is, Sally delivered the baby she was pregnant with when she ran away fifteen years ago and if we could compare a sample of your DNA to his, and it isn't a match, then it really is your word against hers, but the evidence would be in your favour.'

There is silence as the trap is sprung.

'Is that okay, Colonel? I can have one of our forensic technicians collect your sample now, and then we'll have it compared to Sally's son's in our lab where there's no risk of contamination. That way, you'll have a report that backs up what you've told me today.'

Havvard still doesn't respond and I wish I could see his face as he desperately claws at any kind of way out. 'I think I should consult with a solicitor,' he finally says. 'If I'm being accused of this preposterous crime, I don't want to say anything that might limit the compensation due me when I decide to sue you and your force for slander.'

I hadn't heard the lounge door open but I suddenly catch sight of a figure in my periphery rushing towards the open kitchen door. Instinct – or stupidity – kicks in and I'm on my feet, crashing my shoulder into the charging Owen Curtis. My nimble body does little to stop his movement, but I slow him enough to allow Rimmington and Havvard to take evasive manoeuvres.

'Enough, Bill,' Owen says, making no effort to pull me away, maybe grateful that I'm stopping him from making a bigger mistake. 'Stop the bullshit and lies and admit what you did.'

'I'll mind you to hold your tongue, Captain,' Havvard cautions, coming closer.

Owen makes no effort to back off and if I'm not careful I'll end up as the meat in their sandwich. 'I *trusted* you. I've blindly followed you for decades, believing that what we were doing was serving the greater good but it's all bollocks, isn't it? You, this, none of it is serving anything other than *your* greater good.'

'Don't say another word, *Captain*,' Havvard warns again,

his leg brushing against mine as he tries to get as close as he can.

I force myself to straighten and hold my ground until both men ease off. Rimmington nods gratefully at me.

'DI Rimmington, I'd like to make a formal statement when you have a moment,' Owen says, now addressing her.

Havvard stabs a finger towards him, almost catching me in the face as he does. 'Another word out of you and I'll have you court-martialled for insubordination. Do you understand me, Captain Curtis?'

I think back to the passage in Natalie's journal where she described the night Havvard visited her dad and the subsequent conversation. I already know what he's about to say before the confession tumbles from his mouth.

'I know who the body in the woods is,' Owen says. 'Her name is Margaret Kilpatrick.'

Rimmington frowns at the name.

'Fifteen-year-old girl who went missing from the base in 2000,' I tell her.

'Don't do this, Captain,' Havvard cautions.

But Owen is past caring. 'Everyone thought she'd run away, especially when a postcard mysteriously arrived from Denmark. Only she never sent it, did she, Bill?'

'That's enough, Captain.'

'What kind of fifteen-year-old runs off to join a convent?' Owen scoffs, echoing my own doubt.

'Don't listen to a word this imbecile is saying,' Havvard pleads with Rimmington. 'This is obviously some other story he's concocted – probably with that lying bitch of a daughter of his – in order to tarnish my good name ahead of my CBE award.'

'Let him speak,' I snap at Havvard, uncertain where the courage has come from. 'Tell us what happened to Margaret, Owen.'

He glares at Havvard as he speaks. 'Bill called on us in the early hours of New Year's Day. Me and Geoff, his two "boys" – that's what he called us. He said there'd been a terrible accident and he needed our help. We were ready to die for him so of course we went. He took us to the old hut where we found Margaret dead on the cold floor. He reckoned he'd found her hanging from a bit of rope. She'd killed herself, he said. Told us it would be too difficult for her family to deal with and that the best thing we could do for them was to bury her body and make out that she'd run away from home. She was nearly sixteen, he said, and therefore of an age where she might want to start out on her own. The bruising around her neck could have been consistent with strangulation by a rope, but when I asked where it had happened, Bill said he'd already disposed of the rope, which is all the more reason why we needed to handle the situation there and then.'

There is pure hatred in Havvard's bulging eyes, and I'm no longer certain he won't attack me to get at Owen.

'Geoff thought we should just tell her parents the truth, but Bill has a way of forcing his will on others and before I knew it, we were sneaking into those woods and digging a ten-foot trench. It took hours but we managed it before the sun came up.'

That depth would certainly explain why sniffer dogs wouldn't necessarily pick up on the scent when searching for Sally years later.

'It was Geoff's idea to go to Denmark to send the postcard,' Owen continues, 'and we bribed a local to make the statement that she'd seen Margaret in the nunnery, alive and well. I never thought we'd get away with it, but as Sergeant Kilpatrick came to terms with her running away, it became easier to believe we hadn't done anything wrong... that Bill had been right all along.'

'I've had enough of this!' Havvard barks, barging me out of the way and pushing past Owen, making for the front door.

Rimmington moves out of the kitchen and shakes her head when the uniformed officer looks to her to see whether he is allowed to let Havvard leave. 'Colonel William Havvard, I am arresting you on suspicion of causing or inciting a child to engage in sexual activity, contrary to Section 10 of the Sexual Offences Act 2003. You do not have to say anything, but it may harm your defence if you do not mention when questioned something which you later rely on in court. Anything you do say may be given in evidence.'

I'm almost certain the vein throbbing in Havvard's head is going to explode as he stares us down, but she isn't budging and neither am I.

Chapter Forty-Three

NOW

High Wycombe, Buckinghamshire

As I walk into the former country manor, the heat from the crackling fireplaces at either end of the open room hits my cheeks instantly. Now converted into an upmarket bar and restaurant, this is where Maddie has suggested we meet.

We're now in that awkward period between Christmas and New Year's Eve when it isn't clear what the day or time is, and that probably explains why all the tables in the place are filled with families celebrating together.

I'll admit to feeling a tad envious that I'm not able to gather with my family at such a venue; Anna is still missing and Mum is back in Weymouth at her nursing home. After much consideration, and further reassurances from Pam Ratchett, I saw that Rachel was absolutely right. I can't take Mum home and expect us to go back to how things used to be.

I went up to the home on Christmas Day but it wasn't one of her good days. Despite my telling her a dozen times that I was her daughter Emma, she continued to refer to me as one of the nurses. I know it isn't her fault, what with all she's been through in the last few weeks with her fall and the abuse from the other patient. I also know there will be better days and I cling to the hope that the next time I see her will be one of them. I've also made a New Year's Resolution to see Mum a minimum of once a week when I'm in and around Weymouth. She needs me now and I think I need her too. Her illness is only going to get worse and I need to make the most of the limited time we have left.

I can't thank Rachel enough for helping me focus on the positives a new year will bring. Having her at home meant I wasn't rattling around the old place like a spare part. Instead, we went for a long morning walk along the shoreline, made a small but adequate Christmas lunch together, and laughed so much our bellies ached by the time the sun went down. Both of us needed distracting from our messy families and I think we both managed to achieve that ambition.

That's where Rachel is going next. She dropped me at the pub to meet Maddie and is now set to visit her parents in the Cotswolds. How that engagement goes will determine whether I require the hotel room at the Travelodge five minutes from here, or whether she'll be so cross she can't bear to spend the night in their company. I do hope it's the former, as Rachel doesn't realise how lucky she is to have both parents alive and in good health. I just hope that they set aside their bias and bigotry and accept Rachel for who she is. Only time will tell on that one, I fear.

Seeing Maddie wave, I raise my hand in acknowledgement, unfurl my scarf and join her at a small round table which is practically on top of one of the fireplaces. She is back to her smart best, not a hair out of place, her makeup carefully applied. You wouldn't know she'd borne witness to a suicide ten days before.

'I ordered us a bottle of wine,' she begins, 'and I know you aren't much of a drinker but I thought we should have a drop to celebrate.'

'Celebrate?' I ask, hanging my coat on the back of the chair and sitting. 'What are we celebrating?'

Maddie unscrews the lid on the bottle, and pours a measure into each glass. 'After much to-ing and fro-ing, the legal department has given the green light for the publication of *Ransomed*. It is set to hit the printing press next week. Because of the delays, they are eager to get the book released as quickly as possible and the PR team has been given a hefty budget to promote it. You can expect to see displays in most of the tube stations in Zone 1. They're also keen to organise a flurry of signing events across the country if you're willing to support them – all expenses paid for the two of us, taking in a total of twenty venues over a two-week period. You won't be their only author on the tour but you will be the big draw, from all accounts.'

I can feel my face folding in on itself as I squirm and wriggle in my chair. Maddie knows how I feel about making public appearances, even if it is just to sit behind a table signing books.

'Don't look at me like that,' she chastises like a petulant parent. 'I know you aren't keen, which is why I insisted on coming with you. I'll be sitting right beside you the entire time and I'll help with any unwanted or unanswerable questions. Okay? I won't leave you on your own. It'll be good for you,' she adds, raising her glass and angling it towards me. 'It'll help you build resistance to this anxiety you feel when faced with public appearances. Okay?'

I lift my glass and clink it against hers. 'If that's what they want then who am I to question, right?'

'That's the spirit.' She smiles encouragingly, before lowering her glass. 'There was something else I wanted to talk to you about as well. It's about our phone call last week. I said one or two things that I'd rather you not mention to anyone else – specifically, about Jordan.'

I hold my hands up. 'Maddie, I wouldn't, I swear.'

She holds my gaze. 'It isn't that I'm ashamed of him, I just don't want people to feel they need to constantly walk on eggshells when I'm around. That goes for you too. It's eight years since he passed and whilst I miss him every day, I have learned to cope with my grief. What happened with that poor girl last week was a shock to the system and opened an old wound. Taking those few days over Christmas helped me get everything back into perspective. I hope my outburst didn't worry you overly?'

Her eyes are longing for me to say I didn't worry but I don't want to lie. 'Next time it feels like things are getting on top of you, I want you to let me know, okay? I know our relationship is a professional one of author and agent, but I like to think we're more than that, Maddie. You're important to me and I want you to know that I'm here if ever you need me. God knows you've helped me when insecurity looms its head.'

The smile softens her face. 'That's what I'm here to do. It still amazes me that you can't see how talented a writer you are, Emma. Even with a *Sunday Times* Bestseller already under your belt and – if my predictions are correct – a second to follow in the coming weeks and months. Pre-orders of

Ransomed are already through the roof. The fuss Lord Fitzhume's proposed legal case has stirred up has been fabulous pre-launch publicity. Let's hope he makes an even bigger fuss on publication day!'

'I'm thinking about sharing Sally and Natalie's story next,' I say, curious to know how she'll feel about the prospect of her role being brought to life. 'I've already drafted an outline if you want to give it the once-over—'

She presses her hand onto mine. 'I think that would be a fabulous idea. A fifteen-year-old mystery featuring witchcraft, murder and a grisly cast, solved by our intrepid narrator? I can see the marketing team going wild for it already. Yeah, ping the outline over and I'll give it a once-over before forwarding it on to your editor for agreement. If we time it right, and send it the day after *Ransomed* launches, I can see them falling over themselves to offer you a huge advance too. But you let me handle that side of things. Okay?'

I clink my glass against hers again but she is suddenly on her feet and holding her arms open to someone approaching our table. 'Ah, here he is. So pleased you managed to find the place.'

I look up and am stunned to see Jack staring back. 'Hi,' he offers, leaning in as if he's going to give me a kiss on the cheek before reconsidering and thrusting his hand out for me to shake instead. He's wearing dark jeans and a jumper bearing a penguin in a Santa hat.

'What are you doing here?' I ask, as Maddie hurriedly pulls on her coat.

He frowns with confusion. 'One o'clock, right? I know I'm a few minutes late but it took ages to get parked.'

I look back at Maddie who is trying her hardest to keep the

smile from spreading across her face. 'I invited Jack to join us to celebrate the news about *Ransomed* as he played such a pivotal role in the investigation. The thing is, I've just remembered I need to be somewhere else but you two can stay and celebrate without me.'

I'm about to protest at this lame attempt at matchmaking when Maddie pushes away from her chair. 'Take my seat, Jack. And please, finish the wine; I barely touched my glass.'

Maddie leans in and pecks my cheek.

'I could kill you,' I whisper.

'Have a good time,' she whispers back. 'Just relax, okay? And don't chew the sleeve of your cardigan.'

And then she's gone without another word, leaving me with the heat rising to my cheeks.

Jack lifts up Maddie's glass and swirls the wine like some connoisseur before taking a sip. 'Very crisp on the palate,' he comments, before grinning inanely at me. It's hard not to mirror his warmth.

'Did Mila have a good Christmas?'

He nods. 'Yes, as far as I've heard. She was disappointed not to get the horse she was after but her mum and new partner got her an iPad, so she's the envy of all her friends. I think she's happy.'

'And you? How was your Christmas Day?'

'I was working, actually,' he admits. 'I figured there was no point being cooped up in my stuffy flat.'

'Working on anything interesting?'

His eyes narrow. 'I was following up on the contents of Arthur Turgood's hard drive, as it happens.'

I blink several times, my brain questioning the signals from my ears. 'The hard drive? You mean Freddie Mitchell, of course. He told me you'd found videos of him on the same drive that had the one of Anna.'

Jack nods grimly. 'I'm pleased he spoke to you about it and I'm sorry I didn't tell you directly. I wanted to but I know that you and Mr Mitchell are close, and I didn't want to overstep. What else did he tell you?'

Videos of me from years ago… where men are… doing bad things.

The memory sends a shiver through my body.

'He told me Turgood and the others would offer the boys treats if they agreed to be filmed.'

Jack is nodding. 'Yes, that's what he told me as well. None of this came out at the trial and I'm speaking with the CPS at the moment about bringing further charges against the defendants for the production of this illicit material, but it's still early days. We'd need statements from Freddie and the others confirming who was involved in the video making and then we'll see if there's any evidence that proves beyond a reasonable doubt that they were responsible.'

'They were on his hard drive. Isn't that enough?'

Jack takes another sip of the wine, this time without the fuss of before. 'Not necessarily. Turgood could easily argue that he downloaded the videos from somewhere. It's enough for possession but not creation and intent to supply. That's what I was following up on, on Christmas Day actually. Based on the sheer volume of footage found on the hard drive, it's clear that Turgood was purchasing videos from other sources and I've been working with a guy who's trying to unpick the source of the videos, by reviewing hidden meta data. I asked him to do the same with the video of your sister… and we got a hit.'

My heart skips a beat and the breath evaporates form my lungs. 'What are you saying?'

'We've found where the video of Anna was downloaded from. A team raided premises this morning and seized video equipment and computers, and apprehended multiple suspects in simultaneous raids. Now, before you get ahead of yourself, this is merely a distribution network and, given the age of the video on Turgood's hard drive, there's every chance none of the people arrested today had any involvement in the production of the video of Anna. It is, however, a step closer to preventing men like Turgood getting their kicks from exploiting vulnerable and innocent children.'

'Where were these premises?' I ask, my journalistic instincts kicking in. 'What if Anna is still being held somewhere nearby?'

Jack shakes his head. 'As I said, this was merely a distribution network we've uncovered. There is no evidence to suggest that the videos they handle were filmed at the premises. Networks like this can sprout up anywhere there's high-speed broadband and a ready supply of electricity. When they start to feel the heat, they shut up shop and move on. Today's raids have been two days in the planning and were undertaken with only limited surveillance, due to fears the crew would become suspicious and move before they were apprehended. Everything I'm telling you is off the record. Are we clear?'

I nod. 'Where do we go from here?'

'The suspects will be interviewed and will be asked to name names of footage suppliers. Hopefully that might help us turn over a few more rocks but we'll have to wait and see. I want you to know that I won't stop until the final lead has been chased down. Okay? I give you my word.'

I try to force a smile but it's hard when all I can imagine is monsters trying to bribe my sister to do such horrific things. The mood at the table has turned decidedly sour but it isn't Jack's fault. This rendezvous certainly hasn't gone as Maddie – and I'm sure Rachel – would have hoped. But therein lies the problem. It doesn't matter what attraction I feel towards Jack, nor whether it's mutual. Ultimately, with this hanging over us, there can be nothing between us except professional respect.

I do agree with his sentiment, however. I won't stop until I know exactly what happened to my sister and, whether she is still out there or I'm just clinging to false hope, I won't rest until I know the truth.

THE END

Emma Hunter will return in *Trafficked*...

Acknowledgments

I always find writing the acknowledgements in a book so difficult, because there just never seems to be enough space to thank everyone who has had some impact on the production of the story. It could be as simple as a snippet of conversation that inspires a chain of thoughts that leads to an idea for a story, or a previously hidden plot twist.

I still remember meeting with my editorial team in the HarperCollins offices in late summer 2019 and brainstorming ideas for possible new stories. My editor at the time (the brilliant Charlotte Ledger) challenged me to produce an original series with a main protagonist who wasn't the traditional lone police detective or private investigator on a mission. She also suggested that the stories should focus on a subject that is so empathic and frightening that readers would tear through the pages to reach the end. And that's kind of how Emma Hunter was born. That one meeting which lasted all of an hour set off a chain of events in my head that saw me plot out a series of six books that would be released back-to-back in a twelve-month period.

Having received a green light for the series from Charlotte and Kimberley Young, I was put in touch with the effervescent editor Bethan Morgan who picked up the reins and ran with the series. She's been a breath of fresh air in helping me develop Emma Hunter into this nuanced and real character. Sadly, I find myself having conversations with Emma in my head as we mull over plot developments. She is as real as you and me in my head, and I'm dreading the moment the series finishes, and I won't be able to talk to her anymore (though I sense she won't go quietly).

I want to thank Lucy Bennett for her work in producing the series' covers based solely on a few scribbled notes about where the future books would go. Thanks also to Lydia Mason, whose copy edit was relatively painless, and to Tony Russell who kindly completed the proofread to pull out those all embarrassing spelling mistakes. Finally, no book release is complete without the fervent effort of the publicity team, so big thanks to Melanie Price and Claire Fenby for all they've done to raise awareness of the series and encourage new readers to pick up the books.

Ransomed launched so brilliantly in September 2020, and that wouldn't have been possible without the support of Rachel Gilbey who organised the 7-day Blog Tour on my behalf, selling the merits of the concept to all who would listen and ensuring everything ran smoothly. Thank you to Mary Anne Yarde who publicised an interview we did back in August to announce the arrival of this series, and to Karen King and Nicola Mostyn who allowed me to pimp my books on their blogs.

Away from publishing, I wouldn't be a writer if it wasn't for my beautiful and always supportive wife, Hannah. She keeps all the 'behind the scenes' stuff of my life in order and our children's lives would be far greyer if I was left in sole charge. I'd also like to thank my mother-in-law Marina for all the championing of my books she does on social media. Thank you as ever to my best friend Dr Parashar Ramanuj, who never shies away from the awkward medical questions I ask him. Thank you to Alex Shaw and Paul Grzegorzek – authors and dear friends – who are happy to listen to me moan and whinge about the pitfalls of the publishing industry, offering words of encouragement along the way.

And final thanks must go to YOU for picking up and reading *Isolated*. You are the reason I wake up ridiculously early to write every day, and why every free moment is spent devising plot twists. I feel truly honoured to call myself a writer, and it thrills me to know that other people are being entertained by the weird and wonderful visions my imagination creates. I love getting lost in my imagination and the more people who read and enjoy my stories, the more I can do it. Don't be afraid to reach out and let me know if you enjoyed *Isolated* because YOUR message could be the one that brightens my day next.

Stephen

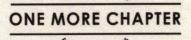

YOUR NUMBER ONE STOP

ONE MORE CHAPTER

FOR PAGETURNING BOOKS

One More Chapter is an
award-winning global
division of HarperCollins.

Sign up to our newsletter to get our
latest eBook deals and stay up to date
with our weekly Book Club!
<u>Subscribe here.</u>

Meet the team at
<u>www.onemorechapter.com</u>

Follow us!

 <u>@OneMoreChapter_</u>
 <u>@OneMoreChapter</u>
◎ <u>@onemorechapterhc</u>

Do you write unputdownable fiction?
We love to hear from new voices.
Find out how to submit your novel at
<u>www.onemorechapter.com/submissions</u>